A Heart Ren

New Hope Falls: Book 4

By

KIMBERLY RAE
JORDAN

THREE**STRAND**
P R E S S

A CORD OF THREE STRANDS IS NOT EASILY BROKEN.

A man, a woman & their God.
Three Strand Press publishes Christian Romance stories
that intertwine love, faith and family. Always clean.
Always heartwarming. Always uplifting.

A Heart Renewed/ Kimberly Rae Jordan. -- 1st ed.
ISBN-13: 978-1-988409-42-9

*The Lord is near to those who have a broken heart
and saves such as have a contrite spirit.
Psalm 34:19 (NKJV)*

CHAPTER ONE

Carter Ward stared at the woman in front of him, a sick feeling in his stomach. Though compassion filled her eyes, her face held a stubborn look. The man beside her had a similar expression. It was one that Carter knew all too well, though it had been years since he'd seen it on the face of the woman he loved—their daughter.

"What are you saying?" he asked, his hands fisted against his thighs.

"You know we love you, Carter." Evelyn Lansdown's gentle smile softened the stubborn set of her jaw. "We only want what's best for you."

"And this." Her husband, Garth, waved at the open doorway they stood in front of. "Isn't it."

"So you're telling me I can't visit her anymore?" Carter swallowed against the wave of nausea that rose up within him.

"No, we're not saying that you can't visit her," Evelyn said. "But we think it's time you visited her less."

"Less?" Carter shook his head. He couldn't do that. He'd already dropped down from nearly daily visits to just three or four a week.

"Son, we're asking you to do this of your own accord," Garth said. "It isn't healthy for you, coming here so much. We'd hoped that leaving Seattle for New Hope Falls would have helped you to move forward, but it hasn't."

"I did as you asked, and I *have* stopped coming to see her as much," Carter pointed out, desperate for them not to force this change on him.

"You have," Evelyn agreed with a nod. "But you're not moving forward. Have you even gone out on a date since the accident?"

"A date?" The word tasted like ash in his mouth. "I can't. We're engaged. It wouldn't be right."

Evelyn reached out and took his fist, rubbing it between her hands. "You're not engaged anymore, Carter. The Suzie we loved is gone. Even if she were to miraculously wake up, she would be different. She might not even remember any of us. As you know, the doctors said that the injury to her brain was significant. And even now, her health is beginning to deteriorate more and more."

Carter shook his head and looked away from Evelyn toward the door that led into Suzanne's room. He knew that what she was saying was right, but he couldn't accept it. Couldn't bring himself to accept that Suzanne wasn't coming back.

"You need to move forward with your life, son," Garth said, his voice holding a gentle note. "It's what Suzanne would have wanted. She would never have expected you to put your life on hold the way you have. I think you know that."

Did he? Carter didn't feel confident about saying he did. It wasn't like they had talked about what they'd want in the event that one of them ended up in a vegetative state. They'd only been twenty-four years old, busy planning for their future. The careers they wanted. The wedding. The home they hoped to share. The children they'd have.

There had never been any conversations about a situation like this one. So he couldn't say with absolute certainty that she would have wanted him to move forward. To move on.

Evelyn turned his hand over and pried open his fist. He looked down in time to see her slip a ring onto his palm. Reflexively, his hand closed, but then Carter tried to give the ring back to her.

"No, Carter, love." Evelyn shook her head. "This is me ending your engagement to Suzanne."

"And you need to cut back on your visits," Garth said.

"And if I don't?" Carter didn't want to hear the answer, but he needed to know what was at stake. They could say the engagement was over. They could give her ring back. But that didn't mean Carter had to accept it as true. They just had to think that he did.

"We'll make sure the staff and security here know that you're not welcome."

Carter's breath caught as a vice tightened around his chest. He shoved his hands into the pockets of his jeans and took a deep breath, staring down at the floor before looking back up at the couple who would have been his in-laws had things worked out differently for him and Suzanne.

"You know we don't hold any ill will toward you because of the accident, Carter," Evelyn said. "We've never blamed you the way you've blamed yourself, and we love you like the son we never had. It's because of that that we want you to move forward. To live your life."

"If I can't come as often as I do now..." Carter swallowed and rubbed the back of his neck. "How often can I come?"

He glanced up to see the couple exchange a glance before Garth spoke. "Once a week. But Carter, we really want to see you making an effort to move forward in your life. There's no reason you can't go on to have another loving relationship. You didn't die in that accident. It's time you start to live again."

Carter wanted to protest that. Wanted to argue that that was impossible. But he kept his mouth shut, realizing even as panic thumped inside him like a living thing, that doing so would only lead to him losing all contact with Suzanne.

"Can I see her now?"

Garth rested his hand on Carter's shoulder. "Yes. Of course."

Without looking at the couple again, Carter stepped into the room.

It was bright and cheerful with a large window that let in plenty of natural light. There were two bouquets of flowers on the wide ledge in front of the window. One was made up of the red, white, and pink roses that he'd brought her on his last visit. The other was an assortment of flowers that changed each week, depending on how Evelyn was feeling. That week, the bouquet was made up of autumnal flowers. Something Suzanne would have loved.

He stood for a moment, looking out the window before he turned his gaze to the bed where Suzanne lay. It had been ten years, and still, he wasn't used to seeing her like that.

Moving quietly, Carter walked to the chair next to her bed and sat down. The bed was elevated slightly, and Suzanne's hands were curled into the blanket that covered her. He reached out and took the hand closest to him and rubbed his thumb over the back of it.

"Hi, Suzie," he said, his voice rough.

Normally, he had a bunch of things he talked to her about, but on that day, all of that was lost to the emotions that threatened to choke him. Thankfully, the worship music that Evelyn always had on played softly in the background to keep the silence from becoming deafening.

As he looked at the woman who lay in the bed in front of him, Carter struggled to see the Suzanne he'd fallen in love with. Her previously long, dark hair was now kept short, and her once-healthy glow had faded. Even though her brown eyes were slightly open at times, and it seemed like she was awake, she never responded to the sound of his voice. Never looked in his direction as he talked to her

Vivacious and full of life, she'd also had a fiery temper that had led to some epic arguments at times. However, she'd never held onto her anger and had been quick to apologize if she thought she'd been in the wrong.

Unfortunately, their last argument had gone unresolved, and they'd never had a chance to make up afterward.

"I won't be able to visit you as much," he finally said. "But I hope you know that it's not because I don't love you anymore.

Your mom and dad just want me to move forward. They say it's what you'd want."

Carter allowed himself to consider what life would be like without his visits to see her. Though he did have other things in his life, his times with Suzanne anchored him. Everything else was just filler between visits.

Now, what would he do?

He still had no answer for that question when Evelyn and Garth joined him in the room half an hour later. Getting to his feet, Carter bent over to press a kiss to Suzanne's forehead.

As he prepared to leave, Evelyn gave him a tight hug. "You take care of yourself, darling. And if you need anything, you let us know."

Even though he was frustrated and upset with them right then, he *did* know that if he needed anything, they'd be there for him.

Once Evelyn let go of him, Garth grasped his shoulder with one hand, while he stuck out his other one. After he shook it, Carter fished the folded check out of his back pocket. He held it out, fully expecting that Garth would argue about taking it, given what they'd asked of him. But instead, the man just took it without comment.

Carter was glad, because even though he'd be visiting Suzanne less, he didn't feel like it released him from the obligation he felt to help cover the expenses for her care. They'd argued about it in the beginning, but when Carter had persisted, they'd finally given in and accepted his checks.

When he left the building where Suzanne had spent the majority of the past ten years, Carter felt like the weight of the world was on his shoulders. He wondered what it would take for Evelyn and Garth to allow him to visit Suzanne more frequently again. Maybe if they had proof that he was moving forward. But what would count as proof?

He'd told them about his involvement at the church and with the men's group. He'd talked about the friends he'd made, and how he even volunteered every couple of weeks with a group that worked with homeless veterans. But none of that had been enough, apparently. No, what they seemed to want from him was to see that he was moving on without Suzanne in *all* areas of his life.

Which meant they wanted to see him with someone new. Someone to take Suzanne's place in his life. A girlfriend.

Carter climbed into his old truck then leaned forward to rest his arms on the steering wheel. Letting out a breath, he stared unseeing out the windshield.

He didn't know how he'd do it, but he'd figure it out.

He just wished that Evelyn and Garth grasped where he was coming from. Didn't they understand that he felt like he couldn't go on and live his life to the fullest when Suzanne couldn't live hers that way too? And if that meant he never lived anything beyond the life he had now, so be it.

It should have been him in that hospital bed. Not Suzanne. Never Suzanne.

Carter didn't want to let the memories of that night take hold when he was out in public, so he sat back and jammed his keys into the ignition and cranked it. He was thankful the old truck started on the first turn, and soon he was on the highway leading from Seattle back to New Hope Falls.

The drive was usually about an hour—give or take—depending on the traffic. He rarely went the speed limit since his truck tended to shimmy at higher speeds, but on that day, he just wanted to get back to New Hope.

As he drew closer to the town, Carter decided to swing by the elementary school. Though he was glad to be back in New Hope, he wasn't in a big rush to return to his apartment. His small, empty apartment. He'd already been alone with his thoughts for the past hour, and he needed a distraction.

The new school year had just started up, and Carter figured it would be a good time to check in with some of the teachers about giving presentations in their classes. He and Kieran Sutherland, the Chief of Police, tried to visit the town's schools regularly, chatting with the kids about the police and fire departments. He enjoyed building a relationship with the youngsters, encouraging them to think about fire safety.

At one time, he'd looked forward to becoming a father. He and Suzanne had often discussed the children they hoped God would bless them with. Now, without that option, he found other ways to interact with children in a meaningful way.

He pulled into the parking lot of the school and swung to a stop in the first empty spot he found. Once inside the building, he proceeded to the office.

"Carter!" Sandra Hernandez, the receptionist, greeted him with a wide smile. "How are you doing?"

There was no way he could answer that honestly right then. "I'm doing alright. How about you?"

"I'm great. Happy to have all the kids back in school."

He could see the genuine affection she held for the students, and he was glad the kids had someone like her to interact with when they had to come to the office. "Is Principal Hughes available for a quick chat?"

"I am, Carter," the man's voice boomed from the open doorway behind the receptionist's desk. "Come on back."

"You heard the man," Sandra said as she gestured behind her.

With a quick smile at the woman, Carter headed for the principal's office, having a momentary flashback as he did. Though he hadn't been a bad kid, he'd somehow managed to end up doing something that upset his teacher a couple of times a week. Either talking out of turn or goofing off. That was usually precipitated by his inability to focus on whatever assignment they were supposed to be working on.

"Good to see you," Trevor Hughes said as he stood and held out his hand. He was a tall, middle-aged man with thinning brown hair and a face that always seemed to wear a smile. Carter knew that he was a man who was loved and appreciated by the students as well as his staff. "You ready to visit some classes?"

Carter shook his hand, then said, "Yep. Thought I'd drop by and see if any teachers were available to chat."

"Sandra can check the schedule. I sure appreciate you and Kieran being so willing to spend time with the students."

"It benefits us, in the long run, to try to build good relationships with the kids at this age, so I'm sure I speak for Kieran when I say that it's a pleasure to be able to do it."

Trevor sat back down and motioned for Carter to do the same. "How's your summer been?"

"It was good. No major fires, so that was a bonus. I anticipate that might change now that we're beginning to move into cooler weather, and people start to light more fires to ward off the chill."

"All the more reason to talk to the kids. Hopefully, they'll lecture their parents about fire safety."

They talked for a few more minutes before Carter went back into the main office. Sandra gave him the names of teachers who might be available to talk with him, and she also reminded him to check the teachers' lounge.

One of the names she'd given him was Jillian Hall's, so he thought he'd go check and see if she was in her classroom first. He knew her from the time he spent with Eli McNamara and the group of people who often gathered to go on hikes and also met for Bible studies. He didn't know her well, but from what he'd seen, she seemed like a nice person.

Walking down the empty hallway, he could hear the chatter in the classrooms he passed in search of Jillian's. When he spotted the 3A label above the door, he headed for the room.

He paused near the doorway when he heard voices.

"C'mon, Jill. I think we'd have a really good time."

"I'm sorry, Martin, but I can't."

"Can't or won't?" the man said. "I know some girls like to play hard to get, but I'm not really into that kind of game."

Carter frowned when he heard the hard edge in Martin's voice. Without thinking twice about it, he moved toward the door.

CHAPTER TWO

Jillian shifted nervously behind her desk. Martin was glaring at her now, and her heart beat a panicked rhythm within her chest. She fought the urge to bolt out of the classroom and run far away from the man.

He'd been asking her out since the first day of school, and it appeared he wasn't keen to take no for an answer. She'd tried avoiding him, but somehow, the man always managed to find and corner her. For some reason, he had determined that they would be perfect for each other.

The very thought threatened to bring forth a full-on panic attack. Anxiety swelled within her, and she began to take quick breaths, her chest tightening painfully. If she hadn't experienced this before, she would have thought she was having a heart attack. Unfortunately, that knowledge didn't help to ease the very physical reaction she was having.

"Hey, sweetheart. Sandra told me you didn't have a class, so I thought I'd stop in and see you."

The man's voice broke through her panic, and Jillian looked over to see Carter Ward walking into the classroom. When his gaze met hers, he gave her a small smile. The panic began to recede a bit, though it was far from gone.

"Who's this?" Martin demanded as he glared at Carter.

Carter held out his hand. "I'm Carter Ward."

Martin hesitated a moment before he shook Carter's hand. "Martin Allen."

"You're a teacher here too?" Carter asked as he moved to stand next to Jillian.

Thankfully, he didn't put his arm around her, but his elbow brushed against her, and for some reason, Jillian felt safe. Carter wouldn't let Martin do anything to her while he was there.

"I teach grade four." He frowned at Carter. "What do you do?"

"I work with the fire department."

"And you're what? Jillian's boyfriend?" Martin's frown deepened. "She's never mentioned you."

Carter glanced down at her and smiled. It was more than he'd ever smiled at her before. "We're still kind of new so haven't really been telling people just yet."

That didn't lessen the scowl on Martin's face, and the look he gave her made Jillian want to step behind Carter. Instead, she crossed her arms as she tried to take a deep breath.

"You didn't have to lead me on," he muttered angrily. "You could have just said you had a boyfriend."

"I believe I just told you why she wouldn't have mentioned that," Carter said, his voice hard. "Her *no* should have been sufficient. She doesn't need to give you details of her life in order to justify turning you down."

Martin gave them an assessing look before gesturing in their direction. "I have a hard time believing this is for real."

"What's that supposed to mean?" Carter growled.

"Just that it's hard to imagine that someone like *you* would be with someone like *her*."

Jillian felt heat rise in her cheeks, and she lowered her gaze to the floor.

"I suggest you leave," Carter said, his voice low with an edge to it. "I will be encouraging Jillian to speak with Principal Hughes if you don't leave her alone."

Martin gave a huff before he turned and walked out of the classroom. Jillian watched him go, hoping with all her heart that this would be the end of his harassment.

However, she wasn't holding her breath.

"Has he been bothering you a lot?"

Jillian looked up at Carter, taking in the surprising concern in his eyes. "He's been asking me out ever since school started. I keep telling him no, that I don't date, but it's like he doesn't believe me." She gave a shrug. "And I suppose now he'll think I was actually lying since it looks like I'm dating you."

Carter grimaced. "I'm sorry. It was the first thing I thought to say when I realized he was hassling you."

"It's fine. As long as you don't actually want to date." Her cheeks flushed. "Uh...not that you would want to."

"Actually," he said, a considering look on his face. "Are you against dating in general? Or is there a specific reason you don't date?"

"I'm not interested in a relationship," she told him. "I mean, most people date with the goal of eventually getting engaged or married. I don't want that."

"If that wasn't something I wanted either, maybe we could help each other out?"

Jillian frowned. "What do you mean?"

"Are your friends trying to set you up?"

She thought about how Cara and Sarah had both hinted that maybe there were guys in the church who had good dating potential. "Yeah. Now that they're in love, they want to help everyone else find that too."

"Yep. I'm getting that from Eli, Beau, and Kieran too."

"So are you suggesting we date to get them off our backs?"

Carter shrugged. "It would help me out if I could say that I have a date for certain things."

"Like Eli and Anna's wedding?"

"Yeah, like that. I'm not saying just the two of us should go out, since neither of us are really looking for that, but having a date for group activities might be beneficial for both of us."

Jillian considered his suggestion, wondering if it could really work. It would be nice to have someone to go with to certain events, especially since her closest friends in town were all in relationships. There were times she felt like a third or fifth wheel when they went out together.

But would anyone actually believe it?

Martin wasn't wrong. The likelihood of someone like Carter ever dating someone like her was pretty slim. But maybe it wouldn't matter what other people thought. If it was what worked for her and Carter, that would be all that mattered. No one needed to know that neither of them was interested in falling in love or having a relationship that eventually led to something serious like marriage.

"I'm not interested in a physical relationship of any type," Jillian blurted out. That was a deal breaker. If he wanted to have that, she couldn't go through with the plan.

"That's fine." Carter gave her a curious look, and she braced herself for him to ask more questions. "Are you okay with me being close to you? Maybe holding your hand?"

She thought about how she'd felt when he'd come to stand next to her to confront Martin and nodded. "That should be alright."

"So Eli and Anna's wedding? We'll go together?"

Jillian stared at him for a moment. "Are you sure about this? Having this sort of...dating relationship with me?"

"I'm sure," he said without hesitation. "I want people to stop pressuring me to date, but at the same time, I'm not in a position to truly date someone. Plus, I don't want to go out with someone who hopes that our relationship will become serious."

Jillian didn't press for his reasons, though she was curious, because if she pushed for answers from Carter, then she'd have to answer any questions he might have for her. And she didn't want to have to do that.

"All I ask is if you change your mind, or meet someone you actually want to date, that you let me know," Jillian said. "I don't want to find out through rumors or gossip."

"Of course," Carter agreed with a nod. "And the same for you."

She wanted to say he had nothing to worry about, but she kept that to herself and just nodded. "People are going to think this is weird."

"Maybe," Carter said with a shrug. "But it's not like we're total strangers. We've known each other for a few months now."

That was true, but she'd never looked at him as a potential boyfriend. She didn't look at *any* man that way anymore. Sarah and Cara might be hard sells for their plan because she wasn't sure she'd ever mentioned Carter to them. They, however, had mentioned him to *her* a few times, and she hadn't been receptive to their hints.

"I guess it doesn't have to be a big deal," Jillian said. "I mean, we'd just be starting out, right?"

"Right."

She was still curious about why Carter would even suggest something like this. And she was pretty sure this was the most she'd heard the guy speak since she'd met him a few months earlier. Eli and Kieran joked about him being the strong, silent dude. She would have agreed with them...until this interaction with him.

Her phone began to chime on her desk, and she leaned over to pick it up. She tapped the screen to stop the alarm. "Well, I've got seven minutes to get myself down to the gym to collect my class." She paused then said, "Were you here for a specific reason?"

"Actually, yes. I was going to see about setting up a time for me to come by and chat with the kids about fire safety."

"Oh, okay."

Carter pulled his phone out of his pocket. "How about we exchange numbers, and I'll call you later to talk about a suitable time, so I don't hold you up now?"

Jillian nodded then rattled off her number for Carter. Within a few seconds, her phone chimed with a text.

"There. Now you have my number too." Carter began to back toward the door as he slid his phone into the pocket of his jeans. "I'll talk to you later."

She watched him turn and disappear out the door into the hallway. Gripping her phone tightly, Jillian considered the bizarre turn her life had taken in the past twenty minutes.

Realizing she couldn't just stand there going over her conversation with Carter, Jillian slid her phone into her purse which she put into the drawer and locked it before leaving her classroom to go to the gym.

Still, as she walked down the hallway, she couldn't help but wonder how this was going to play out. Carter seemed to feel it wouldn't be a big deal, but she had a feeling he'd be able to brush aside queries from the men in their group easier than she would be able to do that with the women.

She didn't have too much time to mull it over before she had to turn her attention to corralling her group of twenty-two third graders as they walked down the hall from the gym to their classroom. Given they'd just spent forty-five minutes or so being physically active, they still had a surprisingly high level of energy.

It took all her efforts to be able to direct their attention to what they needed to do in their last class. Once that was done, she gave them each a coloring sheet then spent the final fifteen minutes of the day reading to them from *Charlie and the Chocolate Factory* while they colored.

They were just finishing up the second week of school, but Jillian already felt hopeful about the year ahead. She loved the kids, and while a few of them were a bit of a handful, it wasn't anything she hadn't been able to handle so far.

Once the last student had left for the day, Jillian began to pack away her things, keeping an eye on the doorway in case Martin decided to pay her another visit now that Carter was gone. When she made it out to her car without seeing him again, she breathed a sigh of relief.

Now that her workday was over, Jillian was eager to get home. She drove the short distance to her grandma's house—her house now—and pulled into the garage. She turned off the engine but allowed the garage door to close before climbing out of the car and entering the house.

She paused to take off her shoes and jacket in the mudroom between the garage and the kitchen. She'd redone that area—along with many other parts of the house—and installed a bench with hooks above it along the wall for jackets and drawers under the padded bench seat for additional storage.

The room and the bench were all painted white. She liked the bright cheery look of things, but the room was really better suited to a family with children than a single person. That was true of most of the house, but since a family was no longer in her future, she had chosen to decorate and renovate with her own enjoyment in mind. If sometimes that led her to decorate in a way that was more suitable to a family than a single woman, so be it.

"Hello, Dolly," Jillian said as a tawny cat wove her way around her ankles. She bent over and picked the cat up, nuzzling against her soft fur.

The cat had been her grandma's, named for her favorite character from the movie by the same name. After her grandma passed away in Portland, Jillian and Dolly had returned to New Hope Falls and to the home they'd both lived in for years.

"How has your day been?" Jillian asked the cat as she set her back down on the floor.

The cat meowed in response. As Jillian made her way to her bedroom, the cat followed behind her, and the two of them kept up their version of a conversation. Sure, it probably made her a crazy cat lady, but she wasn't going to apologize for that. Her grandmother had often talked to Dolly, so their "conversations" were something that soothed them both.

After she'd changed out of her work clothes and into a pair of loose sweats and a baggy T-shirt, Jillian went back to the kitchen. Once she'd set the oven for the frozen lasagna she'd pulled from the freezer, she turned on the television. She usually had it on whenever she was in the house because sometimes the quiet was just too loud.

The Food Network was currently playing, so she left it there since she liked most shows on that channel as well as on HGTV. The interest in the latter was recent, spurred on by the renovations she'd had done on the house.

Once the oven beeped, signaling it was ready, she slid the lasagna in and set the timer. Though she did have some work to do for school, she needed a bit of a break before she tackled it.

She loved her job. Her grandma had been a teacher, and Jillian had always enjoyed school. Although her grandma had taught middle school, Jillian had loved the idea of teaching younger kids. Being a teacher was all she'd ever wanted.

But even with loving her job as much as she did—Martin aside—Jillian always felt the need to unwind for a couple of hours before diving back into the preparation she needed to do for the day or week ahead. The interlude was the perfect time to do a few things around the house, and on that day, she had laundry to finish up.

As she went to the laundry room to pull a load from the dryer, Jillian thought back to her conversation with Carter. She had to admit it was a bit bizarre, and now that she had a little distance from the conversation, she had to wonder if she was making a mistake.

CHAPTER THREE

On the surface, Jillian figured the plan seemed like a decent enough one. They would, essentially, be friends who would be each other's date when necessary without the need for one-on-one or romantic dates. That part of the scheme definitely appealed to her.

It would get Cara and Sarah off her back and hopefully keep Martin at bay. Realistically, however, it wasn't as if guys were banging down her door wanting a date with her these days.

What was giving her a bit of pause was that she didn't know Carter all that well. He seemed perfectly nice, and Eli and Kieran seemed to think highly of him. He held a good job in the town. He attended the same church as she did when his schedule allowed. Definitely all positives.

The downside was that she had no confidence in her ability to judge a guy. At one time, she'd considered herself a good judge of character, but she no longer felt that way.

Back in the living room, she sat down with the full laundry basket and began to fold its contents. Dolly rubbed up against her arm, purring loudly. In between items of clothing, Jillian gave the cat some love since she was always a needy kitty after Jillian had left her alone for an extended period of time.

"What do you think, Dolly?" she murmured. "Did I make a bad decision by agreeing to this?"

Dolly's thoughts on the topic were limited to a single *meow*. Jillian's thoughts on the subject, however, were plentiful and maybe not quite rational.

Though they wouldn't be going on dates by themselves, it would look strange if they showed up to events like Eli and Anna's wedding in two separate vehicles. That meant she would have to be willing to spend time alone with Carter in a car. She'd have to trust that when he picked her up, he would drive her to where they were supposed to go and not take advantage of being in control to drive her somewhere else.

Jillian lowered the shirt she'd been folding into her lap, crumpling it in her hands. Her heart thumped painfully in her chest. She lifted her gaze and stared at the television, focusing on the people on the screen. It was a reality baking competition show, and she forced herself to engage with it.

She began to count, working to calm her rapidly beating heart enough that she could take a deep breath. Finally, Jillian was able to draw in a long breath then let it out, willing all the anxiety and panic to accompany the exhale.

"Should I call Sarah, huh, Dolly?" Jillian said as she scooped up the cat and sat back on the couch. "Maybe she could give me some insight into Carter."

Pulling her phone out, Jillian spent a few minutes rehearsing what she'd say to her friend. She didn't want to lie to her, but she also didn't want to give her all the details that she and Carter had agreed on.

"Hey, Jillian," Sarah said when she answered her phone. "How's life as an elementary teacher?"

"So far, so good. The kids are keeping me on my toes, but I'm loving it."

"That's great. Those kids are blessed to have you," Sarah said with strong conviction in her voice."

Jillian couldn't help the smile that tugged at the corners of her mouth at Sarah's words. She really hoped that the kids felt that way.

She tugged at a piece of her hair before shoving it behind her ear. "Listen, what can you tell me about Carter?"

"Carter?" Sarah asked. "Carter Ward? Firefighter? Mr. Strong and Silent? *That* Carter?"

Jillian sighed. "Yes. *That* Carter."

"I will answer your question about him, but just know that I expect some answers in return. Deal?"

"Sarah..."

"Deal?"

"Fine," Jillian said with a huff. "Deal."

"Perfect!" Jillian could literally *hear* the grin on Sarah's face. "Okay. What do I know about Carter? He's been here for three or four years, maybe more. I'm not altogether sure how long, to be honest. If you need an exact date, I can ask Eli."

"No, you don't need to do that," Jillian said.

"Well, he's worked for the fire department as long as I've known him, and he's attended the church for that length of time too. He and Eli became friends through the men's group in the past year or so."

"Has he ever dated anyone?"

"He's never shown an interest in any of the women at the church that I'm aware of. Whhhhyyy?"

The way Sarah drew out the word made Jillian roll her eyes, but she'd known this was the risk of asking her about Carter.

"I was talking to him today," Jillian began.

"You were?" Sarah exclaimed. "Where?"

"He, uh, came to the school and stopped by my classroom."

"Really? Just came by to see you?"

Jillian tugged at a strand of hair again. "No. He came to arrange a time to do a fire prevention presentation for my class. Martin was there when he came."

"Martin? The guy who's been hassling you for a date?"

"Yeah. Carter put him in his place, and then we got to chatting."

"Got to chatting? Mr. Silent got to chatting?"

Jillian could hardly blame Sarah for her skepticism. She had also been surprised at how much Carter had talked. "Yes. We chatted."

"And now you want to know more about him?" Sarah paused for a moment. "Are you *interested* in him?"

"Well, I'd hardly be asking you about him if I wasn't," Jillian said with a sigh. "We talked about going to Eli and Anna's wedding together. I just thought maybe I should find out a little bit more about him."

"I would imagine that he's a decent guy if Eli considers him a friend. I mean, he's one of Eli's groomsmen, so Eli must think highly of him."

"Who else is standing up with Eli?" Jillian knew that Sarah, her twin sister, Leah, and Anna's assistant, Rebecca, were all bridesmaids, but she hadn't heard who the groomsmen were.

"He wanted to ask Kieran, but no one figured that would be a good idea as long as that detective is still poking around. So he has Carter, Michael Reed, and Andy. He hadn't had a lot of friends to choose from until the last year or so."

"Andy surprises me," Jillian said.

"I know, right? But honestly, Andy's been a rock, so supportive of all of us for a long time, never believing for a moment that Eli had anything to do with Sheila's disappearance. And ever since Eli started organizing the hikes and having Bible study at his place, Andy's been there."

Jillian thought of all the changes that had occurred while she'd been away from New Hope. Though some of them were surprising, most of them were welcome. She liked the more mature group of friends she had now compared to the ones she'd had in high school. Sarah and, to a lesser degree, Leah had been part of both groups, but the stability of the group now appealed to her more.

"So, are you going to go with Carter?"

Jillian tried to put aside her own gut instincts and just think about the things Sarah had told her and what she figured Carter likely had to go through as far as background checks for his job at the fire station. Of course, a finger-print based background check didn't necessarily mean he hadn't committed a crime, just that he hadn't gotten caught for it.

Still, Eli seemed like a good judge of character, so if he wanted this man to stand up with him, then Carter must be a decent guy. "Yes. I think I will."

"Oh, that's so wonderful!" Sarah exclaimed. "Just you wait!"

Jillian stifled a laugh. *No, just* you *wait.* She knew that Sarah would never understand why she was agreeing to do things this way with Carter. Not unless she shared all her reasons. Sarah would understand then, but Jillian didn't want her to have that knowledge.

She'd worked hard to keep people from knowing that part of her life because she didn't want people to treat her differently. In some ways, it felt like a small miracle that Carter not only had agreed to a relationship without a future, but he'd done so without asking *why* she wanted such a thing.

"Are we celebrating the end of the second week of school tomorrow?" Sarah asked.

"Don't you have a better way to spend a Friday evening than eating chocolate fondue with me?" Jillian asked. "Like going for a date with your man?"

"Well, about that," Sarah began.

"If you need to cancel, that's fine."

"Not cancelling," she said quickly. "I just thought maybe we could do a joint evening. Have the guys with us. I wasn't sure at first, but now that you and Carter are a thing, maybe we could invite him too."

"We're not a thing." Jillian sighed. "It's still new. It might not work out."

"Don't think like that," Sarah admonished her. "Don't start out thinking so negatively."

It had taken Jillian ages to get herself out of a constantly negative mindset, but occasionally she slipped back into it. At one time, she'd had the best of expectations when it came to her future. A sucker punch followed by a knock-out blow had done a number on her once positive outlook.

"So are you saying we'll be having a co-ed chocolate fondue?"

"I think that would be fun."

"It's possible Carter will have to work," Jillian said.

"I'll ask him, and if he does, we'll work it out."

Her phone beeped, and she looked at the screen. "Maybe I'll ask him and let you know."

There was a beat of silence. "Is he calling you right now?"

"Yes, so I'm going to go."

"Byeeee," Sarah sang out then hung up.

After Jillian answered Carter's call, he said, "Hi. This is Carter. Just thought I'd call and touch base about the presentation for your class."

"Sure. Just let me check my schedule." Jillian got up from the couch and went to her messenger bag where she pulled out her planner. She sat down at the dining room table and opened it up. "When were you thinking of coming?"

"I probably have a bit more flexible of a schedule than you might," Carter said. "I can work with what is most convenient for you."

For the next several minutes, they discussed possible times and dates before settling on a day. Jillian found that she was curious to see how the reserved man managed to connect with the oft-times hyper students in her class.

"Um, just one more thing," Jillian said as their conversation seemed to be drawing to a close.

"What's that?"

"I was talking to Sarah a couple of minutes ago, and I'd mentioned we might be attending Eli's wedding together." She hesitated. "I hope that was okay."

"That's fine," Carter said. "Was that all?"

"No. She also mentioned that she wanted to include the guys in our ladies' Fondue Friday tomorrow night, and then she wondered if you'd like to come too."

"Fondue Friday?" he asked.

"Yeah. A few months ago, we started meeting on Friday nights every two or three weeks to have chocolate fondue. You're welcome to say no, by the way. Don't feel like you have to come. I mean, especially if you have to work."

"I don't have work tomorrow," he stated.

"Okay. Well, if you'd like to come, you're welcome."

"Time?"

"Oh, uh, we usually meet around six."

"And all you eat is chocolate fondue?" Carter asked.

Jillian wondered if she should feel judged by his assumption that they would eat chocolate fondue as the main course. "Well, we dip fruit in the chocolate."

"So dinner is chocolate dipped fruit?"

"We also dip pound cake."

It was then Jillian heard something she'd never heard from Carter before. A laugh. Seriously, a *laugh.*

"Okay, well that sounds just...yummy."

"It is," Jillian agreed, unable to keep from smiling. "But, to put your mind at ease, we usually do have an actual meal first. Although, it won't be terribly healthy. It's our indulgence meal."

"I guess I'll take my chances."

Sobering, Jillian said, "Just brace yourself. Even though I told Sarah that we're still just getting to know each other, she's excited about this turn of events."

"No worries. I can handle it."

"I'll see you tomorrow then."

After they said goodbye, Jillian returned to her laundry, groaning when she saw that Dolly had knocked over a pile of clothes that she'd already folded.

"Naughty girl," she said as she set about re-folding them all.

She'd only just finished with the laundry when the timer went indicating the lasagna was ready. After setting it on the counter to cool for a few minutes, Jillian went to put away her laundry. Back in the kitchen, she put some food in Dolly's bowl then dished up some lasagna for herself.

While she ate, she watched some television then cleaned up the kitchen. She gathered up her messenger bag and planner before shutting off all the lights and making her way to her bedroom.

Dolly followed behind her and jumped up on the bed as Jillian closed the bedroom door. She turned the television on to provide background noise while she sat at her desk, grading the worksheets the kids had done that day before turning her attention to her lesson plans.

Once she was done with the schoolwork, she took a shower then crawled into bed to watch a bit more television while she played some games on her phone. Before turning off her lamp for the night, she opened her Bible and did her reading for the day. That was usually her way of unwinding and filling her mind with Godly thoughts in hopes that the nightmares would not invade her sleep.

But that night, she found herself spending more time thinking about the situation with Carter. She really hoped that it wasn't going to blow up in her face.

The thought sent anxiety spiralling through her, which made it even more challenging than usual to fall asleep.

CHAPTER FOUR

Carter was dragging by the time he finished talking to Jillian. As he headed to his small bathroom to get ready for bed, he wondered if he'd just hallucinated that conversation with her. The humor of the moment over the chocolate fondue had caught him off-guard.

He was still a bit surprised—no, make that *very* surprised—at the direction things had taken when he'd stepped into Jillian's classroom. All he'd been thinking, once he'd realized that Jillian wasn't interested in a serious relationship, was that maybe that was something that could work for both of them.

Being together would help get Martin off her back, and it would help convince Evelyn and Garth that he was moving forward.

He wasn't sure what to consider it. Fake didn't really describe what they'd discussed. They weren't going to actually fake a relationship. They'd go on dates...just not by themselves.

As soon as he'd walked out of the school, he'd had a moment wondering if he'd lost his mind. But realistically, it was the only type of relationship he could even begin to imagine. One where there would be no expectations of romance or a proposal at some point in the future.

Was it possible that she was only saying that and would change her mind later on?

Carter supposed it was, but she had been the one to bring up the fact that she wasn't interested in a serious relationship. Just as there was something holding him back, there was clearly something holding her back too. She hadn't pressed for answers though, so neither had he.

He hoped that the dinner—which seemed very couple oriented—wouldn't be uncomfortable for either of them. The guys had been talking to him about dating, especially as they'd each found a woman to love, but they hadn't specifically mentioned Jillian. He had no idea what they'd think when they realized they were together, especially because he'd been pretty adamant about not dating.

When he crawled into bed a short time later, Carter was beginning to think that maybe they'd bitten off more than they could chew. He hoped not, though, because it seemed like this could be the answer for both of them.

At least in the short term.

Carter pulled his truck to a stop in front of Eli's place. He'd had to text Jillian to ask where to go since that wasn't something she'd mentioned the night before.

As he stepped out of the truck, he took a deep breath, appreciating the fresh fall air. The sky was a dark gray, making it seem later than it actually was. Even though the days were getting shorter, it was still an hour or so before the sun was due to set. Winter would soon be upon them, and then the new year. That was something he looked forward to and dreaded in equal measure.

But now wasn't the time to dwell on that.

Glancing around, Carter recognized most the cars there, including Jillian's. He frowned as the thought crossed his mind that perhaps he should have offered to pick her up.

After ten years of not dating, he was sorely out of practice. That this wasn't a normal dating relationship made things even more complicated. But as long as he and Jillian were comfortable with their agreed-upon arrangement, it shouldn't matter if others thought they were doing things "wrong."

He took the stairs two at a time, then knocked on Eli's front door. It opened right away to reveal the man himself.

"Hey there," Eli said with a broad smile. "C'mon in."

Carter nodded a greeting as he stepped past his friend.

After closing the door, Eli turned to him. "So this is a surprise. I kind of thought you weren't interested in dating."

Shrugging, Carter said, "Things change."

"I'll say they have." The other man smacked him on the shoulder. "You're a sneaky one."

"Not really. This is new. It's not like we've been sneaking around dating."

Motioning for Carter to follow him, Eli headed over to where the living room was set up in the open floor plan. "I hear you rescued her."

"I guess so. The guy was not taking no for an answer."

"She should probably report him," Kieran said with a frown as Carter sat down on the loveseat across from him.

Beau nodded. "I would agree. Sarah said that Jillian mentioned he'd been asking her out from the first time they met."

"I told her to talk to the principal," Carter said. "I think she worries about rocking the boat when she's a new teacher there."

"Hopefully now that the guy knows you two are dating, he'll back off." Kieran still had a frown on his face. "But if he doesn't, she needs to let Hughes know. I'm almost positive that he would want to know, regardless. He might turn his attention—unwanted attention—on someone else now that Jillian is unavailable."

"I'll talk to her about it again," Carter said.

Eli got to his feet. "I'm just going to check on the food."

Carter watched him walk over to where the kitchen was located, spotting Jillian right away where she sat on a stool at the counter that divided the kitchen space from the dining room area. He realized that perhaps he should have gone over and said hi to Jillian when he arrived, but he wasn't sure if that would have created an awkward situation for them.

Jillian's attention was on Anna as she stirred the contents of a large crock pot, which Carter knew was the source of the rich aroma that filled the air. He inhaled deeply, his stomach rumbling in anticipation. Though he'd had a good breakfast, he'd skipped lunch, figuring he had a tasty meal to look forward to that evening.

Eli put his arm around Anna and dropped a kiss on her head. They were just two weeks away from the wedding, so Carter imagined they were excited that they would be married soon. He knew that if it had been him, he certainly would have been.

Shutting down those thoughts, Carter shifted his attention back to the men he'd come to consider good friends. "How's your new house?"

Beau smiled. "It's great, but I still need to get more furniture. Julianna's been a big help, but we've just purchased the basics so far. Beds. A few couches. Table and chairs. She says I need a lot more."

Carter ignored the pang he felt when Beau mentioned his sister. In a lot of ways, Julianna reminded him of Suzanne, right down to her penchant for designer things. Of course, they both came from wealthy families that had allowed them to indulge that fondness.

If at all possible, Carter limited his interactions with Julianna because she was a poignant reminder of all he'd lost. It was hard enough that he had that reminder whenever he visited Suzanne. He was glad that this particular gathering didn't include Julianna, particularly because this was supposed to be his and Jillian's first...something.

"So Jillian, bro?" Kieran said. "How exactly did that come about? Pretty sure you weren't interested in dating just like...two seconds ago."

"Already had this convo with Eli," Carter grumbled. "Things change."

Kieran's brows rose slightly. "I would say that's true. Things do change."

"Am I going to be constantly explaining everything we do?" Carter wasn't sure he was on board with that.

"I sense that would bug you," Beau commented.

"You sense correctly." Carter leaned back, stretching his legs out. "So no inquisitions please."

"Well, since you said please..." Kieran laughed. "Who am I kidding? The curiosity will kill us if we can't ask you any questions about this."

"RIP you," Carter muttered.

Beau chuckled. "I think we could probably get info from the ladies. I have a feeling they're going to be as curious as we are. Maybe Jillian will be more forthcoming."

When Kieran arched a brow at him, Carter just shrugged. "Time will tell."

Carter honestly couldn't say whether Jillian would spill more details. Even though she did seem more talkative than he was, she could still keep the secret of the true nature of their relationship.

"Have you always been this closemouthed about things?" Kieran asked.

Truthfully, he hadn't. Back when he and Suzanne had met, he'd been a lot more talkative. The sorrow and strain of the past ten years, however, had knocked that out of him. And when he'd moved to New Hope a few years back, he'd already gotten to the point where he only spoke when absolutely necessary. Giving away as little information about himself as possible. That wasn't going to change now.

"I talk when I have something to say," Carter replied.

Kieran rolled his eyes. "You make a rock seem chatty."

"Don't know what kind of rocks you've been around lately."

"Hey, guys," Eli called. "Why don't we sit up at the table?"

The three of them got to their feet and headed to the large dining room table. Anna told them where to sit, and Carter realized that he and Jillian were seated next to each other. When he noticed the other men holding the chairs for the girlfriends, he quickly did the same for Jillian.

She gave him a small smile, and he wondered if she would expect these kinds of gestures all the time. Not that it would matter if she did. It wasn't like it cost him anything to do things like hold her chair. But he was going to have to give himself a crash course in boyfriend behavior if he wanted his friends to buy the story that the two of them were really dating.

Once they were in their seats, Eli said a prayer for the meal, then they began to pass the food around. The tasty beef stew and fresh sourdough bread were perfect for the cool fall evening. It had been a while since he'd had either, so he enjoyed the meal very much. Conversation flowed around him, with Jillian holding her own as she answered questions about how her first couple of weeks at the school had gone.

No one asked about Martin, for which he was glad as he had a feeling that would bring Jillian's upbeat mood down. Though she wasn't over-the-top happy and bubbly the way Sarah was, she had a sort of understated happiness that worked for Carter. At least the Carter he was now.

He could tell by the curious looks they were getting that everyone at the table was trying to get a read on how things were between them. Carter wasn't sure he wanted any of this group to know more about them as a couple. He and Jillian just needed to do things the way they chose and not let other people's expectations force the course of their relationship.

"So you two are coming to our wedding together?" Anna glanced back and forth between him and Jillian.

"Yes," Jillian said. "Is that a problem?"

"Not at all," Anna assured her. "You were both coming anyway, so that doesn't change the numbers."

Now that he thought about it, planning for them to go together to the wedding didn't make a lot of sense, since he'd have other responsibilities demanding his attention and wouldn't be able to devote much time to Jillian.

Once they finished dinner, the dishes were quickly cleared away, and the fondue was set up on the large square coffee table in the living room. Rather than sit on the couches, they all settled on the floor with four small fondue pots set up with an assortment of fruits and cake on medium-size platters next to them.

This was all new to Carter, so he listened as Sarah gave a few instructions before handing out small plates and metal skewer looking things with black handles on one end and a two-pronged fork on the other.

"I like the bananas the best," Jillian said as she leaned close to him, her shoulder brushing against his. "My next favorite is either the strawberries or the pound cake."

He waited while Jillian dipped a chunk of banana and then put it on her plate. Since he liked bananas, Carter decided he'd start there too.

Conversation around the table was of the wedding and all the things that had to occur in the next couple of weeks. There was talk of the upcoming joint bachelor and bachelorette party that Anna and Eli had decided to have rather than two separate parties.

"Did you like the banana?" Jillian asked as he reached out to spear a piece of strawberry.

"It was good," he said, then dipped the strawberry into the warm chocolate.

Jillian went for another piece of banana, waiting until he'd finished with his strawberry before dipping her fork into the pot. He moved onto the pound cake, then a slice of apple, a grape, and an orange, before finding himself back at the bananas.

"Do you want to trade?" Sarah asked, nudging Jillian.

Jillian glanced at him. When he arched a questioning brow at her, she said, "Sarah likes the strawberries. She'll give us bananas in return."

Carter chuckled. "Sure. She can have the strawberries."

He watched as trades went on around the table. The other men laughed as well as they observed the trade process. Carter turned to Eli, who sat kitty-corner to him. "Is this your first time to one of these?"

"Yep, it is."

"So you don't know if this is normal or not?" Carter asked, his voice low as he gestured at the fruit being exchanged.

"From the ease with which these trades are happening, I would say it's quite normal," Eli said, an indulgent smile on his face as he watched Anna slide oranges onto Cara's plate and take some pound cake in return.

Carter enjoyed watching the women interact, and he noticed that the other guys seemed to as well. They were definitely on the ladies' turf now that the dinner was over, and Carter found he was somewhat fascinated by it. It had been forever since he'd shared a meal with other couples while also being part of a couple himself. Sort of.

When his thoughts began to wander to times he and Suzanne had spent with other couple friends, Carter quickly refocused. Though it wasn't the first time Suzanne had come to his thoughts while in the presence of these people, it was the first time he hadn't felt comfortable with those thoughts.

"That banana not to your liking?" Eli asked.

"Hmmm?" Carter looked at him.

"You're frowning like the banana personally offended you."

"No banana offense here," Carter assured him, firmly pushing the thoughts of Suzanne from his mind.

She still had a place in his life, but it wasn't there in that moment. There was a twinge of guilt at that thought, and he knew that it would grow later when he had nothing to distract him.

As the evening progressed, Carter had to admit that he could see why getting together like this would appeal to Jillian. It wasn't really his thing. He preferred the men's group or the Bible study since there was a clear focus for the evening. This reminded him a bit more of the dinners they had following the hikes the group often went on. Of course, that group usually included more than just the couples present there.

"Do you want more apples?" Jillian turned their tray so the apples were closer to him. "You seem to like them better than I do."

"I do." Carter speared an apple. "You can have the rest of the bananas."

Jillian gave him a quick smile. "Thanks. Strange thing, but at any other time, I'm not a huge banana fan, but dunk them into some chocolate, and I can't get enough of them."

It felt a bit intimate to be sharing food the way they were, making Carter shift a bit as he watched Jillian dip another piece of banana into the pot. But even as the thought of that intimacy made him a bit uneasy, he couldn't deny there was a level of comfort present as well.

CHAPTER FIVE

The comfort Carter felt extended to the others at the table. These people—especially the guys—were his friends. They knew not to push him for conversation, though they did give him a hard time on occasion. And that was okay.

Those interactions reminded him of his old friends. The ones who had been left behind when he'd fled Miami for Seattle after Suzanne's parents had brought her back home when it became clear that there was nothing more that could be done for her there.

"What are you doing this weekend, Jillian?" Sarah asked as she leaned against Beau. Her gaze slid Carter's way for a moment, and when she saw he was looking at her, she gave him a beaming smile.

"Just working on stuff around the house." Jillian set her empty fork down on her plate. "I'll probably try to do some painting. I finally picked up the colors I wanted for the guest bedrooms, so I should probably tackle those soon."

"You did a great job on the master bedroom." Cara shifted forward to rest her arms on the coffee table. "I love the colors you chose."

"Your grandma would be happy with the work you're doing on the house," Sarah said.

"Is she buried here?" Eli asked. "I don't remember hearing anything about her passing."

"She wanted to be cremated. I had her ashes interred not long after I got back here. She didn't want to be buried in Portland."

Carter found himself wondering a bit more about Jillian. Did she come from a large family like his? Did her parents live in New Hope?

"That was nice that she left you the house," Sarah said. "Maybe I could come help you do some painting."

"Hang on now," Eli protested, pointing at his sister with his fork. "You didn't offer to help when we were painting the cabins."

Sarah shrugged. "But you had Leah and Anna to help you, and that all worked out in the end."

"Yeah." Eli smiled indulgently at Anna. "Yeah, it sure did."

"I think I'll be okay with it," Jillian said. "But if I want a mural painted, I'll let you know."

"Did you have work done on the house?" Kieran asked. "Or are you just repainting?"

"I had work done. Grandma left me money as well as the house, with express instructions that I use it to renovate the house the way I wanted it." Jillian shifted away from Carter, even though they hadn't been sitting that close together. "So I upgraded the master bathroom and the kitchen and mudroom area. I also replaced the flooring throughout most the house. I mean, I didn't do the work myself. I hired people to do it all."

"It looks really nice," Sarah said. "And I hope that means you're planning to stick around."

"I have no desire to move anywhere else. New Hope is where I feel..." Jillian paused and took a deep breath. "Well, it's where I feel most at home."

Carter could see that Jillian's shoulders were tense, lifted high. Her fingers began to tap lightly on the table.

One. Two. Three. Four. Five. Pause.

One. Two. Three. Four. Five. Pause.

One. Two. Three. Four. Five. Pause.

He stared at her fingers, watching as her light pink coated nails tapped out a rhythm. As the conversation continued on around her, the tapping gradually slowed. He heard her blow out a breath as her fingers curled into a loose fist. Carter found himself wanting to reach out and cover her hand with his.

What was it that had upset her during a conversation about home renovations and decorating? It seemed like a harmless enough topic.

"Are you looking forward to moving out of your cabin, Anna?" Cara asked.

Anna grinned at Eli. "I definitely am." She curled into Eli's side. "Since realizing I loved Eli, I've been anticipating this. The moment we begin the together portion of our lives."

A vice tightened around Carter's chest at her words. He said a quick prayer that nothing would happen between that moment and their wedding. That they would never experience the grief and loss he had.

When he found himself taking deep breaths to ease the tightness around his chest, Carter realized that Jillian had been doing something similar. Had she also experienced something traumatic in her past? Had it just been grief over her grandmother's passing? Or had it been something more?

"When are you two tying the knot, Kieran?" Eli asked.

Kieran glanced at Cara. "We thought we'd let you two get married before we announced anything."

"Oh, you guys didn't have to do that," Anna protested.

Cara laughed. "We haven't actually settled on a date yet. But since we're doing something small, it shouldn't take long to pull things together once we decide."

Carter thought of the many discussions he and Suzanne had had about a wedding date. He hadn't wanted to wait, while Suzanne had insisted that a decent wedding would take at least a year to plan. It had been one of their more heated...discussions. It had been an argument...a fight, really.

He wanted to tell Kieran not to argue with Cara about something so trivial. To let the woman he loved pick whatever date she wanted. But Carter didn't say anything. The likelihood of something happening to them like what had happened to him and Suzanne was pretty slim.

"It's not that *we* can't agree on a date," Kieran said. "It's my mom. She wants a big wedding. We're happy with a smaller one. Once we find common ground, we'll have our date."

"I have a feeling it won't be too long," Cara revealed with a smile. "I think Rose is getting to the point where she just wants us married."

"I'm going to be suspicious of any invitation either of you issue," Sarah said. "We'll all show up for something, and you'll be like *Surprise! We're getting married.*"

Kieran and Cara exchanged a look then laughed with the others. Even Carter smiled. He could imagine that happening.

Even though the mood was light, he struggled to embrace it. The thrum of pain within him didn't allow for lightness. He'd known from the moment Eli had asked him to be part of the wedding that he'd have moments like these. Lots of moments like these.

If it had been anyone else, he would have said no. But Eli was the closest thing he had to a best friend these days. Neither of them was very talkative—though Eli could be when around a group of close friends like he was that night—and the man had never pressed Carter to talk about himself, which Carter definitely appreciated.

With another wedding in the near future, Carter was bracing himself for more painful moments. But really, it was something he should have been used to. It seemed that for the past ten years, his life had been one painful moment after another as they'd hoped and prayed for Suzanne's full recovery.

Next to him, Jillian seemed to have relaxed. Whatever had triggered her earlier tension appeared to have loosened its grip on her.

The conversation wound down as the last of the fruit was eaten. They all pitched in to clean up, though Eli and Anna said they had it all under control.

"I think I'm going to head for home," Jillian said as she approached Anna. "Thanks so much for hosting our Fondue Friday."

Anna gave her a hug. "It was fun to include the guys for a change, but I think I enjoy it more when it's just us girls. Then I don't have to share my favorites."

"You just need to bring more." Eli looped an arm around her shoulders, pulling her against his side. "I rather liked being part of Fondue Friday."

"I guess I'll be leaving as well," Carter said. "Appreciate the invite for tonight."

"See you at church on Sunday?" Eli asked.

"I'm working a twenty-four starting tomorrow morning, so we'll see how tired I am at the end of it."

Eli held out his hand. "Stay safe."

"Always." Carter turned to Jillian. "May I walk you to your car?"

He expected her to make a joking comment about her car not being that far away, but instead, she just nodded.

After saying goodbye to the others, Carter walked outside with Jillian. The evening air held more of a chill than it had when he first arrived, and he was glad he'd worn a heavier jacket. Thankfully, Eli had installed lots of lights along the wide porch and the steps so they could safely walk down them to where the cars were parked.

"I think that went well," Jillian said as they reached her car. "Don't you?"

"It did," Carter agreed. "Not having second thoughts about...this?"

Though he hadn't been specific, Jillian seemed to understand what he was referring to.

She gave him a quick look as she opened her car door. "No second thoughts."

Realizing he should have opened the door for her, Carter moved to take hold of the handle when Jillian slid into the driver's seat. "Drive safe."

She smiled up at him as she tugged her seatbelt into place. "You too."

When she started the car, Carter closed the door and stepped back. He waited until she'd backed out of her spot and headed down the road away from Eli's cabin before he climbed into his truck and followed after her. He was glad that she thought the evening had gone well, and he was especially glad that she hadn't seemed to have any expectations for how it should have ended.

Although maybe a kiss at the end of a first date—which he supposed was technically what this had been—wasn't the norm. However, he and Suzanne *had* kissed on their first date. She had been the one to initiate it, but it wasn't like he'd objected. Not at all.

Though he and Jillian hadn't discussed it, kissing wasn't something he was prepared to indulge in as part of their arrangement. Without the basis of some sort of real relationship with her, it just felt like kissing would cheapen it. Not to mention possibly creating awkwardness between them.

That was the last thing he wanted.

Hopefully she felt the same way.

~ * ~

Jillian stared at herself in the mirror. What was one supposed to wear to a joint bachelor-bachelorette party? It didn't sound like the average pre-wedding bash. From what Anna had said, all they wanted was for their friends to have a good time. And apparently that was going to happen at the town's community center. The three bridesmaids had been in charge of planning it with Anna, but they hadn't been leaking any details.

Not that it really mattered what she looked like, though she didn't want Carter to be embarrassed to be seen with her. She already knew that they made an odd couple, and there were probably going to be more than a few people who would wonder why they were together.

That would have bothered teenage Jillian a whole lot, but it didn't bother adult Jillian as much. Still, she didn't want Carter to regret their plan. She'd had a whole week where Martin had basically left her alone aside from a few remarks in the staff lounge about her new boyfriend.

Carter stepping in the previous week had seemed to do the trick of getting Martin off her back. It helped that he'd also seen that Carter had come by again to give his presentation to the children. Jillian had enjoyed that as much as the kids had as it had given her the opportunity to see a different side of Carter.

With her outfit decided on, she looked herself over in the full-length mirror, hoping the light blue jeans and black sweater would do, then went to finish getting ready. While she waited for the flat iron to heat up, she opened the drawer of her vanity, and putting all the skills she'd learned as a teen to work, Jillian did her best to give herself a flawless complexion then applied eyeshadow shades that she knew accented her eyes the best.

When her hair and makeup were finally done, she went to stand in front of the mirror once again, casting a critical eye over her reflection. People might think that when she looked at herself, she would hate the extra weight she carried. That she'd want to lose that weight. But all she saw when she looked at herself now was safety. Her extra weight represented safety.

Though she doubted that Carter would care what she wore—what she looked like—she hoped that the others there would at least see that she'd made the attempt to look nice. For this to work for her and Carter, they had to at least make sense on some level to the people around them. The ones who needed to believe that they were actually a couple.

Satisfied that she looked okay, Jillian headed downstairs to the mudroom where Dolly greeted her.

"Take care of the house, Dolly-girl." She sat down on the bench and reached into the storage space beneath the seat to pull out the medium-heeled boots she planned to wear. "Be a good kitty."

Dolly's response was some window-rattling purring and meowing. The cat wound her way around Jillian's ankles as she slid the boots on. Getting to her feet, she took a jacket off one of the hooks and put it on before gathering up her phone and purse.

It seemed a bit crazy to drive for all of five minutes to get to the community center, but she wasn't interested in walking, especially at night when it was chilly and drizzly.

There were several vehicles in the parking lot when she pulled in, but Carter's truck wasn't one of them. Frowning, she wondered if she should have checked to make sure he was going to be there. They hadn't been in touch that week except for the brief period he'd been in her classroom, but she'd assumed he'd be there since he was part of the wedding party.

Before she got out of her car, she pulled her phone out and stared at it. Would it be weird to text him to see if he was planning to attend the party? Though they'd discussed attending the wedding together, they hadn't talked about this. Maybe she was jumping the gun to assume that they would be in couple-mode for the party. Still, if she showed up without him, she was going to get asked questions...

Just checking to see if you were working tonight or if you were coming to the party. Don't mean to butt into your business, just want to be able to tell people where you are if you can't make it.

Jillian sat for a couple of minutes, waiting for a reply. When there was no response from Carter, she frowned, wondering what to do. She was almost positive that the moment she walked into the building without Carter by her side, Sarah would ask where he was. A perfectly normal question to ask one half of a couple when the other person wasn't with them.

She bit her lip, staring down at the screen of her phone. There was no sign of the three little dots that meant he was replying to the message she'd sent. Though she didn't want to be sitting out in the parking lot any longer than necessary, she still hesitated to head into the community center.

Thankfully, the parking lot was well-lit, but that didn't quell the sense of unease in her stomach. The longer she sat there, the more her anxiety grew, and so did the idea of abandoning the party.

Clutching her phone tightly, she struggled to take slow, measured breaths. This was not how she'd wanted to start her evening. She should have just gone inside and fended off any questions that might have come her way instead of sitting in the dark in her car, allowing herself to become freaked out.

This was New Hope, not Portland. She was safe here.

A knock on the glass near her shoulder sent a bolt of panic through Jillian. Any chance of taking even breaths was obliterated by the anxiety that spiked within her.

CHAPTER SIX

"Jillian?" The man's muffled voice did nothing to calm her. *He* had known her name.

The car door's handle rattled, and she gasped. Then there was another knock on the glass.

She squeezed her eyes shut, well aware that she was overreacting, but her anxiety and panic were so easily triggered these days. After months of emotional stability—with only her grief over her grandma to deal with—it had all begun to fall apart with Martin's continued harassment, and it didn't matter that he had finally left her alone. She had been thrown back into that emotionally fragile place and hadn't yet managed to pull herself out of it.

Her phone chirped and vibrated in her hand, jarring her enough that the fog of panic cleared just a bit. Enough that she knew she should check the message.

Carter: *It's just me. Are you okay?*

Carter... He'd replied to her text. He was there...at her car.

The anxiety began to ease, but not fast enough for her to be able to brush aside what he'd seen through the window. She could hardly just text him back that she was okay. Instead, she took a shaky breath and reached out to press the button to unlock the door.

Immediately, it opened. "Jillian? Are you okay?"

She glanced over and saw Carter crouched down, bringing him to her eye level. Thanks to the light that had come on inside the car, she was able to clearly see the concern on his face.

Great. Now he was going to think she was crazy. Who in their right mind would have a panic attack over a knock on the window of their car?

"I'm okay." Jillian reached out and rested the fingertips of her hand on the lower portion of the steering wheel. With her heart still pounding, she began to tap out the rhythm she used to settle her breathing and her anxiety. "You just surprised me."

One. Two. Three. Four. Five. Pause.

"I'm sorry about that," Carter said softly. "I didn't read your message until I got here, so I figured I'd just talk to you instead of replying."

One. Two. Three. Four. Five. Pause.

Jillian nodded. "That makes sense. I just wasn't expecting your knock, that's all."

One. Two. Three. Four. Five. Pause.

"Jillian? May I touch your wrist?"

"What?" Jillian looked at him a little more directly.

"Your wrist. May I touch it?"

She searched his gaze for anything threatening, but only saw sincere concern there. Though she was still a bit confused about what he wanted, Jillian nodded.

With slow movements, he pushed the sleeves of her jacket and sweater out of the way then rested the tips of his fingers against the inside of her wrist. It dawned on her then what he was doing...taking her pulse.

Of course he'd recognize what was going on with her. Because of his job, he no doubt dealt with people who were having panic attacks.

Why couldn't she just get past the event that had precipitated all her anxiety and panic attacks? It had only been a week...just seven days...out of a lifetime of weeks and days. And yet that one week had changed everything for her. *Everything.*

"Breathe in," Carter said. "Now out."

In the space of the few moments she'd thought of the kidnapping, her anxiety had begun to spike again. Her mind was her own worst enemy when she got to this point.

Blinking back the tears that stung her eyes, Jillian tried to focus on Carter's voice. She wanted to get past this moment so they could enjoy the rest of the evening. What she really didn't want to do was go back home and miss this special night.

She refused to let *him* rob her of this. He'd robbed her of enough already. It was supposed to be an evening celebrating the love of two special people. And she wanted to be a part of it.

Carter continued to coach her through some breaths until, finally, the panic and anxiety had once again dropped to their normal levels. Normal meaning that they were still there in the background, but they weren't consuming her mind and body.

"I'm okay," she told him, eager to move past the panic of the last few minutes and on with the fun part of the evening.

"Are you sure?" Carter asked, his voice still low...soothing. "I can take you home. I'm sure Anna and Eli would understand."

Jillian shook her head, looking straight ahead out the windshield. Sure, they'd understand, but only after she told them *why* she'd panicked so deeply from just a single knock on the window of her car. "I want to go in."

Carter didn't reply right away, so she looked at him, taking in his furrowed brow. But it seemed that meeting his gaze reassured Carter that she really was okay. He gave a single nod before standing up and moving out from the space between the driver's seat and the open door.

Jillian was glad to find that her hands weren't shaking beyond a slight tremor as she pressed the button to release her seatbelt. She could do this. She *would* do this.

Grabbing her purse, she slipped her phone inside it before getting out of the car. Aware of her tendency to be shaky after an attack, Jillian gripped the top of the door with one hand and the roof edge of the car in the other. Carter didn't say anything as she stood there for a moment before she felt secure enough to step away from the car and close the door.

Carter hovered nearby as she locked the car. Looking up at him, she said, "Ready to go party?"

"I guess so," he replied. "As long as you are."

"I am. I'm fine." She paused, feeling like she owed him a bit more explanation than she'd ever had to give anyone else. "I sometimes have moments like that when I'm surprised. I just wasn't paying attention."

"Well, I'm sorry for the role I played in that. I'll be more careful in the future."

Seeing the seriousness of Carter's expression, Jillian had a feeling that this "relationship" wasn't going to last long. It was one thing to hang out as a couple in group settings. It was something else altogether for him to have to deal with her mental health issues.

She really didn't expect Carter to stick around for moments like the one she'd just had. In fact, she wasn't sure she *wanted* him to be around, even though he had done an excellent job of calming her down. Whatever this was between them, it had an expiration date. They weren't going to live out their entire lives in a casual dating relationship. So she didn't want to become dependent on him physically or emotionally.

This had to be the first and last time he saw her like that.

"Let's go inside."

Carter didn't argue, just walked silently beside her to the entrance of the building, then reached out to open the door for her. Jillian thanked him as she stepped inside the center. There was a big, brightly lit open space, but she knew that Eli and Anna had rented a smaller room since they hadn't invited a lot of people.

A whiteboard sat on an easel near the entrance with the words *Party time with Eli & Anna* written in a flowing font in bright colors. Jillian had a feeling that Sarah was responsible for that. On the sign, an arrow pointed to the back of the community center where there were smaller rooms available for rent. She could hear laughter and music coming from that area, so they moved in that direction.

As they approached the open doorway, Jillian took one more deep breath and shoved down the memory of what had happened in the parking lot. She pasted a smile on her face and stepped into the room with Carter.

The fake smile quickly became a real one as she took in the decorations and the people who were already gathered there. Jillian was glad that she'd pushed through and insisted on coming to the party.

Carter stuck to her side as she sought out Eli and Anna. She laughed when she spotted them. Anna wore a light pink T-shirt that said *Bride-to-be* on the front while Eli's shirt was light blue and said *Groom-to-be* on it.

"Hey, you two." Eli greeted them with a broad smile, obviously enjoying himself already. "Glad you could make it."

Jillian gave Anna a hug then watched as Eli shook Carter's hand, pulling him in for a quick bro hug. With her mind fogged by her panic, she hadn't had a chance to take in what Carter had worn for the evening. His jeans and long-sleeve, dark green Henley weren't much different from what she saw him in most the time.

The irony of the situation she found herself in with Carter was not lost on Jillian. Three years ago, he would have been exactly the sort of guy she would have gone for. She wasn't sure there was a woman alive who would deny that the man was attractive. He looked like he could pose for one of those firefighter calendars.

Jillian had no idea why Carter was still single. From what Sarah had said, he hadn't dated anyone in the time he'd been in New Hope. Why he'd suddenly been willing to make it seem like he was dating now, Jillian had no clue. But since it worked for her too, she wasn't going to question his decision.

"You're here!" Sarah held out her arms as she approached them, wrapping Jillian in a tight hug. "How are you doing?"

"About as good as I was when I talked to you earlier," Jillian said with a smile.

"Yeah, I guess we did chat earlier, didn't we? This day has kind of blurred for me." Sarah gestured at the space. "What do you think?"

Along one side of the room, there was a large table with lots of snack food on it. Smaller tables with chairs were set around the room. And there were balloons...lots of balloons...and flowers.

Jillian wasn't sure about the exact plans for the evening, but hopefully, it would be fun so that she could just enjoy herself and not think about how the evening had started.

~ * ~

As the evening progressed, Carter felt compelled to stick close to Jillian. It was more than just putting on a front for everyone there. When he'd realized he'd triggered some sort of panic attack with her earlier, he'd felt just sick.

Thankfully, she'd let him help her through it. He wasn't sure what he'd have done if she'd told him to leave her alone. When combined with what he'd seen at the fondue the other night, he realized that there was more than just a little anxiety going on with her.

He thought back even further, searching his memory for times when he might have missed something. For most of the time he'd known Jillian, he hadn't really paid that much attention to her. Not any more or less attention than he gave any other woman who was part of his social circle.

Suddenly the memory of the expression on her face when he'd walked into her classroom to find her dealing with Martin came to mind. He'd glanced her way when he'd realized what was happening, but the majority of his attention had been on the guy who was annoying her.

Only now, he could see some of the same things he'd noticed at the fondue. She had a clear issue with anxiety, and there was a part of him that wanted to know why. What had brought it on? Was she getting any help for it?

Carter grimaced at the thought. It was slightly hypocritical to wonder if someone was getting help for something when he'd refused all attempts by his family and by Evelyn and Garth to get him to go for therapy himself.

"You're supposed to look like you're having fun."

He turned to find Jillian in the chair next to him. They'd split the girls and the guys for a game of Pictionary. Not surprisingly, the girls had won, mainly because they'd had Sarah on their team, and that girl could draw everything.

"I am having fun," Carter assured her.

"If you say so." She gave him a skeptical look. "But usually people smile when they're having fun, not frown."

"I'm still trying to figure out how the guys couldn't see that I was drawing a tuxedo."

Jillian laughed. "I'm surprised we actually managed to win that game since we spent most our time watching you guys draw and laughing."

"Sarah should have been disqualified," Carter stated.

Jillian lifted her brows. "I'd say you were a poor loser, but you're probably right. We did have an unfair advantage with her on our team."

Carter dragged a carrot stick through the spoonful of dip he'd put on his plate earlier. "If more than bragging rights had been at stake, I might be more upset by the loss."

"What? Like a trophy?"

"Or a steak dinner."

"So if a steak dinner had been at stake, you'd be more bothered?"

"Exactly." It had been a long time since Carter had enjoyed that kind of banter with a woman. He bantered a bit with the guys in the group or at the station, but not with women since he always worried they'd take it the wrong way.

"Lucky me, the prize was some chocolate," Jillian said as she settled back in her chair.

"If I'd been part of the party planning, there definitely would have been steaks as prizes."

Jillian laughed again, and Carter felt his concern for her fade a bit. He was glad to see that she had apparently been able to let go of the anxiety that had gripped her earlier. Or maybe she was just really good at hiding it.

"Okay, everyone," Rebecca, Anna's assistant, said into the mic she held. "Time for the next game. We've asked a few couples to come up here with Eli and Anna."

When Jillian leaned forward, resting her arms on the table, Carter hooked his arm over the back of her chair, figuring it was a pose that would look natural for a dating couple. He had to admit that so far this dating role with Jillian had been easier than it might have been.

He'd actually been a little surprised that he hadn't heard from her after the fondue night except for the short time he'd spent in her classroom for his presentation. At first, he'd wondered if she'd been upset with him about something, but that didn't appear to be the case. The text she'd sent him earlier had made perfect sense, and as soon as he'd read it, he realized that perhaps they should have at least coordinated things.

"Okay. So we have a dating couple: Beau and Sarah. A newly engaged couple: Cara and Kieran. An almost newlywed couple: Eli and Anna. And a couple who's been married for a couple of years:

Natalie and Evan." Rebecca gestured to each couple. "We're going to play a game to find out how well these couples know each other."

The pairs were split up with the ladies on one side and the guys on the other. They were each given a small whiteboard and a marker. Rebecca called Andy up to give her a hand in reading out the answers.

What followed brought lots of laughter and cheering. For all that Andy could be a little on the quiet side, he and Rebecca actually did a great job playing off each other as they read answers to the questions posed to each couple.

Carter was glad that they hadn't wanted him and Jillian to be part of the game. He wasn't sure he was ready for that, especially since all he really knew about her was that she had some sort of anxiety and panic attacks and that she liked chocolate and bananas. They would have failed miserably at this particular game.

Though he was trying desperately to keep his thoughts in the moment, it was a battle that Carter was not winning. The combination of the wedding/couple-oriented events plus having seen Suzanne earlier that day for his weekly visit, made it nearly impossible to not think about what might have been. He figured that was going to be the case for the next week too with the rehearsal dinner and then the wedding itself coming up.

The guilt was weighty as well because now he was dealing with it from two different directions. He was used to the constant guilt when it came to seeing Suzanne in her current state or doing things without her by his side. That guilt had been around for a decade, but now there was new guilt.

Though things weren't real with Jillian, Carter still felt guilty about it. Part of it stemmed from the feeling that he was moving on, even though he wasn't—at least not in his heart. But the other part was about Jillian. She had no expectations of the relationship, or at least she'd agreed not to have any. However, he still struggled with feeling like he should be more emotionally available. He felt guilty that he wasn't able to offer that kind of support to her.

Not that she seemed concerned with the fact that he wasn't offering her any sort of long-term relationship. Still, she deserved better than a relationship that went nowhere...except that seemed to be what she wanted. So, as long as that was the case, Carter would maintain the status quo, but for both their sakes, if he got even a whiff of her wanting more in the relationship, he'd have to bring a halt to their arrangement.

After much hilarity, the game finally ended with Natalie and Evan winning—no surprise there—but the other three couples came in fairly close. Carter had never been to a joint bachelor/bachelorette party before, and he doubted that Suzanne would have wanted to have a joint party, even though he was pretty sure she would have enjoyed this one.

"I'm really surprised at how well Sarah and Beau did," Jillian said, turning to face Carter. "Especially considering they've only been dating a few months."

As the other people at their table got up, Carter shifted in his seat, moving his arm from the back of her chair. "Guess they must talk a lot."

Jillian's gaze went to where Sarah and Beau stood with their arms around each other, talking to a couple of other people. "They do. Sarah says that ever since Beau came back to New Hope, they spend part of most evenings talking."

Though he and Suzanne had spent a lot of time together, most of that time had been spent hanging out with other friends or being in places that didn't encourage a lot of deep conversation. Not that they hadn't talked...they had...but it seemed that perhaps Sarah and Beau put a significant emphasis on communication.

"They say that communication is important for a successful relationship," Carter said. "So hopefully that's the case for them. I get the feeling that Beau is quite serious about Sarah."

"Sarah is serious about him too. Pretty sure they'll be the next ones to get engaged. There must be something in the New Hope Falls' water supply." She gave him a quick look. "Which is why I only drink the bottled stuff."

Carter lifted his brows. "You seriously don't want any of this?"

After a glance around the room, Jillian said, "A party? Sure."

He waited for her to go on, but she didn't. It shouldn't matter to him why she wasn't interested in marriage, but the fact she'd deliberately misunderstood his question made him curious.

Carter rubbed his chest. The plan with Jillian was supposed to have helped him find some stability after the imposed curtailing of his visitations with Suzanne. Instead, he was feeling even more con-flicted over everything in his life.

He needed to keep their interactions on a less personal level. That was absolutely necessary if things were going to work out how he wanted them to.

CHAPTER SEVEN

Jillian looked up from where she was straightening the books the kids had been reading that day to see Martin coming into her classroom. Her chest tightened, and her heart started thumping.

"Well, hello there," Martin said, giving her a leering grin. "How's school going?"

"It's going just fine." Jillian moved to keep the desk between them. She picked up the papers she planned to take home to grade and straightened their edges, hoping he couldn't see the slight trembling of her fingers.

"And Carter?" he prompted. "How's that working out for you?"

Jillian frowned at Martin. "It's working out just fine."

"Really?" Martin's brows rose. "You expect me to believe that?"

"I don't really care if you believe it or not." Jillian hoped she sounded more sure of herself than she felt. "I don't need to convince you of anything when it comes to my relationship with Carter."

"Your relationship with Carter," Martin scoffed. "That's rich."

"Did you need something, Martin?" Jillian asked, trying to sound brave when all she wanted was for him to leave before she melted down into a panic attack. "Or are you just here to stick your nose into something that isn't your business?"

"Considering you turned me down because you were "dating" Carter," he said, using air quotes. "I think it's my business." He took a step closer to her. "I smell a lie."

Her insides began to shake, and Jillian knew that she needed him to leave...right then. She crossed her arms, desperate to contain the tremors spreading throughout her body, and lifted her chin. "Please leave. I have things I need to do."

"Of course, sweetheart." Martin glanced around. "Is your boyfriend coming by again?"

Jillian tried to stand firm, though everything in her was screaming for her to get out of the classroom and away from the man smirking at her. She didn't say anything in response, certain her voice would shake if she did. She prayed that someone would come along and rescue her.

But in the end, after a final smirk in her direction, Martin wandered back out of her classroom. With her legs suddenly going weak, Jillian grabbed for her chair and sank down into it. She tried to take a deep breath but couldn't inhale past the constrictions that panic had wrapped around her chest.

However, worried that Martin might come back, Jillian quickly began shoving her things into her messenger bag, taking rapid breaths as she did so. With anxiety spiking within her, bringing a panic attack along with it, she had to take a few precious minutes to calm herself down, tapping out a rhythm to help stabilize her breathing.

Jillian didn't want to stay there any longer than necessary. Still, she knew she couldn't drive safely when she was shaking and struggling to breathe. All she wanted was to get to the safety of her home.

After what felt like an eternity, the tightness in her chest finally eased so she could breathe more steadily. The tremors had stopped shaking her extremities enough that she could walk, even though inwardly she still vibrated with them.

Once out in her car, Jillian engaged the door locks then looked around, checking to make sure that Martin wasn't anywhere near her. The last thing she wanted was for him to follow her home. She didn't know if he'd take his obsession with her that far, but then, she hadn't suspected he'd get to the point of harassing her the way he was either.

Rather than go straight home, Jillian took a drive, eventually heading into Everett. Even though she really didn't need anything, she stopped at a store and did a little shopping, desperately needing a little normalcy. After that, she picked up some dinner at a drive-thru before heading home.

Part of her wanted to phone Carter to tell him what had happened, but it wasn't his problem. If they'd been a real couple, she would have called him right away. But Martin wasn't wrong to question the validity of their relationship. They didn't make sense as a couple to him, because they weren't one.

Once again, they hadn't spoken since the party for Eli and Anna, four nights earlier. That hadn't bothered her until that moment when she really wanted to tell him what was going on.

But she didn't think that was how their deal worked. They were casually dating, which meant that she could tell Martin that Carter was her boyfriend in order to keep him off her back. However, that didn't mean that Carter was available to come around and act like a boyfriend every time Jillian needed him. Plus, she had an idea of what he'd tell her to do if he called her about this: Go talk to Principal Hughes.

Though she understood why he thought she should report Martin, Jillian felt like he didn't really grasp why she was reticent to. She was aware that Martin had worked at the school for several years. Clearly, if he had a history of harassing female teachers, he wouldn't still be working there. And she'd only been there a month. The last thing she wanted was to make it seem like she was a troublemaker.

So for now, she'd keep the situation to herself and hope that Martin would lose interest in her soon.

Why was it that she was a magnet for men like him? Men who liked to harass and prey on women. It made her want to lock herself in her house and never come out. But that would be giving him more power than he already had.

Plus, she wanted to teach. It had been her dream, and she'd already had to give up on other things she'd wanted for her life. She didn't want to lose this, too, because she was let go for causing problems at the school by reporting him.

When she finally pulled into her garage, Jillian let out a sigh of relief. The first thing she did once she was inside the house—even before greeting Dolly—was to make sure the alarm was set, all the doors and windows were secure, and the curtains were closed. Only then did she go back to the mudroom to take off her jacket and shoes.

She scooped Dolly up and nuzzled her, wishing so much that she'd come home to not just her grandma's cat, but to her grandma. Missing her had lessened from an acute pain to a dull ache...most of the time. Right then, it hurt enough to bring tears of grief to her eyes.

Blinking rapidly, she set Dolly down, then picked up her bags and went into the kitchen. She put away the few groceries she'd bought, then took her dinner and messenger bag to her room. It was the one place in the house that she felt truly safe. She'd decorated it and the attached master bathroom to her own preferences, so being inside the room brought her a calmness that she desperately needed.

Gradually, as she picked at her food and watched the shows she enjoyed, the tension from the confrontation with Martin eased away. When she finally turned her attention to the papers she needed to grade and the lesson planning, Jillian had almost been able to convince herself that she'd overreacted to the meeting with Martin.

After a restless night, the next day passed without incident, thankfully. However, she'd spent her time at school on high alert, just waiting for Martin to appear once again.

She was taking her dinner out of the oven when she heard a text come in. Figuring it was Sarah, Jillian didn't pick up her phone right away, choosing to wait until she'd finished serving herself a helping of the chicken pot pie she'd heated up.

She tucked her phone into her pocket, then carried her plate and drink into the living room. Dolly came with her, meowing loudly even though she'd already eaten.

Once she'd settled onto the couch and said a prayer of thanks for her food, Jillian pulled her phone out to check Sarah's message.

Carter: *Eli just let me know that you'd be welcome to come with me to the rehearsal and dinner tomorrow night.*

Jillian set her fork back on the plate as she stared at the message. She'd assumed they'd go to the wedding and reception together, but she hadn't even thought about the rehearsal.

Sure. What time would I need to be there?

Carter: *The rehearsal is at 5 at the church.*

Okay. I'll be there at five.

He didn't respond, so Jillian assumed the conversation was over. She put her phone down and began to eat her dinner while watching bakers compete to come up with cupcakes made from weird ingredients and flavors.

When her phone's text alert went off again, she stared at it for a moment before picking it up.

Carter: *I could pick you up if you'd like.*

Well...hmmm...

That was totally unexpected, and Jillian wasn't sure how to respond to his offer. For appearances' sake, it probably made sense that they should arrive together. However, she didn't really feel it was necessary, unless he did.

I don't mind just meeting you there since I don't live that far from the church.

Carter: *Sounds good but let me know if you change your mind. I'll see you there.*

Yep. See you there.

She wondered if Carter had felt obligated to offer her a ride. Maybe he'd thought it was something he should offer for appearances. Should she have taken him up on it?

She'd dated while in college, but after one experience that had gone so terribly, terribly wrong, she didn't want to ever date again. So no, she wasn't going to change her mind about the ride to the church for the rehearsal.

If he asked again for the wedding itself, she might take him up on it. Or not. If too many people questioned why they didn't arrive together, they could talk about it and decide if it was necessary.

~ * ~

Carter pulled his truck into a spot in the church parking lot and glanced at the clock on the dash. He was about ten minutes early, so it wasn't a big surprise that Jillian wasn't there yet. After a brief debate with himself, he decided to wait in the truck until she arrived so they could go into the church together.

Picking up his phone, he checked for a text from Evelyn. He'd taken to texting her to let her know when he planned to visit Suzanne. With the rehearsal dinner that evening and then the wedding on Saturday afternoon, he only had the next day—Friday—available to visit her. He planned to go the next morning, leaving the afternoon free in case Eli needed him for anything.

There was no message from Evelyn, and Carter hoped that didn't indicate an issue with his plans. He'd abided by their request that he only visit once a week, so they shouldn't have a problem with his plan to see Suzanne the next day. He hated feeling like he wasn't in control of his own decisions. Like he was at their mercy for something that was such a large part of his life.

Letting out a forceful sigh, Carter stared unseeing at the church. There was no denying that all this wedding stuff was wearing on him. He'd been naïve to think he could be so involved in a wedding and not have his past intrude on his thoughts.

Still, he'd told Eli he'd stand up with him, so he would do it. But even though he hated to think it, he couldn't wait until all of it was over. There would be at least one more wedding in the near future, from the sound of things. However, Kieran hadn't said anything about him being part of the wedding party, so he hoped that for that wedding, he could just show up for the ceremony and reception and not have to be so involved.

When a car pulled up next to his truck, Carter looked over to see that Jillian had arrived. He slipped his phone into the pocket of the button-down shirt he wore and removed his keys from the ignition before getting out of the truck.

By the time he'd walked around the front of the truck, Jillian was standing there waiting for him.

"Hi," she said, a small smile on her face.

He noted that her face seemed to hold some strain, and even though she wore makeup, he could see dark smudges beneath her eyes. It made him wonder if she'd had another panic attack.

"Hey." There was a moment of awkwardness, making him wonder if he should offer her a physical greeting like a hug. But he held back because that wasn't the type of relationship they'd agreed to. "How're you doing?"

"I'm fine," she said as they fell into step. "How about you?"

"Yeah, I'm fine too." When they reached the large doors leading into the church, Carter reached out and grasped the handle to pull it open for Jillian. "Hoping I don't mess up during this rehearsal."

"I doubt it's going to be too complex," Jillian remarked. "From what Anna's said, they're keeping things pretty simple."

"Since I'm the best man, I know I have to do a few extra things. Like hold the rings."

Jillian reached out and rested her hand briefly on his forearm. "I think you're going to do just fine. Have you been in a wedding before?"

Carter nodded. "It's been a while, though. My older brother got married about twelve years ago, and I was in his wedding."

The doors to the sanctuary stood open, and Carter could see that people were already gathered there. He and Jillian walked in and made their way down the aisle to the front.

Eli spotted them and immediately headed in their direction, a broad smile on his face. "Glad you could both come."

"Someone's excited," Jillian said with a laugh.

"I am," Eli admitted without hesitation. "It's only been a few months since we got engaged, but it feels like I've been waiting for this day forever."

"Where are you guys headed for your honeymoon?" Jillian asked as Anna joined them.

Before answering, Anna gave Jillian a hug. "We haven't really told anyone. You'll just have to stay tuned to our social media to see where we end up. I'm going to do a little vlogging."

They didn't chat too long as Rebecca soon called for all the wedding party to meet at the front of the sanctuary.

"I'll just sit here," Jillian said, gesturing to a row of chairs nearby. "Good luck."

Carter nodded. "Thanks."

Once he was at the front with the rest of the wedding party, Rebecca began to give some instructions to them. Carter listened intently, determined to stay in the present and not let thoughts of the past encroach on what was going on.

As Jillian had said, it appeared to be a reasonably straightforward ceremony. Pastor Evans and Rebecca guided them through the rehearsal without too many issues popping up. Even though the service was simple, there were little things that made it unique to Eli and Anna.

The unity candle at the front was something the two of them had worked on together. Eli had carved the base with their initials on it while Anna had made the candle that sat on it. For the first time ever, Carter heard Leah sing, and he was stunned at the beauty of her voice. He was even more impressed when he found out that the song was one she'd written specifically for the couple.

As he stood at the front with Eli, his gaze met Jillian's. She gave him a small smile and a thumbs up that almost made him laugh. He appreciated the distraction she presented as he worked to keep his thoughts on the rehearsal.

After it was all done, Eli invited them to the newly built hall that was attached to the church for the rehearsal dinner. Carter approached Jillian, where she stood talking to Sarah.

"If you have nothing to do tomorrow night, I'm sure Anna would love your help to decorate the church and hall."

"Friday night?" Jillian said. "Pretty sure I've got nothing going on."

Sarah glanced at Carter then back to Jillian. "Thought maybe the two of you might have a date or something."

Jillian gave him a quick glance then said, "Not this weekend. With Carter being involved with the wedding, that's kind of our focus. There's always next Friday."

For a moment, Carter wondered if she was hinting at something, but they'd agreed that this wasn't a case of them going on dates with just the two of them.

"I'm not the most creative person," Jillian continued. "But if someone will tell me what to do, I'm happy to do it."

"Great! We'll probably have pizza or something since we'll be here around dinner time. Taylor, Michael's sister, is doing the flowers, so she'll be around to help us do the décor."

Rebecca approached them, a paper in her hand. She gave Carter a friendly, if slightly flirtatious, smile. "Just wanted to make sure that you were comfortable with everything."

"Uh...yep. Seemed pretty straightforward."

"And you have your suit, and it fits you well?" Rebecca's gaze traveled down his body then back up again, making Carter feel more than a little uncomfortable.

He'd already sensed her interest as she'd tucked her hand in his arm as they'd walked down the aisle. Given their roles in the wedding, they were partnered together, but he didn't want her reading anything more into it. Hadn't she seen him and Jillian arrive together?

"Rebecca," Sarah said with a smile. "I don't think you've met Jillian yet. She's Carter's girlfriend."

CHAPTER EIGHT

It felt weird to Carter to hear that term used in reference to him, but it also felt right, given the circumstances. Sarah's voice had been friendly, but it also held an edge of warning.

Rebecca's eyebrows rose as she looked at Jillian and gave her the same assessing look she'd given Carter, only this time, her expression held a bit of disbelief. Anger flared within Carter. He didn't like that people somehow thought that he and Jillian didn't belong together.

It wasn't that he didn't understand why people reacted that way. He got it. And ten years ago, they probably would have been right to be skeptical of the two of them together. Carter wasn't proud of that fact, but he'd like to think that with age, he was a better man, more likely to look beyond the physical to what the person was like on the inside.

Though he appeared more physically fit than most, he wasn't that way because he was heavily into health and fitness. It was partly because of his job that he worked out so much, but working out was also his outlet. It was how he got rid of frustrations and, now that he wasn't visiting Suzanne as much, also how he filled some of his free time.

"It's nice to meet you," Jillian said, giving Rebecca a smile that looked utterly genuine.

Surely she had picked up on Rebecca's assessment of her, but it didn't appear to have bothered her. That meant that either she didn't care what Rebecca thought since they weren't really dating anyway, or she was secure enough in herself that what Rebecca thought wasn't important enough to bother her.

Having seen Jillian in a very vulnerable state, Carter hoped that it was the latter. He liked the idea that she didn't let what others thought bother her.

Glancing at the doorway that the others were disappearing through, Carter stepped closer to Jillian and lightly rested his hand on her back, not wanting to push any physical boundaries, but also wanting to reinforce Sarah's words with actions. "We should probably go to the hall."

Jillian glanced up at him, then nodded. She didn't move away from his side, allowing Sarah and Rebecca to head up the aisle first. Carter waited until she took a step in that direction before letting his hand fall away from her back. He wasn't sure if he should say anything about what had just happened with Rebecca, but in the end, he just decided to let it go.

If Jillian was bothered at all by what Rebecca had said, the best thing Carter could do was to just stick close to her and let Rebecca see that whatever assumption she'd made about him and Jillian was wrong.

As they stepped into the hall, they were greeted by the rich aroma of the dinner they'd be eating soon. There were a couple round tables set up, and along one side of the room was a long rectangle table that was set up as a buffet.

"Come sit with Beau and me," Sarah said, gesturing to where Beau stood near a table.

Carter was more than happy with that suggestion and followed Sarah and Jillian as they made their way toward Beau. Andy and Leah and Michael and his sister were also at their table. Rebecca was at a table with Eli and Anna and their parents, along with Pastor Evans.

When Pastor Evans instructed them to find their seats, Carter held the chair for Jillian then sat down beside her. Once the pastor had said a blessing for the food, they waited until Eli and Anna's table had dished up their plates, then their table got up to get their food.

Carter stuck close to Jillian as they lined up, and he took the plate she handed him with a smile. With so few people there, it didn't take long to go through the buffet line and return to the table.

"What would you like to drink?" Carter asked Jillian, gesturing to the pitchers in the middle of the table.

"Just water, please."

Reaching out, he picked up the water pitcher and proceeded to pour them each a glass.

"Thank you," Jillian said when he set a glass next to her plate.

The smile she gave him brought a responding one to his face. "You're welcome."

Conversation during the meal covered a variety of topics, some of which interested Carter more than others. Partway through the meal, his phone vibrated in his pocket. Since Jillian was with him, that meant it could only be Evelyn or work.

He pulled his phone out and looked down at the screen.

Evelyn: *It's fine for you to come tomorrow, but just be prepared. Suzie hasn't had a good week. She's picked up some sort of bug which has left her congested.*

The words sent a chill through Carter. He knew that something like pneumonia could be deadly for Suzanne because of her already weakened physical condition. It wouldn't be the first time she'd gotten sick with something like that, but the risk was higher each time she did. It seemed that after every such bout, she never quite made it back to the level of health she'd had before getting ill.

With that news, it made him all the more determined to go see her the next day.

"Is everything okay?" Jillian asked, her voice soft.

Carter glanced up, having forgotten where he was as he'd digested the news in Evelyn's text. "Uh, yeah. Just...someone I know is sick."

A look of concern crossed Jillian's face. "I'm sorry to hear that."

"I'm making arrangements to go see them tomorrow morning."

"Oh, I'm sure they'll appreciate that."

Carter wished that Suzanne was cognizant enough to know that he was there for her, but these visits were more for him than for her. "They're in Seattle, so I'll be back in time to help with stuff in the afternoon. I just need to let them know what time I'll be there."

Jillian nodded, then turned her attention back to Sarah.

Thanks for letting me know. I'll be there around ten o'clock.

Evelyn: *I'll probably be there, although Garth has meetings so he can't join us. I'll see you then. xoxo*

Carter tried to take a surreptitious breath to loosen the vice that had tightened around his chest when he'd read Evelyn's text. He hated the idea of seeing Suzanne sick, but he'd be there. He owed her that much...and so much more.

The text left him a little distracted for the rest of the evening, and he could tell that Jillian noticed, but she didn't ask any questions. Just continued to chat with the others at the table while giving him quick concerned looks. Part of him wished that he could tell her all about Suzanne, but for some reason, he couldn't bring himself to do that.

Would she think differently of him if she knew the whole story of how Suzanne had come to be in the state she was? For some reason, he really hoped not.

Once the meal was over, and they were finishing up their desserts, Anna and Eli stood up, and after a short speech, they handed out gifts to the members of their wedding party.

"We just want you to know how much we appreciate each of you and your willingness to stand up with us as we pledge our love and our lives to each other," Eli said.

Anna nodded, then added, "Our special day is all the more special because you are part of it. Thank you for your support and help as we planned our wedding. We can't wait for Saturday."

There was laughter and clapping at their words. As conversation went on around them, Carter unwrapped the flat square box Eli had handed him. Once unwrapped, he opened the top of it and stared at the wooden keychain that had his initials delicately carved into the wood. He touched it with his finger before lifting it from the box.

As it dangled from his finger, something else on it caught his attention. On the back side of the initials, a Bible reference had been burned into the wood. The reference was familiar, but it took him a moment to recall the verse itself. The verse had been part of a study they'd done in their men's group. At that time, Carter had mentioned that he found it particularly meaningful, even though he hadn't shared the details of why he'd felt that way about it.

That Eli had remembered and put that reference on this gift meant a lot to Carter.

When he'd left Miami for Seattle and then left Seattle for New Hope, he hadn't imagined ending up with a group of friends like he had now. He'd continued to go to church because he knew that it was what his parents and Evelyn and Garth wanted him to do. In the process, he'd found men who, even without knowing the details of his life, had offered him friendship and support.

"That's beautiful," Jillian said as she leaned close to him.

Carter held the keychain out so that she could take it. When she turned it over and saw the reference on the back, she murmured, "*The Lord is near to those who have a broken heart and saves such as have a contrite spirit.*"

Hearing Jillian recite the familiar words surprised Carter. "You know the verse."

Jillian nodded, her gaze still on the keychain, her fingertips tracing the reference that was burned into the wood. "I've memorized a lot of verses over the years."

"Really?" Carter asked.

"Yeah." She looked up at him then, a smile on her lips but sadness in her eyes. "I memorized a lot when I was in Sunday school as a kid, but my grandma was insistent that I learn even more. She always felt that memorizing Scripture verses was important, so she had verses for me to learn each week." She shrugged. "It wasn't a big deal for me as memorizing came really easy for me."

"Wow, you're lucky," Carter said. "I've always struggled to memorize things, whether it was verses at church or the periodic table in science."

"Sometimes, I'm surprised that I actually remember some of the stuff I do, like this verse, but it has come in so handy at times." The sadness in her gaze deepened. "I'm not memorizing as much as I used to. I kind of stopped once I moved away, and then my grandma passed away..."

"Death can change things," Carter said. And so could near death...or living in a vegetative state the way Suzanne did. As much as the accident had changed her life, it had changed his and her parents' lives as well.

He waited for Jillian to ask how he knew that, but instead, she just nodded then handed the keychain back to him. "Eli really did a beautiful job on that."

"He did. The guy has a lot of talent."

"He and Anna make a good pair in that regard. Both so creative in what they do." Jillian smiled, the sadness easing from her expression. "And then there's Sarah and Leah. That whole family is creative in one way or another."

"Are you creative?" Carter asked, wondering, even as he spoke, where the curiosity about her was coming from.

"Not really. My memory is my superpower." She paused. "Or my curse, depending on how you look at it."

"Your curse?" Carter frowned. "What do you mean?"

She met his gaze for a moment then looked away. "Not everything is something I want to remember."

Oh. Well, he could understand that. There was definitely stuff he didn't want to remember either. But unfortunately, even though he didn't have the memory that Jillian had, he had a clear recollection of the night that changed everything for him.

"What about you?" Jillian asked. "Any creative outlet for you?"

Carter sighed. "Can't say that there is. I tend to just appreciate the creativity of those around me."

"Me too. I especially enjoy Sarah's. I hadn't known about Leah's creative side until today. How neat is it that she wrote that song for Eli and Anna?"

Carter nodded. "A special gift, that's for sure."

"Well, we're done for tonight," Pastor Evans said, interrupting their conversation. "There will be some decorating here tomorrow night, and then, of course, the ceremony is at three o'clock on Saturday. Keep your phones on in case the bride or groom needs to get hold of you. I don't know about you, but I'm really looking forward to this special event. Let's pray a blessing on the couple and the wedding."

Carter bowed his head and listened as Pastor Evans prayed. He always appreciated the man and the simple way he approached his faith. Though Carter had originally started going to church in New Hope because he'd wanted to appease Evelyn and Garth, to show them that he was thriving in his new hometown. He'd ended up at Pastor Evan's church because of an invitation from a guy at the fire station.

He had gone on to get more involved in the church, even though it hadn't ever been his intention. Carter didn't regret that involvement, but sometimes his heart felt very fractured. He wanted the peace that Pastor Evans promised could be his, but at the same time, he couldn't let go of the responsibility he felt for what had happened to Suzanne.

"So, are you going to help us out tomorrow?" Sarah asked after Pastor Evans finished his prayer, and people began to get ready to leave.

"I'll be here," Jillian promised.

"And you too, Carter?" Sarah prompted.

Carter nodded. "If this is where Eli needs me, then this is where I'll be."

Sarah beamed at them then turned to greet Beau as he came to her side and slid an arm around her waist. "Ready to go?"

When the four of them walked out of the church, Carter noticed that the sun had gone down, leaving them swathed in twilight as they headed for their vehicles. The other couple called goodnight as they veered off to climb into Beau's luxury SUV.

"I guess I'll see you tomorrow," Jillian said as they stood near the front bumpers of their vehicles.

There was a moment of awkwardness before Jillian said goodnight and stepped to her car. As she opened the door and slid behind the wheel, Carter took hold of the door handle.

"Good night," he said, giving her a smile and nod before he closed her door.

He once again waited until she was on her way out of the parking lot before getting in his truck and heading home. As he let himself into his apartment a short time later, he sighed.

This studio apartment wasn't exactly where he'd figured he'd be living at this point in his life, but since he gave the majority of his income to Evelyn and Garth to help care for Suzanne, there wasn't much left for his monthly expenses. Still, even though it wasn't the apartment he would have picked if he'd had a real choice, it was home.

He took a quick shower, then got ready for bed, eager to put that day behind him, even as he dreaded the two that were yet to come.

His double bed was pushed into one corner of his room with a small nightstand next to it with his lamp and his Bible on it. He usually tried to do some Bible reading before sleeping, but as he sat propped up against his headboard with his Bible open on his lap, Carter struggled to focus on the passage.

Being bombarded by wedding stuff, he was fighting the memories of the past. From the first time he'd met Suzanne to the night he proposed and then to the moment when everything went tragically wrong. He couldn't, for the life of him, figure out how to move forward the way Evelyn and Garth wanted him to.

He had yet to figure out how to get through a day without thinking of Suzanne, wondering how she was doing, which inevitably led to all the other thoughts. This wedding stuff was just making everything so much worse.

His gaze went to the chest of drawers at the foot of his bed. The top drawer held the small box where he'd put the ring that Evelyn had returned to him. He knew that in doing that, she had essentially freed him from the engagement...whether he wanted to be freed or not. In her and Garth's mind, he was no longer their daughter's fiancé.

He'd accepted it...that was the only way he could have entered into the arrangement he had with Jillian. Still, he struggled to view himself as anything other than Suzanne's fiancé. After all, he'd been that for over a decade.

Closing the Bible, he set it back on the nightstand. He turned off the lamp, then settled down against his pillows and chose to focus instead on the verse that Eli had carved into his keychain. *The Lord is near to those who have a broken heart and saves such as have a contrite spirit.*

Right then, his heart felt even more broken than it ever had before. The wedding activities were punching at his already bruised and broken heart, making it hurt in a way it hadn't in a long time. Saturday evening couldn't come soon enough. Then he'd just have to get through Cara and Kieran's wedding...then probably Beau and Sarah's.

Please, Father, heal my heart. Take away the pain.

CHAPTER NINE

Jillian hurried from her car into the church, anxious to see familiar and friendly faces. Normally, she would have waited for Carter, but that wasn't an option right then. Her hand trembled slightly as she reached out to pull open the door, and she glanced over her shoulder before she stepped into the foyer.

Martin had stopped by her classroom again. It had been lunchtime, and he hadn't stuck around long, but his visit had shaken her up enough that once the school day was over, she started a panicked packing up of her stuff. Her low-level anxiety had spiked by the time she made it out to her car.

She'd gone straight home because she'd known that she wouldn't be able to stave off the panic attack that usually accompanied the anxiety if she didn't feel safe. Thankfully, she didn't live too far from the school because even though she'd realized she wasn't in great shape to drive, she'd done it anyway. She'd just had to get out of the school before Martin showed up again.

Not knowing what else to do, she'd gone home, fallen apart and then tried her best to put herself back together again so she could face her friends.

"Jillian!" Sarah called out as soon as she walked into the sanctuary. She hurried over and wrapped her in a tight hug. "I'm so glad to see you."

Tears pricked at Jillian's eyes, but she blinked them away before Sarah released her from the hug and stepped back. "How is the decorating going?"

Sarah grimaced. "I love Anna to death, but Rebecca is driving me...and a few others...a bit crazy."

"Why's that?" Jillian had her own feelings about Rebecca, but she wasn't going to voice them. She had a feeling that Sarah was already well aware of what they might be.

"She has her own ideas of how things should be decorated even though Anna already worked out a plan with Taylor. I think Taylor is about ready to lose her cool with Rebecca."

"Isn't Anna here?" Jillian asked.

"She'll be here in a bit," Sarah said. "She and her mom went into Everett to pick up some things."

"Well, we'll just have to make sure that we keep asking Taylor what to do and not Rebecca."

"I think Rebecca is used to bossing people around, and she thinks that she knows exactly what Anna wants because she's known her the longest." Sarah suddenly smiled as she looked past Jillian. "Well, look who's here."

Expecting it to be Beau, Jillian was surprised to see Carter walking toward them. As she watched him, she could see the tension in his expression and the set of his shoulders. Remembering that he'd planned to visit a sick friend that morning, she hoped that nothing serious had happened to them. That wouldn't be a good thing for Carter since he had a wedding to deal with.

As he neared where they stood, Jillian found herself with the very foreign—and unwanted—urge to hug him. The very idea of such an action kept her frozen in place, and she worked hard to dispel the urge. She couldn't cross that line with Carter, fearful it would send the wrong message to him.

The unexpected urge to hug Carter, along with the ongoing issues with Martin, caused anxiety to begin to build within her again. Sarah's voice receded a bit as Jillian began to tap her fingers.

Carter spoke to Sarah for a couple of minutes before turning his attention more fully on Jillian. "Are you okay?"

"What?" Jillian fought to stay focused on him, barely noticing that Sarah had slipped away.

Carter frowned as his gaze dropped to where Jillian's fingers were tapping out a five-count on her thigh. "What's upset you?"

Jillian wanted to deny that anything was wrong. To insist that nothing had upset her. But it was clear that Carter was already aware of some of the things she did to calm herself. "I'm okay."

Carter reached out and lightly rested his hand on her upper back, guiding her to a chair in the back corner of the sanctuary. Jillian sank down on it, grateful to no longer have to trust her legs to hold her up.

"I need to help," Jillian said as she gestured to the room.

"They can wait." Carter sat down beside her. "You can take a few minutes, if you need to."

With a nod, Jillian stared down at her hand, watching and feeling each tap of her fingertips on her leg. Carter didn't say anything right away, just sat with his body angled to block out the rest of the room.

His actions allowed her to focus on pulling her thoughts back from the dark place they'd been heading toward. To calm the panicky feelings welling up inside her. She heard Sarah ask Carter if she was okay, then some murmured conversation before Sarah moved away again.

Jillian struggled to accept that her mental health issues were worsening once again. She'd been doing better when she'd first moved back to New Hope Falls. So much better, in fact, that she hadn't bothered to reconnect with her old therapist in Portland or follow up on the referrals she'd given her for a new therapist in Everett.

After she'd returned to New Hope, she'd gone off all the medications she'd been prescribed for her panic and anxiety, just wanting to be normal again. And she'd been doing well enough that it had seemed like the right decision. Now she was worried that she was going to have to go back on the meds in order to regain the emotional stability she'd lost since the harassment by Martin had started.

"Do you want to talk about it?" Carter asked softly.

She looked up at him. "Do you want to talk about why you're upset today too?"

He stared at her for a moment, his eyes narrowing briefly, then he shook his head. "Just...if Martin's still bothering you, you need to talk to Principal Hughes. He's a decent guy, and he wouldn't be happy that harassment is going on in his school."

Jillian wasn't sure she believed that. Well, not that Principal Hughes wanted stuff like that in his school, but that it would be that easy to address it with him. She had no doubt at all that Martin would deny her claims.

"Or if you'd prefer, I'll have another talk with him," Carter said. "Martin, that is. I wouldn't interfere with your actual employment situation."

Though Jillian would have liked to take Carter up on his offer, she wasn't sure it would help. After all, even though Carter had made it clear to Martin that they were dating, he was still bothering her. True, he wasn't asking her out anymore, but he definitely wasn't leaving her alone.

Looking down again, Jillian continued to tap, timing her breaths to the rhythm. She needed the panic to subside so she could do what she'd come to the church to do. Once again, she was surprised but grateful that Carter stayed with her, a silent but steady support.

When the anxiety eased enough that nothing within her shook, she was able to focus on why she was at the church rather than on all the reasons why she wanted to run for home. Still, she was quite sure that she could actually leave, and it wouldn't impact the decorating significantly. But she didn't want to do that. She wanted to be there to help prepare for Eli and Anna's special day.

"I'm okay now," she said, looking up.

Carter regarded her for a moment, as if he was searching for the truth in her expression rather than in her words. Finally, he nodded. "Let's see what we can do."

It took her aback when, after they'd stood up, he held out his hand to her. She hesitated for a moment, feeling like this was going to change things between them. Not a lot, but enough to make her really think about it.

However, the move could be explained away because of the presence of others. Not strangers—although there were a few of them—but mainly these were their friends. People who knew them. The same people who they'd been trying to convince they were a couple starting out on their way to a possible serious relationship.

"Doing okay, sweetie?" Sarah asked when Jillian and Carter approached her.

"Yeah. I'm fine. Just had a moment."

"Sorry to hear that." Sarah gave her a quick hug. "I'm glad that you had Carter to help you through it."

Jillian glanced sideways at Carter, giving him a smile. "Yeah. Me too."

And she was surprised by how much she meant those words.

Sarah glanced around, then leaned forward and whispered, "Please, help us keep everyone from running Rebecca out of town. She seemed like a perfectly lovely person until the past two days. Anna might not be a bridezilla, but she's got a bridezilla assistant."

"Tell us what to do," Carter said.

Gesturing for them to follow her, Sarah headed in Taylor's direction. "Oh, and I'm starting to feel like I have another Cece on my hands with Rebecca. She's flirting with all the men except Eli."

"Even Beau?" Jillian asked.

"Yeah," Sarah growled as the man walked up to her and slid his arm around her waist. "Even Beau."

"Well, I don't know about Beau," Carter said, "but I have little respect for women who flirt with men who are clearly taken."

"I feel the same way." Beau pressed a kiss to Sarah's temple. "You're the only woman for me, darlin'."

Taylor set them to work draping fairy lights along the sides of the sanctuary while she decorated the arch where Eli and Anna would stand to exchange their vows. But each time Rebecca approached them to try and redirect the guys to help her with whatever it was she was doing, Taylor left her work and stepped in.

"Taylor does that really well," Sarah said. "She doesn't let it rattle her. Me, on the other hand...I'm ready to throw fists whenever Rebecca heads in Beau's direction."

Jillian didn't feel jealous when Rebecca focused her attention on Carter. What bothered her more was how dismissive Rebecca was of her. However, Carter didn't let Rebecca get away with it. He made it clear as often as possible that he was with Jillian, and that he wasn't interested in anyone else.

If this had been three years earlier, his words would have meant the world to her, especially if they had been in a serious relationship. But as it was, they still touched her, and she couldn't help but be grateful for his presence. They might not have a future as a couple, but she hoped that they'd have one as friends.

When Eli and Anna arrived, things with Rebecca settled down a bit, and once the majority of the decorating of the sanctuary had been done, the pizza arrived. They headed to the hall to eat, and when they were done, they began to decorate the large room where the reception would be held.

The guys were put to work setting up the round tables to Taylor's specifications throughout the hall. The ladies followed behind, putting dark burgundy tablecloths over the tables then laying orange squares in the center. It was a color combination that Jillian wouldn't have thought would work, but after seeing the decorations in the sanctuary as well as in the hall, she decided that it really worked nicely. Especially for an autumn wedding.

"Are you guys wearing orange or burgundy?" Jillian asked Sarah as they spread an orange square into place.

"Thankfully, burgundy. I don't mind orange, but it's not a color I like to wear."

"No argument over the color between the three of you?"

Sarah laughed. "Surprisingly, no. We didn't have to think too much about that, and I think it was a good choice since our flowers are an autumnal mix of oranges, yellows, and a bit of green."

"Sounds lovely. I can't wait to see you all tomorrow."

Sarah grinned. "Can you believe we managed to get Leah to go to a spa with us today?"

"No, actually, I can't."

"I think I might have even convinced her to give it another go in the future." Sarah jostled Jillian with her elbow. "And we'll take you and Cara with us."

That sounded terrific, and Jillian found she couldn't wait.

They didn't stay around long once the last of the decorations were in place.

"Are you sure you're okay?" Carter asked as they stood outside the church a short time later.

Most of the people in the wedding party had left right away, no doubt hoping to get a good night's sleep before the big day, so it was just them and Michael and Taylor still in the parking lot. The brother and sister appeared to be in the midst of some sort of argument, if the raised voices and flailing arms were anything to go by.

"I'm sure." Looking away from the siblings, she tried to give him a reassuring smile. "You've seen me like that before, and I've been fine."

"I don't like seeing you like that, though. No matter how well you manage to bounce back." He hesitated. "I don't suppose you want to talk about it?"

"No. Not really. But it's not you," she hurried to say. "I've discussed it with professionals, so it's not like I haven't talked to anyone about what causes my anxiety."

"Okay." Carter seemed to accept that she wasn't going to spill her guts to him. "But, you know...if you change your mind."

"I know where to find you."

"Or at least how to get hold of me."

"Well, true. I don't know where you live." And Jillian was fine with that since she still wasn't sure she wanted him to know where she lived either. "But if I need you for something, I'll give you a call."

She wasn't surprised when he waited to say goodnight until she was in her car and then he shut her door. It wasn't lost on her that, yet again, he waited until she left the parking lot before pulling out himself. The first time he'd done that, she'd hesitated to go straight home and had driven around a bit just to make sure he wasn't following her.

He hadn't been then, nor the previous night, and from the look of it, he wasn't following her that night either. Still, she was glad to get home and behind locked doors.

As she got ready for bed with Dolly for company, she hoped that the next day would pass without incident. The last thing she wanted was to have yet *another* panic attack. Still, more than that, she didn't want anything to detract from the wedding festivities. Especially if it would mean taking Carter's attention from his duties as best man.

That was the absolute last thing she wanted to do.

CHAPTER TEN

Carter made it until noon before he finally caved and phoned Evelyn.

"Hello, Carter," Evelyn greeted him warmly. "Today's the big day, eh?"

"Yep. The wedding starts in about three hours."

"I'm so proud of you for accepting the role of best man for your friend," Evelyn said. "I'm sure it hasn't been easy."

"No, it hasn't been, but I was happy to help him out. Eli's one of my best friends here."

"I'm glad that you've been able to forge those friendships. It gives Garth and I both a sense of peace for you."

Carter thought about asking if it was enough to prove that he was moving forward so that he could visit Suzanne more frequently, but he had a feeling that it wouldn't matter. They wanted to see him move forward in *all* areas of his life.

"Do you have a date for the wedding?"

The question shouldn't have surprised him, but it did. Thankfully, he could answer her honestly. "Yes. Actually, I do."

"Really?" Evelyn sounded surprised. "Tell me about her."

"Her name is Jillian. She's been part of our Bible study group from church," Carter told her. "And she's a grade three teacher at the elementary school here in town."

"Well, Carter, I'm so pleased to hear that. Have someone take a picture of the two of you. I want a picture of you in your fancy suit and with your lovely date as well."

If Carter didn't know her so well, he might have thought she was trying to figure out if he was telling the truth. He had a feeling, however, that she just wanted to be a part of the day. Since Suzanne had been their only child, Evelyn's only opportunity to be personally involved in a wedding had died with the accident.

The doctors had made it clear from the very start that the longer Suzanne was in her vegetative state, the less likely it would be that she'd be able to recover in any meaningful way. Given she'd been in the coma for ten years now, the physical effects of a severely damaged brain were already very apparent.

So, while he still felt tied to Suzanne, he had accepted—sort of—that the Suzanne he'd fallen in love with, wouldn't be the one who would be present even if she woke up. But regardless, he wanted to be there for her.

"I will try to remember to have someone take a picture of us," Carter told her then paused, hoping Evelyn would give him the information he wanted. "How is Suzanne doing today?"

"Better," Evelyn said without hesitation. "It seems like the antibiotics are working, but we'll have to see how she responds over the next couple of days."

"Will you keep me updated on how she's doing?"

"I will, sweetheart."

Though he'd never marry her daughter, Evelyn had always treated him like a son. And Carter knew that even in telling him he needed to move forward, they were doing it out of their love for him. Didn't make it any easier to accept, however.

"Thank you. I really appreciate that."

"Just know for today that she's doing better, and try not to think about her too much. Enjoy your friend's wedding."

"I'll try."

"That's all I can ask."

After they said goodbye, Carter tossed his phone on his bed before sinking down onto the mattress. He leaned forward, resting his elbows on his thighs, and slid his hands into his hair.

How was it possible to feel pulled in so many directions? To have one event make him feel both happy and sad? To feel excitement and dread?

Part of him wanted to just head back to bed, but retreat wasn't how he usually dealt with things. Though realistically, he hadn't ever dealt with something like this before. This was the first wedding since the accident that he'd been a part of. Two of his sisters had gotten married in the years since. However, it had still been too soon after the accident, so he'd limited his involvement to flying into Miami, attending the ceremony, and flying out again.

His abrupt arrival and departure had upset his family, but it was all he'd been able to handle mentally or emotionally. When Eli had asked him to be his best man, his first instinct had been to say no, but he'd hoped that being ten years out from the accident, he might be more able to handle it.

Right at that moment, he felt like maybe he'd been mistaken. He couldn't do anything to change things now, however. He had to buck up and deal with it. Focus on Eli and Anna and do his best not to think about Suzanne and his own emotional pain when it came to weddings.

He'd gone to the gym earlier and worked out for an hour, but now he needed to shower then head over to Eli's place. The ladies were all meeting at the lodge while the guys were getting ready at Eli's cabin. So far, he hadn't received any calls from the groom needing him to do anything, so Carter assumed things were going smoothly.

With a sigh, he pushed to his feet and headed for the bathroom. It was time to get the day he'd been dreading underway.

"One would think you were the one getting married," Eli said with a laugh. "I think you're more nervous than I am."

Carter smoothed a hand down the front of his vest. "I just don't want to screw anything up."

The two of them were waiting in a small room off the sanctuary while Andy and Michael were out in the foyer, ushering people to their seats. They'd walk out with Pastor Evans once it was time for the ceremony to begin.

When Eli had first asked him to stand up with him, Carter had assumed that they'd wear something more along the lines of jeans and flannel shirts since that was about all he'd ever seen Eli in. As the planning went on, it seemed that Eli became willing to ditch his usual attire for the sake of his wife-to-be, and somehow, they'd all ended up in suits.

He considered the suits they wore to be a medium shade of gray with some very faint sort of pattern, but according to Anna and Rebecca, they were something called cool gray. They all wore burgundy ties that were chosen to match the ladies' dresses, and they had an orange rose pinned to their lapels.

It had certainly been a while since Carter had dressed up that much. Thankfully, Anna and Eli had covered the cost of their outfits, as Carter wasn't sure he could have afforded a five-hundred-dollar suit. He'd asked why they hadn't just rented, but Anna had wanted the guys to be able to keep the suits after the wedding. For what purpose, Carter had no idea.

Pastor Evans walked into the room where they waited, giving them a broad smile. "It's almost time."

"Best news I've heard all day," Eli said, rubbing his hands together.

Carter checked his pocket to make sure he had both rings, determined to not mess up any part of this day for his friends. He also had a few tissues. Though he wasn't one to cry, he had no idea what his emotions were going to be like during the ceremony, and he didn't want to be caught without any.

"How about we say a word of prayer before heading out?" Pastor Evans suggested.

As the three of them stood close together, the pastor prayed God's blessing on the ceremony and on Eli and Anna. It was a quick but heartfelt prayer, and Carter was sure Eli appreciated it.

They walked the short distance from the room to the door leading to the front of the sanctuary. Carter knew Jillian was there as she'd texted him earlier, before he shut his phone off, to let him know.

Taking a deep breath, he followed Pastor Evans and Eli through the door and up onto the stage. As soon as they were in position, the music for the processional began. Rather than watch the rest of the wedding party make their way to the front, Carter glanced out over the sanctuary.

He wasn't surprised at how full the church was. Eli's family wasn't small, plus Eli had said they'd invited most the people from the church. He saw lots of familiar faces, but it wasn't until he saw Jillian that a smile tugged at his lips. She happened to be looking at him and smiled in return.

Once the ceremony was underway, it passed rather quickly. Carter was grateful that he was able to stay present in the moment and could appreciate the personalized vows that Eli and Anna exchanged. The words they shared with each other and the people gathered there were heartfelt and emotional, though Carter managed to not need the tissues in his pocket.

Carter also managed to pass off the rings to Pastor Evans without dropping them. While Leah sang, Eli and Anna lit their unity candle. Then he and Rebecca joined the couple to sign the marriage certificate. When the pastor pronounced them husband and wife, Carter happily clapped along with the guests, feeling the first prick of tears at the realization his friends were starting onto the next stage of their lives. A stage he would never have with Suzanne.

Blinking rapidly, he was glad that everyone's attention was on the couple and not him. When the recessional music began to play, he walked to the center of the stage to offer his arm to Rebecca, then they followed Eli and Anna up the aisle to the foyer.

As planned, the wedding party and Anna and Eli's families made their way to Beau's property for pictures. Taylor and Michael, along with Anna and Eli, had set up a garden resplendent with autumn flowers for their picture taking. Carter wished Jillian had been able to go with them, but when he didn't see her after the ceremony, he figured she was in the hall with Taylor, making sure it was all ready for the reception.

Thankfully, the picture-taking went smoothly, and they were on their way back to the church within an hour.

When they got there, Eli and Anna took a few minutes in one of the rooms while the rest of them went into the reception hall. Most of the tables were already full, so it took Carter a couple of minutes to find Jillian. She was sitting at a table with Cara and Kieran, along with a few others. He wished he could sit with her, but he'd be at the head table with the rest of the wedding party.

He made his way over to their table and settled into an empty seat next to Jillian. Putting his arm across the back of her chair, he said, "Hey."

Carter was happy to see that there was no sign of tension or anxiety on her face as she smiled at him. "You did a great job."

He chuckled. "Thanks. Considering my main responsibility was to not lose the rings, I'd consider it a success."

"And all of you looked just stunning," Cara said. "Anna sure knew how to pick her colors. And everything here is beautiful too."

"Does it give you inspiration for your wedding?" Jillian asked.

"It does," Cara said with a glance at Kieran. "I may have to ask Anna for some help since Kieran's eyes glaze over when I start to talk about colors and flowers."

Kieran shrugged. "I can't help it if I'm a little bored by décor talk. I just want to focus on the things we actually need to get married. Like the license and stuff."

"Did you two coordinate your outfits?" Cara asked, her gaze going back and forth between Carter and Jillian. "Because you look great."

"No, we didn't," Jillian said. "But I knew the colors were burgundy and orange, so I figured navy blue would be appropriate. I didn't want to wear something that would clash with the tablecloths and flowers."

"Oh, the things we think about." Cara grinned. "Let me take a picture of you two."

Jillian gave Carter a quick look, as if to check that was okay with him.

"I'm usually not one for pictures," Carter said. "But I'll make an exception today, as long as Jillian's okay with it."

"Sure. Why not?"

Cara picked up her phone then gestured for them to move closer together. After a moment's hesitation, Carter shifted so his leg pressed against Jillian's then leaned his head toward hers. Her shoulder brushed his chest as she positioned herself, then they both held still as Cara took a couple of pictures.

"Let me take some of you two," Carter offered, pulling out his phone after she declared the pictures perfect.

Cara and Kieran happily posed for a couple of pictures, then they began to share the images from their phones. Carter wasn't sure what Jillian would do with her copies of the photographs, but he planned to send one of them to Evelyn.

"Sorry to interrupt," Rebecca said as she stepped up to the table, resting her hand on his shoulder briefly. "We're ready for Anna and Eli to come in, so we need the wedding party at the front."

Carter shifted away from Rebecca as he turned to Jillian. "I'll see you a bit later."

She nodded. "I'll be here."

He got to his feet and followed Rebecca back to the head table. She directed them all to their seats, then everyone stood as the emcee for the evening introduced the newly married couple.

Once the evening was underway, and dinner was being served, Carter pulled out his phone and sent one of the pictures to Evelyn.

Evelyn: *Oh, sweetheart! You both look just lovely. She's beautiful.*

It wasn't something he'd focused on, but Carter supposed she was. Her dark blue dress had looked nice on her, and he realized he probably should have told her that. He was severely out of practice when it came to the finer points of dating. If they were going to be convincing, he needed to up his game.

CHAPTER ELEVEN

Jillian was glad that she was at a table with Cara and Kieran, since she at least had someone to talk to. She knew the others seated at the table, but not as well as she knew Cara.

This was the first wedding she'd been to since everything had gone so wrong in her life, and she'd had a hard time controlling her emotions at times. The vows Eli and Anna had shared had been so touching that she'd had to blink back tears. She was happy for them, even though it was hard not to mourn what she'd lost. The future that could never be hers.

"This food is terrific," Cara said as they finished their dessert and coffee. "I'm going to have to find out who catered it."

"It must be a real bonus to attend a wedding while you're planning your own."

"I hadn't really thought about it, but yep, it turns out that I'm learning lots from what Anna and Eli have done for theirs." Cara glanced around. "There's only one thing that I know for sure will be different, and that's the number of guests we'll have."

"Yeah. There's no way we're going to have this many people at our wedding," Kieran said. "It helps that we both have small families."

Jillian knew all about small families. At one time, it had been her hope that her grandmother would be at her wedding, but tragedy and cancer had robbed them both of that. At least, Cara had a brother, and Kieran had his mother, so they wouldn't be completely bereft of family at their wedding.

She had no idea where her mom and half-sister were. It had been over ten years since she'd last heard from them. She didn't even know if her mom was aware that her own mother had passed away. Or if she would even have cared if she'd heard.

Carter was still at the head table, having stayed in his seat beside Eli throughout the meal. When it came time for them to do all the fun things couples did at wedding receptions, he left the table and headed over to where Jillian sat.

People were up and wandering around, chatting with other guests. That meant there were a couple of empty seats at their table, and he settled into the one next to her that had been vacated by Taylor.

He didn't sit there for too long as the emcee began to call for all the single men to come to the clear area in the center of the room.

"Aren't you coming?" he asked Kieran.

"Nope. I don't need to catch a garter to tell me I'm getting married next. I already know that."

"Well, I don't want to go either," Carter muttered.

"You don't have a choice, my man," Kieran said with a broad grin. "You're the best man. It's practically in the job description if you're a single guy."

"Whatever." Carter got to his feet and headed over to join the other single guys.

Jillian had a feeling he wasn't going to make any effort to catch the garter, and she couldn't blame him for that. She knew she'd have to go up when the bouquet was tossed, but she had no intention of trying for it. She was sure there were plenty of other single women who'd be more than happy to catch it.

Rebecca...Taylor...Sarah...probably not Leah, however.

Eli stood with his back to the group of guys, then waited while someone led a countdown, letting the garter fly when it reached zero. It appeared that Carter wasn't the only one not too interested in catching the garter.

Rather than a mad scramble to grab it, there was more of a parting of the sea as all the guys stepped back...except for Beau. With a grin, he reached out and snagged it as it flew past him. There were claps and whistles as he bowed.

Then they called the women forward.

"Guess you're not coming?" Jillian said to Cara as she stood up.

"Nope. If Kieran didn't go, I'm not going either."

"Maybe I don't need to go then. There are plenty of women who actually *want* to catch the bouquet."

Cara frowned. "You don't want to catch it?"

"Not really," Jillian said. "Nothing like just starting to date someone and then catching a bouquet that has the meaning attached to it that *I'll be the next to get married*. Talk about pressure."

"Ah," Cara said with a nod. "I can see that."

Sarah appeared at their table and grabbed Jillian's arm. "C'mon. Let's go."

"Why do you want me there?" she asked. "It's just more competition for you."

"It's all just in fun," she said. "C'mon."

"Fine. But I'm not going to try to catch it." Jillian allowed herself to be led to the floor, then took a spot at the very back of the group.

Carter stood off to the side with Eli, Beau, and Andy, looking down at his phone while the others were talking.

"Think Carter would be happy if you caught the bouquet?" Rebecca asked as she caught sight of Jillian.

"Well, I doubt he'd be mad if I did. It's just for fun, after all," she replied, borrowing Sarah's words.

Before Rebecca could respond to that, Anna got into position with the bouquet. She didn't hesitate at all when the countdown hit zero, whipping the bouquet up and over her head. It sailed for quite a distance, and just when Jillian thought she might have to actually catch the silly thing, so it didn't end up on the floor, Rebecca dove in and grabbed it, literally snatching it from right in front of Jillian.

"Hey," Sarah said. "You can't just take it from her like that."

Rebecca turned toward Jillian, a surprising look of contrition on her face. When she held the bouquet toward her, Jillian lifted her hands, palms out, and shook her head. "It's all yours."

Rebecca looked off to the side, where Jillian knew Carter stood, then asked, "Are you sure?"

"Very."

"If you're sure..."

"I am." Jillian gave her a smile then turned to Sarah. "It's fine."

Sarah stared at her for a moment before smiling and hooking her arm through Jillian's and guiding her over to where Beau stood. "Can you take a picture of us, babe?"

"I'd love to."

With her arm around Sarah's waist, Jillian smiled at Beau. Pictures weren't her favorite thing these days, but she'd prepared herself for the possibility she'd have to be in a few since it was a wedding. It wasn't like she had to look at them herself afterward.

After he'd taken the picture, Beau handed Sarah the phone. "Make sure it meets your high standards."

Sarah looked at it, then showed it to Jillian. "I think it's perfect."

Jillian was pretty sure she'd never used the term *perfect* to describe anything she was a part of, but it wasn't a bad photo.

"Our colors go so well together," Sarah added. "And that shade looks amazing with your complexion."

That made Jillian smile, especially since she'd gone back and forth that morning, trying to figure out what to wear. Not that she had all that many dressy outfits to choose from. If she had two more weddings to attend, she was going to need to invest in a couple more nice dresses.

One of the things she'd discovered about buying clothes since gaining weight was that her options for styles that she liked herself in had diminished considerably. When she'd been smaller, she'd worn almost any style, but that wasn't the case anymore.

However, the loss of style options wasn't enough to regret the weight gain.

"By the way," Sarah began, her voice low. "I still think that bouquet should have been yours."

"I agree with her," Beau said.

"Agree with her about what?" Carter asked as he joined them.

"That Jillian should have won that bouquet toss." Sarah crossed her arms. "She was robbed."

Jillian gave a huff of laughter. "I was only robbed if I'd actually wanted to catch it. Which I didn't."

"You should have elbowed your way to victory," Carter suggested. "Like Beau did."

"Yeah. It was a real battle elbowing the air," Beau said with a chuckle. "No one else was interested in grabbing that thing. I didn't want Eli to feel bad."

"You're such a sweetie." Sarah went up on her toes to press a kiss to Beau's cheek. "That's why I love you."

Jillian looked away from the couple, making sure to also keep her gaze averted from Carter. Moments like that created a quagmire of emotion within her. She was happy for Sarah and Beau, she really was, but mixed with that happiness was anger at the circumstances that had robbed her of the desire and ability to find that kind of relationship for herself.

Not now, Jilly. Not now.

"Time to cut some cake," the emcee announced. "Can I get the bride and groom over to the cake table?"

Grateful for the reprieve from her thoughts, Jillian followed Sarah and Beau with Carter by her side. They stayed back from the table so that the photographer could take pictures of the couple as they cut, then each ate a piece of the cake.

"I sure hope it's not poisoned," Sarah muttered.

Jillian glanced at her. "Why would you say that?"

"They got the cake from the bakery in town. You know, the one where Cece works."

She looked from Sarah to the cake that Eli and Anna were currently enjoying, then back to her friend. "Why did they use *that* bakery?"

"They wanted to go local if at all possible."

"I suppose that's a good plan, but I think I'd have made an exception if the woman who had a crush on my fiancé worked where she had the opportunity to sabotage a part of my wedding. Anna's a bigger woman than me." Jillian hesitated. "Well, emotionally, anyway."

"Oh stop," Sarah said, giving Jillian a light jab in her side. "I agree with you, though. I'm not entirely sure I'd go there for *my* cake."

"Do you think Cara would be safe if she got her cake there?"

"I think she should be," Sarah said. "Cece never had her sights set on Kieran."

"Don't you think you're overreacting just a tad?" Carter asked.

Sarah turned to look at him and Beau. "Have you *met* Cece?"

Carter hesitated then said, "Well, yes. I know she's caused you a few issues."

"Things have gotten worse with her this past year." She shrugged. "It's mainly been verbal stuff with her. Hurtful jabs are her forte."

Jillian remembered the night things had finally reached a boiling point with Cece and Sarah. She had so appreciated Sarah and the other girls sticking up for her, but a part of her felt sorry for Cece. For some reason, whatever caused her to act the way she did was stronger than her desire to maintain good friendships.

"Let's focus on the positive stuff today," Beau said, drawing Sarah into his side. "I'm pretty sure that there's no poison in the cake."

Sarah nodded. "I'm pretty sure too. Still not sure if I want a piece, though."

"You're crazy, darlin'." Beau grinned then pressed a kiss to her head.

Sarah beamed up at him. "Crazy for you."

Between Anna and Eli and Sarah and Beau, the sweetness level was almost cavity-inducing. But that was to be expected at a wedding, Jillian supposed.

Once the cake portion of the evening was over, music began to play. Some guests started to dance, but Jillian had no desire to join them. Thankfully, it appeared that Carter felt the same way because he didn't argue when she said she was going to sit down again.

"Are you glad your best man role is almost over?" she asked as they settled in the seats at the table she'd sat at earlier. It was only the two of them at the table right then.

"I am," he said with a nod, leaning back in his chair and resting his arm across the empty chair on his other side. "Have you ever been part of a wedding?"

Jillian frowned as she recalled the one wedding she should have been part of but hadn't been. "No."

Carter appeared to be waiting for a longer response, but Jillian wasn't sure what more to say. That she hadn't been a close enough friend for anyone to ask her to be in their wedding party? Or that her own mother hadn't wanted her as part of her wedding?

Music filled the silence between them, and while Jillian wanted to move past her awkward abrupt single word answer to his question, she wasn't sure what direction to take the conversation. Thankfully, Cara and Kieran rejoined them at the table.

"Did you get some of the cake?" Cara asked as they each sat down with a small plate with a piece of cake on it. "It looks delicious."

Jillian shared a look with Carter before smiling. "No. We didn't get any."

"Do you want some?" Carter asked. "I can get us a couple pieces."

"Sure. Why not? Let's live dangerously."

Carter gave her a quick grin as he got to his feet. Before heading for the cake table, he took off his suit coat and hung it on the back of his chair, leaving him in a long sleeve shirt and a vest. As he walked away, he began to roll up the sleeves of his shirt.

"What's that all about?" Cara asked as she lifted her fork and took a bite.

"Oh. Well, Sarah and I were discussing the chances of the cake being poisoned since they got it at the bakery where Cece works."

Kieran choked out a laugh and reached for his glass of water. "You might have wanted to lead with that before, you know, we took a bite."

"I think we came to the conclusion that it was unlikely."

"Unlikely?" he asked. "Or impossible?"

"Well, considering that Carter's just gone to get us some, I think we can go with impossible."

"Good," Cara said. "Because it's delicious, and I wouldn't mind getting our cake from that bakery."

After she took her first bite once Carter returned with pieces for them, Jillian had to agree. "I haven't had much opportunity to go into the bakery to try their stuff because of what happened with Cece, me, and Sarah. Maybe I need to just risk it and pay the bakery a visit."

Jillian was sure that people would assume she was on a diet, but even if she had been, she probably would have made an exception for a wedding.

Thankfully, with Kieran and Cara back at the table, and a few minutes later, Michael and Taylor, Jillian didn't have to worry about any more awkward pauses between her and Carter. Beau and Sarah also wandered over for a bit before they all gathered to send the newlyweds off.

Once Eli and Anna were gone, and a lot of the guests had also left, Jillian slipped off her shoes in order to be more comfortable as she helped with cleaning up the hall. The rest of their group also stuck around, and they made quick work of removing the center-pieces and tablecloths so that the men could put away the tables and chairs.

Taylor and Michael took care of preparing the flowers for transport. Jillian heard them discussing that some of the center-pieces would be going to the lodge, while the remainder would be delivered to the personal care home where Beau's grandfather lived. The caterers were also packaging up the leftover food, and at Eli and Anna's request, it would be given to a nearby shelter.

Jillian loved to see the generosity of the pair even with some-thing like their wedding. It fell in line with everything she'd come to know about Anna and Eli in recent months.

Once the hall was all cleaned up, Jillian looked around for her shoes and found them with Carter. He held them by their straps as he stood talking with Kieran. For a moment, Jillian felt as if she was truly part of a real couple.

Giving herself a shake, she headed over to Carter. He turned to smile at her as she approached, causing a flutter in her stomach.

It's nothing, she reminded herself. *Nothing but a role.*

And she didn't want it to be anything but a role they were both playing.

"Thank you for rescuing my shoes," she said as she took them from him.

With all the chairs put away, she wobbled while trying to put on the first one. When Carter held out his arm for her to hold onto, she took it. Once she had them on, she said, "I think I'm going to head home."

"Me too," Carter said. "I'm exhausted. Being a best man is hard work."

Kieran laughed as he thumped Carter on the back. "Don't I know it. After all, I'm the best man every day."

"You wish," Carter tossed back.

Cara slipped her arm around Kieran's waist and tucked herself against his side. "Oh, I can verify that he is, in fact, the very best man."

The four of them laughed before they headed for the exit of the hall. They said goodnight to the others who were also leaving. Jillian was sure that Eli and Anna's families were glad the day was over. For all that it had been a beautiful day to celebrate their union, Jillian knew that it had been a lot of work in the days leading up to the happy event.

"I guess I'll see you tomorrow," Jillian said as she slid into her car.

Carter shook his head. "I'm back to work."

"Oh. Well, I hope you have a safe shift."

"You and me both." He gave her a quick smile before saying goodnight and shutting her door.

After he stepped back, she pulled out of her parking spot. He stood in place until she began to drive to the exit of the lot. In her rear-view mirror, she could see him head toward his truck. It was a weird sort of pattern they'd fallen into. Thankfully, it seemed like maybe they'd found a way to get past their awkward goodnights.

If they'd been a normal couple, they wouldn't have been saying goodnight in parking lots. Still, it was what worked for them, and if it could make things a little less awkward, why not?

When she got home, Jillian was only too happy to slip out of her wedding outfit and into some much more comfortable pajamas. As she removed her make-up in the bathroom, Dolly wound around her ankles and meowed her protest of being left alone for several hours. That led Jillian to settle into her bed with her remote and the cat.

Though the day had held a few emotional pitfalls, it had been one of the most enjoyable times she'd had in the past few years. She knew that her grandma would have enjoyed the wedding too, and Jillian really wished she could have been there with her.

She'd been watching television for several minutes when she remembered the pictures that had been taken at the wedding. They'd done an airdrop with the photos between their phones, so she had copies of all that had been taken during the evening.

Jillian reached for her phone on the nightstand, then opened her photos. She couldn't help but smile at the one of her and Sarah. Her friend absolutely beamed in the picture, looking beautiful in her bridesmaid's dress. The rich burgundy looked amazing on Sarah and Leah with their dark hair and fair skin. Leah had worn her hair up, but Sarah's had been more of a half updo with part of it up in an elaborate twist and the rest left loose in curls.

While she wasn't smiling quite as broadly as Sarah, Jillian was sort of happy with the pictures Beau had taken of them. She was a little less eager to look at the photos of her and Carter. No matter how real the picture might seem, she knew that it wasn't.

She swiped the screen and paused on the first one of her and Carter. The way they were sitting did make them look like a real couple, and the smiles on their faces looked genuine. Well, hers had been genuine, though small. Carter's smile didn't look stilted either, though, like hers, it was nowhere near as beaming as Sarah's had been.

His wavy blond hair looked more styled than usual. And though she'd only ever seen him in casual clothes, he seemed just as comfortable in the suit he wore. He was definitely a handsome man, and Jillian had to wonder what his story was. Why was he interested in a relationship with no future?

Again, that was not a question that she'd be posing to him since she didn't want it directed back at her. But regardless of that, it was a question she kept circling back around to.

"But we're not going to ask, are we, Dolly-girl?" Jillian said as she scratched behind the cat's ears. "Because we're not going to take a chance on your life. No matter how curious we are."

The cat's loud purring seemed to show her appreciation of Jillian not giving voice to her curiosity to Carter. After a moment's hesitation, she set the picture of her and Carter as the lock screen on her phone. She figured that if Martin or anyone else saw her phone, having that on her screen would lend credence to their claim of being a couple.

That done, Jillian set her phone back on the nightstand, then slid down further in the bed. With the television still flickering and Dolly curled up against her hip, she let go of everything about the week and that day and watched as the bakers on a reality competition show tried to wrangle their recipes into impressive displays for the judges.

CHAPTER TWELVE

Carter pulled his truck to a stop in front of Eli's cabin. Well, now it was Eli and Anna's cabin. They'd gotten back a couple of days earlier from their ten-day honeymoon.

He'd thought they'd end up at some fancy resort in the Caribbean, so it had been interesting to see that they'd set off in an RV on a road trip up into Canada. Judging from the pictures they'd posted on their private joint Instagram account, they'd had a wonderful time.

He was looking forward to seeing Eli as well as the rest of their group. He hadn't seen anyone but Beau and Michael in the days since the wedding. He'd worked every third day, and on his days off, he'd been sleeping, working out, and making his weekly trip to Seattle to see Suzanne.

With no reason to contact Jillian, Carter hadn't been sure what to do. Meeting up for a meal or calling to chat seemed a bit out of the bounds of their...relationship, so he hadn't done either. He just hoped that she hadn't had any more anxiety issues. Though he'd told her to let him know if she wanted him to talk to Martin again, he'd doubted that she would.

He'd been right.

"Welcome home," Carter said when Eli answered the door.

"Thanks, man." Eli grinned. "Though I have to say that I could have handled another couple of weeks away."

When they stepped into the cabin, he could hear female voices and looked in their direction. He spotted Cara, Sarah, and Anna in the kitchen, but there was no sign of Jillian. He'd seen her briefly before the service that morning, but once it was over, she hadn't been around. Though at the time he'd suspected she was either in the nursery or working with the kids' church, he wasn't so sure now.

"No Jillian?" Sarah asked when she spotted him.

He shook his head. "We didn't make plans to come together. I'm sure she'll be here soon."

Sarah frowned as she came closer to him and murmured, "Is everything okay with you two?"

"As far as I know." He frowned back at her. "Why? Do you know something I don't?"

It was bad enough to see any sort of frown on Sarah's face, but when her frown deepened further, it was even worse. "I have no idea. She hasn't really been talking much to me this week."

That didn't make Carter feel very good. He realized that he'd been counting on Jillian keeping in contact with her friends to help her out if she was struggling. Now he was wondering if they were aware that she suffered from anxiety and panic attacks.

Pulling out his phone, Carter headed for the front door. "I'll be back."

"Okay," Sarah called after him.

There was a chill in the air as he stepped out onto the porch, letting the door close behind him. They'd generally kept in contact through text, but right then, he felt like he should call. Still, he hesitated, hoping he wasn't overreacting. Because really, when it came right down to it, it wasn't his place to overreact.

Except...she was a friend. Or at least he considered her one. Hopefully, she felt the same way about him and would accept his call in that mindset.

After staring at Jillian's contact information for another minute, Carter sighed and tapped the screen to call her. He lifted the phone to his ear, turning to stare out at the forest around Eli's place. The scenery eased a bit of the worry he had so that by the time Jillian answered after three rings, he felt calmer.

"Hey, Jillian. It's Carter," he said when she answered. "Just here at Eli's, and...uh...." He lifted a hand to rub the back of his neck. "A few of us are wondering if you're coming this evening."

"Yep." She didn't hesitate in her response. "Just running a bit late."

"Okay. Good. I'll let them know."

"See you in a few," she said.

Once the call had ended, Carter lingered on the porch for a couple more minutes before heading back inside.

"Is she coming?" Sarah asked.

"Yes. She said she's just running a bit late, but she'll be here soon." Carter frowned at Sarah. "How come you didn't just call her?"

"Oh. Well." She didn't meet his gaze. "I...uh...just thought maybe you should be the one to call her."

Carter mulled over her response for a moment before it dawned on him. "You thought we'd broken up or something?"

Sarah shrugged. "Maybe? It just seemed like you two weren't talking to each other."

"You need to stop looking at everyone else's relationship through the lens of your and Beau's. Trust me when I say that Jillian and I are both fine with how things are between us. We're just starting out in our relationship, so just give us some space."

"Okay." Sarah looked back at him. "You're right. I guess I just want everything to work out for you guys."

"I understand. Just know that whether or not it does, that will be on Jillian and me."

"You can't fault me for caring about the two of you."

"I don't. It's a good quality to have in a friend, so don't stop caring. Just stop worrying."

Sarah gave a huff. "I'll try."

He felt much more relaxed now that he knew that Jillian was okay, and also that he'd gotten Sarah to back off a bit. Still, it didn't keep him from glancing over every time the front door opened.

As the minutes ticked by, Carter managed to work himself up again. His mindset hadn't been helped by the fact that over the past week and a half, Suzanne's health had continued to teetertotter. One day Evelyn would call and tell him she was doing better, only to call him back a couple of days later to say that she had worsened again.

He'd asked about going in to see her more than just once that week, but Evelyn had brushed him aside, telling him that she'd let him know if he needed to come in between his weekly visits. It was frustrating, but he didn't want to push his luck and have them revoke even the weekly visit.

When Eli finally opened the door to reveal Jillian standing on the porch, Carter breathed a sigh of relief as he walked over to greet her by the door. "Hey."

While they may have figured out how to get beyond the awkward goodnights, the greetings when others were around were a different story. Obviously feeling the same tension, Jillian took the bull by the horns and reached out to give him a hug.

It didn't last long, but it was enough for Carter to feel the awkwardness dissipate. It also gave him a whiff of the shampoo she used. A light floral scent that kind of made him feel like he was sniffing a bouquet.

"Are you doing okay?" he asked when she stepped back from the hug.

She smiled up at him. "I'm fine. How about you?"

"Doing good," he said. "Just working and stuff."

"How's your friend doing?"

It took a second for Carter to figure out she was talking about Suzanne. "It's been up and down, but they seem to be doing a bit better."

"That's good. I could see that you were worried about them last week."

Carter nodded. He wasn't sure how he felt talking to Jillian about Suzanne. It was like his past and present were colliding...although it was a rather soft collision since Jillian was unaware of who Suzanne was to him.

"Jillian!" Sarah exclaimed as she joined them. "I was beginning to think you might not be coming."

"Well, I'm here. I was kind of hoping that I might miss the walk and just get here for the food."

"Ha. You have yet to actually time that correctly." Sarah bumped her shoulder against Jillian's. "Even though you keep saying that's what you want to do."

This was the first time they'd been back at Eli's for a hike in almost a month. Between the wedding and the pair being off on their honeymoon, it just hadn't worked out.

"Is everyone here?" Eli asked. "We probably need to get going because it looks like we might get some rain. I hope you all brought rain gear."

A few people stopped by their cars to pick up jackets, then they all headed up the trail behind Eli's. Carter waited to fall into step with Jillian, realizing as he did that this was the first time they'd gone on a hike since agreeing to be a couple...of sorts.

"You don't need to walk with me," she said. "I'm not the fastest hiker."

"I don't come on these hikes for exercise," he told her. "I go to the gym for that."

"I was going to ask how often you go to the gym, but I have a feeling the question should probably be, how long do you spend at the gym each day?"

Carter chuckled. "Yeah. I do work out daily. If I can't make it to the gym because of work, I use the equipment at the firehouse."

"I consider chasing twenty-plus eight-year-olds and lifting my hefty cat to be my exercise for the day."

"You have a cat?"

"Yeah, I do. Her name's Dolly. She was my grandma's cat." She glanced up at him. "Are you a cat or a dog person?"

"I don't have a real preference," Carter said. "Growing up, we had plenty of both around."

"Did you have a favorite?"

It had been a long time since he'd thought of his growing up years. As memories came to him, he couldn't help but smile. "I suppose it would have been a golden retriever named Aslan."

"Wait." She gripped his arm. "A *dog* named Aslan?"

At her question, he had to smile. "Yeah. That was what my parents said, but we were determined. He lived up to his name, though. Best dog ever."

"My grandma loved musicals, and one of her favorites was *Hello, Dolly!* so that's how the cat got her name."

"You know, my youngest sister had a teddy bear that she named Dolly."

Jillian giggled. "Your family has a thing for contrary names."

"My family has a thing for names in general."

"Really? How's that?"

"All of us have names that start with C and J."

"How many is *all* of you?"

"There are five of us. Two boys and three girls."

"That's a lot of C and J names. I was thinking like three."

"Nope. My parents took the *be fruitful and multiply* command to heart."

"So, what are all the names?" She grinned up at him. "Consider it a pop quiz from the teacher."

"Well, let's see. In order of age: Christopher James, Catherine Jill, Candace Janelle, me, and Charlotte Joy."

"And yours?"

"My name?" He glanced down at her in time to see her arch a brow at him. Giving a huff of laughter, he said, "Julian. Carter Julian Ward."

"Any of you go by CJ?"

"My oldest brother claimed that and left the rest of us having to stick with our actual names." Figuring he could safely ask a few questions, he said, "So what is your sibling and name story?"

When she didn't reply right away, Carter looked away from the path so he could see her expression. Any of the levity from just moments ago was gone from her face.

"I have one half-sister...that I know of."

"That you know of?"

"Yeah." She sighed. "Do you really want the whole sordid story?"

"Sure. If you want to share it." Carter found that he really hoped she did.

"Okay. Well, you asked for it." She paused before she said, "I don't know who my dad is. If my mom is to be believed, she slept with some random guy who was in town for the Fall Festival. She never got his name.

"My mom was in high school when she had me, so my grandparents helped take care of me since she was still living at home. She had boyfriends off and on throughout my childhood, but she didn't get serious about any of them until I was about ten. That was when she met Seth. She got pregnant and moved in with him, but they only had a one-bedroom apartment, so I stayed with my grandma. My sister, Vivian, was born just before I turned eleven."

"That's quite an age gap," Carter commented when she didn't go on right away.

"It was. My mom and Seth ended up getting married, then decided to move away from New Hope Falls. The only problem was that Seth decided he didn't want someone else's kid, so my mom terminated her parental rights, and they left me behind with my grandma."

"That's terrible."

"It would have been a lot worse if I hadn't had my grandparents there for me, plus they went on to legally adopt me. After my grandpa died, it was just my grandma and me, and we did okay. She loved me so much that I never really felt like anything was lacking in my life."

Carter wondered if she had managed to truly convince herself of that. He couldn't imagine a person would ever really get over a parent abandoning them. But he wasn't going to press her to delve into her emotional baggage when he had absolute trunk-loads of it himself.

Thankfully, they both got a reprieve as they joined the others at the bench that usually marked the halfway point up the trail. That day, however, Carter had a feeling the bench was going to be the turning-back point.

"Think we'd better not push our luck," Eli said as he looked up at the sky.

Even through the canopy of trees, Carter was hit with a splattering of raindrops. "I would agree."

No one argued, so they were soon headed back down the trail. Since Carter didn't want to prod more at Jillian's emotional pain, he didn't revisit the topic once they began to walk again.

"How has Martin been behaving?" Okay, so maybe he wasn't completely leaving things alone.

He'd hoped for an immediate answer, but her hesitation was noticeable. Carter supposed he should be happy that she thought twice before lying to him.

"He's...fine."

"Okay. But how are you with regards to Martin?"

"He's not entirely convinced that we're a real couple," she said with a sigh. "So he comes around frequently to let me know that."

"Why didn't you tell me? That was one of the reasons..." He glanced around. "Well, you know."

"I know. I just didn't want to bug you."

"Bug away. I agreed to do this to help you out," he said, keeping his voice low. "We'll fix that this week."

Already his mind was at work, and after he got home that night, he texted Jillian to find out when Martin was most likely to show up to harass her. He had to work a few days in the coming week, but he could fit in a visit or two at the school to see Jillian.

Once he had a better idea of what he was working with, Carter began to plan out the best way to tackle the problem of Martin. He didn't want to completely rob Jillian of her power to stand up for herself, but if he could let her know that she wasn't alone in that, he wanted to do that.

CHAPTER THIRTEEN

On Monday morning, Jillian stood in her bathroom, swallowing against the nausea that had been plaguing her since her alarm had woken her. There had been times—especially when she'd been in high school and college—when she hadn't viewed Monday mornings with any fondness. However, at no time had she ever felt this level of dread.

Carter had said he'd help her out, but she also knew he was busy with his own life, and it might not be until later in the week that he could do something. Almost worse than Martin's visits to her classroom was the dread as she waited to see what he was going to say or do next.

She breathed in and out several times, trying to bring her anxiety under control so she could go to school and teach her class. A job that she loved...even if the atmosphere there currently sucked.

At least she knew that while class was actually going on, she was safe from him.

It was just before lunch when there was a page asking her to go to the office. Wondering what could be going on, Jillian waited until the kids were off for their lunch break before heading to the office as requested.

"Hey, Jillian," Sandra said when she walked into the office, giving her a beaming smile. "Look what came for you."

Jillian looked over to where Sandra gestured, her eyes widening when she spotted the huge bouquet of flowers that sat there. "That's for me?"

"That's what the card says," the woman told her. "You don't have someone who would give you flowers?"

Well, when Carter had said he'd do something, she'd kind of assumed it would be him paying her a visit, not sending her a massive bouquet of flowers. "I do, yes."

"Then good on him. That's a beautiful bouquet."

It really was, Jillian agreed.

"I don't suppose you'd leave it here for all of us to enjoy."

Normally, Jillian might have considered it, but since this bouquet was there to serve a purpose beyond a boyfriend giving his girlfriend flowers, she would have to take it back to her classroom. "Sorry. I think I'm going to keep these flowers in my room so I can enjoy them."

"I don't blame you for that," the secretary said with an indulgent smile. "If I'd received that, I'd want to keep it within eyesight too."

Jillian picked the bouquet up, surprised at the weight of it. The vase it was in was almost as beautiful as the flowers themselves. She wondered if Carter had gotten the bouquet from Michael and Taylor's flower shop.

Back in her classroom, she set the flowers on the corner of her desk then took the card from the bouquet. After pulling out her insulated lunch bag, she sat down to eat her sandwich and bag of chips.

As she ate, she opened the card. She'd kind of anticipated that it would be blank, more for show than anything.

Hope this makes your Monday more beautiful. -C

It was written in a script that looked masculine, making her wonder if he'd gone to the shop directly instead of just phoning in the order.

The thought made her smile, so she picked up her phone and sent Carter a text.

Thank you for the gorgeous flowers! So amazing! I really appreciate them.

She didn't know if he was at work that day, but if he'd had a chance to write the note with the flowers, Jillian thought maybe not. Still, he didn't reply right away, so she focused on her lunch.

She was done her sandwich and halfway through her bag of chips when she decided to take a picture to send the girls. Getting up, she carried the bouquet over to the bookcase that sat in front of the window so that it was bathed in natural light, making it a great spot to take a picture.

Though she didn't know the names of the flowers, the autumn colors were beautiful and so appropriate for the season. After moving the bouquet around so she could see it from a few different directions, Jillian settled on one angle and snapped a couple of pictures of it.

"Boyfriend finally come through?"

Jillian gripped her phone and took a deep breath before turning around. Her heart began to pound, thumping so hard it felt like it was going to jump right out of her chest.

"He's been coming through all along," Jillian said, lifting her chin in hopes that she could steel herself against the anxiety that was fast rising within her. "He has exceeded all of my expectations."

Martin scoffed. "Then you must have pathetically low standards."

"No. I do not." She paused. "If I did, I would have agreed to go out with you."

As soon as the words left her mouth, Jillian wished she could take them back. Especially when she saw Martin's expression darken. He stepped in her direction, and if the bookcase hadn't already been pressing against her back, she would have taken a step away from him.

A knowing smirk crossed his face, leaving Jillian to wonder how the man—a teacher of young impressionable children—had developed such a cruel streak? Was she really the first woman he'd treated this way?

Suddenly, worry about her own safety gave way to worry about the children in his class. Even though she was weak in caring about her own safety, she had to be strong for the sake of the students.

"You need to leave," she said, the tremor in her voice weakening the command.

"I'll leave when I want to." Martin crossed his arms. "I'm not sure how you think you can make me."

"Perhaps I need to talk to Principal Hughes about your unwillingness to leave me alone." She said a prayer that Martin wouldn't press her. Being strong was horribly frightening, and she wasn't sure she could continue to stand against him if he didn't leave.

The bell rang before Martin could respond, and he stared hard at her before he turned and left her classroom. Jillian slumped back against the bookcase, feeling the tickle of the flowers against her neck.

As she looked into the faces of her students a short time later, Jillian knew she needed to stay strong. Carter had told her to go to the principal, and maybe that was what was needed at that point. For the sake of the kids, and for her own sanity, she had to do it. If she didn't, she might as well quit her job. She couldn't continue on like this.

Her anxiety hadn't been this high in months. Since returning to New Hope earlier that year, she'd found that the anxiety and panic had lessened to a manageable level. While there was always a thrum of anxiety within her, she had felt fully functional for the first time since her grandma's death.

However, since things with Martin had started, her anxiety baseline had risen to the point where everything seemed to set her off. Case in point, her reaction to Carter's knock on her car window the night at Anna and Eli's party.

By the time the students had left for the day, Jillian still wasn't sure if she should go ahead and talk to the principal or give Martin a chance to smarten up. After sitting at her desk and praying for a few minutes, she knew that the right thing was to protect the children. If talking to the principal ultimately cost Jillian her job, then so be it. At least she'd know in her heart that she'd done the right thing.

With her anxiety level spiking once more, she walked on shaky legs to the office. What did it say about her that she wished Carter was with her? Probably that she was weak.

At one point in her life, she never would have thought in terms of being weak or strong. She would have just known that she could take on the world. Or at least her small part of it.

"Back for more flowers?" Sandra asked with a smile as Jillian walked into the office.

Jillian tried to smile back. "Uh. No. I'm happy with the one bouquet I've received."

"You should be. It was gorgeous." The woman tilted her head. "So, who's the man?"

"Carter Ward."

Sandra's eyebrows rose as her eyes widened, which only served to feed the negative emotions within Jillian. She had yet to tell someone they were dating without receiving some sort of surprised reaction.

"He's a lovely man," the woman said. "You're very lucky."

Jillian couldn't argue with that. He'd been amazing with her anxiety and was willing to work within the constraints she'd put on their relationship. He'd put no pressure on her about anything except that she consider telling Principal Hughes about Martin.

On the other hand, she was pretty sure that no one would consider Carter lucky for having her as a girlfriend.

"Yes. I am." And there was no word of a lie in that. "I was wondering if Principal Hughes was in."

"He's not, actually. Is there something I can help you with?"

"No. I just need to discuss something with him." Jillian felt the small amount of strength that had carried her from her classroom to the office begin to seep away. She needed to shore it back up again if she was going to go through with this. "Could I make an appointment to speak with him?"

"Sure thing." The woman tapped a few keys on her computer. "This time tomorrow afternoon?"

"That would be perfect." As long as she didn't lose all her nerve overnight.

She'd just stepped out of the office and turned in the direction of her classroom when she spotted Martin heading toward her. Her first instinct was to turn and head for the doors at the front of the school, but all her things—including the beautiful bouquet—were still in her classroom.

Lifting her chin, she continued toward her room, determined to walk past Martin without acknowledging him. Her plan might have worked, if only he hadn't grabbed her arm, forcing her to turn and face him.

"What were you doing in the office?" Martin demanded. Though he wasn't as big as Carter, he still loomed over her, his expression threatening.

Jillian tried to jerk her arm free, but when she couldn't, her breathing became rapid and labored as panic began to well and truly sink its claws into her. Martin was still talking to her, but she couldn't hear him past the whooshing of blood in her ears.

She heard muffled shouts, and suddenly Martin's grip on her arm was gone. Voices carried on around her as strong arms engulfed her. But after a moment of struggle, the scent of a familiar cologne registered with her. She might have only smelled it a few times, but she already knew who it belonged to.

Carter.

Feeling safe, she slumped against his chest, letting him support her as her legs threatened to give way. Gripping one of his arms in both her hands, she began to tap against the sleeve of his jacket.

Words floated around her, muffled and distant, but in the midst of it, she heard a whispered *I've got you.* She let the words sink into her heart as she focused on the things she needed to in order to bring herself back to the events at hand.

"Jillian?" A woman's voice had Jillian taking a deep breath before opening her eyes. Sandra was standing close to her and Carter, a concerned look on her face. "Was this what you came to speak to Principal Hughes about?"

Jillian stared at her for a moment before nodding.

"I think perhaps you should speak to him first thing in the morning," she said. "I'll arrange for someone to cover your class."

"Have there never been issues with that man before?" Carter asked, his voice rumbling beneath her ear.

Sandra glanced up at him, then back at Jillian before her gaze dropped, and she sighed. When she didn't say anything further, Jillian closed her eyes again.

"Let the principal know what happened here because I'm not sure Jillian has a clear recollection of everything," Carter told the woman. "If Hughes has any questions about this incident, he can give me a call."

"I'll tell him." Jillian felt a touch on her hand and opened her eyes to meet Sandra's gaze. "I'm so sorry this happened to you. We'll get it sorted. I promise."

"Thank you."

The woman gave a nod then headed back down the hallway.

Still feeling a tightness in her chest, Jillian took a few deep breaths with Carter's encouragement before he said, "Let's go to your classroom."

Carter lowered his arms and rested his hand on her back to guide her down the hallway to her room. As soon as she stepped through the doorway, a cry of dismay escaped her as she took in the sight of the flowers of her bouquet strewn across the floor. Rushing over, she dropped to her knees, her legs finally giving out, and began to pick them up with trembling fingers, realizing as she did that the blossoms had been crushed.

"Hey. Hey." Carter knelt down beside her and took the bruised flowers from her hands. "They're only flowers."

"I know," Jillian whispered. "But they were so beautiful."

Working in silence, they began to clear up the flowers. When everything had been dropped into the garbage, Carter stuck close as Jillian gathered up all her things. She was still really shaky, and all she wanted was to go home, crawl into bed, and decompress from everything that had just happened.

Carter stayed quiet as she worked, which she appreciated. She felt frustrated, sad, angry, and embarrassed. And shaky. Yeah, that still hadn't abated as much as she wished it had.

Never mind making the decision to talk to the principal, she had another decision she needed to make. Or maybe it wasn't a decision, so much as an acceptance. It was time to see a therapist again. Everything was going downhill, and if that moment in the hall wasn't rock bottom, she wasn't sure she wanted to see what that would be.

Feeling drained at the thought, she slid her phone into her pocket then reached for her messenger and lunch bags.

"Let me," Carter said, taking the messenger bag from her.

Looking up at him for the first time since she'd become aware of his presence in the hallway, she said, "Thank you."

He held her gaze for a long moment before he replied. "Always."

Maybe if she wasn't so drained, her emotions might have reacted in some sort of way, but all she felt was...dead. All the emotions from just moments ago had faded away, just leaving a dead feeling inside her.

"Let's go."

He kept pace with her slower steps as they headed down the hall. There was no sign of Martin, and she was extremely grateful for that. She had no idea where he'd gone after everything had erupted in the hallway, but as long as it wasn't anywhere near her, she didn't care.

"I know you plan to talk to the principal," Carter said as they neared her car. "But, I think you should talk to Kieran about Martin as well."

Jillian frowned. "Talk to Kieran?"

"Yes. We have no idea what Martin might do next. What this latest confrontation might do to his mindset. He seems a bit unstable, and who knows if this might send him round the bend."

Fear sparked in her heart. "So you think I should talk to the police?"

"Yes. I do." Once she'd unlocked the car, Carter opened the rear passenger door and set her bag on the back seat. "I'll go with you if you'd like."

"Right now?"

"Right now. In case Martin does anything more, it would be good if the police had a record of what just happened at the school."

Jillian hated—absolutely hated—the idea of having to speak to the police again. It brought back memories she didn't want. "I just want to speak to Kieran. No one else."

When Carter didn't respond right away, she looked up to find him watching her closely. "Okay. Let me call and make sure he's in the office."

Carter pulled his phone out and placed the call. With the phone pressed to his ear, he paced a few steps away from the car, then turned and stared at the school. Jillian opened her car door then slid behind the wheel. She gripped the wheel as she listened to Carter as he spoke to Kieran.

"Hey, man. Are you at the station?" He paused, glancing down at her. "I need to bring Jillian in to talk to you."

Jillian looked away as tears pricked her eyes. What was it about her that drew the attention of men who wanted to hurt or abuse women? And how was she supposed to deal with having Carter so entwined in her life? He was only supposed to be on the edge of it. A casual boyfriend for those times when having a date was beneficial for them both.

She didn't want to rely on him emotionally or physically, but Martin had taken that choice away from her. And she was sure that this wasn't what Carter had signed up for either.

"He's at the station," Carter said as he stepped close to the car.

"Okay." Jillian looked up at him. "You don't need to come with me."

He shook his head as he lowered himself down so that he was more at eye level with her as she sat in the car. "I need to be able to tell him what happened from my perspective."

When she was in the midst of her panic attack, he meant. She dropped her gaze to her hands. "I'm sorry."

She saw Carter's hand reach for her, his fingers gently touching her chin, applying just the faintest bit of pressure until she lifted her head. His blue gaze was serious yet gentle.

"Don't apologize. None of this is your fault. The only person who should be apologizing in all of this is Martin. I don't have anything else that's demanding my time right now, so don't worry about taking me away from anything."

Jillian let out a shaky breath. "Okay. Let's go."

"Why don't you let me drive?" Carter suggested.

She wanted to turn him down, but she also knew that she wasn't in any condition to drive. Though the tightness in her chest had loosened, the shakiness hadn't completely left.

"You want to drive my car?" she asked.

"Sure. Or we could just take my truck."

"I'm a bit nervous about leaving my car here," she said, looking around at the lot that was emptier than it was during official school hours. "I don't know if Martin knows what I drive."

"That's a good point." Carter straightened up. "My truck is parked out on the street, so it should be okay."

He stepped back as she got out of the car and handed him the keys. "Oh, you'll need to push the seat back."

Carter walked with her around the car and opened the door for her. By the time she was buckled in, Carter was in the driver's seat. Though she'd never felt that her mid-size SUV was small, exactly, it kind of felt that way with Carter in it. His presence in her car felt a bit like his presence in her life. Steady and in control.

But she knew she shouldn't get used to it. Their relationship was casual and temporary...they'd both agreed to those parameters. She had to remember that she didn't want anything more than that. The emotional baggage she carried was too overwhelming for her to unpack, let alone someone else.

CHAPTER FOURTEEN

The anger within Carter had settled into a low simmer, down from the absolute wildfire it had been when he'd walked into the school and seen Martin with his hands on Jillian. All he could think about was what might have happened if he hadn't decided to stop by the school to see how things had gone for Jillian that day.

By the time he'd reached her side, he'd been able to see that she was well into the throes of a panic attack. Up until that moment, he'd been careful to not cross physical boundaries, even though they hadn't really discussed them beyond holding hands. But when he'd seen that Jillian was barely able to hold herself up, let alone walk away, he'd reacted on instinct.

He was just glad that she'd agreed to speak to Kieran. There were plenty of stories of men who became fixated on someone, stalked them and eventually did horrible things. Carter knew he couldn't just stand by and hope for the best.

It didn't take too long to get to the station, and there was a parking spot right in front, so he swung into it. After he turned off the engine, he turned to look at Jillian, not too surprised to find her just sitting there staring straight ahead. He'd seen her reluctance to speak with Kieran back at the school.

"Ready to go?" he asked, trying to keep his tone gentle.

The look she gave him told him that she was absolutely not ready at all. Rather than push, he just sat quietly, waiting for her to make the decision to go inside and tell Kieran her story of harassment.

He had a momentary urge to offer to pray with her before going in, but he'd just barely gotten to the point where he felt comfortable talking about spiritual things with the men's group. Praying with someone was still beyond anything he'd done recently.

When he'd been involved with the church as a younger man, the group he'd been part of had been large and full of charismatic people who happily took on the responsibility of leading and praying aloud. So, while he felt the urge, he didn't respond, choosing rather to just pray silently for her.

He heard her sigh, and when he looked over at her again, she said, "Let's go."

Before he could respond, she had her door open and was climbing out of the car. He hurried to join her on the sidewalk in front of the station. After a brief moment of hesitation, he reached out and offered her his hand. She took it, tightening her fingers around his.

"Hi, Lois," Carter said to the woman behind the receptionist's desk in the foyer of the station. "We're here to see Kieran."

"Sure thing, hun." She smiled at them, her gaze briefly dropping to their joined hands. "He said you were coming and to just send you on back."

"Thanks." Carter led the way through the door into the back area then to Kieran's office, where he rapped on the door frame.

Kieran looked up then waved them in. His smile was friendly but reserved. "Have a seat, you two."

Carter led Jillian to the two chairs in front of Kieran's desk then let go of her hand so he could close the door. Kieran regarded him with lifted brows as he returned to sit down beside Jillian.

"What's up?" Kieran asked.

Though he could have said something, Carter really wanted Jillian to find her own voice. She glanced at him, and he gave her a smile of encouragement.

"I want to report a...harassment."

"A harassment?" Kieran frowned. "Sexual harassment?"

"Um...maybe?"

"How about you tell me what's happened," Kieran said, his expression clearing as he glanced at Carter. Had he remembered the brief conversation they'd had about Martin and his actions toward Jillian? "Do you mind if I record this?"

Jillian shook her head then shifted on her seat while Kieran got himself set up, making note after he started the recording of who was with him.

"Okay then, Jillian." He gave her a reassuring smile. "Tell me what's happened."

Carter realized a bit late that by encouraging Jillian to share what had been going on, she was going to have to share how they'd come to be together. Not that he really cared. Kieran would keep their confidence if they asked him to.

He came to another realization as she spoke, and that was that she'd downplayed to him how much Martin had been harassing her. She hadn't told him everything, and Carter's anger began to build once again. However, he tried to keep it under control because he needed to be clearheaded when he told his part of the story.

"So today, he actually put his hands on you?" Kieran asked.

Jillian nodded. "He grabbed my arm to keep me from walking past him."

"And then what happened?"

She sighed, rubbing her temple with her fingertips. "I can't remember. I started to have a panic attack, and things got a bit fuzzy."

"That's when I came in," Carter said.

"You were at the school?" Kieran asked, shifting his attention from Jillian.

"Yes. I stopped by to see how Jillian's day had gone. As I was headed to her classroom, I noticed the two of them in the hallway."

"Was there anyone else around?"

Carter sighed. "I'm not sure. I was totally focused on the two of them."

"What happened then?"

"I yelled at him to let her go, and he did. Sandra Hernandez, the receptionist at the school, must have heard me because she showed up."

"What did Martin do then?"

"Sandra was talking to him while I tried to help Jillian. She was in the midst of a panic attack, and my attention needed to be on her."

"That's understandable," Kieran said with a nod. "So you don't know where Martin went?"

Carter shook his head. "I saw him head off down the hallway, but I don't know where he went."

"He ruined my bouquet," Jillian said, her voice sad.

"I'll get you another one," Carter promised.

"What bouquet was that?"

"Carter sent me a bouquet this morning. When we walked back to my classroom, we found all the flowers on the floor. They'd been crushed."

Kieran frowned. "Did you see him come out of your room?"

Jillian shook her head. "No. I mean, he was coming from that direction, when I first saw him in the hall, but all the classrooms are that way."

"Who else would it have been?" Carter demanded, anger once again flaring up within him. "No one else has been harassing Jillian about our relationship."

"I understand that," Kieran said. "But we need a bit more than that to say for certain that he was the one who ruined the bouquet."

"I'm sorry if we've wasted your time," Jillian said, her shoulders slumping.

"No, I'm not saying that at all," Kieran assured her. "I'm just talking about the flowers, not the harassment. His actions are definitely escalating, so we need to make sure that he is stopped."

"She's talking with the principal in the morning," Carter told him. "And when I asked the receptionist if they'd had other issues with Martin, she didn't come out and say yes, but her reaction seemed to lean in that direction."

"Okay." Kieran made a couple of notes on the pad in front of him. "Do you think he knows where you live, Jillian?"

She shrugged. "I don't know. I've been taking a different route home from school each day for the past couple of weeks. In case he was following me."

"Do you have a security system?" Kieran asked.

"Yes."

He regarded her for a moment then said, "Do you feel safe in your home? I'm sure you could stay at the lodge if you don't."

Carter could see the war within Jillian. "Maybe you should go there for at least tonight. Until we know what's going on with Martin."

"I would agree with Carter. Give Sarah a call and see if you can stay out there."

Jillian sighed. "Okay. I just hate to drag everyone into my problems."

Carter reached out and rested his hand on hers where they were clenched together in her lap. "We're all your friends, and friends stick together in good and bad. I feel confident in saying that Sarah would be quite upset if she found out about this and that you hadn't called her for help."

"Carter's not wrong," Kieran said as he reached for his phone and turned off the recording feature. "I think Cara would even give you her couch if you'd rather stay with her. And her couch is quite comfy."

"Okay. I'll call Sarah."

As they got up, Kieran circled around the desk and came to stand in front of Jillian. "I can't pretend to understand what you're feeling right now, but Carter is absolutely correct. We're here for you. Also, I think you may want to consider getting a restraining order."

"Okay. Thank you."

"Be sure to call if anything else happens. If Martin phones you or contacts you in any way, you call."

"I will."

Kieran looked up at Carter, his expression speaking volumes. From *you have some explaining to do* to *take care of her.*

He gave the man a nod then guided Jillian out of the station to her car. Once they were seated inside it, he said, "Why don't you call Sarah? I'll take you to your place to pick up some stuff then drive you to the lodge."

"How will you get your truck?" she asked, rubbing her forehead.

"I'm sure Eli will give me a ride back into town."

Jillian sighed. "I'm causing so many problems."

"No, you're not. *Martin* is causing all these problems. You need to stop taking on responsibility for his actions. You've done nothing to bring all this on."

"I know, but it seems that I attract this sort of man." She seemed to realize she'd revealed something she might not have wanted to because she fell quiet.

"Have you had a stalker or an abusive boyfriend before?" Carter asked. It would certainly explain the panic attacks she seemed prone to. And also why she was willing to agree to the type of relationship they had.

"No, but I have attracted the wrong type of attention before."

He waited to see if she'd reveal anything more, but when she didn't, he said, "Go ahead and call Sarah."

While she did that, he sent a quick text to Eli.

Any chance I can get you to give me a ride back into town?

Eli: *Sure. What's going on?*

Carter glanced at Jillian, gathering from the part of the conversation he could hear that Sarah had said she could stay out there.

Jillian is going to be staying at the lodge tonight, and I'm giving her a ride out there.

Eli: *I'll get the rest of the story on the ride back in.*

Thanks, man. See you in half an hour or so.

Eli sent him back a thumb's up.

"Where do you live?" Carter asked once Jillian was off the phone with Sarah.

The hesitation before she replied with her address was barely there, but he caught it, nonetheless. Though he understood why she might be reticent to trust him with that information, it stung a bit to think she had even the slightest bit of a worry that he would use that information to hurt her in some way.

Once they reached her house, Carter pulled into the driveway. "I'll just wait here."

If she hadn't been entirely comfortable with him knowing where she lived, he couldn't imagine she'd want him in her home.

"You can come in, if you want."

Okay. So apparently he was wrong about that.

She leaned over to push a button on the garage door opener attached to the visor over the steering wheel, then she tugged on her door handle and got out of the car.

As Carter followed her through the garage to the door leading inside, he noticed how clean and neat it was. He waited as she pressed the button to close the garage door, then unlocked the interior door and turned off the alarm.

The mudroom he stepped into was as neat and tidy as the garage, and as he took off his shoes, he noticed how brightly it was decorated.

A fluffy orange cat appeared and began to weave its way around Jillian's ankles, meowing loudly. She bent and picked the cat up, nuzzling her face in its fur.

"I'm guessing that's Dolly," Carter said.

Jillian looked up and smiled a truly genuine smile for the first time since the incident with Martin. "Yep. This is Dolly."

Carter reached out and rubbed the cat behind her ear. Her purring was loud in the quiet of the room. "Guess she likes me."

"She likes most people," Jillian said, giving him a small smile. "You give her attention, and she'll love you."

"Will she be okay if you're not here?" Carter asked.

"Yes. I'll leave fresh food and water for her. She'll be fine. I'll be back to check on her tomorrow."

"Guess it's good you have a cat and not a dog. You can't leave dogs for extended times like you can cats."

"Very true." Jillian bent to put Dolly back on the floor then led him from the mudroom into the kitchen, which, like the mudroom, was bright and airy. "Would you like something to drink? Water? Coffee? Tea?"

Carter hesitated for a moment before he said, "How would you feel about grabbing a bite to eat before we head out to the lodge?"

Her brow furrowed for a moment as she glanced at the clock on the wall. "I didn't realize how late it was already."

"So you'd be okay stopping by *Norma's*?"

"Yeah. I think I would be."

"Good. Then I'll wait to get something to drink there."

"You can wait in the living room, if you want," Jillian said, gesturing to where a large couch sat. "I'll be back in a few minutes. The remote for the television is on the coffee table."

Carter watched as she walked away with Dolly in her wake, then looked around. He was curious about her home, he had to admit. Walking further into the house, he could see the personal touches she'd added to the décor. He went to look at the pictures that sat on the mantel above the fireplace.

For a moment, he didn't realize that the person with the older woman in a few of the photos was Jillian. She was thinner and had a wide beaming smile. She looked happy and relaxed, and though he'd seen Jillian smile, there was something different about her smile in the pictures. She was more reserved now, and Carter knew with certainty that something had happened between when those photos had been taken and the present that had changed her.

The couch looked comfy with a blanket thrown across the back of it. He had no trouble picturing her curled up on the couch with the blanket over her, watching the television that was set up across the room.

With a sigh, he sat down on the couch, happy to find that it was, in fact, as comfy as it looked. He took out his phone to send Eli another text.

Slight change in plans. Going to take Jillian out for some supper before we head to the lodge. Still work out for you to bring me back into town?

Eli: *I'm not an old man going to bed at 8pm you know.*

Carter chuckled then tapped out a reply. *You're an old married man now, so I wasn't sure.*

Eli: *Ha! You're older than me. If anything, Anna keeps me young.*

He felt a brief surge of jealousy. He was happy for his friends, but he missed what he could have had.

Glad to hear it! Tell her I'm sorry for taking you away for a little while.

Eli: *She says it's fine. I'll make it up to her. Lol Text me when you're at the lodge.*

Will do.

As he waited for Jillian to reappear, Carter checked in with Evelyn to see how Suzanne was doing. This particular bout of illness had lasted longer than ones in the past, which had been particularly worrisome for him as well as for her parents.

Thankfully, over the past few days, it seemed that the latest round of antibiotics had finally kicked whatever it was that hadn't wanted to leave her body. That news had helped to ease the worry he'd been dealing with lately regarding her health.

Carter knew that there would likely come a day when an infection like that would take hold and not let up. The doctors had said that was the most likely thing that would rob Suzanne of her life. And he could see—and he was sure that Evelyn and Garth could as well—that even though Suzanne recovered from these bouts of illness, each time she was weaker afterward. Her health would plateau in between illnesses, but she'd never be as strong as she was before she got sick.

For the duration of this last illness, he'd spent each day dreading that he'd get a phone call from Evelyn or Garth with the worst news ever. Now that she was doing better, he felt like he could breathe again.

Except now, another woman he cared for was at risk, and the worry and dread were back...tenfold.

CHAPTER FIFTEEN

The realization that his emotions were now engaged with Jillian had Carter looking up from his phone to stare blankly at the fireplace. He'd considered Jillian enough of a friend to say hi to her at church or when he saw her out and about in town, but Carter had never sought her out or initiated a conversation with her.

Now, however, he had no problem imagining starting a conversation with her at their friend gatherings or at church, and he would definitely go out of his way to say hi if he saw her in town. He hadn't thought about how things might change for them when he'd first proposed their arrangement. Clearly, that had been pretty naïve of him.

He'd anticipated an uncomplicated arrangement. Something that would benefit them both. That would be there when they needed it, but not something that would take a lot of effort on the part of either of them.

He had a feeling that Jillian had viewed their agreement the same way, if the amount of time that elapsed between their conversations over the past couple of weeks was any indication. Everything about how she'd reacted to this situation with Martin told him she wished she hadn't had to rely on him for any sort of help.

And for her sake, he kinda wished she hadn't had to rely on him either. He was glad to be able to help her, but he'd much rather she not have to face this particular situation at all.

"I'm ready."

Carter pushed to his feet and turned to see her standing next to the end of the couch, a floral duffle bag in her hand. She'd also changed out of her teaching clothes into something that looked more comfortable. Her hair was pulled up in a messy knot on the top of her head, and she looked weary.

He walked over and took the duffle from her. That she released it without argument told Carter how worn out she was from everything that had happened in the past few hours. She probably would have crashed if not for having to go to the lodge, which was why he wanted to get some food into her. If she did crash once she got there, at least she'd have something in her stomach, which might help her sleep better.

His mom always believed that a full stomach solved everything. That had led to all of them experiencing what they'd come to refer to as the *awkward years*, which referred to the middle school years when they'd all carried a bit of baby fat. Once he and his brother had gained significant height in high school, they'd thinned out. His sisters, however, had struggled with the extra pounds longer, and even now, his youngest sister continued to battle her weight.

"I just want to grab a couple of things and put out fresh food and water for Dolly," she said, going into the kitchen.

Carter carried her bag into the mudroom and put on his shoes while he waited, hearing what sounded like a radio come on. No doubt she'd turned it on to keep the cat company while she was home alone for an extended period of time. Jillian appeared a couple of minutes later with a grocery bag in her hand. Unzipping the duffle, she shoved the bag inside it before closing it again.

After she locked and secured the house, they made their way in silence to the car. Carter didn't know if he should be trying to make conversation with her, but honestly, he didn't like to force stuff like that. He wasn't called strong and silent these days for no reason.

"Still okay for *Norma's*?" he asked as he opened the car door for her.

"Yes."

Though her answers were short, she wasn't hesitating about going to eat, which told him she was comfortable with him. Or at least, he hoped that was the case.

It was past the dinner rush, so the restaurant wasn't too busy when they got there. The sign near the hostess stand said to seat themselves, so Carter led Jillian to a booth in the corner.

As soon as they were seated, a server approached them. Carter didn't recognize the young teen, but she was friendly and greeted them with a smile as she laid menus down on the table. She rattled off the specials then left to get them their drinks.

Now that everything had settled down, Carter found that he was ravenous. He hadn't had anything to eat but a quick sandwich around eleven just before he'd gone to the gym.

"Are you ready to order?" the server asked when she returned, setting their drinks on the table in front of them.

Carter glanced at Jillian, who nodded. He waited as she placed an order for some chicken strips and fries, then he told the waitress he wanted a double cheeseburger with bacon and fries. He didn't usually eat at *Norma's* since his budget didn't support eating out too often, so he was going to indulge a little bit.

His bank account had a tiny amount of savings, so the flowers and this meal wouldn't eat into the money he had set aside for rent, bills, and groceries. But if he was going to be laying out money like that in the future, he'd have to look for other ways to tighten his belt financially.

Though he was sure Evelyn and Garth would tell him he didn't need to pay them as much—or at all—he didn't want to stop doing that if at all possible.

"So, how are you enjoying the school year?" Carter asked, then realized that was probably a stupid question. "With your class, I mean."

She gave him a small smile that showed she understood what he meant. "I love my class."

"What made you decide to teach grade three?"

"I didn't decide on the grade, per se. I can teach any elementary grade, but I do really like grades three and four. By that age, kids have learned a lot of the fundamentals, so I get to build on that, which I really enjoy."

"And did you always want to be a teacher?"

Jillian nodded. "Yep. My grandma taught, and I saw how much joy it brought her. Because of that, I decided that was what I wanted to do. Plus, I had a couple of really great teachers who made a big difference in my life. I wanted to be that kind of teacher."

"Did you go to college in Seattle?"

She hesitated for a moment before shaking her head. "I moved to Portland for college, then my grandma came to live with me a couple years ago."

The server returned with their food, and once she left them again, Carter offered to say grace for their meal—that was a prayer he could say aloud. When Jillian nodded, he said a quick prayer, thanking God for the food. Then, after a moment's hesitation, he prayed that God would resolve the situation with Martin quickly.

When he was done, they ate in silence for a few minutes before Jillian said, "Are you from around here?"

Carter had just taken a bite of his burger, so he had a bit of time to try and come up with an answer that didn't give away too many details he'd then have to explain.

"I'm from Miami, originally."

Her brows rose briefly. "You literally moved to the other side of the country."

He nodded. "I moved to Seattle first, but then I had a chance at a job here, so I made the move."

"Did you always want to be a firefighter?"

Grateful that she hadn't pressed for more information on why he'd moved from one corner of the country to the other, Carter said, "It was either a firefighter or a cop. I had family members that were both, so early on, I knew I wanted to be one or the other."

"How did you decide which route to take?"

"After there was a string of arsons in the town where we lived, I became interested in how they determined which fires were arson and which weren't, and how they solved that question. I was originally going to try to become an arson investigator, but I've been happy with my role in the station now."

"What do you enjoy most about your job?"

"I like that there is a lot of variety. I work in the field and go out on calls, but I also have admin responsibilities. Probably my favorite part of it all is doing the presentations at the schools or having classes come to the fire station."

"You haven't really struck me as much of a people person, in the short time I've known you," Jillian said, a curious look on her face.

Carter gave a quick laugh. "True. But kids are different. I enjoy being around them, talking with them."

"I could see that when you came for your presentation. I look forward to seeing you do it again sometime." Her smile slid from her face, a frown replacing it. "If I still have a job, that is."

"You'll still have a job," Carter assured her.

"You can't know that for sure."

Carter shrugged. "I've known Trevor Hughes for several years now, and he seems like a decent guy."

"That doesn't necessarily mean he'll believe me."

"I think he will, but even if he didn't, this time, you have witnesses." The despair on her face hurt Carter's heart. "But, I honestly think you have nothing to worry about where Martin is concerned."

"What I don't understand is why Sandra made it seem like there had been problems with Martin before."

"Yeah." Carter sighed. "I got that feeling as well, and I'm not sure why they wouldn't have done something about it unless the woman involved decided not to say anything."

Jillian's shoulders slumped as her gaze dropped to her plate. "Which is why I have to follow through with this, even if it makes me sick to my stomach and I just want to ignore it all. I need to make sure he doesn't make another woman feel the way I do."

"You're not alone." Carter just barely caught the endearment he wanted to tack onto the end of that. "I believe you. Kieran believes you, and I know Sarah and the others will believe you as well. If and when you decide to tell them. You are not alone."

Her gaze lifted, and she gave him a tremulous smile. "Thank you. You have no idea how much that means to me."

They finished their meal in silence, then when the bill came, Jillian insisted on paying for her own meal. Carter tried to argue, but she persisted, so he let her do as she wanted.

The sun had fully set by the time they left the restaurant, so they made the trip out to the lodge in the dark. Warm lights glowed invitingly from the windows as he pulled to a stop in front of the large building. He had texted Eli just before he left the restaurant, so it wasn't a surprise to see his truck there already.

For some reason, the air at the lodge seemed crisper and more fall-like as he stepped out of the car. He took a deep breath then retrieved Jillian's bags from the back seat before following her up the front steps of the lodge.

Once inside, he set the bags on the floor then turned to Jillian. "Text me when you're done speaking with the principal tomorrow. If you want me to be there, let me know. I have to work, but as long as there's nothing going on, I can take some time off. My boss will understand."

"I think I'll be okay," Jillian said. "But I so appreciate everything you did for me today. You went far above what we'd agreed on, I know that."

"You're right, I did, but don't let that stop you from calling me if you need some moral support. The only reason I wish this hadn't happened is because I hate what you've had to endure. Being there for you through it? That's been the easy part. I would do it again in a heartbeat."

He wanted to give her a hug, but because he suspected that she'd experienced some sort of negative encounter with men before this situation with Martin, he held back. If she made the first move, he would have given her a hug. But she didn't, so he left well enough alone.

"I'll be praying you sleep well."

"Thank you."

"Jillian?" Sarah's voice had them both turning toward the lodge's kitchen. She held out her arms and wrapped Jillian in a hug, showing none of Carter's reticence to embrace her. "What's going on?"

Jillian sighed. "Can I tell you about it once I get to my room?"

"Oh, of course. Definitely." Sarah picked up one of her bags. "I'll take you upstairs. We've only got one guest in the lodge tonight, so we have plenty of room for you."

Jillian turned back to him. "Thank you again for everything."

With a nod and smile, Carter said, "Always. I'll talk to you tomorrow."

Eli had wandered out of the kitchen by then. "Ready to go?"

"Yep. Appreciate the ride."

"You're more than welcome."

With one last look at Jillian, Carter left the lodge with Eli, bracing himself for the many questions that were likely to come his way.

CHAPTER SIXTEEN

"What's going on?" Sarah asked as she curled up on one end of the loveseat in the beautiful room she'd shown Jillian to.

Jillian sank down on the other end, wanting more than anything to take a shower then fall into bed. Unfortunately, it was also the last thing she wanted to do. She had a feeling that even though she *could* have panic attacks without nightmares...and more panic attacks...following, that wouldn't be the case that night.

Thankfully, her nightmares didn't usually end with her screaming. Her grandma had told her that she'd never heard her scream when she had them, so she hoped that was still the case. Maybe she should have asked for a cabin instead. Except that she much preferred the security of the lodge.

"You don't have to tell me, if you don't want to," Sarah said. "But maybe talking about it will help?"

Jillian wasn't sure if it would help, but for the first time since everything had happened—everything, not just this latest twist with Martin—she wanted to talk.

"Have you heard of the Portland Predator?" Jillian asked.

Sarah's eyes widened as she nodded. "He was that guy who used a dating app to kidnap women, then torture and kill them, right?"

Jillian nodded. "I was victim number nine."

Her friend's mouth dropped open. "What? I remember hearing they'd arrested him and rescued a couple of the women he'd taken. One of them was you?"

"Yes."

"Wait." Sarah sat up straight. "The people who testified during his trial said he did terrible things to the women he took." Her face paled. "Did he do those things to you?"

Jillian swallowed and looked down. "Yes."

"Oh my word," Sarah whispered. "I'm so sorry, Jillian. I never knew."

"My lawyer did her best to protect my privacy, and my grandma agreed to keep it quiet too, figuring it would be hard enough for me to adjust back to life without the world looking at me as a victim."

"So what happened today? Did something happen with that guy?"

"No. I just wanted you to know that part of my life to give perspective to what's been going on lately."

Sarah frowned. "What's been going on lately?"

Taking a deep breath, Jillian began to tell her everything, including how she and Carter had ended up together...sort of.

"I can't believe that things escalated like that with Martin. I would have thought he'd leave you alone once you and Carter started dating."

"I feel like I have some sort of target painted on me," Jillian confessed. "First, that guy in Portland targeted me, then Martin."

"But not Carter," Sarah said with confidence. "Carter would never do anything like that to you."

"I know. He knew what was going on with Martin before he suggested we date."

"So I'm confused about that," Sarah said, drawing her legs up to wrap her arms around them. "Are you guys together or not?"

"Yes?" Jillian said. "I mean, we're together in that if we need a date for something, we'll go with each other. But we're not going to be going out on dates with just the two of us. I'm not looking for a serious relationship, and I don't think Carter is either. I don't know his reasons."

"But your reason is because of what happened?" Sarah asked.

Jillian hated that that time still held so much of her life in its grip. Her grandma would have told her that she was letting the monster win by denying herself something she'd always wanted. "Yes. I can't see myself getting married."

"But marriage was something you used to want so much," Sarah said, her voice sad.

Jillian shrugged. "Sometimes life changes things for us."

"I still can't believe what's happened to you." Sarah rested her chin on her knees. "You're absolutely amazing to have come through all that and still be as happy as you are."

"I was happy to be back in New Hope and had hoped that moving back would be a fresh start for me. I didn't want anyone here to know about what had happened in Portland."

"I won't tell anyone, I promise," Sarah said. "Not even Leah."

"I don't mind if you tell her." Jillian gave her a small smile. "I know that you tell her everything, and I also know that Leah never tells anyone anything."

"You do know us so well."

"You can even tell Beau, if you want, but I'd prefer it go no further. Even Carter doesn't know the details of what happened. He just knows what's going on now with Martin."

"I'm glad that he's been there for you," Sarah said. "I think you need a man in your corner, and I really don't think there's a better one than Carter. Well, Beau might be better, but he's kind of taken."

Jillian gave a huff of laughter. "I don't think *kind of* is the right description there."

"Well, it's not official," Sarah remarked. "I mean, he hasn't proposed yet."

"He will."

Sarah straightened, her eyes going wide. "Has he said something to you?"

"Like he has to. I think the only question is *when* he's going to propose, not *if*."

"Feel free to tell him that sooner would be better than later."

"If he comes to me for advice, I'll be sure to pass that on."

Sarah fell silent then. It was a weighty silence that pressed down on Jillian, making her suddenly feel exhausted. The emotional turmoil of the day was finally catching up with her.

"You're tired," Sarah stated as she lowered her feet to the floor. "Can I do anything for you?"

"Just giving me a safe place to stay is more than enough." She waved her hand at the room. "Thank you so much for this."

"You're welcome. I'm glad you felt comfortable enough to ask rather than go home where you didn't feel safe."

Sarah leaned over to give Jillian a hug. But before she wrapped her arms around her, she sat back, dropping her arms.

"I just realized that maybe you don't like to be touched." A look of consternation crossed her face. "Have I been hugging you this whole time when you haven't wanted it? Oh, I'm so sorry."

Jillian held up a hand. "Stop. Please. Just stop."

"Okay. Okay. I will. No more hugs, I promise."

"That's not what I meant." Jillian sighed as tears pricked her eyes. "Don't treat me differently, please. It's why I didn't want anyone to know about my past."

"Oh, sweetie, I'm so sorry." Sarah instantly wrapped her arms around Jillian. "I won't. It's just such a lot to take in. I wasn't sure how to react, but if you want it all to stay the same, I'll do my best to do that."

"Thank you." Jillian leaned her head against Sarah's for a moment, soaking in the affection she offered.

Sarah gave her a quick squeeze then sat back. "Anything for you, my friend. Anything."

After they'd said goodnight, Sarah left her alone in the room. Jillian stayed on the edge of the bed for a few minutes, trying to gather herself together to face the night ahead. She prayed that there would be no nightmares, but the reality was that it was highly unlikely that she would have a calm night.

She put a worship playlist on her phone as she began to prepare for bed. It was a little earlier than she'd normally call it a night, but since she anticipated a restless night, allowing extra hours for sleep was probably a good idea. She didn't have the luxury of staying in bed late the next morning.

With the music playing in the background, Jillian went through the motions of preparing for bed. Removing her makeup, taking a shower, laying out her clothes for the next day. Finally, with no small amount of trepidation, she went around, turning off the lights and making sure the curtains were closed. She needed the room to be completely dark.

People would probably assume that she would need light after a nightmare, but the quickest way for her to break free from her nightmares was to be able to open her eyes and see darkness. When she'd been held captive, darkness had meant safety while light had meant she was in the place that had brought her way too much pain and horror.

As she lay there in the dark, the memory that was a curse when it came to recalling details of her time in captivity, was a blessing as she recited verses, bracing herself as sleep and nightmares drew ever closer.

The nightmare swept in like a raging storm, bringing with it all the sights, feelings, and sounds of that time. It was hard to say which memory was the worst, but at any given time, one of them was battering her. Finally, when a particularly painful one jolted her so hard that she had no choice but to wake, she broke free of sleep.

Darkness.

I'm safe...for now.

After that initial thought, the panic and fear eased back a bit, but not fast enough. The vice around her chest made drawing a deep breath nearly impossible, so while the nightmare began to fade, the panic started to build as she struggled to draw breath.

Count with me, Jillian. Carter's voice cut through the panic.

One. Two. Three. Inhale.

One. Two. Three. Exhale.

She gripped the sheets, registering how soft they were.

One. Two. Three. Inhale.

One. Two. Three. Exhale.

The pillow beneath her head was fluffy.

One. Two. Three. Inhale.

One. Two. Three. Exhale.

The air was cool and lightly scented with flowers.

One. Two. Three. Inhale.

One. Two. Three. Exhale.

Slowly...ever so slowly, Jillian was able to return to the present. She lifted shaky hands to brush at the tears that had slipped from her eyes. Then after a moment, she sat up and reached for the lamp she knew was on the nightstand. Light flooded that area of the room, and she flopped back on the bed. She stared up at the ceiling, trying to think about anything but the details of her nightmare.

For months following her time in captivity, she'd barely been able to go an hour, let alone a day, without reliving the details. A year out, the nightmares had lessened to only a few every week. By the time she'd returned to New Hope, the nightmares had tended to only come when that time had been in her thoughts throughout the day, or if she'd had a panic attack brought on by a very physical reminder.

That had been the case with Martin grabbing hold of her, followed by Carter hugging her. Not that she'd wanted to be free of

Carter's embrace once she'd realized who it was. But being held that way had at first felt as if she was being restrained.

Finally able to take in a steady and deep breath, Jillian swung her feet over the edge of the bed and sat up. She took a long drink from the bottle of water she'd left on the nightstand then reached for the chocolates she'd set there earlier.

It wasn't that she thought they really made a big difference. Still, she'd fallen into the habit of chasing the bad aftertaste of a nightmare with something that brought her joy. As she ate the chocolate, she thought back to hearing Carter's voice as she'd fought to come back to the present.

She didn't know what to make of his presence in her nightmare recovery, but she was thankful for it. Like her chocolate, his voice had been a pleasant thing to surface to.

Though she didn't want to go back to sleep, it was only 1:23 in the morning, so she'd only had about four hours of sleep. It hadn't been restful, however. She felt as exhausted as she had when she'd fallen asleep the first time.

With a sigh, she got up and went to the bathroom to use the toilet, then wash her hands, rinsing away the bits of chocolate that still remained. She brushed her teeth and took another drink of water before heading back to bed.

In the darkness once more, she again recited Bible verses. They weren't so much to ward off the nightmares—that hadn't worked in the past—as to give her enough peace in her heart and mind to fall back asleep.

"He'll see you now," Sandra said, her demeanor definitely less perky than usual. "Don't worry. Everything is going to be just fine."

The smile Jillian gave her didn't feel too steady, but she felt better than she might have had she been on her own before leaving for school. Instead, she'd been surrounded by the McNamara family.

Nadine had assured her that she could stay at the lodge for as long as necessary, all the while giving her a tight hug. Sarah had whispered that she hadn't told her mom anything, but it appeared that news of the altercation had already spread through the town. Jillian hated the idea that her business had become the town's latest gossip scandal, but such was life in a small place like New Hope.

From what she understood, Martin wasn't a town native, so people would probably give her the benefit of the doubt in the situation. Not that she wanted people to judge by rumor and not fact, but in this case, the truth was that Martin was in the wrong.

"C'mon in, Jillian," Principal Hughes said when she stepped into his open doorway. "Please have a seat."

When she turned to close the door, he said, "You can leave it open if that would make you feel more comfortable."

It wasn't like Sandra hadn't witnessed what had happened, but Jillian wanted for things to be normal. And normal, in this regard, meant she would have closed the door for a private conversation with the principal. So she did. The door had a large glass window in it, so she wasn't too afraid of being alone with the man.

After she'd taken a seat in one of the chairs across the desk from the principal, he regarded her with an expression that seemed to be a mix of compassion and sadness. Giving a sigh, he settled back in his chair.

"I've already had a conversation with the police chief this morning, and I gave him all the information I had on Martin." Sitting forward, he met her gaze directly. "Can you share with me what's been happening?"

Like with Kieran, she just started at the beginning, although she did gloss over the part about her and Carter's arrangement.

"It definitely did escalate," the principal observed. "I understand it can be difficult to let someone know when things like this are happening. But was there something in particular that prevented you from approaching me sooner to let me know what was going on?"

"It wasn't anything about you. I was just...worried about being the new teacher and already causing waves. Martin had been here longer, and I was so new."

Principal Hughes nodded. "I understand, but I want you to know that I would have listened to anyone who had come to me with this. Male. Female. New teacher or old. I want a happy and safe work environment for each of my teachers and, of course, for the students."

"Had there been anything mentioned about Martin's behaviour, before?" Jillian asked, half-afraid of his answer.

The principal sighed. "Nothing to this extent. Last year, he had a similar situation with another teacher. He asked her out, and she said no. He continued to ask her out, so she came to me, and I spoke to him about it. Things calmed down after that, and there wasn't anything more brought to my attention. I had no idea that he made a habit of harassing women in this way."

"So maybe if I had come to you..." Jillian's shoulders slumped.

"No. Don't think that. You couldn't have known how things would escalate." The man paused. "Unfortunately, I don't think he learned from last year, and his decision to pick on you was quite calculated."

"And I played right into it, huh? Showing my reluctance to trust that you'd believe me since I was the new teacher."

"I think he didn't foresee Carter coming into the picture, and that probably helped take his crazy to a new level. But none of that is your fault," Principal Hughes stated. "You should be allowed to live your life without worry that someone is going to take offense to a choice you made and retaliate just because they don't like it."

Jillian nodded, but she knew that once a crazy or insane person had you in their sights, it didn't much matter what you did. Short of agreeing to everything they said—and even then, it didn't always matter—you didn't have much hope of escaping completely un-scathed. Still, she wished she'd gone to the principal sooner when it had become apparent that Martin didn't want to take no for an answer. Maybe then Carter would have been spared being dragged into her mess.

"I want to reassure you that your job here is quite secure, and Martin's employment has been terminated."

"Have you seen him since yesterday?" Jillian wasn't sure what to do. She wanted to go back home, but as long as Martin was un-accounted for, she didn't think she should.

"No. And he didn't answer my call earlier." The principal shook his head and sighed before looking at her again. "Like I said, your position here is secure, so if you'd like to take the rest of the day off, you're more than welcome to. We have a substitute in for you already."

She thought of the parting advice that Kieran had given her as they'd left his office the night before, suggesting that she should get a restraining order. Eli had offered her the name of a lawyer that morning who would be able to help her since she had no idea how to proceed. "Okay. I think I should do that as I need to see about getting a restraining order."

"Excellent idea. I'll let the police know if Martin turns up here."

"Thank you," she said.

"Please, in the future, feel free to come to me about anything. I want happy teachers here for the sake of the students, so if you have a concern, I want to hear about it."

"Okay. I'll keep that in mind." Jillian got to her feet, which also brought the principal to his.

As she left the school, she felt a sense of relief in knowing that at least her job was secure. She slid behind the wheel of her car, then closed and locked the door. Though she wasn't sure she wanted to be alone in her home, Jillian knew she needed to spend a little time there to make sure Dolly was okay.

After spending about an hour there, cuddling with Dolly, and making sure she had enough food and water for another day, she left. On the way back to the lodge, she did make a quick stop at the bakery—a place she'd avoided until recently because of Cece—and picked up a flavored coffee and some baked treats.

The lodge was quiet when Jillian returned, so she headed up to her room. She settled down at the desk with her coffee and baked goods, then she set about making some calls, and, as promised, she texted Carter to give him an update.

CHAPTER SEVENTEEN

"You got a woman not getting back to you?" one of the guys at the station asked, his question no doubt prompted by Carter's repeated checking of his phone.

"Something like that," Carter muttered.

"Seriously?" the guy asked, surprise evident in his voice. "I was just kind of joking with you, man. After all, a woman? When have you *ever* had anything to do with a woman? Or a man, for that matter."

Carter scowled at him. "It would be a woman, and you don't know everything about my life."

"Clearly." The man gestured to his phone. "So, tell us about her."

"No." He usually took the ribbing from the guys in stride, but that day didn't find him long on tolerance or patience.

The silence that followed his single-word response had Carter looking up. All the guys in the lounge part of the station were staring at him with various degrees of surprise. Carter understood why. He was usually steady and patient, more so than a lot of the guys in the station, but his worry for Jillian had him on edge.

A brief conversation with Eli earlier let him know that Jillian had seemed okay when he'd seen her before she'd left for school. So now he was just waiting to hear how things had gone with the principal. He really didn't think there was any question that the man would support Jillian, but he hoped that she was in a good enough mental place to deal with it regardless.

"It's personal," he said.

They'd teased him before about his lack of relationships, and while it had been annoying, he'd made the choice to keep things about Suzanne private, so he'd just accepted the ribbing. But with Jillian, it was probably just a matter of time before word got out that they were...something.

"Of course, it's personal," one of the guys said. "Most relationships are."

"Sorry," Carter said with a sigh. "There's just some stuff going on that I can't discuss."

"Say no more," the man said. "I'm just glad to discover you're human."

Carter looked over at him. "You thought I wasn't human?"

"Well, others thought maybe alien, but I was betting on a robot. After all, I think even aliens might have emotions."

Carter just shook his head and looked back down at his phone. It was almost ten o'clock, and for some reason, he had thought she'd be done with her meeting with Hughes by then.

He got up and went to the kitchen to grab another cup of coffee. He'd had three so far since arriving at the station at seven that morning. Sipping the strong bitter liquid, he stared out over the street in front of the station. He'd been praying non-stop that Jillian was doing okay that day, and that everything had gone smoothly with the principal. He was also praying that Martin was staying far, far away from her.

That was a big concern he had since when he'd talked to Kieran earlier, the man had told him that there had been no sign of Martin after the incident at the school the previous day. They'd checked out his residence, but there'd been no sign of him.

Carter really didn't think that Martin would take Jillian's rebuff lying down. He'd lost his job...or at least he'd better have...so there was really no need for him to stick around in New Hope Falls. However, as long as he was roaming free, Jillian wouldn't be able to relax, and the last thing she needed with her anxiety issues was to have that uncertainty hanging over her head. He hoped that she'd be willing to stay out at the lodge for the time being.

His phone buzzed in his hand, jerking him from his thoughts. Blowing out a breath, he looked down at the screen.

Jillian: *Everything went well with the principal. I'm taking the rest of the day off and going back to the lodge to figure out what I need to do to get a restraining order.*

Relief flooded Carter as he read her words, and he was glad to hear she was heading back to the lodge. At least she'd be safe there. He knew that the McNamaras would take good care of her.

Glad that your meeting went well. Let me know what you need to do for the restraining order. I'm on shift til tomorrow morning, but if you need anything, feel free to text me.

Jillian: *I will. Going to stick close to the lodge since no one seems to know where Martin is.*

Good plan. Just take someone with you if you decide to leave the lodge.

She sent him back a thumb's up, which he hoped meant she'd taken him seriously. He kind of thought that she would. He was still convinced that something traumatic had happened to her in the past, which hopefully meant that she'd take all precautions necessary until Martin was dealt with...whatever that meant.

Carter had assumed that once he'd received her text letting him know how the meeting had gone with the principal and that she was safe, he'd be able to shift his focus back to work. That didn't appear to be the case, however, because he still felt unsettled as he moved on with the daily routine of the station.

He'd thought that the only woman he'd ever feel such concern and worry over would be Suzanne. However, now he was finding himself with an overwhelming desire to keep Jillian safe—not just physically, but emotionally as well. He didn't know what to think about that, but he knew that he wasn't about to back away from her now. At least not until the situation with Martin had been resolved satisfactorily.

"You doing okay?" Stuart Price, the fire chief, gave him a concerned look as he went to fill his coffee mug. "You seem a bit unsettled."

Carter took a sip of his coffee, contemplating if he should confide in his boss or not. He knew that Stuart believed in making sure his staff was in a good place physically and mentally since distraction could cause life-threatening slip-ups when dealing with an emergency.

"Why don't we go into my office and have a chat?" the man suggested. "Grab a couple of cookies. My wife made them fresh yesterday."

Carter did as he suggested and grabbed two of the oatmeal chocolate chip cookies that he knew from previous experience were amazing, then followed Stuart into his office.

"Are you having some issues with the guys?" Stuart asked as he rounded his desk and settled into his chair. "Is that what's bothering you?"

Carter shook his head, then decided to just dive in. He told him about what had been going on with Jillian, including that they were dating, and how he was still worried since Martin was on the loose.

"First of all, I'm sorry to hear you and Jillian have been dealing with this. Second, I'm relieved—and happy—to hear you have someone special. I've always worried that you were lonely since you didn't seem to have anyone in your life, let alone a special woman."

Carter wanted to protest the significance of Jillian in his life. Still, in that moment, he realized that he couldn't do that without it being a lie. "She is special, and certainly doesn't deserve the stuff she's dealing with."

Stuart shook his head. "Just can't figure out what gets into the head of some of those guys. Why they think it's okay to harass a woman simply because she's not interested in them is beyond me."

Carter couldn't argue with the man about that. The same thought had been going through his mind ever since this situation had developed back before Eli and Anna's wedding. "I just want this to be dealt with, so she doesn't have to constantly look over her shoulder as she tries to go about her daily life."

"Her job's not in jeopardy, though, right?" Stuart clarified. "I'd hate to have to have a word with Trevor Hughes about it."

"He's assured her that her job is secure, so that's not a problem. The most important thing is finding Martin. I don't worry too much about her when she's at the lodge or at the school, but walking to and from her car—especially at school—or going anywhere alone is risky."

"She'll be safe at the lodge, so it's good she's there."

Carter nodded. "But it's not a good long-term solution."

"Well, if there's anything we can do, just say the word." Stuart paused, his brow furrowing. "Do you need to take some time off?"

"Not right now." Carter wasn't sure what he'd do with time off except hang around the lodge or drive Jillian to and from the school. And somehow, he didn't think she'd be on board with that idea. However, if she gave even a hint of wanting that, he would definitely do that for her.

"Let me know if that changes," Stuart said before moving on to station-related issues.

By the time Carter got off shift the next morning, there had still been no news on Martin. He was thankful that Jillian had been able to get her restraining order. Of course, they hadn't been able to serve Martin with the order since the man was apparently in the wind. But that didn't matter. If he came around Jillian, she could call the police on him, and that gave Carter a little peace of mind.

He had thought about heading out to the lodge once he was done his shift, but it was too early, plus he was tired. They hadn't had a lot of call-outs the previous night, but they'd had enough of them that it had been a bit of a chopped up night in terms of sleep.

Though he wasn't sure if Jillian was awake, he sent her a text anyway. *Are you heading to school today? If you want me to give you a ride, send me a text.*

He went to his kitchen and pulled out stuff for his breakfast. After filling a bowl with cereal and milk, he stood leaning against the counter as he ate it. Cereal wasn't his favorite breakfast, but he'd long ago given up the eggs, bacon, and pancake meals he'd once enjoyed.

Though he was tempted to have another cup of coffee, he did hope to get a few hours of sleep once he heard from Jillian. After he finished eating, he washed his dishes, then set them in the drainer to dry.

He had just finished cleaning up when his phone beeped. Drying his hands, he picked up his phone to see a message from Jillian.

Jillian: *Yes. I need to get back to my class. I don't think I need you to come out here to give me a ride though.*

Carter frowned. He'd suspected that she'd turn him down, but that didn't mean he wasn't still worried about Martin waylaying her along the way.

After a moment, he tapped out a reply. *How about I meet you at the school?*

He held his breath as he waited for her reply. Again, he was pretty certain she'd turn him down. That was why her *okay* in response took him a bit by surprise.

What time do you arrive at the school?

Jillian: *I usually try to be there by 8:15.*

Carter glanced at his watch. 7:50.

Okay. I'll be there.

Jillian: *Thank you.*

Running a hand through his hair, Carter grabbed his jacket and pulled it back on. It had been a cool misty morning when he'd walked out of the station, so he knew he'd need it.

Though he'd hated to do it, he'd spent some time through the night trying to get into the mind of a crazy man, asking himself what he would have done in his shoes. The one thing he'd come up with was how someone like that would want to take their victim by surprise. To lie in wait for them.

Would he do it this soon after the latest confrontation? Or would he take his time, plot it out, all the while allowing his target to stew in worry and fear?

That was the big question.

Carter hoped that Martin wasn't smart enough to try for the second option. That would most likely lead to a worse result for Jillian.

He had no idea if Martin knew what he drove, but he was kind of hoping that the man was still subscribing to the theory that he and Jillian weren't a real couple. If so, Martin might not think to be on the lookout for Carter's truck.

When Carter reached the school, he glanced at the vehicles close to it as he drove down the street. Since he had extra time, he circled the parking lot then went to make one more loop of the streets around the school. It was on that trip that he spotted a car driving slowly past the parking lot. He missed his chance to check out the driver, so he pulled over to the curb right away and used his phone to take a picture of the license plate in his driver's side mirror.

He called Kieran as he went to the picture on his phone app, then flipped it around since it was a mirror image. "Does Martin drive a white Cavalier?"

"Yes. Why?"

"There's one by the school." He gave him the license plate number. "Jillian's on her way, and I said I'd meet her here to walk her in."

"Call and tell her to wait in her car, okay?" Kieran said. "We want him to approach her so that we can grab him. If he's in his car, he can take off. If he's on foot, we have a better chance of catching him without endangering others."

Kieran hung up before Carter could respond, so he went ahead and called Jillian.

"Carter?"

"You need to pull into your usual spot in the parking lot, but then stay in your car with the doors locked."

"What's going on?" Jillian asked, fear evident in her voice.

"Martin's been spotted in the area. The cops are on their way, and they want you to stay in your car, so he gets out of his in order to avoid a car chase through New Hope." Carter wasn't thrilled about her being bait, but at the same time, putting an end to this would be beneficial all around. Especially for Jillian. "I'll be parked not too far away, so I'll be right there as soon as everything is over."

"I don't know," Jillian whispered.

"You can do this, Jillian," Carter told her. "You're strong and brave. You can absolutely do this. The cops are going to be there, and I'll be nearby too."

He heard her take in a deep breath and let it out, and he questioned his decision to phone her with this news while she was driving. But he'd really had no choice. This was a case of striking while the iron was hot.

"Okay." Her response was tremulous, but there was a thin thread of strength in there too.

"Just park your car, then pretend you're on a call," he said. "Well, you won't have to pretend because I'm going to stay on the phone with you."

"I'm almost there."

"You can do this." Carter watched as her car approached and turned into the lot. "Just think, when they catch Martin, this will all be over. You can go back to what you love without this hanging over your head. Won't that be nice?"

"It will be." She sighed. "It really will be."

His heart began to pound when he noticed Martin's white car appear on the road. Without hesitation, it swung into the parking lot.

"We'll go out for dinner to celebrate," Carter said. "Where would you like to go?"

"For dinner?"

"Yeah. For dinner." Carter kept an eye on the parking lot, wondering where Kieran and his men were.

"I don't know." He heard a swift intake of breath and knew that she'd spotted Martin. "He's here, Carter."

"Just sit tight and breathe for me, okay?" Carter began to count, hoping to keep her calm, all the while praying for Kieran and his officers to show up.

Another car approached and pulled into the parking lot, but Carter couldn't see if it was a cop or a teacher. Dread filled him at the sudden thought that Martin might be armed. Why hadn't he thought of that? He could only hope that Kieran had.

He watched as the newest car parked, and someone got out. It appeared to be a teacher since they made their way right to the doors leading inside.

"Where are the police, Carter?" Before he could answer, he heard her breathe, "Oh no. Oh, no."

"What's wrong?" Carter reached for the handle of the door. "Jillian?"

"He's got a gun. Carter, he's got a *gun!*"

CHAPTER EIGHTEEN

The note of hysteria in Jillian's voice had Carter pushing open his door and exiting his truck. "Duck down, sweetheart."

He was running across the street with his phone pressed to his ear when he heard the whoop of a police siren. Glancing over, he saw a cop car pull into the parking lot and come to a stop. Carter slowed, not wanting to get in the way of the police, but also not wanting to be too far away from Jillian.

"Put your hands up, Martin."

The words had Carter coming to a complete stop. He didn't want to. He wanted to get to Jillian, but his training held him back. The last thing the cops needed was yet another body on the scene that didn't need to be there.

"Martin! Lay your weapon on the ground and step back with your hands in the air." The latest command told Carter they'd just realized he was armed, and that realization no doubt meant the school had been ordered into lockdown mode. "Martin, lay your weapon down."

Carter's heart began to slam against his ribs, and he could hear Jillian breathing rapidly in his ear. He counted breaths for her, even as he tried to listen to what was going on with the cops and Martin. If Martin resisted the police directives, it made him even more unpredictable.

Please, God, keep Jillian safe. Don't let her get hurt. Frozen in place, he just kept repeating the prayer even as he tried to help Jillian stay calm.

Suddenly, a shot rang out, quickly followed by two more. Shocked silence reigned for several seconds, then there were more shouts. This time, they were not commands directed at Martin. Instead, he heard Kieran shouting out orders, telling his officers to clear the way for the ambulance.

Fear for Jillian galvanized Carter into action. He ran for the parking lot, jumping over the low metal railing surrounding it. Reaching her car, he paused just long enough to look for blood before jerking on the door handle. It snapped back, reminding him that he'd told Jillian to lock the door.

Pressing his hands to the window, he bent over. "Jillian. Open the door. It's me. Carter."

When she didn't move, he wondered if somehow she'd been injured despite there being no sign of blood or a broken window. She was bent over the center console, arms tucked under her. Since the car wasn't running, he didn't know if her phone was still hooked up to the vehicle's Bluetooth. He could still hear her, but he wasn't sure she could hear him through the phone.

"Jillian." He raised his voice, hoping she could hear it within the confines of the car. "I want you to breathe with me. One. Two. Three. Inhale. You can do it."

He had no idea who was hurt, but he really hoped it wasn't any of the cops. At least he knew for sure it wasn't Kieran. Keeping his attention on Jillian, he focused on getting her to come back to the present. She was his priority.

"Can you unlock the door?" he asked after he'd counted with her for a couple of minutes. "Unlock the door, please, Jillian."

For a moment, he thought she wasn't going to do as he'd requested, but then he heard the thunk of the locks releasing. Moving quickly, he pulled on the handle again, relief filling him as the door opened.

Bending over so he could move a little way into the car, he rested his hand on her shoulder, taking in the way she'd tucked her arms in close to her chest, her head bent down against the console. "Jilly. Sweetheart. It's all over. You're safe."

He could feel tremors running through her body. Though he wanted to pull her out of the car, he left his hand on her shoulder and continued to count breaths for her. When he felt her breathing come more in line with his counts, Carter hoped that they were getting closer to the end of this ordeal.

"Does she require medical assistance?" a male voice asked from behind him.

"I think she's okay," Carter said, not sure how Jillian would react to a stranger at that moment. He figured that she would feel more comfortable with him than with someone she didn't know. "Just having a bit of a panic attack."

"Maybe you should let me check her out."

"Back off," Carter said, moving back enough so that he could look at the person behind him. "I know her."

"Oh. Sorry, Deputy Chief." The man lifted his hands and backed away. "I'll just...uh...leave you to it."

Carter would talk to the guy later and make things right, but at that moment, Jillian needed him more. Jillian mattered more. He turned his attention back to her, murmuring reassurances in between counts for her breathing.

He could hear the bedlam going on around him, and he suspected it wasn't all from the incident with Martin. It happened to be prime time for student drop-offs, and even if the school was in lockdown, the word wouldn't have spread to parents already en route to the school with their children in tow.

Hopefully, they'd positioned cops on the streets around the school to divert cars. He had no idea what the principal might do about the school day. And he wasn't sure that Jillian would be in any shape to teach her class.

Sudden movement beneath his hand had him shifting back a bit, giving Jillian space as she slowly sat up. She brushed back her hair with a hand that was still visibly shaking as she stared out the front window.

"Jillian?" Carter wasn't sure she needed to see what was going on around them. He reached out and took her hand. "Hey."

She squeezed his fingers a couple of times before she finally looked at him. He could see that she was still taking measured breaths.

"Keep breathing slowly and deeply," he encouraged. "You're doing so well."

He stayed crouched beside her, remembering the night he'd done the same thing outside Eli's house. It seemed ages ago, though it really hadn't been that long.

"Thank you," she whispered after a few minutes.

"You don't have to thank me," Carter told her. "I'm just glad I could be here for you."

"Did they catch him?"

He wasn't entirely sure what had happened, but he said, "Yes. It's all over now."

Her shoulders slumped, and she blew out a breath. "I should get inside for my class."

"I'm not sure what the principal is doing about classes at the moment."

She looked toward the school. "I should check with him."

"I'll go with you, but Kieran might need to talk to you."

With a nod, she reached for her messenger bag from the passenger seat. "I just want this done. It wasn't supposed to be like this when I came back to New Hope."

Carter didn't know what to say, so he just moved back and let her climb from the car. He took the messenger bag from her, then offered his hand. When she grasped his fingers, he could still feel the trembling, so he held it firm, hoping to steady her more.

As they moved toward the school, Kieran jogged over to them. "Doing okay, Jillian?"

"Yeah. Better. Had a panic attack." She looked embarrassed by the confession.

"I think I'd have been more surprised if you hadn't. This was an unusual situation, for sure."

"You arrested him?"

Kieran glanced at Carter than back at Jillian. "Yes. However, he, along with one of my officers, was shot, so they're both on their way to the hospital."

"Oh, no. I'm sorry to hear about your officer." She paused, then said, "He won't be able to leave the hospital, will he?"

"Martin? No. He'll be under guard."

"Okay. Good."

Kieran asked her to come by the station at some point to give a statement then left them. They headed into the school, nodding at the cop stationed by the door, and made their way to the office.

"Oh, Jillian," Sandra said when she spotted them. "Are you okay?"

"I'm alright."

"What's happening with the school?" Carter asked. "Classes as usual?"

"Yes. We were in lockdown mode, but that was lifted a few minutes ago, and we were told parents were safe to approach the building at the main entrance, not the parking lot one." She looked at Jillian. "I had one of the other teachers take in any of your students who had already arrived. I was just getting ready to call in a sub for you."

"No. I'll be okay to teach."

The other woman gave her a skeptical look. "Are you sure? It sounded a bit traumatic out there."

Jillian shrugged. "I need to be with my class."

Sandra hesitated before nodding. "But if you change your mind, call me, okay?"

"Give me a few minutes, then I'll be ready for the kids."

"I'll let Lis know to keep your kids for a few more minutes."

They left the office and headed for the classroom. When they reached it, Carter went in with her and placed her messenger bag on her chair.

"You can do this," Carter said with a smile. "You're so strong for coming in here to teach after what you've just been through."

"I don't feel strong." Jillian frowned for a moment. "I just need to be with the kids. They're my world right now."

"Can I do anything else for you?"

She shook her head. "You've already done so much. More than you'll ever know."

"How about we head out for dinner once you're done later to-day?"

"I have to go home and check on Dolly first."

Carter was a bit surprised that she agreed to his suggestion, but he didn't comment on it. "Sounds like a plan. Give me a call when you're ready, and we can decide where to go. Think about what you'd like to eat."

"Okay. I will."

"See you later then," Carter told her then left her classroom.

He headed back out to the parking lot, wanting to get a few more details on the take-down now that he knew Jillian was going to be okay.

~ * ~

Jillian watched the last of her students leave the room then let out a long breath as she sank back in her chair. She'd made it.

Once she'd made up her mind to go ahead with the school day, she knew she needed to do it. She wasn't going to let yet another madman rob her of something she loved.

Being with the children had slowly driven out the shakiness, and doing the things that she loved with them had helped to center her once again. She hadn't focused too much on lessons since it was apparent from what some of the kids were saying, they were aware that something bad had happened before school had started.

So they'd mainly sang songs, read stories, drew pictures, and generally just had a bit of a day of fun—even though she had tried to make sure that each of the things they did in some way tied in with things they'd been working on since the beginning of the school year. It was just what she'd needed, and from the smiles on the kids' faces as they left at the end of the day, it had been what they'd needed too.

For the first time in weeks, she didn't dread being alone in her classroom. When lunchtime had come, there'd been no spike in her anxiety. No sick feeling of panic in her stomach. Just a sense of peace that came from knowing that Martin was in custody. There was no longer any chance of him coming to her classroom and harassing her.

She honestly had a hard time believing that the situation was truly over, and there was a part of her waiting for the other shoe to drop.

As she gathered up her things, Jillian had to wonder if this was going to be the last time she had to deal with a man set on taking advantage of her. Or did she need to brace herself for it happening again in the future? Would she need to look at every man who came into her life, wondering if he would be the one to hurt her again?

Carter came to mind as she left the school building a short time later. He'd been so good to her, but did that mean he'd stay that way? She knew nothing about him except that he was a firefighter and a good friend of Eli's. Of course, she also knew about his family, the pets he'd had growing up, and his middle name.

Moving across the parking lot that was now empty of emergency vehicles and policemen, she felt her anxiety start to rise a bit from its usual low hum. She hurried to her car, pushing the button on her fob to unlock the door before she got there. It allowed her to open her door right away.

Though she got a bit jammed with her messenger bag sand-
wiched between her and the steering wheel, Jillian was able to get
the car door closed and locked. She sat there, trying to breathe and
keep the panic at bay, unable to keep from flashing back to the
moment when she'd seen Martin coming toward her, gun in hand.

Her breaths started coming more rapidly as she clutched her
messenger bag close. A vice tightened painfully around her chest,
making it impossible to draw a deep breath.

She didn't want to have a panic attack—not when everything was
finally over—but her mind and her body had other ideas, wrestling
control over her will. Utilizing all the tools she'd been given during
her therapy, Jillian fought the panic, praying for relief from it.
Carter's insistence that she was strong played distantly in her mind.

It seemed to take forever before she felt the panic begin to ebb.
Her heart was still pounding, but she was able to tap out her counts
and focus on her surroundings.

When the anxiety and panic finally dropped to a manageable
level, Jillian slumped over her messenger bag. Instead of letting her
thoughts go to the attack and what had caused it, Jillian began to
make a mental list of things she needed to do.

Drive home.

Spend time with Dolly.

Think of where to go for dinner.

Let Carter know.

Get changed and freshen up.

Go to dinner.

It was a fairly pathetic list, as far as to-do lists went, but it was
enough to help her focus on the present and the future rather than
the past.

With her shakiness down to slight internal tremors, Jillian
moved her messenger bag over to the passenger seat then loosened
her grip on her keys enough to find the ignition key. She was

surprised that she actually managed to get the key engaged on the first attempt.

She slowly made her way out of the parking lot and headed for home, glad that she'd put the bag she'd taken to the lodge in her car that morning. There had been a big chance she'd end up back at the lodge that night, but she'd been hopeful that Kieran would be able to find Martin, so she'd brought her bag with her in anticipation of being able to return home.

Her phone rang as she drove, so she tapped the screen to answer it through her car's Bluetooth.

"Jillian!" Sarah's voice held a worried edge. "Are you okay?"

"I'm fine," she said, even though that wasn't entirely true. Considering how things could have ended that day, however, she was going to go with *fine*. "Martin won't be bothering me anymore."

"But he had a *gun*?"

"Yeah." Jillian's hands tightened around the steering wheel. "The cops were here, though, and they got him."

"Why didn't you call me?"

"I went to work once it was over. I needed something normal, you know?"

Sarah sighed. "I understand." She hesitated then said, "Are you sure you're okay? Do you want to come back here again tonight?"

"No. I'm going to dinner with Carter, and then I'm looking forward to sleeping in my own bed tonight. No offense to your beds. They are very comfortable."

With a laugh, Sarah said, "No offense taken. I much prefer my own bed to any other."

"Thank you for putting up with me for two nights, and thank your mom for not charging me. I didn't expect that."

Sarah scoffed. "Of course you should have expected that. You're like family, not a guest."

Sarah's words warmed her heart. "Well, regardless. I'm so thankful for everything you all did for me."

"Just know that we'll always be there for you, so don't ever hesitate to come to me or any of the rest of the family if you need something." She paused. "And have a nice dinner with Carter."

"It's not like that, Sarah. I told you what our deal is."

"He's been good to you," Sarah said.

"Yes. He absolutely has been, and I'm very grateful for that. I'm not sure I could have made it through this without him." Jillian knew that she wasn't exaggerating. "But that doesn't change things."

"Okay. Okay. Can't blame me for trying."

Jillian couldn't, but she also knew that what had transpired hadn't changed anything for them. Carter had his reasons for not wanting a serious relationship, and as far as she knew, that hadn't changed. And, of course, things hadn't changed for her either.

They said goodbye as she approached her garage, pulling right in once the garage door was up. Though the danger Martin had presented to her was gone, she still wasn't prepared to be completely lax in how she approached her safety.

CHAPTER NINETEEN

Dolly came running to greet her as soon as Jillian stepped into the mudroom. After taking off her jacket and shoes, she scooped the cat up and went into the living room. She cuddled Dolly close, taking comfort in her loud purring.

"Did you miss me, Dolly-girl?"

She often found herself interacting with the cat the way her grandma had. She had adopted Dolly as a young kitten from a no-kill shelter when Jillian had been a teen, and she'd brought Dolly with her when she'd moved to Portland to be with Jillian during her recovery and the trial that followed. Dolly had become a source of comfort during that time for both of them. And even more so for her grandma as she'd dealt with her cancer treatment.

And again, Dolly offered Jillian comfort and a reminder of her grandma's unfailing love and support through the most difficult times in her life. Though she tried not to think of all she'd lost with her grandma's passing, she felt it keenly right then.

"Where should we go for dinner, do you think?" Jillian asked Dolly. "Mexican? No? Yeah, I'm not feeling that tonight. Chinese? Hmmm. No. I think I'm in the mood for pasta. Yep. Italian, for sure."

Having made up her mind, she fished her phone out of her pocket and texted Carter.

I was thinking about pasta. Would that work for you?

His response came back in a flash.

Carter: *Sounds good. I'm glad you don't want to go to Norma's. I'm sure you'd rather not deal with the curious masses of New Hope.*

You're quite right.

Carter: *How soon would you like to go?*

Maybe around five?

Carter: *Sounds good. I'll come by around then.*

Jillian toyed with the idea of telling him she'd just meet him at the restaurant, but it was time to move past her fear of being alone with Carter in a vehicle. She'd already gone with him once, but it had been in her car, and for some reason, that had been okay. Alone with him in his vehicle? That thought gave her a little bit of pause.

But if she couldn't trust those closest to her, then what kind of life would she end up with? Carter had proven he could be trusted with her mental health issues, so maybe it was time to trust him with a bit more.

She sat cuddling Dolly a little longer, then got up and headed to her bedroom to change out of her work clothes. At the last minute, she decided to take a quick shower to wash away the turmoil of the day beneath the hot spray and her favorite shower gel of peony, apple, and vanilla sandalwood.

Once she was done, she dressed in a pair of black fitted jeans and an oversize light-weight denim blouse that extended well past her hips. She had a cropped black denim jacket that she planned to wear over top of it since the evening air was holding more and more of a chill as they moved deeper into fall.

By the time she spotted Carter's truck pulling up outside, she had her jacket and boots on, so all she had to do was grab her purse and phone. She was just stepping out of the front door when Carter came up the walk to the house.

"I guess you're ready to go," he said with a smile.

"I am."

Together they walked to his truck, where he opened the passenger door for her. As she buckled her seatbelt, Jillian was a bit surprised that he didn't have a nicer truck. It was clean and smelled nice, though, so it seemed he took care of the vehicle, regardless of its age—probably better care than she took of hers, in fact.

"How were the kids today?" Carter asked as he guided the truck to Main Street.

"Well, don't tell the principal, but we had a bit of a fun day today. Music. Games. Reading stories. It was a day we all needed, I think."

Carter gave her a smile. "Well, you would have been my favorite teacher if I'd had a day like that when I was in third grade."

"Unfortunately, I can't give them fun days every day."

"More's the pity. But somehow, I think you still make learning fun for them."

"I try my best."

Jillian noticed that he wasn't specifically addressing the day's events, and she was beyond grateful for that. Instead, they talked a bit more about what she'd done with her class. He also volunteered some information about his own day, which had included a visit to the gym—surprise, surprise—after he'd gotten some sleep.

When they arrived at the Italian restaurant that Carter had chosen for their dinner, they were able to get seated right away. Jillian was glad for that as she was actually feeling quite hungry. The hostess showed them to a table in a corner. It had a red gingham tablecloth and a fat white candle sitting on a small square mirror in the middle of it.

She slipped off her jacket and laid it on one of the chairs, and Carter did the same on his side of the table. They were just settling into their seats when their waiter appeared carrying a pitcher of water.

After greeting them cheerfully, he offered to answer any questions they might have about the menu. When they had none, he left them to decide on their meals, promising to return in a few minutes to take their orders.

Jillian perused the menu, going back and forth on what she was in the mood for beyond just *pasta*. Her younger self was whispering in the back of her mind that she should just order a salad, but it had been a few years since she'd listened to that voice.

And after the day she'd had, getting what she really wanted would be a celebration that she and Carter had both survived. It hadn't escaped her notice that by being there for her that morning, Carter had been in danger from Martin as well. So yes, she was going to celebrate that they had both survived, and she would be praying that the officer injured that day would make a full recovery.

"Do you know what you're going to have?" Carter asked.

"It all looks so good," she admitted. "But I'm leaning toward Chicken Parmigiana. How about you?"

"I'm going for some lasagna. That seems like a nice meal to have on this chilly fall evening."

"This is one of my favorite times of the year," Jillian said. "My house has a wood-burning fireplace, and my grandma taught me how to light it. Sitting in front of a blazing fire when it's chilly out is something I enjoy very much."

"Does Dolly enjoy it too?" Carter asked with a smile.

Jillian felt a smile tug at her lips in response. "Dolly enjoys being wherever I am, so yes, if I'm sitting on the couch with a fire going, she'll be right there with me."

"Kinda makes me miss the pets I had growing up."

"Why don't you get a dog or a cat?" Jillian asked.

"I'm not sure they'd let me have pets in my place. Aside from a goldfish, I would imagine."

"I've never had a fish. I think Dolly might find that a little too interesting. I'd come home from school to find an empty fishbowl."

The waiter returned with their drinks and some breadsticks, then took their orders.

"Have you been here before?" Jillian asked.

"No, I don't eat out much. But I asked Kieran and Eli for a suggestion for Italian food, and they both agreed this was the place."

"It looks nice. I like the ambiance."

"It's very Italian looking. I hope the food is as good."

Jillian felt herself relaxing as they talked, and she almost laughed when she thought about how the members of their friend group called Carter *Mr. Strong and Silent.* While she was sure the *strong* applied, she wasn't so sure about the *silent* anymore. She would have expected a lot more awkward pauses or stilted conversation if Carter hadn't been comfortable talking.

When their food arrived a short time later, Carter said a brief prayer, then they dug in. Too late, she remembered that ordering noodles on a date wasn't a wise move. Of course, this wasn't really a date, but messy eating wasn't something she enjoyed when she was with anyone but her closest of friends.

"Is your food as good as you'd hoped it would be?"

Jillian looked up from trying to wind some noodles on her fork and nodded. "It's delicious. How about yours?"

"Eli and Kieran were right." Carter eyed the breadsticks before reaching out and taking one. "Not that I doubted them, really."

As they talked about a bunch of stuff—nothing too heavy—Jillian was so grateful that Carter hadn't taken advantage of their time together to rehash everything that had happened that day. Her anxiety was at its usual low-level hum. Still, if they'd started discussing the day's events, it surely would have spiked again. She really didn't want to have another panic attack that day—two was enough—and she really, really didn't want Carter to have to deal with yet another one either.

When they had finished their meal, Carter insisted on paying even though Jillian offered. The evening was even chillier when they left the restaurant, and Jillian pulled the collar of her jacket up.

The drive back to New Hope was quiet, with only music drifting softly from the radio. With the end of the day in sight, Jillian felt her exhaustion from the day begin to weigh down on her. The warmth of the truck was making her drowsy, and if the drive had taken any longer, she probably would have fallen asleep.

When Carter pulled to a stop in front of her house, Jillian was a little sad that the evening was coming to an end, even though she really did want to just crawl into her bed. Light from a streetlamp in front of them cast a bit of light into the truck, so she could see Carter when she turned toward him.

"Thank you so much for everything today," Jillian said. "You've really gone above and beyond. This was all probably way more than you'd thought you'd have to deal with when you suggested this...uh...thing between us." She looked away from him, staring out the windshield. "I'll completely understand if you'd like to put an end to our arrangement."

"Jillian," Carter said softly, but then he didn't continue. When it seemed like he wasn't going to, she looked over at him, their gazes meeting in the dimly lit cab of the truck. "I'm glad that I was able to help. And no, I don't want to put an end to our arrangement. Unless you want to, then, of course, we can."

She thought about it for just a moment then shook her head. "No. I don't want that either."

"Then we continue on as we have been." Carter turned off the truck. "Let me walk you to your door."

Jillian wasn't going to argue with that, but when they got to the door, she braced herself for an awkward goodbye.

"I'm covering a shift starting tomorrow morning for the next twenty-four, but feel free to text me if you need something or if you want to tell me how your day went with the kids."

"Okay. I hope you have a safe shift."

Carter flashed her a smile. "From your lips to God's ears. I'll let you know how it goes. And I'll be praying you have a restful night and a good day tomorrow."

He waited while she unlocked the door and disarmed the alarm before he said goodnight and jogged back to his truck. As Jillian closed the door and armed the alarm once again, she heard the rumble of his truck's engine as he pulled away from the curb.

As she headed to her room a short time later, Jillian knew that the night ahead was going to be another rough one. She put a water bottle and some chocolates on her nightstand, then got ready for bed. After she'd finished her usual nighttime bathroom routine and changed into her pajamas, she went to the bed and slid under her comforter.

She lifted her Bible and Bible study book from her nightstand. Once Anna had returned from her honeymoon, she'd reached out to Jillian, inviting her to become part of a ladies' Bible study group at the church. Anna had given each of the ladies the book she wanted to use for the study on the previous Sunday, with instructions to work through the first chapter before they met for the initial bi-weekly study the next week.

The study appeared to be focused on different women in the Bible, and the assigned chapter was on Esther. As she read the passage of scripture which was related to the first few questions, she felt a calmness settle over her.

Normally, after such a traumatic day, she would have been a mess, fighting panic and anxiety. She thought of the assurances of Sarah and Nadine that they'd be praying for her. She thought of Carter saying he'd be praying she would have a restful night.

For once, she knew that their assurances were more than just lip service. The sense of peace she felt when she usually wouldn't have felt anything close to that, told her that they were indeed praying for her.

After she finished with the study, she turned off the light then slid down into her bed, feeling the comforting press of Dolly against her side. She spent some time in prayer, thanking God for protecting everyone that day and asking for healing for the officer who had been injured.

Rather than focusing on herself, she thanked God for Nadine, Sarah, and her other friends, but most especially, Carter. It may have been a weird set of circumstances that brought the two of them together, but she was so grateful for his presence in her life.

So while she was quite sure that there would be at least one nightmare waiting for her in her sleep, she didn't fear it as much, knowing that when she woke, she wasn't alone. God would be right there with her.

A verse she'd often clung to came to her mind as she began to drift toward sleep. *Fear not, for I am with you; Be not dismayed, for I am your God. I will strengthen you, Yes, I will help you, I will uphold you with My righteous right hand.*

CHAPTER TWENTY

"It's been quite a week, Suzy-Q," Carter said, giving Suzanne's hand a light squeeze. "Truly unbelievable."

He'd shown up a little while ago for his weekly visit. Evelyn and Garth weren't there, but he wouldn't be surprised if one or both of them showed up before his visit was over.

As he gazed at Suzanne, he struggled to see the woman he'd fallen in love with. And it wasn't just that she'd undergone significant physical changes. She had been a vivacious, outgoing woman, who had moved through life with so much...well...life. That quality was one of the first things about her he'd fallen in love with.

To see her quiet and unmoving was to see her without the very essence of what had made her Suzanne. Evelyn and Garth had both been telling him for several years that even if she woke up, she wouldn't be the same Suzanne. After all, he wasn't the same person he'd been when the accident had happened either. Though he'd not suffered physically from the accident beyond some bumps and bruises, he certainly bore mental and emotional scars.

Was it possible to move on?

The question had barely flicked through his mind when he rejected it. Perhaps if she'd lapsed into a coma for a reason other than one that he felt responsible for, he might feel differently. But why should he get to move on with his life and pursue his dreams when she couldn't?

Truth be told, however, he'd enjoyed the times he'd spent with Jillian. He'd forgotten what it was like to be with someone, just the two of them, sharing food, talking about their day, and supporting each other physically and emotionally. Being there for Jillian had brought something to life in him that he hadn't even realized had died.

Given his job, he was often there for people during stressful and traumatic times in their lives. Jillian's weren't the first panic attacks he'd dealt with, and likely wouldn't be the last. Still, being able to be there for her during such an awful time had fed something within him.

"Carter, sweetheart." Evelyn's voice had him looking up, then getting to his feet to give her a hug. "How are you doing?"

He pulled one of the other seats in the room closer to the bed, then waited until she'd settled into it before sitting back down in his. "I'm doing okay." Pausing for a moment, he debated telling her what had happened. "But I've had quite a week."

Evelyn arched a brow. "Do tell."

So, he did. Still leaving out the part about how he and Jillian had first gotten together, he told her about the situation with Martin and the events of the week.

"Wow. You've had some excitement in your small town," Evelyn said. "And how is Jillian doing?"

"She was already prone to panic attacks, so everything that happened kind of exacerbated things. I think she's had at least one more this week, though I wasn't with her when it happened. She's powered through in the very best way that she can."

"I'm so sorry to hear about what she's gone through," Evelyn said. "But she couldn't have anyone better by her side for the rough bits. If I know you—and I think I do by now—you are the perfect person to help her through all of this. I'm so pleased that you have someone special in your life now."

Carter wanted to argue that he already had that, but he knew that wasn't what she wanted to hear. She wanted to believe that there was a future for him and Jillian. Hearing that they weren't viewing it that way wouldn't make Evelyn happy at all. So, he kept his mouth shut and turned his gaze back to Suzanne.

"She would be happy for you, Carter," Evelyn said gently. "Have you told Jillian about her?"

Carter shook his head. "Not yet."

Evelyn laid her hand on his arm. "You need to tell her. It's so much about who you are. Telling her will help her understand you even more."

Yeah, except it might cause her to look at him differently, and Carter wasn't sure he wanted that. It was one of the reasons he hadn't shared about that part of his life with anyone in New Hope Falls.

"And I'd really love to meet her," Evelyn said. "Garth would too."

Carter wasn't sure when—or if—that would ever happen, but he nodded. He just hoped they didn't try to force an introduction by suggesting he cut down further on his visits with Suzanne.

Thankfully, their conversation moved on to other things, and by the time he left shortly after lunch, he found he was eager to get back to New Hope. He wasn't going to see Jillian that night. He was meeting up with Kieran, Eli, and Michael for dinner while Jillian was having a fondue night with Sarah, Anna, and Cara at Cara's place.

He was looking forward to spending time with the men he considered among his closest friends. It would be a good way to end a crazy week.

~ * ~

Jillian approached the door to Cara's studio, her fruit contribution for the evening in the bag she carried. The door swung open to reveal Sarah standing there with a broad smile on her face.

"Hey!" She grabbed Jillian into a quick, tight hug before letting her go. "Let's head up. Cara's finishing up dinner prep. We're having some sort of fancy chicken dish. Not sure what it's called, but Anna seemed to know what it was. All I know is that it smells divine."

Jillian had to agree when she stepped into Cara's apartment a couple minutes later. She handed over her strawberries and bananas, then hugged the other two women.

"You doing okay, sweetie?" Cara asked as she stepped back from the hug, keeping a hold on Jillian's arms. "Kieran told me how crazy things were for you a couple days ago."

"I'm doing surprisingly well," Jillian assured her. "And I know that is due to so many people praying for me."

Cara gave her another hug. "It's our privilege to be able to pray for each other, so I do that happily for you."

Jillian blinked back tears as she whispered, "Thank you."

"Any time." Cara gave her a smile. "Now, let's get this meal on the table."

As they ate, Jillian felt the stress of the week slip away. The other three asked her if she wanted to talk about what had happened, but when she'd said no, they let it go, moving on to other lighter topics.

Sarah was upbeat, and every smile was beaming. She had them laughing as she talked about the latest adjustments to small-town life that Beau and his siblings had experienced.

Everything felt so normal, not like she'd just had another experience when her life had been in jeopardy. It was just what she needed, and she was so thankful for it.

"Let's go to the coffee table in the living room," Cara said when they'd finished cleaning up from their dinner.

They carried the two chocolate fondue pots and all the food, working to set it up so they could easily reach the pots. Jillian sank down onto the floor, and the others did as well, Cara doing so in the most graceful way of them all.

They'd been chatting and eating their chocolate-dunked fruit and pound cake when Cara said, "I want to talk to you guys about something."

When all their gazes moved in her direction, she smiled. "Nothing too serious. But first, Anna, I wanted you here because even though we all agreed that it was best not to have us participating in your wedding or you participating in ours, I wanted you to know that if it was possible, I absolutely would have both you and Eli stand up with us."

Anna gave Cara a sad smile. "I wish it could be different. But as long as that detective considers Eli a suspect in Sheila's disappearance, we can't be that closely connected. However, if I can do anything else to be a part of your wedding, you only have to ask."

"Actually, I do want to ask you if you'd be willing to help me with the organizational side of things. Your wedding was so beautiful that I know you'd be a big help. Of course, we're doing ours on a much smaller scale, and we've decided on the first Saturday in January as our wedding date."

"That's not too far away," Anna commented.

"I know. We wanted to wait until after you two had your wedding before we announced our date. We also didn't want to have a long engagement."

"I think we can plan a really nice wedding even though we only have just over three months. Just tell me what you want me to do."

"Thank you," Cara said, a relieved look on her face as she turned to face Jillian. "I know we haven't known each other that long, Jillian, but you've become a good friend, and it would be such a blessing to have you stand up with me as one of my bridesmaids."

"Really?" Cara nodded, and Jillian's throat tightened with emotion. "If you're sure, I would be honored."

"I'm very sure." Cara reached out and squeezed her hand. "You're important to me."

Tears pricked the back of her eyes for the second time that night. When she'd come back to New Hope Falls, she hadn't thought she'd end up with people like Cara, Sarah, and Anna as such good friends. These women had become the support she needed in the town that was supposed to have been a safe haven for her.

"You're important to me, too," Jillian told her. "I'm so thankful for your friendship."

"When I moved here almost five years ago, I hadn't planned to connect too closely with anyone. I'd lost a lot in my life and didn't want to lose even more. But then I met Kieran, and everything changed. Suddenly I found I wanted the connection not just of love, but of friendship."

Cara turned to Sarah. "You were there for me when I thought I'd lost something—someone—again. When things ended with Kieran, all I wanted was to leave New Hope, but I'm so thankful that God closed all the doors I tried to open when it came to figuring out where to go. You were there, praying for Kieran and me. I didn't think God would answer your prayer, but then He did. And in the process, He gave me a friend like I'd never had before. Would you do me the honor of being my maid of honor?"

"Of course," Sarah said, her voice thick with emotion. "Oh, my word, yes, for sure. I can't wait!"

Cara laughed. "Well, thankfully, you won't have to wait too long."

Their discussion turned to the wedding and what Cara was already considering for it. Jillian didn't have much to contribute since she'd stopped thinking about weddings two years ago. Still, it was kind of fun to listen to the discussion. Sarah had some definite ideas as well, so Jillian figured that she was already thinking about wedding stuff even though Beau hadn't proposed yet.

"I think you'll need to get Sarah and Jillian to try on dresses soon," Anna said. "I can give you the name of the place where we got the dresses for our bridesmaids. They were excellent."

"I think we'd like a deep purple," Cara said. "That should look nice on both of you."

"It would," Anna agreed. "And a good color with purple is yellow."

"Ooo. I love yellow," Sarah said. "It's my favorite color."

"Do you think purple and yellow are good colors for winter?" Cara asked.

"I do," Anna said with a nod. "The purple would be good for the dresses, then they could carry yellow bouquets. The guys could wear gray suits with matching vests or ties, depending on how fancy you plan to get."

"I do want Kieran and the guys in suits, even though he's not so sure about it."

Sarah laughed. "I think Beau is probably the only guy who enjoys wearing a suit."

"Yeah, I can see that," Anna said. "Eli wasn't sure about the suit thing, but he went along with it when he realized it was what I really wanted."

"Who is standing up with Kieran?" Sarah asked.

"He's asking Carter and Michael tonight." At the sound of Carter's name, Jillian perked up. "He wants Carter to be his best man?"

Jillian wasn't sure why she was disappointed that she wouldn't be partnered with Carter at the wedding. It was just nice that they were both going to be part of such a special event. She was sure that he would agree to stand up with Kieran since he had done it for Eli.

"The guys could wear the suits they wore for our wedding," Anna said. "Just change out their vests to match the girls' dresses."

"That's a good idea," Cara agreed. "As long as you don't mind us using them for our wedding too."

"I don't mind at all. The guys might as well get more use out of them."

Though Jillian was happy that Cara wanted her to be part of her wedding, she felt a bit self-conscious. She wasn't going to look like Sarah in whatever dress they chose. Or maybe they could each choose their own style.

"Would you two have time to go looking at dresses sometime this week?" Cara asked.

"As long as it's after school, I should be able to go," Jillian said. "I do have a staff meeting on Monday, so it would have to be after that if you wanted to go then."

"I'm pretty flexible with my schedule." Sarah leaned forward to dip a piece of apple in the pot closest to her. "Though Friday probably isn't the best as Mom likes to have us around to help with guests who are arriving for the weekend."

They talked a bit more about possible times before Cara said she'd phone the wedding shop to see what their hours were and then make an appointment for them. Jillian had planned to make a couple of phone calls to see about an appointment with a therapist, but that could probably wait another week.

As Jillian ate the banana she'd just dipped in the chocolate, her phone buzzed. She picked it up from the spot on the coffee table where she'd set it when they'd sat down earlier.

Carter: *I hear we're going to be in a wedding.*

Jillian smiled as she tapped out a reply. *I suppose it was bound to happen with so many of our friends dating or engaged.*

Carter: *True. Still have Sarah and Beau to go. Think we'll be in that one too? I'm going to end up with more suits than I'll know what to do with.*

She chuckled. *Well, you're in luck. I think you're going to wear the same suit for Cara and Kieran's wedding that you wore for Eli and Anna's.*

Carter: *Well, that would be practical. I could get on board with that.*

I, on the other hand, will have to get a new dress which isn't something I'm really looking forward to.

Carter: *I'm sure you'll look beautiful in whatever dress you choose.*

Jillian stared at the screen as heat crept up her cheeks. Had Carter seriously just called her beautiful? She had a hard time believing it was more than just a platitude—something to make her feel better.

We shall see!

Carter: *Are you still at Cara's?*

Yep. Just enjoying some fondue.

Carter: *I'll let you get back to it. Have a good rest of the evening.*

Thanks. You too!

She set her phone down then looked up to find the three women regarding her with big smiles.

"What?"

"Let me guess," Sarah said. "That was Carter."

"Uh, yes, it was. Why?"

"You were smiling." Sarah beamed at her. "As if hearing from him made your day."

She wanted to deny it, but she couldn't. Somehow Carter had become an important part of her days. He'd become a really good friend.

"I think that's so sweet," Anna said. "Eli said that Carter was always adamant that he wasn't interested in dating. I'm glad that you were able to change his mind."

Jillian glanced at Sarah. "It's not really like that."

Cara frowned. "What do you mean?"

It felt wrong to let those closest to them believe their relationship was something it wasn't. "It's true that we're dating, but it's more that we've agreed to go with each other to events where having a date would be nice. Neither of us is interested in a serious relationship. We're not going to get engaged or married."

Now Anna was frowning while Sarah just looked sad. "Why would you date if there was no hope of the relationship turning serious?"

Jillian took a deep breath then explained how things had developed, starting with that day Carter had appeared in her classroom when Martin was harassing her.

"So it started off as Carter pretending he was your boyfriend to get Martin off your back?" Anna asked.

Jillian nodded. "And I think Carter has his own reasons for wanting something like this."

"You really don't want a serious relationship or to get married?" Cara asked.

Dropping her gaze, Jillian stared at the table. Her heart rate increased, and she could feel a knot of anxiety start to tighten in her stomach. She began to tap on her leg, then she felt an arm come around her and realized that Sarah had moved to sit beside her.

"You're safe," Sarah said softly. "You're okay."

Jillian hated that just the thought of explaining why she couldn't get married was sending her into a panic attack once again. She hated how weak it made her feel that she couldn't even have a conversation with friends without melting down. Maybe that phone call to the therapist *couldn't* wait another week.

"I'm sorry, sweetie," Cara murmured. "I didn't mean to upset you."

Jillian struggled to take deep breaths while Sarah whispered words of encouragement to her and even prayed for her. Finally, the panic began to recede, and she could think clearly, though her chest was still tight with anxiety.

"I'm sorry," she whispered.

"Do not apologize," Cara said. "I'm sorry for pressing you."

It was then she realized that maybe it would be good for them to know at least part of her story. She didn't necessarily want to go into detail about what had happened to her the way she'd explained it to Sarah, though.

"I was kidnapped and raped," she said, getting the words out as quickly as she could.

CHAPTER TWENTY-ONE

There was stunned silence for a moment before Anna said, "I'm *so* sorry to hear that."

"I had no idea..." Cara's words trailed off, and Jillian knew she was probably struggling to know what to say.

"You had no reason to know. I came back here because I'd hoped to put it all behind me. It seems God has other plans, I guess. It's been a challenge to handle the flashbacks, especially when faced with Martin's harassment."

"That's just awful," Anna said. "It's bad enough that the guy harassed you like that. Have you been having lots of panic attacks?"

Jillian sighed. "Unfortunately, yes. I hadn't had hardly any until it became apparent that Martin wasn't going to take no for an answer. Then they started to be almost daily, with varying degrees of severity."

"How have you been dealing with them?" Cara asked.

"Back in Portland, my therapist helped me figure out tools that would help me, so I've been trying to use them." She hesitated, knowing that if she explained about Carter, they would read things into that that weren't true. But it seemed wrong to not give him credit for how he'd handled everything. "Carter's also been a big help. He knew right away what was happening when I had my first panic attack around him. Honestly, he was great through that whole situation with Martin."

"Kieran has said he's excellent at his job. Very steady under pressure."

Jillian nodded. "I would agree with that. He's never freaked out when I'm having an attack. Unfortunately, things have gotten worse. Like you just saw, I'm very easily triggered right now."

"So, you had therapy after your rape?" Cara asked.

"Yes. My grandma insisted. She said that just like the doctors in the hospital helped me heal my body after what happened, a good Christian therapist could help me heal my mind." Jillian let out a sigh. "I thought I was doing better—I *was* doing better—when I moved back from Portland, so I didn't pursue getting another therapist here."

"Maybe it's time to change that?" Anna suggested gently.

"Yeah. I've already come to that conclusion. Even though the situation with Martin is over, I'm still struggling with panic attacks and anxiety. Lately, though, even the tools the therapist gave me haven't been working as well as they once did."

"Do you know of a therapist around here?" Sarah asked. "Mom might be able to give you a name if you need a recommendation."

"My therapist in Portland gave me a list for the area of ones she recommended. I just need to call one of them."

"Well, if there's anything we can do to help, I'm sure I speak for all of us that all you need to do is let us know," Cara said. "You're important to us, so if you're struggling, let us offer you support."

"Thank you." Jillian slumped against Sarah. "Just don't treat me differently. That was why I didn't want to tell anyone about what happened. I don't want people to feel like they have to be wary of how they interact with me."

"Does Carter know?" Anna asked.

Jillian shook her head. "It's the reason I don't want to get married, but I haven't told him. Just like he hasn't told me his reasons. The arrangement we've agreed on is what works best for us."

She didn't bother to add that she was sure that if he *was* interested in getting married, she wouldn't be his first choice.

Anna seemed to consider her words before shrugging. "If this is what works for the two of you, then who are we to argue with you about it."

"I understand why your point of view is different, but for me, the prospect of marrying is terrifying. It's not like I can find out before we get married if we can have sex or if I'll have a panic attack in the midst of it." Jillian shrugged. "Maybe it would be different if I could try to have a physical relationship with someone before marrying them, but you know that's not possible."

"I guess I can see that, but there's more to marriage than sex," Anna said. "If you love someone enough, you can work together with a therapist to build the physical side of your relationship."

Jillian thought back to her first therapist, and the conversations they'd had on the subject. The therapist had also told her that she could have an intimate relationship, but it would take work for both her and her partner. Even if she was willing to take the chance, she just couldn't see how that man could ever be Carter.

"I'll be praying for you as you go to a new therapist," Sarah said, giving her shoulder a squeeze before moving back to where she'd been sitting.

"I'm nervous about having to tell them everything. It's like reliving it all over again, plus now I have the stuff with Martin." Jillian shuddered. "Sometimes it just feels like too much to deal with. Other times, I just want to push it all down and focus on my job—which I love again now that Martin is gone—and being with my friends."

"I would imagine that pushing it all down only means that it all comes back up at some point," Cara said. "I've been there, though obviously not to the degree you have. I had trauma in my life when my mom was killed in a car accident that I survived. It took me a while to deal with that."

"Yes. Trauma doesn't like to be ignored," Jillian said. "Which is why I hope to at least be able to get back to the point I was at when I left Portland. I was having hardly any nightmares, and my panic attacks were few and far between."

"We'll pray to that end," Anna said, and the other two nodded.

"Sorry for kind of hijacking your evening with this," Jillian said. "Maybe we can go back to discussing something lighter."

"I'm not upset that we discussed this," Cara assured her. "I feel more than ever that I made the right choice of the people I chose to stand up with me."

"I think I'm going to eat my feelings now," Jillian said, picking up her fork and stabbing a piece of banana.

"I don't want to offend you," Sarah said. "But, well, you've gained weight since high school. Was that tied to the attack?"

Though some might find it a touchy subject, Jillian didn't mind discussing it. "After I was kidnapped, all I could think was that if I'd been bigger—heavier—he wouldn't have been able to move me as easily as he did. After he sedated me, he was able to carry me to where he held me captive. All of the women he kidnapped were about the same size. Easily manageable for him." Anxiety began to ping in her stomach again. Jillian took a deep breath and let it out. "I purposely gained weight so that a guy would see my weight as a challenge if he wanted to be able to move me against my will."

Sarah stared at her for a moment, then nodded. "So it wasn't because you hoped you'd be unattractive to a man? Which you aren't, by the way. You're still as beautiful as you ever were."

Jillian shook her head. "Though this guy had a type of woman he preyed upon, rapes aren't always the result of attraction. It's about power, and for some, it's about a set of circumstances that they need to fulfill a fantasy. So I basically decided to gain weight to make it more difficult for any man that tried to target me again. I realize that it wouldn't deter every attacker, but it would likely have deterred mine."

"That does make sense," Sarah said. "I'm just so sorry that you had to deal with any of that. In high school, you were the one we all thought was going to get married and have a bunch of kids right away."

Jillian shrugged. "Things change. Now I'm focused on my career and loving the kids I'm teaching."

"I'll bet you're a terrific teacher," Cara said with a gentle smile.

"I really try to be. The kids deserve my best effort, so I try to give them that."

"Have Kieran and Carter come to do a presentation yet?" Cara asked.

Once again, the conversation drifted away from Jillian's past and her emotional trauma, and she was able to relax and enjoy the rest of the evening. She wasn't sure yet if all of this talk would trigger another nightmare that night, but she wasn't going to dwell on that because she'd yet to have an untroubled night since the take-down episode with Martin.

Instead, she'd enjoy the rest of the evening as best she could and then deal with whatever came later.

~ * ~

Carter parked his truck then headed into the church. He'd gotten off shift at eight that morning, and since it had been a Saturday night, they'd gotten a few more call-outs than they would have on a weekday night. Once his shift was over, he'd gone home and tried to sleep for a couple of hours before getting up to go to church.

A lot of times, he just crawled into bed and slept until he woke up, but on Sundays, he tried to make an effort to wake up to his alarm, even if it was just a couple of hours after he went to sleep. That morning, however, he'd dragged his way through a shower and into suitable clothes, praying the whole time he wouldn't fall asleep in the middle of Pastor Evan's sermon.

As tired as he was in body, he was feeling a similar sort of way in spirit. His visit with Suzanne and Evelyn had gone as usual, though her insistence that he tell Jillian about Suzanne weighed on him. Then going to Kieran's, only to be asked to participate in yet another wedding, had him fighting to keep from slipping into a negative headspace that seemed to accompany reminders of what he wasn't going to experience in his own life the way he'd planned with Suzanne.

Evelyn would tell him that the only reason he wasn't going to experience those things was because he was holding himself back from them. And there was truth to that, but the guilt and responsibility he felt for what had happened that night ten years ago prevented him from fully embracing any of that stuff.

How could he get engaged, marry, and have a family, when he felt a lot of responsibility for having robbed Suzanne of experiencing those things? It was the knowledge that he lived with on a daily basis. No one could convince him otherwise.

So he entered the church that day needing refreshment in spirit as much as in body.

Carter smiled and nodded at the people in the foyer who greeted him but continued into the sanctuary to find a seat before the service started. He glanced around at the people already there, seeing plenty of familiar faces. When his gaze landed on Eli and Anna neared the front of the room, he headed in their direction.

As he reached them, he noticed that Beau and Sarah were there as well, already seated in the row next to where Eli and Anna stood talking to another couple. He saw that Jillian was sitting next to Sarah, and without thinking it through, he walked to the front of the sanctuary so he could get around to where Jillian sat.

He settled onto the seat next to her and gave her a smile. "Morning."

"Good morning," she said with an answering smile. "I thought you might be sleeping since you just got off work."

"I got a couple of hours, but I'll sleep more this afternoon before heading to Eli's for the study tonight."

"Is that enough sleep for you?" Jillian asked, her brow furrowed.

Carter shrugged. "I've never really needed eight hours of sleep a night, so if there's stuff I have to do on the day following my shift, I just grab sleep where I can then conk out for the night."

"I need at least eight hours of sleep a night," she said. "Otherwise, I'm dragging and more prone to...you know."

Carter nodded, knowing she was referring to her panic attacks. "That makes sense."

Just then, the worship leader stood up on the stage and asked for people to find their seats. The worship team began to play, so Carter shifted to face the front, his shoulder pressing against Jillian's.

It only dawned on him then that he maybe should have asked if it was okay to sit with her. The decision to sit beside her had been natural. No thought had been required. That was probably something he needed to think more about, but not right then.

After they'd moved through the first part of the service with singing, scripture reading, and the offering, Pastor Evans got up, a familiar figure behind the podium.

"Good morning, everyone," he said, beaming out at the congregation. "I hope you've all had a good week and that you've had some opportunities to share God's love and grace with others."

Carter thought back over his week, realizing that perhaps even if there had been opportunities, he hadn't taken advantage of them the way he should have.

"We are in our first week of exploring how to live our lives as Christians so as to be lights in a dark world. However, I'm not diving right into how to show that light to the world just yet. I've chosen rather to use a lantern to help us visualize how our light can be affected. We're focusing first on growing our flame. The bigger the flame, the brighter will be the light. Next week, we're going to look at how to clean the glass of your lantern so others can see your bright flame."

He led them in prayer, then delved into his sermon.

"I hope we all know the song *This Little Light of Mine,* and though it's thought of as a children's song, it has such a great message for adults too. There's a line in the song that I want to use as I begin my sermon. *This little light of mine, I'm gonna let it shine.* Notice the indication that we're choosing to let our light shine." Pastor Evans came to stand next to the podium as he asked them to open their Bibles. "This song is based on Matthew 5:14-16."

Carter pulled out his silenced phone and opened his Bible app to the reference given. He followed along as the pastor read the verses.

"*You are the light of the world. A city that is set on a hill cannot be hidden. Nor do they light a lamp and put it under a basket, but on a lampstand, and it gives light to all who are in the house. Let your light so shine before men, that they may see your good works and glorify your Father in heaven.*"

"Amid the busy-ness of our lives, we sometimes forget to let our lights shine, especially if we have issues in our lives that are weakening our light. What sorts of things, you might be wondering? Well, I'm so glad you asked." He returned to stand behind the podium. "So, before anything else, we need to acknowledge that we're going to let our light shine."

"We all know that becoming a Christian doesn't mean we never sin. It just means that through God's grace, we are forgiven. Unfortunately, any sin in our lives that we continue to commit can dim that light. Certain emotions can dim the light. Things like self-recrimination. Self-doubt. Guilt. Anger. Hypocrisy. Dishonesty. And just because I might not have mentioned your particular sin or negative emotion doesn't mean that it is exempt. I think we are all quite aware of the things in our lives that dim our light."

Carter shifted on his seat, starting to wish he'd just shut off his alarm and stayed in bed. He took a deep breath then blew it out. With his phone held tightly in his hand, he tried to stay focused on what the pastor was saying as he expounded on the points he was trying to make. At least with all the emotions coursing through him, there was no danger of him falling asleep.

"As I close out this sermon, I want you to think of your life for a moment, then consider how you interact with others. How you interact with yourself. How you interact with your God." He paused then said, "Then I want you to ask yourself one question about each of those things: Does how I act or react, does what motivates me, bring glory to God?"

Carter stared down at his phone. He knew what it was in his life that he'd need to ask that question about, but he just couldn't bring himself to do that, let alone shine a light on it. Surely he could still shine a light to the world that would draw others to Christ without having to let go of the responsibility he felt for the accident.

As he sat there, he refused to think of that emotion as guilt. Claiming it was *responsibility* that chained him to the past and refusing to forgive himself seemed more acceptable than naming it as *guilt.*

"If what you're feeling, saying, or doing doesn't bring glory to God, your light is going to be dimmed. You might feel differently, that you're still able to shine regardless of what might be going on within you or in secret in your home, but God sees. God knows. And if you're struggling with these things, it will affect how you feel towards God. It will also affect how brightly your light will shine."

Carter wanted to argue with Pastor Evans, but the reality was that he *was* very reserved in his spiritual life. Even at the Bible study, he contributed to the discussion, but he didn't lead in the way that Eli and Kieran did. They had a genuineness to their interactions with people, and while Eli hadn't always been the most vocal about his faith, in the past year, he'd definitely become more that way.

Though he'd tried to pass off his subdued approach to things as just his personality, in reality, Carter knew it was more.

As he ended his sermon, Pastor Evans led them in prayer, encouraging them to search their hearts and ask God to reveal those areas in their life that might dim their light. Carter's leg jiggled as he sat there, his eyes open as he stared at the floor.

He had never been more relieved for a pastor to end a sermon. If only he'd been seated at the back of the sanctuary, he would have been able to make a quick getaway. Instead, he had to spend at least a few minutes chatting with people before he could make his escape.

After exchanging a few words with those around him, he stepped to Jillian's side and bent his head to say, "I'm going to head home and try to get some sleep."

Jillian smiled at him. "I guess I'll see you at Eli's later."

Carter nodded, even though, right then, attending the study wasn't very appealing. But he'd go because others—including Jillian—expected him to be there.

He said goodbye to the others standing with them then headed up the center aisle of the sanctuary. Pastor Evans was talking with someone at the exit, letting Carter breathe a sigh of relief as he slipped past them out into the gray day. He jogged down the wide cement steps and crossed the sidewalk to the parking lot.

As he drove home, all Carter let himself think about was his bed, glad that he was so tired that he wasn't going to have any trouble falling asleep. Though he was a bit hungry, he didn't bother with a meal, just settled for a protein bar and a glass of water, then peeled out of his clothes and dropped into bed.

He took a moment to set his alarm, choosing a time that would likely make him a bit late to the study, but he needed the sleep.

CHAPTER TWENTY-TWO

Carter drove his truck up the incline to Eli's and pulled to a stop beside Jillian's car. He was still tired, but not as tired as he'd been when he'd tumbled into bed after church. His mind was still a bit of a mess, though, but at least he had a better grip on his emotions.

Eli answered the door, giving him a wide smile. "Was wondering if you were going to make it."

"I'm sorry," Carter said as he stepped into the house. "I pushed the snooze on my alarm more than I should have."

"Totally understandable." Eli thumped him on the back. "Coming off a twenty-four shift must be brutal."

"Especially this one as we had enough call-outs through the night that we didn't get any real rest. I still wouldn't trade this job though."

"Well, come and grab some food. Thanks to Leah, we've got plenty."

Carter wandered over to the food, his gaze searching the room as he walked. It wasn't until his gaze met Jillian's and he realized she'd been watching him that he knew she was who he'd been looking for. He gave her a quick smile then made his way to where the food was spread out on the island.

As he surveyed all the food, he wondered if anyone would mind if he just piled it all on one of the platters. He hadn't eaten a decent meal since...well, the previous night when a couple of the guys at the station had made stew for them. It had been delicious, but he was ready for more than the bowl of cereal he'd had for breakfast, and the protein bar he'd had for lunch.

Once he'd filled a plate with as much food as he could manage, Carter turned to find an empty seat. Leah got up from where she'd been sitting next to Jillian and waved him over.

"I'm done already," she said as she picked up her empty plate and glass.

Carter thanked her, then set his plate down and went to pour himself a drink from the selection of pop bottles that sat on a nearby table. He wasn't a huge fan of pop, so he only poured half a glass then grabbed a water bottle.

"How's life treating you?" Beau asked after Carter had bowed his head to say a silent prayer of thanks for his food. He was seated across the table with Sarah.

"Can't complain," Carter said with a nod. "How about you?"

"Making some progress with getting my business off the ground, so I'm pleased about that."

"Your brother and sister around?" Carter asked, remembering the funny stories that Sarah and Beau had shared about Beau's siblings' adjustments to small-town life.

"Not this weekend," Beau said. "They've headed off to New York for some sort of fundraising event they were invited to. I think they plan to spend the week there to be immersed in a big city once again."

"Better them than me," Carter replied. "I may have lived in big cities over the years, but I'm really a small-town boy at heart."

"Small town like New Hope Falls?" Sarah asked.

"Basically." Carter took a bite of the pasta salad and moaned in appreciation. "This is delicious."

"Jillian made it," Sarah volunteered with a broad smile. "It's amazing, isn't it? *She's* amazing."

Carter glanced at Jillian to see her cheeks had pinked, and she had an embarrassed look on her face. "Yep. I agree with both those things."

Jillian's gaze met his for a brief second before dropping to her empty plate. "Stop, you guys."

"Could we cook burgers on those cheeks?" Sarah asked with a laugh as she reached out to touch Jillian's face.

Jillian batted her hand away. "Probably, thanks to you."

"You're welcome." Sarah leaned against Beau. "Any time."

"I'll keep that in mind." Jillian picked up her glass of pop and took a sip. "And never take you up on it."

Carter enjoyed the banter around the table between Jillian, Sarah, Beau, and Andy while he ate. When his alarm had first gone off, he hadn't been sure he'd be up to coming to the study, which was why he'd hit his snooze so many times that he'd ended up being late. Still, now that he was there, he was glad he'd made the effort to come.

After most had finished eating, they began to clean up the food. People pitched in to clear away empty plates and cups and to put the food away in the fridge. The aroma of coffee soon began to float through the air, and Carter knew he'd be drinking at least one cup to help him wake up a bit more.

Desserts were also set out, though Carter was a bit too full to indulge just yet. The treats would be available throughout the Bible study for people to eat as they wanted. Jillian had gone to the kitchen to help with the clean-up, so Carter just concentrated on finishing up the food he'd taken. Once he was done, he carried his plate and glass to the kitchen. Jillian took them from him with a smile then turned to add them to the dishwasher.

Once everything was cleared away, people began to make their way to the large open area of Eli's living room. *Eli and Anna's,* Carter corrected himself. Nothing much had changed with Anna moving into the cabin, but that was probably because a lot of changes had been taking place even before they'd gotten married.

Anna had begun to incorporate lots of personal touches from both her and Eli over the past few months. There were plenty of photos of the two of them scattered throughout the main floor of the cabin. And already there were some casual wedding pictures of the two of them in frames on the mantel above the fireplace.

"There's space for you here, Carter," Sarah called out.

He found her seated with Beau and Jillian on one of the couches. As he headed toward them, Sarah tugged Jillian closer to her in the middle of the couch, leaving room for Carter on the other side of her. He was sure that Jillian had explained to Sarah about the true nature of their relationship, but it seemed she was determined to continue to force them into close, couple-y contact.

Not that Carter was going to complain. He enjoyed spending time with Jillian, and she'd shown no interest in changing the original parameters of their arrangement, so he felt quite comfortable sitting next to her on the couch.

Michael Reed settled on the floor, his guitar in hand. At Eli's prompting, Michael led them through several worship songs that were familiar enough that no one needed the words in order to sing them.

Kieran was in charge of the study that night, and Carter's heart sank a bit when he started out with letting the group know that he thought it would be good to build on the pastor's sermon that morning. That wasn't exactly an unusual occurrence. There had been plenty of times they'd done just that.

Thankfully, he wasn't usually as active a participant for these larger group studies as he was in the smaller men's group. So, the fact that he was quiet throughout the discussions wouldn't make anyone think that he was struggling with the topic.

Each study—which was held bi-weekly—seemed to have the same people participating. There were definitely some in the group who enjoyed talking and sharing their lives and struggles. In some ways, it seemed that they fell into two groups that were reflected in the McNamara twins. Sarah represented the group that seemed willing to share freely—both about themselves as well as in the encouragement of others—while Leah was definitely more reserved in both areas.

It seemed that both he and Jillian fell into Leah's group. He'd noticed that about Jillian even before they'd grown closer. Still, since then, he'd discovered that the closer Jillian got to people, the more she opened up. The more she smiled. The more she laughed.

It was just too bad that the events with Martin had suppressed both the laughter and the smiles. He understood that it might take some time to bring both those back entirely. But if they didn't return, he might feel like he had to hunt Martin down to exact some vengeance for stealing away Jillian's smiles and laughter.

As the study progressed, Carter came to the realization that plenty of others had been impacted by the pastor's sermon that morning. Some spoke of holding unforgiveness or anger in their hearts toward someone. Others spoke of feeling like their anger hurt those around them, even when they felt justified in being upset.

Even though Carter didn't feel alone in his struggles, he didn't want to share them. At least not with such a large group.

Once the study ended, people raided the dessert offerings. They stood around chatting for a bit before some began to leave. Carter stayed until Jillian was ready to go. After they said goodnight to their friends, he walked her out to her car.

"So, are you ready for another week?" Carter asked as they stood in front of her vehicle.

"I'll tell you what. I'm not just ready for another week. I'm ready for an uneventful, absolutely boring week where the most excitement I experience is someone spilling a juice box during snack time."

Carter chuckled. "I hear you. I'd kind of like to have that kind of exciting week myself, as opposed to the excitement I tend to run into."

"Well, I hope we both have quiet weeks," Jillian said. "And thank you again for everything you did for me last week. It was definitely above and beyond anything I deserved or expected."

"Maybe for just a friend," Carter agreed. "But I'm your *boyfriend*, remember?"

"Right." Jillian laughed softly. "How could I have forgotten?"

"I have *no* idea."

When she laughed again, Carter felt hope fill his heart that she'd be back to normal—*her* normal—sooner rather than later. He didn't know what had happened to her that caused her panic attacks, but something told him she needed to be at a place where she could laugh and smile to balance that out.

"I'll try to remember in the future."

"I would appreciate that, as I'm not sure my ego can survive you forgetting again."

"Well, on that lovely note, I should probably head home. I need to finish up a few things for school tomorrow."

"Drive safe," Carter said as he followed her to the driver's door. He held it open as she slid behind the wheel. "Talk to you soon."

"Yep." She pulled her seatbelt across and clicked it into place. "Have a good week."

As she started the engine, Carter shut her door and walked to the front of the car, then turned to watch her back out. He lifted his hand, then walked to his truck and climbed behind the wheel.

He'd just driven past the lodge when his phone rang. Since he didn't have Bluetooth in his truck, he pulled over to see who was calling. He frowned as he answered it, worried that something had happened to his family. They usually only talked every couple of weeks, and he'd just had a brief conversation with his dad the previous week.

"Carter Julian Ward," his mom said when he answered. "Why is it that I had to hear from Evelyn that you are dating?"

Carter winced as her voice gained altitude as her sentence progressed. "It's new, Mom. Really new."

He switched the call to speakerphone then snapped his phone into the cell holder attached to the truck's vents. Putting the truck in gear, he checked to make sure no other cars were coming before pulling back onto the narrow road leading off the lodge property.

"Not so new you didn't mention it to Evelyn."

Though her words might have made it seem like she was jealous of Suzanne's mother, she wasn't. She'd told Carter that she understood he needed to be there with them. They'd lost their only child, and she didn't mind sharing one of hers with them. Still, he was sure that Evelyn had assumed he'd mentioned Jillian to his mother.

"I'm sorry, Mom. I guess I should have told you when I mentioned it to her." He'd definitely not thought through his plan with Jillian beyond satisfying Evelyn and Garth's requirement.

"Well, never mind that," his mom said, and Carter could picture her waving her hand dismissively. "Tell me about her."

Carter let out a breath, suddenly aware he was digging himself in even deeper. But what could he do? It wasn't a request from his mother that he could deny unless he wanted to answer a ton more questions.

"Her name is Jillian, and she teaches grade three at the elementary school here in town."

"A teacher? That's lovely. How did you meet?"

"We've been part of the same church group for the last few months."

"So you were friends first? That's good."

Carter didn't bother to state that *acquaintance* might be a more accurate description of their prior relationship. He'd definitely class them as friends now, however.

"So what have you been doing? What sort of dates have you been taking her on?"

"We've attended a wedding and gone out to dinner. Like I said, it's new."

"Do you have a picture from the wedding?" she asked. "One with her, I mean. Not that I wouldn't mind seeing you all dressed up on your own."

"I have one I'll send you. I'm driving at the moment, though, so I'll have to wait until I get home."

"Oh, I can wait. In the meantime, tell me how you've been."

Given that his life was pretty much in a rut, there really wasn't much to tell, so once he'd given her a brief recap, he asked about his siblings. That was enough to keep her talking for the remainder of his trip home.

As he walked into his apartment a short time later, he was glad that she couldn't see where he lived. While she continued to talk about how his oldest brother's wife's pregnancy was going, he thumbed through to the picture of him and Jillian then sent it off to his mom.

He could tell when she got it because she suddenly went quiet. "Oh, Carter. She's just beautiful. Does she make you happy?"

He answered with an automatic *yes*, but even as he said the word, he realized that it wasn't a lie. She made him laugh, and even when he was with her in the midst of a panic attack, he'd never wished he could be somewhere else.

"I'm glad to hear that, darling. I wish we could meet her. Do you think you might bring her to Florida to meet us?"

The idea made Carter's stomach clench. "Maybe. Like I said Mom, it's still new."

"Well, we'll be praying for you both." She paused and gave a little sigh. "I've been waiting so long for this moment."

"Please don't get your hopes up too much, Mom. We're taking it slow."

"That's fine. Probably a good idea, actually. It still makes me happy."

"Sorry again about not telling you sooner."

"It's okay, darling. I forgive you...this time. But don't let it happen again."

Carter rubbed the back of his neck as he settled onto the edge of his bed. "I'll try my best."

"Well, I'm off to bed," she said. "Love you, honey. Sleep well!"

"Love you too, Mom."

After they said goodbye, Carter sat staring at the floor. This was starting to get a little bit out of control. Establishing the relationship had made a lot of sense in that moment in Jillian's classroom, but now he wasn't so sure.

People would expect things to become more serious between them. That would mean more dates with just each other. More affection between them. Things they hadn't planned on including as part of their arrangement. The only good thing was that they were both fairly private people, so for at least a little while longer, they could probably get away with not being as overtly affectionate like Sarah and Beau were.

Still...he was going to have to talk to Jillian about the situation soon. He really hoped that she didn't decide to end things. There wasn't much of a chance that he'd find someone else who would be willing to accept that he wasn't looking for more. So far, Jillian hadn't seemed to be interested in anything more either, which made her a perfect fit for him.

All in all, if they could just continue on with the way things were for as long as possible, it would be for the best for both of them. If they staged a "break up" in a few months, Evelyn might give him a bit of a reprieve before encouraging him to date again. And if they continued to date, it would give him the opportunity to be available to support Jillian if she was still struggling with her anxiety and panic attacks.

Rubbing his hands over his face, Carter decided that was all a mess for another day. He got up and headed for his small bathroom to get ready for bed. Though he'd had some sleep throughout the day, he needed more. If for no other reason than to escape the thoughts going round and round in his head.

CHAPTER TWENTY-THREE

Jillian parked in the church parking lot, then got out and carefully lifted the box from the back of her car. She had tried to pack it well, so hopefully the contents were still okay. Heading for the church doors, she was grateful that the drizzle that had been going on throughout the day, had stopped. At least for the time being.

She held the box with one arm then pulled the door open to let herself into the church. There were voices in the foyer, and she spotted a handful of people standing around. They smiled as she passed them on the way to the hall where people were setting up for the fall festival.

Sarah was there already and came over to greet her. "Are those your baked goods?"

"Yep," Jillian said. "I hope everything survived the trip."

"Well, let's take them to the kitchen." Sarah led the way to where her mom was working with a couple of other women.

"What have you got there?" Nadine asked with a smile.

Jillian slid the box onto an empty spot on the counter. "Just a few goodies for the church booth tomorrow."

Nadine opened the box and lifted out the pies and set them on the counter. "Oh, these look lovely, Jillian. And cupcakes too."

"I'm sure they're not as good as Leah's, but I enjoyed baking them."

"And I'm sure that people will enjoy eating them," Nadine assured her.

"Come help me," Sarah said, grabbing her arm. "I'm doing flowers with Anna to decorate the tables for the pie judging contest."

Jillian followed Sarah out of the kitchen and toward where Anna was seated with heaps of flowers on the table in front of her.

"Hey there," Anna said with a wide smile. "Glad you could make it."

"Me, too. What can I do? I'm not terribly creative."

"Oh, don't hand me that," Sarah said as she settled on a seat at the table. "I've seen your house. You have done a wonderful job with decorating."

"Well, we shall see. Tell me what to do."

She got to work with the other women, happy to be with them and helping out for the fall festival. It had been ages since she'd last been to one, and that had been when her grandma was still alive.

They spent some time chatting about the dress try-on they'd done earlier that week. Cara had been happy to let them each choose their own style as long as they both were in the same dark purple color. Jillian had spent some time in advance looking at plus-size models wearing different styles, so by the time she went to try on dresses, she had some ideas of what would look flattering and what wouldn't.

The saleswoman had been patient and also very experienced, so it didn't take as long as Jillian had thought it might to find a dress she loved. She'd gone there thinking she'd be lucky if she got a dress she liked, but she'd actually ended up with one she loved. It had turned an experience she'd kind of dreaded into one she'd really enjoyed.

"It Carter coming?" Anna asked.

"He's working today." Jillian gathered up a few flowers and arranged them like Anna had shown her. "He'll be off early tomorrow morning."

"How long are his shifts?" Sarah asked.

"Twenty-four hours."

"Those are some long shifts," Anna said. "I bet he's exhausted when he's done."

"Sometimes he can sleep during the shift, depending on how busy they are."

Anna tilted her head as she looked at the flower display in front of her. "You guys are working the booth tomorrow afternoon, right?"

"Yep. We're there from three to four."

"I think this is Carter's first time working the booth," Sarah said. "You're a good influence on him."

Jillian gave a shake of her head. "I doubt that."

"He seems to be more engaged with us than before you and he got together. I think you're good for each other."

Frowning, Jillian met Sarah's gaze. Her friend knew the truth of their arrangement, but for some reason, she persisted in acting like they were in a relationship that was moving toward something more serious.

Sarah gave her a smile and shrugged. "Just sayin'."

"She's not wrong," Anna added. "I know what you told us about how things are between the two of you, but there's no denying that it seems that you bring out the best in each other."

"We've become friends," Jillian admitted. "Good friends, I would even say. But probably the fastest way to get us to change our arrangement is to be constantly trying to force us into something we're not interested in. If that keeps happening, we'll probably just call it off altogether."

This time, Sarah frowned. "I just think you and Carter are too close to the situation, too determined to only see it one way, to admit how good you are together."

"Well, of course, we're close to the situation," Jillian said. "We're *in* the situation."

Sarah and Anna exchanged glances, then Anna said, "Okay. You're right. At the end of the day, it's your and Carter's lives. None of us can truly know the situation the way you two do."

Jillian saw the concern on her friends' faces and sighed. "Carter and I are in a good place. What we have works for us. So yeah, we're happy right now, even though we know our arrangement is not going to lead to anything more."

Sarah looked a little sad as she focused her attention on the flowers in front of her. Jillian felt bad that she had to disappoint her friends, but even though they knew about her past trauma, they just didn't seem to understand where she was coming from when it came to marriage and having an intimate relationship.

"Hello, lovely ladies," Eli said as he appeared at the table. He moved to Anna's side, and when she lifted her head, he bent down to press a lingering kiss to her lips. "How's it going here?"

"It's going well," Anna told him. "Are you here to set up the tables and chairs?"

"Yep." Eli grabbed a chair and set it next to Anna's. "Just waiting for a few more of the guys to show up."

"Beau plans to be here," Sarah said. "And maybe Rhett, if he's recovered from his trip to the big city."

"He and Julianna are back?" Anna asked.

Sarah nodded. "They arrived back yesterday."

Jillian hadn't spent a lot of time with the pair, but she had struggled at times with the idea of who Julianna was...especially lately. Though she wasn't as short as Julianna, she'd once been small like the other woman was...back in her high school and college years. She'd worked hard to achieve and maintain that size, confident that by looking that way, she'd be able to attract the type of man she wanted to marry.

Even though she no longer was focused on marriage, Jillian could admit that seeing the looks of interest Julianna had given Carter had left her with emotions she hadn't wanted to think too deeply about. Wistful, maybe. A little jealous that she no longer could give a man those looks of interest without anxiety and panic attacks following them.

Julianna and Carter would have made a cute couple if he'd been at all interested in her. Jillian had no idea why he wasn't. Why he couldn't have just had a normal relationship with someone like Julianna instead of a casual one with her.

A thought occurred to Jillian in that moment that made her feel a little sick. Had Carter figured that the arrangement he wanted would be safe with Jillian because he knew he wouldn't be tempted to want anything more with her?

It hurt to think that, but at the same time, Jillian reminded herself that it didn't matter. She shouldn't care whether Carter found her attractive or not. In fact, she should be glad that he didn't. He treated her well, and considering their agreement, that should be enough for her.

Still, the voice of her teenage self lamented not being attractive to a good-looking guy. During her teenage years, she'd always wanted guys to think she was the prettiest girl around. Her grandma had reminded her often that a man worth having was one who could appreciate outer beauty, but who understood that inner beauty was more important. And that if they had to choose between the two, would choose the girl with inner beauty.

Back then, Jillian had just rolled her eyes, feeling her grandma was too old to understand how teenage boys were. In time, however, she came to realize that they were both right. Her grandmother's description of the qualities a woman should want to find in a man was accurate. Still, the chances of finding those qualities in a teenage boy were fairly slim. Not impossible, but definitely a challenge.

Of course, Jillian couldn't exactly judge those teenage boys when she'd been pretty much the same way...certainly preferring the attention of the cute boys over the not-so-cute ones. She would have liked to think she'd grown up in that regard, but since she'd gone out with a guy based solely on the fact he was handsome and rich, it was clear she hadn't. Too bad that guy had turned out to be a predator of the very worst kind.

Carter's looks hadn't played a role one way or the other in her decision to agree to his suggestion of a casual relationship. She kind of wished she could say the same for Carter with regards to her. But short of asking him, she wouldn't know.

"Jillian?" Sarah said, her voice raised just slightly.

She looked up from the flowers she was holding...but not arranging. "Sorry. What?"

Sarah's brows drew together. "Nothing." She gave her a quick smile. "Nothing."

Jillian glanced around at the others, noticing as she did so that Beau had arrived with Rhett and Julianna in tow.

"Carter not here?" Julianna asked as she sat down next to Jillian.

"No. He's working his shift at the station," she said.

"That's too bad. I'm sure the guys would have appreciated the help of his muscles in moving the tables and chairs."

Jillian gave her a smile. "I think they'll do just fine without him since most also have muscles of their own."

"Most?" Julianna laughed. "Are you referring to my brothers' lack of muscles?"

Jillian lifted her brows. "I would never presume to judge a man's muscles or lack thereof."

"Except for Carter, of course."

"Uh, I suppose. Though I have to say that Carter has a lot more going for him than just his muscles." That was definitely the truth. But rather than continue on with a discussion about Carter, she gestured to the flowers. "Are you here to help with the decorations?"

"I'm more used to *being* the decoration than creating them."

"Juli," Beau said with a laugh. "Nothing like reinforcing any ideas people might have about you being vain and useless."

"Who am I to disappoint?" Julianna said with a shrug as she curved her fingers and inspected her perfectly manicured, deep red fingernails.

"You're the perfect Allerton princess," Rhett said with a heavy dose of sarcasm in his voice. "You never disappoint."

As the banter went back and forth between Beau's younger siblings, Jillian tuned them out. Having grown up as basically an only child, she'd never really gotten into sibling banter, and it wasn't something she necessarily enjoyed listening to. Particularly these two, as the banter seemed to go a step beyond the teasing she'd seen from Sarah and her siblings over the years.

Jillian was glad when the guys moved off to begin setting up tables and chairs, taking Rhett with them. They'd pretty much finished with all the decorations, so once the tables were in place in the center of the room, they began to cover them with tablecloths and centerpieces.

"Are you going to go to the festival tonight?" Sarah asked her as they stood by the door leading out of the church once everything had been done in the hall.

"No. I think I'm going to head home. I'm ready for a bit of downtime after a fun-filled week with energetic little ones."

"Just you, Dolly, and the Food Network channel?"

"Sounds perfect," Jillian agreed. "And maybe a cupcake."

Sarah slid her arm around Jillian's shoulders and gave her a hug. "Well, we'll see you tomorrow, right?"

"Yep. I'll be there."

"And maybe we can do some stuff in the evening."

"I'd like that."

Jillian breathed a sigh of relief when she walked through the door of her house a short time later. Dolly seemed just as relieved to have her home. She hadn't had time to eat dinner between getting home from school, packaging up the pies and cupcakes she'd made the night before, and going to the church.

So after feeding Dolly, she changed into her pajamas then made herself something to eat. Curled up on the couch with her food and her favorite show on television was the perfect ending to a decent week. Definitely a better week than the one previous. She'd still had nightmares and panic attacks, but that wasn't unexpected, and thankfully, nothing had triggered her while she'd been with her class.

Though she'd put off calling the therapist until about midweek, they had fit her in for an appointment for early the following week. That had her feeling a little apprehensive since she knew that delving back into the time of the attack was going to bring a lot of unwelcome memories to the surface. All of that would leave her emotionally drained, and nightmares and panic attacks that would continue to occur would drain her physically.

Once she got passed the worst of it, things would settle down. She hoped...

In the meantime, comfort food and a few episodes of her favorite reality cooking shows with Dolly curled up next to her would be the perfect evening.

CHAPTER TWENTY-FOUR

The next morning, Jillian was slow to wake after having had another nightmare-plagued night. She'd set her alarm for eleven, just to make sure she was up by then for sure, though she hadn't figured she'd actually sleep that long. And she hadn't, but it still had been close to ten by the time she'd woken and grabbed her phone to peruse her social media and news sites.

What she spotted first was a message from Carter.

Carter: *Hoping to grab a few hours of sleep. Will be by to pick you up at 1. See you then!*

Rather than reply and chance waking him if he didn't mute his phone because of the possibility of emergency work calls, Jillian decided to wait to send him a message until after noon. Since she still had a few hours before Carter would be there, she took her time getting out of bed and into the shower.

Shortly before one, she was ready for a few hours at the festival. She wore a pair of black jeans that had some stretch to them along with a burnt orange sweater that had a cowl neck and ended just past her hips. The denim jacket she wore was the same color as her jeans and ended just at her waist.

Knowing she was going to be on her feet for several hours, she chose a pair of brown knee-high boots with just a bit of a heel. Her hair was up in a twist, and she'd chosen a pair of gold teardrop earrings as well as a few rings on her fingers for her jewelry.

She'd always liked wearing rings on several fingers, but she'd gotten out of that habit in recent years. Some of her favorite rings had gone missing during her kidnapping, but she'd recently begun to replace them, and that day seemed like the perfect time to show them off.

When her doorbell chimed, Jillian hurried to open the door, smiling at Carter when she spotted him standing on her porch. "Hey. C'mon in. I just need to grab my purse and phone."

"Well, hello, Dolly," Carter said, then chuckled. "Did your grandma get a kick out of people saying that to her cat?"

"Yes, I think she did." Jillian went back to the front entryway, looking down at where Carter had knelt to pet Dolly. "After a while, I think people who visited us often did it just to hear Grandma laugh."

Carter got to his feet. "Did your grandma attend the church we do now?"

Jillian shook her head. "She attended one of the other churches in town. It was the one she and my grandpa went to when they first moved here."

"I did wonder why I didn't recognize her when I realized that she would have still been in town when I moved here."

"Yeah. She was very much attached to her church social group. They'd supported her...and me too when I was younger...through quite a bit."

"Did you come back much over that time?"

"Not a lot, no. I only came back for things like Thanksgiving and Christmas, and when I was here, I went to church with her. During the summer, I stayed in Portland to work. There were more job opportunities there."

"I guess that explains why our paths didn't cross before now."

"Yeah. I tended to stick close to home and Grandma when I was here." After she'd set the alarm, they left the house and climbed into Carter's truck.

"I think I'm going to park at the church, then we can walk to Main Street."

"Sounds like a good plan, as I would think parking on the streets around it will be a bit of a nightmare. That's if the festival is as popular as it used to be."

"Oh, it's still popular. Very popular."

Jillian could see what he meant a short time later as they walked toward the street. A Ferris Wheel, as well as a few smaller rides for younger kids, took up a section of the street that had been blocked off, and all around the area, booths had been set up with food and crafts for sale. They wandered along the street, checking out the various stalls for a bit before they had to report for duty at the church booth.

At some point, as they'd wandered through a crowd, Carter had taken her hand then never let it go. When they showed up at the church booth, the couple who had been manning it greeted them with smiles.

"Carter, good to see you," the man said as he held out his hand. "I assume you're our replacements."

Carter shook his hand. "Yes, we are."

"It's been fairly steady," the woman said. "Leah and Nadine went to fetch some more stuff from the church."

The couple took a few minutes to show them the ropes, then they headed off to enjoy the festival. Leah and Nadine showed up a few minutes later with more goodies, but they didn't linger.

It didn't take long for people to begin approaching the booth. She and Carter quickly fell into roles with Carter filling orders and Jillian taking care of payments. Though all the baked goods had been donated by church members, they were charging for the items in order to raise money for a homeless shelter in Everett.

Jillian once again noticed the looks of interest sent in Carter's direction, but as usual, he ignored them all. Except when it was a particularly persistent flirter, then he would touch Jillian on the back or call her sweetheart. That seemed to do the trick most of the time, but if someone made a second trip back to flirt some more, Carter just filled their order while Jillian happily took their money for the second time, and they still left without having gained his attention.

The hour flew by surprisingly fast, and the next people in charge of the booth showed up to relieve them. Carter snagged a couple of chocolate chip cookies and handed over some money for them before giving one to Jillian.

"Let's go wander a bit more," Carter said. "Maybe find some hot cider or cocoa."

"I'm on board with that."

Carter offered his arm, and they began to make their way down the street, munching on cookies. "Let's hope we have no excitement at this Festival like we had last year."

"What happened last year?"

"Sheila's mom attacked Anna during the Festival because she was apparently convinced that as long as Eli was dating Anna, Sheila wouldn't come back."

"What?" Jillian looked up at Carter. "Isn't it presumed that Sheila is dead?"

Carter shrugged. "Honestly, the theory seems to vary depending on who you talk to. Of course, most of the people do hope she's somewhere still alive."

"Well, then yes, I do hope we don't have that type of excitement this year."

They found a booth where they purchased drinks. Carter chose a hot cider while Jillian opted for hot cocoa. She took his offered arm again as they continued walking around, sipping on their drinks.

Jillian was drawn to the craft booths that were set up alongside the food ones. She didn't remember those from her times at the Festival as a teen, but that didn't mean they hadn't been there, since at that age she hadn't really been on the look-out for them.

Carter didn't seem impatient with her as she looked over the crafts that people were selling. She found one of the booths that was selling knitted things, and she was immediately thrown back to the times she'd spent in front of the fireplace on cold evenings with her grandma, learning how to knit. Jillian had loved those moments because it was during those times she'd known without a doubt that she was loved and that she didn't have to be anyone but herself.

She could take off her makeup, change out of the fashionable attire she wore to school into something more comfortable, and just relax. They'd talked about so much, just the two of them, and Jillian treasured the memory of those moments even more now that her grandma was gone.

Running her fingers over the knitted products at the booth, Jillian made the decision that she was going to get back to knitting. Maybe it would be something that would help her with her anxiety, as she'd always found it a calming hobby. She'd done a little of it after her grandma had moved to Portland. As her health had declined, it was one thing her grandma could still do, though much more slowly than she'd once been able to.

Resolved to dig out the yarn and knitting needles she'd never gotten rid of after her grandmother's death, Jillian turned away from the booth. She noticed that Carter was talking to a couple of guys. They had a similar build to Carter, and as the three stood there together, she realized that it was likely they also worked at the fire station.

She and Carter had agreed to be public about their relationship with their friends and at church, but she wasn't sure how he felt about his co-workers knowing about them. Rather than joining him, she wandered away to look at more craft booths. They were supposed to meet up with some of the others from their group around five, so they still had time to kill.

When Carter caught up with her a short time later, he said, "That is what I'd imagine having a child would be like."

"What do you mean?"

"One minute you were there, the next you were gone." He gave a soft chuckle. "I thought I'd lost you."

Jillian laughed. "You looked busy, so I figured I'd just keep looking at the crafts."

"It was just some of the guys from my shift at the station. As if I didn't spend enough time with them yesterday."

They wandered away from the craft booths, moving slowly through the ever-increasing crowds. As the day wore on, there seemed to be a steady influx of teens who appeared to be more interested in the rides and the food than in the crafts.

"Sometimes, I feel like I was never that young," Carter said.

"You're not *that* old," Jillian said then paused. "Are you?"

"I'm older than you."

She laughed. "I had sort of figured that out."

"Let's just say I'm in my thirties and leave it at that."

"Well, we can say I'm in my mid-twenties and leave it at that."

They were stopped a few more times by people they knew. Some were people from school. Some from the church.

Then an older African American couple, an imposing man with a bald head, and a curvy woman with a friendly smile and sparkling eyes, greeted Carter with obvious affection.

"Carter," the man said with a wide smile as he smacked Carter on the shoulder. "I'm so glad to see you out and about enjoying the festival."

"And who is this enjoying it with you?" the woman asked, curiosity clear on her face as she looked from Carter to Jillian.

"This is Jillian Hall." Carter's hand rested briefly on her back. "Jillian, this is Stuart and Vera Price. Stuart is the fire chief. In other words, my boss."

"And what a privilege it is to boss him around," the man said with a deep laugh. "But seriously, it's an absolute joy to have Carter in my station. He's a wonderful man."

"Yes." Jillian glanced up at Carter. "He certainly is."

"I'm just so glad to meet *you*," Vera said as she reached out and took Jillian's hand in hers. "You and Carter must come for dinner."

Jillian looked at Carter again, still not sure how he wanted to play this with the people from his work. However, all he did was smile.

"That would be lovely," she said, looking back at Vera.

"What do you do for work?" the older woman asked.

"I teach third grade at the elementary school."

"Really?" The answer seemed to please the woman immensely. "I was a teacher too. I taught sixth grade before I decided to retire."

"My grandma taught middle school," Jillian said.

"Here in New Hope?" When Jillian nodded, Vera asked, "What was her name?"

"Margaret Hall."

"Oh, I remember Margaret. She's a lovely woman and such a great teacher. The students definitely loved her."

"They did. I loved her too. Very much."

Vera frowned at her words. "How is she?"

"My grandma passed away earlier this year."

"I don't remember hearing about that."

"She was living with me in Portland when she was diagnosed with cancer last year."

"I'm so sorry to hear that," Vera said, moving to wrap her arms around Jillian. She gave her a tight squeeze then stepped back. "You have my condolences on your loss."

"Thank you." Jillian felt a pang of loss, but it was still nice to meet someone who had known her grandma and spoke so highly of her.

"Well, we'll let you two continue on with your Festival experience," Stuart said as he laid his arm on his wife's shoulder, tucking her against his side. "But we'll line up a meal soon."

After they said goodbye, Jillian walked in silence, her mind caught up in how their lives were getting more complicated. As far as she was concerned, they could continue on with the initial agreement until one of them called it quits on the casual relationship. She was comfortable with Carter in a way she hadn't expected to ever be with a man again, but what they had was friendship. Nothing more.

However, she was also well aware that they couldn't just go on as a casual couple indefinitely. Eventually, people would start to ask when they'd be getting engaged and married.

"You okay?" Carter asked.

She glanced at him, then nodded. "Just realizing we never really talked about whether you wanted your co-workers to know about us."

"That's not a problem. I don't care if they know. Maybe it will help to get them off my back. They always want to set me up with their single friends, or their girlfriends' best friend, or their sisters. Now, hopefully, that will all stop."

"Is that why you wanted this arrangement?" Jillian asked.

Carter hesitated before he said, "Partly. I have other reasons, as well."

She waited for him to expound on the 'other reasons,' but he didn't say anything more. "Your boss and his wife seem very nice."

"They are. He's a great boss. I hope that I'm even half as good in my dealings with the people at the station as he is."

"I'm sure you are," Jillian assured him. "You've always been wonderfully patient with me, so I'm sure you've been that way with your co-workers."

"I try."

Jillian found herself even more curious about Carter's motives, and for the first time ever, she considered sharing her reasons with him. But the Fall Festival was hardly the time or place to have such a discussion, even if she was one hundred percent convinced she wanted to share that part of her life with him...Which she wasn't.

Letting the subject go for the time being, she took his arm once again as they made their way toward the church where they were going to meet their friends.

"Your pies and cupcakes all sold," Leah told Jillian when they got back to the hall at the church.

"Oh, that's good news." Jillian had worried that hers would be the only ones left over. Her grandma would have been happy that her baking lessons over the years had taken root.

"You didn't tell me which ones you made," Carter said. "Did you save any for me?"

"I do have some left at the house. When you drop me off, I'll get them for you." She'd planned to give them to him anyway.

Sarah came into the hall with Beau, Rhett, and Julianna in tow. When she spotted Jillian, she came right over to her. "How's your day going? Enjoying the Festival?"

"I am. Though I have to say, it's a little different attending now than when we were teens."

Sarah laughed. "Isn't that the truth? Although I'm quite happy I'm here with Beau over any of those boys I thought were cute in high school."

"Can't argue with that," Jillian agreed.

"Nice you've been able to join us today, Carter," Julianna said as she smiled in his direction.

"Work took precedence yesterday," Carter said. "But Jillian takes precedence today."

"Lucky girl," Julianna replied.

"No." Carter shook his head. "I'm the lucky one."

Jillian felt warmth spread through her. The thing was, Carter sounded quite sincere. He was definitely a great actor, but really, Julianna was correct. Jillian *was* lucky to have Carter in her life. His help with her panic attacks. His willingness to take on Martin. His patience. His consideration.

Yeah, she was definitely getting more from Carter than he was from her. Even as far as friendships go, it was fairly one-sided. That didn't make Jillian feel good at all.

"So, what's the plan?" Beau asked.

Jillian suddenly wished her plan was to go home and hide for the rest of the night while she tried to figure out a way to make what she had with Carter a little less lopsided. Unfortunately, that wasn't the plan that she'd agreed to earlier.

"There's food," Carter said. "If you don't mind typical fair food."

"What is typical fair food?" Rhett asked.

"Well, in the case of this fair, a variety of food truck types of food. Hotdogs. French fries."

"Corn dogs. Hamburgers. Pulled pork buns. Fried pickles," Kieran added.

Julianna groaned. "That all sounds so fatty. Usually, I'm all about tasty food, but honestly, this sounds too much, even for me."

"I'm ready," Rhett said, rubbing his hands together. "Point me to the pulled pork buns and fried pickles."

"I'll show you the way, young man," Kieran said. "Let's go."

And with that, they left the church again after promising Nadine they'd be back to help clear away the tables and chairs before the evening was over.

Back up on Main Street, it took a bit for people to decide on the food they wanted, then they all headed up to Cara's apartment to eat. Being able to eat while looking out over the crowds was kind of fun. It was a beautiful sight as the sun began to set, and the lights on the Ferris Wheel were more clearly visible. Lights were also strung up around booths and between the lamp posts on the street.

Jillian stood close to the glass after she'd finished her food, soaking it all in. Her grandma would have loved this view, then she would have wanted to go back down to immerse herself in the sights, sounds, and smells of the Festival.

"Everyone ready to head back?" Kieran called out.

Jillian turned away from the window and let her gaze sweep over the group gathered there before moving to help Cara and Sarah clean up. It didn't take long, and soon they were back out on the street.

"I want to go on the Ferris Wheel," Sarah said, hooking her arm through Jillian's. "Are you coming?"

Jillian peered up at the large rotating wheel and decided that she would like to see what the town looked like from up there. "Sure. Why not?"

"Do you think Carter might want to go too?" Sarah asked, looking around.

"No clue. We didn't really talk about it."

"Beau said he'd go, so let's talk Carter into going so he can ride with you."

"Maybe Leah would like to go up with me," Jillian said.

Sarah gave her a perplexed look. "You'd rather go on the Ferris Wheel with Leah than with Carter?"

"Not saying that. Just that maybe Leah would like to go up, and if so, I'll go with her."

"She might," Sarah said with a shrug. "She could go with Rhett or Julianna."

Jillian shifted closer and lowered her voice. "But would she *want* to go with Rhett or Julianna?"

Sarah laughed. "I think we both know the answer to that."

"Well, let's see who all wants to go."

After much discussion, Rhett revealed a slight fear of heights so passed on the ride. Kieran, Cara, Julianna, and Leah also decided not to go up. In the end, it was just Beau and Sarah, Anna and Eli, and Jillian going up. Carter had disappeared somewhere between Cara's and the Ferris Wheel.

Jillian told herself that enjoying the view was not dependent on Carter being with her. In fact, having him along might have turned it into too much of a romantic outing, which wasn't what they needed. So she got in line with the two couples and a lot of teenagers.

CHAPTER TWENTY-FIVE

Carter looked around to see if he could spot his friends. He'd been on his way with the group heading toward the Ferris Wheel when he'd felt his phone vibrate. After he'd seen Evelyn's name on the screen, he knew he needed to answer it. He'd let Kieran know he had to take a call since Jillian was walking a bit in front of him with Sarah and Cara, then he'd stepped out of the way of others on the road to answer the call.

Unfortunately, it hadn't been a great conversation, especially since it hadn't been that long ago since Suzanne had been sick. For some reason, fall was the time that illness found Suzanne over and over again. After receiving the news that she was sick again, the last place he wanted to be was surrounded by the lights and laughter of the Fall Festival.

Letting out a sigh, he slowly walked closer to the Ferris Wheel. After looking around a bit more, he finally spotted Kieran and Cara and made his way over to where they stood. When he joined them, he saw others from their group with the couple, but there was no sign of Jillian.

"Where's Jillian?" he asked as he joined them.

Julianna laughed. "Did you lose your girlfriend?"

Carter felt anger rise within him, not just because he wasn't in the mood for humor, but because even though Suzanne technically was no longer his girlfriend, the idea he might lose her created a piercing ache in his chest. Knowing that she meant Jillian, he just ignored Julianna and turned to look at Kieran. The man lifted his brows, then pointed up.

"She's on the Ferris Wheel?"

"Yep. She went on it with Beau, Sarah, Eli and Anna."

Carter felt like he'd let Jillian down by not being there to go up with her, but they hadn't discussed going on the ride before he'd stopped to take the phone call from Evelyn.

With a sigh, he put his hands on his hips and stared up at the wheel, watching as it did a slow turn then came to a stop. He wondered if Jillian was at the top, looking out over the Festival. Though he might be unhappy with the news Evelyn had given him about Suzanne suffering from yet another respiratory infection, he thought that maybe a turn on the ride with Jillian might have been soothing.

He stayed with the group, listening to them chat as he waited for Jillian to reappear. When he finally spotted her walking away from the ride with the others, Carter headed toward her.

"Fancy another go 'round?" Carter asked when he reached her.

"You want to go for a ride?"

"Sure. If you don't mind going again."

"I don't mind at all," she said. "I'm sorry. I would have waited if I'd known you wanted to go."

"Let me just talk to Kieran for a second." At her nod, he went to Kieran. "I'm going to go up on the wheel with Jillian, then I think we might leave for a bit. If you could text me when you guys are headed back to the church to clean up, I'll meet you there to help."

Kieran reached out and gripped his shoulder. "Everything okay?"

Carter hesitated then said, "Just got a bit of not-so-great news."

"Anything you want to share?" the man asked.

"Not at the moment."

"Fair enough. I'll be praying for you. If you need to talk, you know where to find me."

"Thanks." Carter walked to where Jillian waited and took her hand as they headed back to the Ferris Wheel.

There was a bit of a wait, but Carter didn't feel obliged to hold a conversation as it was quite noisy around them. When it was finally their turn to get on, Carter waited as Jillian settled on the seat before sitting down beside her. It was a bit of a tight fit, so he rested his arm along the back of the seat, gripping her shoulder as the ride lurched into motion.

The wheel had a few stops and starts before it started to gain a bit more speed. As they reached the top of the wheel, Carter stared out at the twinkling lights of the town below. He took a deep breath and let it out, allowing the soothing movement and the beauty of the view along with Jillian's presence to calm him.

When they reached the top and stayed there for a bit, Carter asked, "Do you mind if we maybe head back to your place after this ride?"

Without any hesitation, she said, "Not at all."

They finished the ride in silence, and when they got off, Carter said, "Thank you for taking another ride on the wheel."

"Believe me, it wasn't a hardship."

"And you're sure you're okay with leaving a bit early?"

"I'm perfectly fine with it, actually."

Dodging groups of young people, they made their way back to the church where his truck waited. From there, it didn't take long to get back to her house.

"Did you want to come in and get your baked goods?" Jillian asked.

"Sure. I'd like that."

He followed her into the house, stooping to pick Dolly up while Jillian took off her jacket.

"Would you like a cup of coffee?" Jillian asked after she'd hung up her jacket and taken off her boots, smiling when she caught sight of him with Dolly in his arms.

"That would be nice. Thank you."

When Jillian headed for the kitchen, Carter set Dolly back down then followed her.

"Do you prefer decaf?" Jillian asked as she headed to a cupboard. "Go ahead and have a seat, if you'd like."

Carter settled onto one of the dark, padded, high back bar stools at the island counter. "Regular is fine."

Though he could see a fancy coffee machine on the counter, Jillian ignored that and went about making coffee in a glass pitcher-looking thing. He was used to his twenty-dollar coffee maker, and he had never paid for the fancy coffees that other people seemed to really like. Over the years, he'd learned to enjoy a plain cup of coffee without any cream or sugar.

As he sat there, taking in the beautiful bright kitchen, Carter was struck by how perfect the home was for a family. "Have you lived here long?"

Jillian turned from the cupboard with a mug in her hand. "You could say that. Until I moved to Portland for college, this was the only place I'd ever lived. My grandpa built this house just before I was born. When she left the hospital, my mom brought me home to this house."

"And you inherited it?"

Jillian nodded. "We haven't heard from my mom in years. We lost contact with her within a couple of years of her leaving New Hope. She didn't come to my graduation from high school or college. I'm not even sure where she is anymore. Anyway, since my grandma had adopted me, I was legally her daughter, so she left me everything. She also left me some money, and before she passed away, she told me to renovate the house exactly as I'd want it."

"You've done a good job. It looks really nice."

"Thank you." She gave him a quick smile then pressed a plunger looking thing on the top of the glass pitcher. As she poured the coffee into the mug, she asked, "Cream or sugar?"

"Just black, thanks."

She set the mug in front of him, then went back to the counter, picked up a couple of covered containers and brought them to the island. "So you have the option of a cupcake—chocolate or lemon— or banana bread with chocolate chips. I do have pie as well, but I figured I'd just send the whole thing home with you."

"Wow. I feel spoiled with so much choice."

Jillian smiled. "Or you can have one of everything. I won't tell anyone."

"How about I start with a lemon cupcake."

"It has raspberry frosting. Hope that's okay."

"That sounds delicious."

"I hope it tastes great. I'm not the baker Leah is, but my grandma made sure I knew the baking basics, which to her was banana bread and apple pie. She said it was prudent to know how to use up fruit that might be going bad, so I didn't have to throw it away."

"That sounds kind of like my mom." Carter had to admit that it had been forever since he'd felt a sense of home. His apartment, both the old one and the one he'd just moved into, had never been more than a place to lay his head.

He lifted his mug and took a sip of the coffee. "This is amazing."

"It is, isn't it," Jillian agreed. "I like good coffee."

"Well, this isn't just good coffee. This is *great* coffee."

When she put a plate with a cupcake on it in front of him, Carter stared at it for a long moment, suddenly feeling a deep longing to see his mom and the rest of his family. It had been a couple of years since he'd last seen them anywhere but on the small screen of his phone. His mom had been after him to come home for Christmas, but he'd always had an excuse, which usually was that he was covering shifts for guys who had families.

"I promise it tastes better than it looks," Jillian said softly. "I can bake pretty good, but my decorating skills aren't that great."

Carter looked up at her. "Sorry. It wasn't that at all."

He reached for the cupcake and began to peel the paper back from around it.

"Is everything okay?" she asked as she made herself a drink that had some frothy milk in it.

She wasn't looking at him, so it might have seemed that she didn't really care, but somehow, he knew that wasn't the case. Maybe she thought he'd be more apt to share if she wasn't focused on him, and he couldn't help but think that she was right.

He felt safe with her. Somewhere along the path of their casual dating arrangement, they'd become friends. He'd seen her at her most vulnerable, and he knew she trusted him. Suddenly he wanted her to know he trusted her too. He wanted her to know, to understand, the thing that made him most vulnerable.

"My friend is sick again."

Jillian came to stand across the island from him with her mug and a piece of banana bread. "The same one who was sick during Anna and Eli's wedding?"

Carter nodded as he broke off a piece of cupcake, but he just held it instead of eating it right away. "Her name is Suzanne, and she is...she *was* my fiancée."

Jillian's eyes went wide as her brows rose. "I'm sorry to hear that she's sick again."

"I worry because she had a traumatic brain injury ten years ago, and she's been in a vegetative state ever since."

The shock was clear on Jillian's face. "I...I don't know what to say."

Carter nodded. "It's a situation most people haven't faced."

"Is she around here? Are you able to see her?"

"Yes. She's in a care home in Seattle."

"Were you still engaged when she was injured?"

Carter ate the bite of cupcake he held then took a sip of coffee. "I was still engaged to her until the day I first came by your classroom last month."

Jillian's brow furrowed. "I'm afraid I don't understand."

Through bites of cupcake and sips of coffee, Carter started at the beginning, telling her everything. At some point, Jillian came around to sit on one of the bar stools. She angled her seat so she could still see him. Never asking him questions, just letting him talk.

"I'm so sorry you had to go through that," Jillian said when he stopped talking. "And that Suzanne was injured so badly."

"I hope you're still okay with our arrangement, knowing all of that."

"Of course, I am. It doesn't change anything for me."

"If someday you'd like to meet Evelyn and Garth, I know they'd like to meet you."

"But they don't know that we have an arrangement, right?"

"No, and I'd like to keep it that way. They just want something for me that I'm not interested in, so if you're still willing to keep things as they've been, I'd appreciate that."

She gave him a quick smile. "I'm fine with keeping things as they've been."

"I'm glad because, honestly, I don't think I'd want to have this understanding with anyone else."

A look passed across Jillian's face that Carter couldn't identify. But it disappeared too quickly for him to figure it out.

"Does anyone else know about this?" Jillian asked. "Like Eli or Kieran?"

Carter shook his head. "It really doesn't paint me in the best light. Plus, it felt like I would be letting people too close if I told them."

"You don't feel that way about me?"

He lifted his mug to take another sip, only to discover it was empty. "No. I don't mind letting you that close. I get the feeling that even knowing the worst parts of the story, you're not judging me."

"I'm not. We all have moments of frustration and weakness. I think that makes us human, not monsters. I might feel differently if I felt you were trying to justify how you were in the right in the argument you and Suzanne were having, instead of admitting that you could have handled things differently."

"Thank you for being so understanding," Carter said, a sense of peace and relief washing over him.

"Going back to Suzanne being sick," Jillian began. "How serious is it for her?"

Carter explained what the doctors had been telling them over the years and how worrying it was whenever she got sick because of her ever-weakening body.

"I can understand now why you're so concerned for her," Jillian said. "And it must be so hard on her parents."

"It is," Carter agreed. "She's their only child, so I worry that once she's gone, they'll really struggle. Though her dad still works, her mom spends every day at the care home with Suzanne. She'll be lost without her."

"Will you leave New Hope if something happens to her?"

Carter paused for a moment to consider her words. That wasn't anything he'd really thought about, mainly because he didn't like thinking about the time when Suzanne would no longer be with them. But thinking about it then, the answer came pretty quickly to him.

"No. I've made a home here, plus I have a job here that I really enjoy."

"I wasn't sure I'd ever come back to New Hope. It had been my plan, with my grandma's encouragement and blessing, to pursue a life away from here. But there came a point when my grandma passed away that I needed the comfort and safety of home."

Having experienced her panic attacks, he could understand that. He wanted to ask her more about what might have caused them, but something told him that while she trusted him enough to rely on him during the attacks, she wasn't ready to tell him more.

His phone beeped, and since he was expecting a text from Kieran, he pulled it out of his pocket.

Kieran: *Don't worry about coming back to the church. We had enough guys to get everything put away. Hope you're okay. Call me if you want to chat.*

Carter hadn't even realized the time, but when he did, he figured he should probably head for home soon.

Thanks for letting me know. Appreciate the offer to listen. Will keep it in mind.

Kieran: *Anytime. See you tomorrow.*

Carter sent him a thumbs up then slid his phone back into his pocket. When he looked up, he saw that Jillian had cleared away their cups and plates.

"Thank you so much for the coffee, cupcake, and for listening."

She smiled at him as she moved the containers to the island and opened them up. "I'm glad it all helped."

"My mom was a firm believer in feeding us tasty treats, so we'd feel better. And it was her way of making us talk too."

"My grandma was the same way."

He watched as she set an empty container on the counter and began to transfer cupcakes and some banana bread into it. When she was done, she put the lid on it then set another container on top of it.

"Hope you like apple pie," she said, tapping the top container.

"I do," Carter confirmed. "It's my second favorite pie."

Jillian tilted her head. "What's your first favorite?"

"Chocolate with whipped cream," Carter said with a shrug. "What can I say? It was the pie my mom made the most, and all us kids loved it."

"I'll keep that in mind if I get the urge to make pie again. I haven't baked as much as I did these past few days in quite a while."

"Well, it was much appreciated, and not just by me."

Jillian's cheeks pinked a bit as she smiled. She lifted the containers to the raised portion of the island in front of him. "Just bring me back the empty containers."

"That won't be a problem." Carter got to his feet. "But I should probably head home. I'm feeling the effects of not enough sleep in the past twenty-four hours."

"I'm glad you were able to come to the Festival for a few hours." Jillian followed him as he walked from the kitchen to the front door. "I enjoyed attending it again after a few years away."

"Goodnight, Dolly," Carter said, bending over to pet the cat. "Goodnight, Jillian. See you tomorrow."

As Carter drove home from Jillian's, he was glad that he'd taken a chance on telling her about everything. That he'd been right in assuming she'd offer him a safe place to share.

People might have questioned if entering into a casual dating arrangement with Jillian was a good idea. Still, Carter knew that it was the best decision he'd made in a very long time.

CHAPTER TWENTY-SIX

Jillian couldn't find a parking spot close to the gallery, so she circled around the block again and settled for one a bit further away. Once she'd parked, she sat back in her seat and glared at the rain that streaked down the windows. It was bad enough that she was late, but now she was going to be late and *wet.*

She should have been used to the rain after having lived in the northwest for her whole life, but that didn't make it any more tolerable when she was dressed up. Though she had an umbrella, she sat there for a few more minutes, waiting to see if it would let up.

The past two weeks had been a roller coaster ride...and not necessarily the fun kind. As she'd expected, her life had become rockier once she started meeting with her new therapist, with more nightmares and heightened baseline anxiety. The nightmares had trigged the panic attacks, which created a double whammy that was hard for her to recover from each night.

But she had survived, even if she was exhausted, and now she wanted to enjoy the evening celebrating the opening of Sarah's art show. If only the rain would lighten up.

Though she'd planned to be there right at the opening, she'd come home from school and crashed for a couple of hours—an hour longer than she'd planned. That meant that after taking the time to make herself presentable, she was fashionably late.

Leaning over, Jillian opened her glove box and pulled out the folded umbrella she kept there. It took a bit of quick handwork to get her door opened and the umbrella up and opened so that she didn't get soaked, but she managed it.

The light from streetlamps overhead reflected in the puddles of water that had collected on the sidewalk. Most businesses, like the bookstore, were closed—their windows dark. The gallery, however, was lit up, warm light spilling out of its large glass windows—a bright beacon in the dark October night.

Jillian paused for a moment with her umbrella, taking in the sight through the window. There was a good number of people milling around inside. Not that there had been much doubt that their whole friend group, along with Sarah's family, would be out in force for the opening.

Exhaustion teased the edges of her mind, but she pushed it away and headed inside.

"Hey, Jillian," Cara said with a sparkling smile as she approached her. "I wasn't sure if you were going to make it."

"It's been a bit of a week," Jillian admitted. Cara, Anna, and Sarah were aware of her return to therapy, and she'd let them know that she was struggling with having to recount the trauma in her past and in more recent events.

"Ah, sweetie." Cara gave her a quick hug. "I've been praying for you."

"Thank you. I really appreciate that."

"I'm glad you are able to be here. Come look at some paintings."

Jillian glanced around, her gaze landing on Carter, where he stood talking with Rhett, Julianna, and Kieran. She felt a pang of something in her chest. Something she wasn't interested in analyzing, so she turned back to Cara.

"You're in some of these, right?"

Cara looped her arm through Jillian's. "I am, but not my face."

"Well, show me."

It didn't take long to weave through the crowd to get to where the paintings of Cara hung. They were a variety of sizes and done with various mediums. Jillian had known Sarah was talented, but seeing the evidence displayed in this artwork took her breath away.

"She is *so* talented, and you are *so* beautiful."

"I think Sarah's talents came into play more than my looks."

Jillian decided not to argue with her, given that Cara was one to brush away compliments all the time. "Did she do one for you and Kieran to keep?"

"She did, but it was a bit different. Kieran's in it with me. We called it our engagement photo. I'll show you next time you're over." Cara tugged on her arm. "You need to see the ones of Beau."

Jillian allowed herself to be led around to the different paintings. There was a real variety in the show, and from the murmured conversation she heard as they moved around the gallery, people were very impressed by Sarah's work.

When they finally found Sarah, she was standing with Beau, talking to a couple of people in front of a painting of Eli's cabin. As she waited to speak with Sarah, Jillian fought against another wave of weariness.

She knew that she should speak with Carter too. They hadn't spent much time together since that evening when he'd told her about Suzanne. It hadn't been intentional on her part. Their work schedules had kept them both busy, plus her therapy had tied up a couple of evenings each week. He'd also worked the previous Sunday, so they hadn't even seen each other at church that day.

The thing was, while she'd missed being around him and would have appreciated his support as she'd struggled with her therapy sessions, the distance had been necessary.

She'd had a realization after Carter had laid his past out for her. While her mind and body might be determined to not ever allow physical intimacies with a man to develop, her heart didn't necessarily feel the same way. Her heart wanted more...too much more.

Just the fact that every now and then she felt a twinge of jealousy—even if she didn't want to acknowledge it—was evidence enough that her heart was vulnerable. And Carter, with his silent strength that he offered her without reservation, was everything she might have once wanted in a man...in a husband.

"I was starting to get worried." Carter's voice made her heart skip a beat, and warmth flooded her cheeks. "Have you been here long?"

She turned to face him, taking in the pressed black slacks he wore along with a long-sleeve button-up shirt in a shade of blue that closely matched his eyes. His wavy blond hair was styled, and his face was clean-shaven.

"Not too long. I was late getting here, then Cara took me to see her paintings."

Carter stared at her for a moment before glancing around. "Sarah is truly talented. I really had no idea."

"She was always drawing in class when we were in school, and her drawings were always so impressive, but she's improved even more since then. I could never do much beyond stick figures. I honestly think some of my students now already draw better than I do."

"Well, I'm right there with you."

"Hey, you two," Beau said as he approached them. "So glad you could make it."

"Wouldn't have missed it for the world," Jillian told him. "Even if I was a bit late."

"I know Sarah is just glad you're here."

"He's right," Sarah said, slipping her arm around Beau's waist. "I'm so grateful you could make it."

Sarah moved from Beau's side to give Jillian a hug. "You doing okay?"

"I'm fine," Jillian said. "Just tired."

"I can imagine. Still having trouble sleeping?"

Jillian might have neglected to mention to Sarah and the other women that she hadn't told Carter about her trips to therapy yet or the toll it was taking on her. She could feel Carter's gaze on her as she shrugged.

"Some nights are better than others."

"I'm sure you're glad it's the weekend."

"I am," Jillian agreed. "I love my class, but I'm ready for a couple days to myself."

"Well, if you need to talk, feel free to call me. Once this is over, I'll have some breathing room. Maybe we can go for coffee."

"Are we still up for Fondue Friday next week?" Jillian asked.

"We'd better be. After canceling the last one, I'm ready for this one."

"Me, too. We can have it at my place."

"As long as it's not too much work for you."

"It'll be fine." Or at least Jillian hoped it would be since she had a couple more sessions with the therapist that week.

"I'd better keep circulating." Sarah gave her another hug. "Thank you both for coming."

After Sarah and Beau had moved away, Jillian braced herself for questions from Carter. He'd always been concerned about her well-being. And while she had appreciated that from him in the past, she was starting to worry about becoming too dependent on him. Too vulnerable to him.

As far as she was concerned, dependency and vulnerability had no place in their casual dating arrangement. But she'd started to develop both early on because of her panic attacks. However, while it was clear that Carter's emotions and heart were still engaged in his fiancée—ex-fiancée—which meant there was no danger of him developing feelings for her, the same wasn't true for Jillian.

She felt Carter's hand on her back as he guided them off to the side. There was classical music playing softly, the perfect background to the murmurs of conversation throughout the gallery. For a moment, she wished they were somewhere that the music or other conversations would preclude them from having one themselves.

"What's been going on?" Carter asked, bending his head down closer to hers. "Sarah seemed concerned about you."

Jillian crossed her arms, running her hands up and down her biceps to ward off the sudden chill that had invaded her body. "I've been going to therapy. It's been bringing up some old stuff that has been...draining."

"Why didn't you tell me?"

She glanced up at him. "There was nothing you could do."

He frowned. "Maybe not. But at the very least, I could have prayed for you."

"I'm sorry."

"No," he said softly as he took her hand gently. "Don't apologize. I don't mean to force you to confide in me. I just want you to know that I'm there for you the way you were there for me. It's a two-way street, you know. I'd like to think that, at the very least, we have a friendship."

"We do," Jillian assured him. "But it's hard for me..."

She knew she couldn't tell him why it was hard for her. Not without telling him everything, and that just wasn't going to happen.

"What would make it easier? Is there something I'm doing that's making it difficult for you to confide in me?"

If only he knew. "I'm just not used to confiding in guys, to be honest. It's easier to share with my female friends."

"I get that. I really do." He sighed, his hand tightening around hers briefly. "I guess I just want to feel like you trust me."

"I *do* trust you," she told him earnestly, needing him to believe that. "If I didn't, I wouldn't have let you help me with my panic attacks."

Carter gave a huff of laughter, rather humorless if Jillian interpreted it correctly. "You didn't have much of a choice, if I recall."

"Maybe, but I also let you into my home, which honestly, is a huge step of trust for me."

He nodded at that. "Still, I wish..." He lifted his hand and rubbed the back of his neck. "I want to have more trust between us."

"You know that's not necessary for our arrangement, right?" she asked.

"I know," he said with a nod. "However, I've been feeling like our friendship could be one of the best ones I've ever had. But maybe I'm alone in thinking that."

Jillian dropped her gaze to the floor. Her heart wanted that. Oh, how it wanted that. And it was because of that longing that she knew it just wasn't something she could offer him. Still, she didn't want to hurt him because he had come to mean something to her, whether she wanted to fully accept that or not.

"I do appreciate our friendship. More than you will ever know." And it was no word of a lie. "I'll try to share things with you, but is just some stuff I can't tell you."

"I understand that," Carter said. "I just want you to know you can come to me with anything."

"I know that." Jillian looked up to meet his gaze and gave him a small smile—all she felt capable of at that moment. She wished that she could tell him that he was helping to restore her faith in men, but that would lead to too many questions.

She knew that his concern for her was just a part of who he was. The fact that he'd stayed engaged to his fiancée for so long, even after knowing that she'd never recover from the severe brain injury, revealed how deeply he cared. His concern each time Suzanne got sick. His devotion to visiting her each week. His choice of career.

All of it added up to a person who seemed to need to care for those close to him. But that care and concern—when it was aimed at her especially—tugged at her heartstrings. In a lot of ways, he reminded her of her grandpa. He'd always been so gentle with her, but he'd had a strength that she'd only learned about later from her grandma when she'd talked about how he dealt with his job as a trauma surgeon. Until a heart attack had taken him from them.

"This probably wasn't the best place to have this discussion," Carter said with a frown as he glanced over his shoulder. "Have you had a drink or anything to eat? Leah must've been baking for weeks if the amount of food is any indication."

"I haven't had anything yet." Because of the extra-long nap, she'd run out of time to eat dinner.

"Then let's find something." Carter offered his arm then walked her through the small groups of people to the part of the gallery where food and drink had been set up for the evening.

Jillian had no idea if food and drink was a usual part of the opening for a show like Sarah's since she'd never been to one before. Still, it didn't surprise her to find it there. Likely it was Leah's way of being part of her sister's special event.

"My word," she said as she stared at the large table covered with yellow and blue tablecloths. "This is incredible."

Platters with a wide variety of bite-size appetizers covered the surface. There was a variety of different beverages, and though Jillian was tempted to opt for coffee, she also wanted to sleep that night...as long as there were no nightmares...so she settled for a glass of sparkling grape juice. After putting a few of the appetizers on a small plate, she followed Carter over to where some of their friends stood talking.

Neither she nor Carter joined in the conversation, and Jillian's thoughts kept drifting to the slowly deepening complexities of her arrangement with the man. She just didn't know what to do about them.

She couldn't allow herself to want anything more with Carter. She knew that, but her heart was wanting to beat just for him. So far, her mind and body were managing to overrule that feeling, but how long would that last?

And even if she was willing to let her heart take the lead, it wouldn't matter. She was pretty sure that guys like Carter would never want anything serious with a bigger girl like her. He could have his pick of any woman—like Julianna, for instance.

So why would he ever settle for someone like her? Someone with so much baggage. Someone whose emotional state was so fragile. Someone who no longer fit in with the world's conventional definition of beauty.

Yeah. She had so many reasons to keep her heart's desire from being what led her forward. If only those reasons could safeguard her heart.

CHAPTER TWENTY-SEVEN

November swept in with cooler temperatures, something that Carter felt right to his bones.

For so much of the past ten years, aside from one or two pivotal moments like when he made the move from Miami to Seattle and then Seattle to New Hope, his days and weeks had held to a pattern. It was a pattern marked by his shifts—one day on, two days off—his visits with Suzanne, time spent at the gym and church when his work allowed it.

His emotional journey during that time was also fairly steady. While most people had good days and bad days, he tended to have...so-so days and bad days. Days he considered "good" were the ones when he didn't receive any bad news about Suzanne. But any day when Suzanne didn't wake up could hardly be considered a good day. So, most days seemed to be a version of bad.

When he'd suggested the arrangement with Jillian, Carter had naively believed that things would continue on as usual. Sure, some things were still the same, but between Suzanne's continued health issues and his deepening concern for Jillian, he was starting to feel a bit overwhelmed.

At one time in his life, he'd embraced the whole range of his emotions.

His mom had always been a big proponent of expressing emotion—good or bad. She'd always told him it was okay to feel angry and sad, and to express that, as long he didn't say things he'd later regret. He remembered plenty of times when he'd get frustrated and angry as a teen. She'd listen to him, then encourage him to go spend some time by himself so he could vent his feelings without hurting anyone with his words.

She'd also encouraged him to express his happiness and love when he was feeling those things. And she'd led by example, showering her family with love and affection, showing them when she was happy, letting them know when she was sad or upset. He'd never feared emotions.

But the accident had changed everything. After the crushing weight of anguish and fear that first year, acceptance of his new normal had deadened his emotions. It had made dealing with everything easier. New people he'd met had just assumed he was introverted and quiet, not realizing that at one time, people had considered him the life of the party.

That day in Jillian's classroom had started a slow trickle of connection between him and his emotions once again. It hadn't been a jumpstart of things, just a subtle flow of emotion that had strengthened in the almost two months since that day. He was feeling things he hadn't felt in a long time. Things that he hadn't thought he'd ever feel again.

Suzanne would always hold a part of his heart, but it was as if his heart was now letting him know that it had room for more. So much more. He hadn't expected that to happen with anyone, let alone with Jillian.

But there was something about her—something about the two of them together—that had sparked a light in his heart that refused to be extinguished. The unfortunate thing was that he didn't think that Jillian felt the same way, and he wasn't sure what to do about that.

When he'd discovered he had feelings for Suzanne, he hadn't hesitated to tell her. To take a chance in hopes that she felt the same way. Something about Jillian, however, made Carter reluctant to be as open, and that made him a bit sad. While his feelings for Jillian were different than what he'd felt for Suzanne because he was a different man now, he knew that, given the opportunity, they could grow their relationship into something just as strong and solid.

As he pulled to a stop at the curb in front of Jillian's house, he pushed all those thoughts aside for the time being. The guys had been invited to another Fondue Friday with the ladies, and this time, Jillian was hosting it. They'd had to accommodate his schedule but had finally found a date that worked for everyone.

Carter was showing up a little earlier to help her, not that he thought she needed his help, but he didn't have anything else to do, and well, he wanted to spend some time with just her.

When he rang the doorbell, it took a few minutes before she answered, but when she did, she gave him a smile and stepped back to let him in. She wore a pair of fitted black pants and a long sweater in deep purple.

"It smells wonderful in here," he said as he took off his jacket. Dolly immediately greeted him with ankle rubs and meowing. "Hello there."

"She's going to be in heaven tonight with so much attention," Jillian said as she hung up his jacket then headed back to the kitchen. "Dolly is definitely not a selective cat when it comes to loving people. She just loves everyone. I'd always heard that cats were aloof sort of animals. Some days I think she's a dog in a cat's body."

"I like that about her," Carter said. "It makes me happy when she greets me like that."

Jillian gave him a curious look before she turned her attention to a pot on the stove. "I have to admit that her greeting is nice to come home to."

"So what are we having for dinner?" he asked as he joined her at the stove to look into the pot. "It smells delicious."

"After much debate, I decided on chicken and dumplings. My grandma's recipe. Today seemed like a good day for it."

"It's a perfect day for it," Carter agreed. "What can I do to help?"

"If you want to finish setting the table for me, that would be great." She pointed to the island. "I put everything out there."

Carter rounded the island and noticed the dark burgundy table-cloth that she'd already put on the table. There were chairs for eight people, so he picked up the stack of dishes and began to set them out.

"So two plates and these wide bowl things at each place?" Carter asked.

Jillian came over to the table. "Yeah. I was going to put the smaller plate under the pasta bowls, then this other plate up here to use for the salad."

"Okay." As he set out the plates, he asked her how her day had gone.

"Pretty good. Now that we're a couple of months into the school year, we've gotten into a good rhythm. Plus, I'm getting to know the kids better, and they're getting to know me. I'm really enjoying it."

As he came back to get the silverware, he asked, "Did you have therapy this week?"

They'd texted off and on through over the past several days, but he hesitated to start that discussion over text when he'd rather talk to her about it in person.

Her reply was slow in coming, and when he looked over at her, she was staring at the contents of the large pot on the stove. Finally, she said, "Yes. Just one session, though."

"Is that good? Just having one session?"

"Maybe?"

Jillian fell quiet for a moment as she dropped biscuit dough into the pot. Carter didn't say anything more, just continued setting the table while he waited for her to continue if she wanted to. He'd finished putting the glasses at each spot when she finally spoke again.

"The first few weeks, the therapist wanted two sessions a week because I was reliving some pretty...hard stuff."

"More than just the Martin stuff?" Carter asked, though he was sure he knew the answer.

"Yeah. More than the Martin stuff. Unfortunately, it meant that I've had more nightmares, along with more panic attacks. Thankfully, I didn't have any at school since there wasn't anything there to trigger me, now that Martin's gone."

At the mention of Martin and the school, Carter suddenly had a memory of how upset she'd been over the flowers the man had destroyed. He'd meant to get her another bouquet, but he'd been distracted by other stuff over the past several weeks. He would have to remedy that.

"Would you ever tell me what happened to you?"

The fact that she didn't shake her head right away encouraged him, but as she stood staring down at the stove, he could sense a battle within her.

"I don't like telling people about it," she finally said.

"Why?"

She picked up a cloth and began to wipe down the counter. Carter wondered again if she was going to respond, and he realized that he'd probably chosen a really bad time to question her about this. Going to her side, he lightly rested his hand on her back.

"You don't have to answer that," he told her. "It's none of my business."

She glanced over at him, her expression hard to read. "I don't want people to treat me differently."

Carter frowned. "Haven't you told anyone about it? Besides your therapist?"

"Yes. Sarah knows all of it, and she probably told Leah—with my permission. Cara and Anna know some of it."

"They don't seem to be treating you differently," Carter observed.

She shrugged, her gaze dropping to the dishcloth that she held tightly in her fists. "They did at first."

Carter was almost to the point of begging her to confide in him because it would mean that she trusted him, felt close enough to him, to tell him all about it. But his concern for her outweighed his need, so he pushed aside that desperate feeling and blew out a breath.

"I'm sorry." She looked up at his apology, a questioning look on her face. "I don't mean to push you to share more than you're comfortable with. I just want you to know that you're not alone. That there are people who care about you. Who have your back."

"I know that. I really do," she said.

There was something in her eyes then. Something that gave him hope. Not a lot, but enough that it fanned the flame that flickered in his heart to burn a bit brighter.

The ringing of the doorbell had them both turning toward the front door. Carter rubbed her back lightly before dropping his hand. "Want me to get that?"

"Do you mind?"

"Not at all." In fact, he liked that she accepted his presence in her home enough to allow him to answer the door.

"Good to see you, man," Eli greeted him as he gave him a quick bro hug.

Anna also gave him a hug, and Carter was reminded of a time when he hugged everyone he considered a friend. Maybe it was time to resurrect that part of him too.

They hadn't even left the entryway when the bell rang again. This time it was Sarah and Beau, and Cara and Kieran arrived shortly after. They all came bearing food for the fondue. While the women crowded into the kitchen with Jillian, Carter stayed with the men in the living room. With the open design of the area, however, it made it feel like they were still all together.

As he soaked in the atmosphere, Carter felt a brief pang of grief as he realized that this was once something he'd wanted to share with Suzanne. This gathering of friends. People who cared about him and who he cared about.

He hadn't thought that he'd ever be open to something like this again. But like his feelings for Jillian, it had snuck up on him, drawing him in before he'd really known what was happening.

A hand landed on his shoulder. "You okay?"

Carter looked from Jillian to Kieran. "I'm fine. Just realizing some things."

Kieran arched a brow. "Do tell."

"It's not really the time or place."

The other man's gaze shifted to the kitchen, where the women were helping Jillian finish up with the dinner. "I suppose not, but don't think I'll forget about it."

Carter grinned. "I know you won't."

As they gathered around the delicious food Jillian had prepared, conversation flowed smoothly. Some of it centered on the upcoming wedding, which Anna was helping Cara organize. Jillian and Sarah had been to try on dresses, and since they had only a short time until the wedding, it had been a bit urgent they find something they liked quickly.

Carter was glad to see that Jillian seemed to be enjoying the evening. He really needed to work on his timing of approaching things with her. But for now, he was going to stop asking her to share about her past. He wanted to focus on the future, and if that meant giving her space about her past, he'd do that.

They stayed at the table for the fondue part of the evening, and this time, since Carter knew what to expect, he found himself enjoying it more. Each time he gathered with these friends, he felt more settled.

When the evening was drawing to a close, and the couples were preparing to leave, Kieran shook his hand and said, "I won't forget."

Carter chuckled as he gave his head a shake. "Talk to you soon."

He had to work the next morning, so even though he would have liked to stay once the others had left, he couldn't. They'd all pitched in with the cleanup, so at least he wasn't leaving Jillian with a mess.

"I hope you enjoy your Saturday," he said as he shrugged into his jacket.

"Thank you. I plan to take it easy. I think it's supposed to rain, so I'm just going to stick close to home. Do a few things around the house."

"I'll be working, but feel free to text if you want. I'll answer when I can."

"Okay." Jillian crossed her arms, hugging herself as he turned to open the door. "Be safe."

"I'll certainly try."

Carter wanted to give her a hug, to just hold her close for a moment, but he held back. Until he had a chance to tell her how he felt about her, and she had an opportunity to respond, he wouldn't push for that. He wanted it to happen as soon as possible, but since he wasn't one hundred percent confident that she returned his feelings, he was also wary of doing it too soon.

So instead of doing what he longed to do, he just said goodnight then headed for his truck. As he pulled away from her house, Carter resolved to pray more, and maybe ask the guys to also pray for him and Jillian. If deepening this relationship wasn't God's will, then he didn't want to force things. But in his heart, he truly felt that God had been leading them in this direction, despite the unorthodox start to things.

"Do you have plans for Thanksgiving?" Eli asked him at church on the following Sunday.

"I usually work it, but Stuart insisted that for once, I take the holiday myself."

"So was that a yes, you have plans, or a no, you don't?"

Carter chuckled. "That was a no, I don't have plans."

"Okay, then," Eli said. "Come to the lodge at three on Thursday."

Carter hesitated. "I planned to check and see what Jillian was doing."

"No worries. She'll be there too."

"Then I'll see you on Thursday," Carter said. "What can I bring?"

Eli laughed. "I think Mom, Leah, and Anna have it all well in hand. So just bring yourself."

"I'll be there."

With a nod, Eli headed off, leaving Carter to look around for Jillian. He'd sat with her during the service, but once it was over, she'd gone to talk to someone while Eli had waylaid him. He'd wanted to see if she'd go for lunch with him.

When he spotted her standing at the back with Sarah and Leah, he scooted down the row then made his way up the aisle to where they stood.

"Hey, Carter," Sarah said as he joined them. "How's life?"

"Can't complain too much."

"Glad to hear it." She smiled at him. "What are your plans for Thanksgiving?"

"Apparently, I'm coming to the lodge." He glanced at Leah. "And Eli said I didn't need to bring anything."

"You don't," she agreed. "We've got everything covered."

"We're going to have a full house," Sarah said. "I'm excited for it."

Carter found that he was excited as well, and that was new for him. Typically, the holidays held no appeal. He tended to take the holiday shifts to give the guys with families the day off, but this year, he hadn't argued with Stuart about sticking to his regular shift schedule instead of switching around to free up the day for other firefighters.

He'd stated that Carter needed to spend the time with Jillian since their relationship was still so new. Carter hadn't bothered to enlighten him about their arrangement, and he'd happily taken the opportunity to spend more time with Jillian.

"Would you care to join me at *Norma's* for lunch?" Carter asked when Sarah and Leah had left them.

"Sure," Jillian said with only the barest of hesitation. "Haven't been there in a while."

"Then we must remedy that," Carter told her, hoping to coax a smile from her. He got the faintest of one and counted it a win. "Do you want to ride with me? I'll bring you back to your car afterward."

Jillian nodded. "That should be okay."

Given he'd expected her to say she'd drive herself, he was surprised but happy that she'd agreed to come with him. It was a bit ridiculous how happy it made him because it was only about a five-minute drive away.

As they walked into the restaurant, the hostess standing at the entryway greeted them with a friendly smile. She led them to a booth next to the windows at the front of the restaurant. After she left them with their menus, Carter glanced around the restaurant, recognizing quite a few faces.

They talked about the menu for a few minutes, so they were ready to place their order when the server appeared. Jillian entertained him with stories about her week with the kids as they waited for their food. Since he'd seen some of the kids' antics when he'd given presentations at the elementary school, Carter could believe even the more outlandish stories.

Once their food came, they gave thanks for it, then ate in silence for a few minutes before Jillian said, "How is Suzanne doing?"

For a moment, Carter wasn't sure he wanted to talk about Suzanne. She was a huge part of his life, but suddenly there was something in him that wanted to keep the various parts of his life separated, and he wasn't sure why. Suzanne would always be his first serious love, but it had taken a shove by Evelyn and then the arrangement with Jillian to make him wake up to the reality of his situation.

Suzanne wasn't coming back. Even if she woke up from her vegetative state, she wouldn't be the same person she'd been ten years ago. The toll her brain injury had taken on her physically would no doubt be apparent on her mentally as well. They would never have the relationship they'd once had.

If they'd been married, there would be no doubt that he would have stuck by her regardless. He would have been responsible for a wife in a way that he hadn't been for Suzanne as his fiancée. From the very start, her parents had made all the decisions when it came to Suzanne's care. They'd made it clear with their actions and words that they felt she was still more their responsibility than his.

Now that he was moving forward—now that the scale was tipping more toward the present and future than it had ever been before—he was struggling to find the new balance in his life.

"She's doing okay. It took some time for her to respond since it always seems that the first round of antibiotics they try never work. I'm not sure why that is. The one that worked previously doesn't always work the next time."

"That must be very hard on you and her parents."

Carter nodded. "Especially her mom, because she's the one who deals with the doctors and is with Suzanne nearly every day.

I'm sure the load of responsibility weighs heavily on her, particularly when she gets sick."

"When my grandma started to decline, it was horrible to have to make decisions when she no longer could. Even though she'd made her end of life choices clear, there were other decisions to be made. When you love someone, you just want to do the best for them, but pain and the impending loss make every decision seem like the wrong one."

"Why did your grandma move to Portland?" Carter asked. It was something he'd been wondering but hadn't yet asked Jillian. "Since she had a house here and everything?"

Jillian frowned, her gaze dropping to her food. She picked up a fry, but other than dragging it through the blob of ketchup on her plate, she didn't do anything with it.

Finally, she said, "Following my...traumatic event, my grandma came to stay with me while I dealt with the aftermath. I was hospitalized for a while, then needed intensive therapy, plus there was legal stuff to deal with."

CHAPTER TWENTY-EIGHT

There was a whole lot for Carter to unpack in that single sentence. *Hospitalized. Therapy. Legal stuff.* He'd come to the conclusion after witnessing her panic attacks that she'd experienced some sort of trauma, possibly an attack of some kind, but this sounded like something much more.

For some men, the idea of being involved with a woman who had that many issues might have been enough to drive them away. But not him. It didn't daunt him at all. If he could stand by someone for ten years who couldn't even interact with him, the idea of being there for Jillian, regardless of what had contributed to the issues she struggled with, didn't scare him at all.

"Did your grandma know she had cancer when she moved?"

Jillian shook her head. "She hadn't been feeling well, but she ignored her own health concerns while helping me deal with my stuff. By the time the doctors diagnosed her, the cancer was already fairly advanced. She fought as hard as she could, determined to be with me for as long as possible, but in the end, her body gave out, even though her mind was strong to the end."

Carter reached out and covered her hand with his. "I'm so sorry for your loss."

"Thank you." She blinked rapidly, then gave him a small smile. "I wish our final times together held happier memories. Grandma died not knowing if I'd be able to pick up the pieces of my life, though that was what she wanted for me more than anything."

Carter didn't know what to say, how to respond to her revelations.

"It had only been the two of us for so long," Jillian said, her expression going distant. "It should have been me moving back here to help her. She should have spent those last months in the comfort of the home she'd shared with the man she loved, instead of in a small apartment in a strange city with a granddaughter who was physically and mentally a mess." Her brows drew together, and she swallowed audibly. "I hate him for that."

"Hate who?" Carter asked.

Jillian seemed to break free of whatever had pulled her into the past, and she turned her gaze back to him, her eyes glistening with unshed tears. "The man who...hurt me. He robbed me of those last months with my grandmother. I didn't know how to support her when I was barely able to function myself. She deserved better than that. After all she'd done for me, she deserved so much more than what I was able to give her."

In her words, Carter heard anger and hurt that absolutely resonated with him. She felt robbed in the same way that he had, all the while feeling responsible for what had happened.

"Do you wonder why God allowed it to happen?" he asked.

She took a breath and let it out, her gaze dropping momentarily to her food before meeting his again. "All the time. All. The. Time. There are times when I feel like I've accepted everything, trusting that God had a plan in all of it, but other times..."

"I'm that way with what happened with Suzanne. It all seemed so senseless. I used to wonder what good could possibly come from it."

"Used to wonder? Does that mean you've accepted it now?"

Carter thought about that for a moment. "I've accepted it in the sense that I know not accepting it won't change anything. I don't question it as much as I used to."

"What's changed?" Jillian asked.

He hesitated to answer, not even sure how to put it in words. "It happened gradually, so I have a hard time pinpointing just one thing that changed. I suppose it began when Evelyn and Garth started encouraging me to move forward, which is when I moved here from Seattle. Then it was a series of things. Finding a church here. Meeting people like Stuart, Kieran, and Eli, who took the time to patiently encourage and uplift me. Having you become part of my life."

He said the last sentence slowly, not sure how it might be received. It didn't take long to get his answer.

Her eyes widened briefly before her face lost all expression, and she said, "I suppose that while my traumatic event was something major, it will take a lot of smaller steps to recover from it. Which I guess is what therapy is...a series of small steps. Sometimes forward. Sometimes backward."

Disappointment threatened the small flame in his heart, but he refused to let it be extinguished. She had so much to deal with already. He didn't want to add to it. No, he wanted to help her shoulder all those things that weighed her down.

So he let go of his expectation of a different response from her and nodded. "I think that's why I resisted moving forward for as long as I did. I wanted it all to be better in the blink of an eye, just like how it was all torn apart."

"It doesn't seem to work that way," Jillian murmured. "But yeah, I wish things could be fixed that easily." Her shoulders slumped, and the mask that had slid over her expression earlier slipped away to reveal her weariness. "Someone else made a mess of my life, but I'm the one that has to do all the hard work to clean it up and reclaim what was taken from me. Sometimes I just want to do enough to be functional. Not all the really hard work."

"But that would mean living life just surviving rather than thriving," he said softly, not by way of condemning her, but more as an acknowledgment that he understood. Oh, how he understood.

Jillian sighed and nodded. "My grandma said the same thing. She didn't want me to just survive. Some of her last words to me were to let God help me learn to thrive again. To not let my attacker win. To not let his evil actions triumph when God could bring victory if I'd just let Him."

"Is he in prison?" Carter asked.

Her gaze flitted to his before she nodded. "But he's appealing his conviction."

That sentence felt like a gut punch, and Carter could only imagine how hearing that news would have affected Jillian. "Is there a chance he'll win his appeal?"

She shrugged and bit her lip. "There's always a chance."

Carter wanted to know more. To ask for more details about the case. "I'll pray that doesn't happen."

When her gaze dropped again, he looked down as well and noticed that her hands were shaking. Abandoning his side of the booth, he slid in next to her, settling his arm along the back of the booth and placing his hand over hers.

"If the worst should happen and he wins his appeal, you need to remember that you're not alone. I'm here for you." His heart thumped in his chest when her hand turned over, and her fingers intertwined with his. "And so many others are here for you too. No matter what happens, we'll always be here for you."

Her head pressed against his shoulder, and though he wanted to wrap his arms around her, he wasn't sure that would be welcome. Particularly now that he knew a few more details of the trauma she had experienced. In that moment, he was just so grateful that she allowed him to get as close as he was.

They sat there in silence for a few minutes, but Carter had never felt more connected to Jillian than he did right then. Just like with his own healing and moving forward, things with Jillian weren't going to happen as quickly as he'd hoped. But if the past ten years had taught him anything, it was how to be patient.

When her grip loosened on his hand and she lifted her head from his shoulder, Carter knew she had reached her limit of emotional conversation. He reluctantly moved back to the other side of the booth.

"So, I guess we'll be celebrating Thanksgiving at the lodge, huh?"

A smile briefly flitted across her face then. "I'm sure it will be a wonderful time."

"Do you know who all's been invited?"

"I imagine Beau and his siblings will be there since Sarah said they didn't plan to go back to Houston. I think Cara and Kieran will be spending the day with his mom, though I'm not totally sure about that. Maybe Michael and Taylor?"

"I think maybe the only thing we know for sure is that there will be lots of amazing food."

When Jillian laughed at that, Carter felt the knot inside him loosen. How he wished she could have more moments of laughter than pain, but he knew that as long as the past had a tight hold on her, his wish wasn't likely to come true. He was only just coming to realize that was true for himself as well. For too long, he'd let the past to weigh him down.

Once they'd finished eating, Carter took care of the bill, this time refusing to allow Jillian to pay her half. There weren't many ways he could take care of her—and he was well aware that she was probably in a better place financially than he was—but it made him feel good to do that small thing.

"Are you going to Eli's later?" he asked as he drove her back to her car at the church.

"I plan to. I don't think we're hiking, are we?"

Carter glanced at the gray clouds that hung low over the town. "I kind of doubt it. It's been a bit too chilly and cold the past couple of days to consider it, I think. Do you want me to pick you up?"

He wasn't offended when she took a moment before answering, and then declined his offer. "I think I'll just drive myself."

"Well, if you change your mind, you have my number," he said as he pulled into the empty space next to her car.

"Thank you for lunch."

"You're welcome," Carter said as he opened his door. He wished she'd wait so he could open her door for her, but he knew that by the time he got around to her side, she'd already be out, and he wasn't wrong.

She already standing outside the vehicle when he came around the truck to her vehicle. "I'll see you later."

As Carter stood watching her pull out of the church parking lot, he wondered if Kieran knew anything about her attack. It was better to hear the details from her, but that didn't mean he wasn't tempted to see if Kieran could find out anything for him. But it was a temptation he wouldn't yield to.

~ * ~

Jillian wasn't sure what to do.

She was seated on the couch at Eli's with Carter sitting on the floor at her feet. There was a part of her that just wanted to relax into whatever was developing between them. But thinking about that too long caused anxiety to spike within her.

During her latest therapy session, her arrangement with Carter had come up in the discussion. The therapist had asked her why she didn't think her casual relationship with him could develop into something more. At first, she'd thought the woman was joking, but it soon became clear that the therapist was quite serious.

Though she had a hard time believing it, there was something in Carter's gaze lately, and in his actions toward her, that hinted at him actually being interested in her. She didn't think it was just her imagination...or wishful thinking. Wishful thinking that made absolutely no sense since she didn't want a physical relationship with *any* man, not just Carter.

They'd spent the Bible study time discussing that morning's sermon in more detail. Over the past few weeks, Pastor Evans had been focusing on what a Christian should do to make sure their light could shine brightly in a dark world. As she'd listened to each sermon, Jillian had despaired of ever being in a position where her light would shine as brightly as it should.

Feeling like she was a complete mess, Jillian wasn't sure how she could ever shine in a way that would draw people to God. She pleaded with God each night to take away her anxiety and fears. But each day, she woke with a familiar low hum of anxiety in her gut. She went through each day with a sense of dreadful anticipation of something happening that would trigger a panic attack.

The only time she felt truly relaxed was within the walls of her own home when no one else was around, and she had nowhere to be. Even at school, she wasn't completely relaxed because a panic attack there would be horrible since the children would bear witness to it. So she was constantly on edge, watching for the thing that might trigger her.

How was she supposed to shine brightly when she felt her brightest when no one else was around?

"Jillian?" A hand touched her knee, drawing her back to the present.

She looked up to find Carter watching her with a familiar expression of concern. It was an expression she was getting weary of seeing from not just him but from others as well. She understood why it was there. She knew it came from a place of love and affection. But she wanted to be strong enough to not need that constant concern. She wanted to be the one offering support and understanding, not the one needing it.

"I'm fine. Just thinking about what we were discussing."

Carter nodded, the concern fading away. "It's been...challenging to think about."

"Why would you find it challenging?" she asked as people moved around them, talking with each other and eating the desserts

Leah had brought. "With the way you care about people, you shine God's love so brightly. I see it every time we're together."

Carter's brows rose. "I guess I don't see it that way. I feel like I have a lot of work to do to shine that brightly."

"Well, if you have work to do, then there's no hope for me. In case you haven't noticed, I'm a bit of a mess."

"We're all a bit of a mess. And yeah, some of us may be more of a mess than others, but that doesn't mean that God can't shine through us. That He can't use us to reach others. As I recall, some of the people He used in the Bible had lives that were a bit of a mess. David's life was a *real* mess at times, yet God still used him. So don't think that just because you see a mess when you look at your life, God can't still shine through you."

Jillian found that his words were a balm for the ache that seemed to always be present in her heart. Still, she couldn't help but wish that she was in a different place, that her life hadn't been torn asunder in such a way that had left her feeling as if she'd never be whole again.

"And just so you know, I'm saying this all to myself as much as I am to you," Carter said. "I still feel like things with Suzanne are a mess because of my own actions, and that's hard to deal with."

She understood then what Carter was saying. It would be easy for her to point out how the accident wasn't his fault—that the person responsible had been the drunk driver who'd hit them. But there were enough circumstances surrounding the accident that he could claim responsibility for, that he wouldn't accept that he wasn't at least partially at fault for what had happened.

When they were in the midst of their own mess, it was hard to have an accurate view of things. There were plenty of things in her situation that she felt responsible for...that she blamed herself for. If only she hadn't decided to accept a date from a dating app. If only she had told someone where she was going and who she was going to meet. If only... If only...

"Just don't feel discouraged, okay?" Carter said, his gaze serious as he looked at her. "And I'm going to try and take some of my own advice."

"It is easier to give it than to live it." Jillian couldn't help but smile at the rhyme.

"Well, isn't that the truth." Carter got to his feet and held out his hand. "And now, why don't we get some dessert?"

Jillian took his hand and allowed him to help her up from the couch that, while wonderfully comfortable, was also terribly hard to get out of. He kept a gentle hold on her hand as they made their way to where the goodies were set out.

Later, as she lay in the quiet of her room, hoping and praying for a peaceful night, Jillian allowed herself to think about the look in Carter's eyes and wonder what she should do about it.

Though a large part of her wasn't convinced that Carter could actually feel any way about her other than friendship, he'd become closer to her than any other man, and most of it was his own doing. She wasn't pursuing him, and for the most part, had only allowed him to help her with panic attacks because he'd already been present when they'd happened.

He had definitely been the one who initiated time together like at lunch earlier that day. That just meant that she was going to end up hurting him. One way or another, she was going to cause him pain when she couldn't give him what he wanted.

But it would also hurt her too because he was a good man. A man who had stepped in to protect her when another man had wanted to hurt her. And she didn't doubt that he would do that for her as often as necessary.

She wanted that in her life so much, but what could she offer him in return? Nothing that didn't involve waiting while she tried to work through her mess, with no guarantee that she'd ever be ready for a genuine relationship.

CHAPTER TWENTY-NINE

Carter headed back from Seattle, hoping he'd make it to the lodge before the Thanksgiving dinner started. Both Evelyn and Garth had been at the care home, so he'd visited with them as they'd spent time with Suzanne.

This time, when Evelyn had asked him if he'd told Jillian about Suzanne, Carter was glad he could say yes. Evelyn had seemed pleased at that, though she was still asking when she could meet Jillian. Carter wasn't sure when—or if—that would ever happen.

After both their conversations the previous Sunday, he'd kind of hoped that things between them might move in a more serious direction. Jillian, however, didn't seem inclined that way. Their interactions in the days since Sunday had been few. Not even one text conversation a day.

Carter understood better what he was facing now that she'd shared a bit more about her past, so he knew he needed to be patient. It was hard, though. He wasn't getting any younger, and his visits with Suzanne were a blatant reminder that things could change in an instant. But he had no choice but to wait, hoping that in time, Jillian would feel about him the way he felt about her.

When he finally arrived at the lodge, Carter found he had just a few minutes to spare. He jogged up the steps and knocked on the large wooden door.

It opened a minute later to reveal Beau's smiling face. "Pretty sure you didn't need to knock, man."

"Well, to be honest, I'm never quite sure since the family lives here too."

"Yeah, I get that," Beau said as he closed the door behind Carter. "I think you're good to just walk in when they're expecting you, though."

"I'll keep that in mind."

The delicious aroma of turkey drifted through the air, and Carter inhaled deeply as he walked further into the lodge with Beau. Evelyn had been delighted to hear that he had plans to join Jillian at a Thanksgiving dinner with friends.

"We've been banished from the kitchen," Beau said as he gestured for Carter to go into the living room. "Something about us getting in the way. However, I also heard we're on clean-up duty."

"You can count on it," Eli said from where he sat on one end of the couch. "That's kind of always been the deal for family meals like this."

Carter settled on the other end of the couch. "No guests in the house?"

"No. We still take reservations for the cabins over Thanksgiving though we let anyone planning to rent one know that they are on their own for meals today. As it turns out, this year we don't have anyone in the cabins either. We do have people arriving tomorrow, though, I believe."

Glancing around the room, Carter saw that it was mainly guys in the living room except for Julianna. She sat in one of the wing-back chairs, legs crossed, her foot swinging loosely as she stared at her phone. He glanced away before she looked up because he wasn't interested in having any kind of interaction with her.

It wasn't that she blatantly flirted with him, but she seemed to have figured out that things with Jillian weren't serious. It seemed that to her, that knowledge meant it was okay to be slightly flirtatious with him. Like he might suddenly change his mind and decide to go out with her instead of with Jillian.

Even as a younger guy, he hadn't wanted to date more than one girl at a time. If he wasn't ready to commit to just one woman for however long things lasted, he just stayed as friends. That hadn't changed about him, so even if things with Jillian were still technically casual, he wasn't interested in spending time with any other woman.

He couldn't deny that at one time, back before everything had gone wrong, Julianna would have been the exact type of woman he was attracted to. Not for the first time, he acknowledged that she and Suzanne had a lot of similarities, and maybe if he'd consciously made the decision to date seriously, he might have chosen someone like Julianna.

But instead, he'd kind of fallen into what had now become a deeply meaningful relationship with Jillian, and Carter found that it wasn't something he wanted to change.

With that thought in mind, he glanced toward the kitchen. He had just assumed that Jillian was there already and hadn't even looked for her car outside. Suddenly, he wanted—needed—to see her.

He leaned forward, preparing to get to his feet when a hand landed on his shoulder. Glancing over, he found Eli looking at him. "She's in the kitchen with the ladies. You'll just be in the way."

"I just wanted to see her," Carter muttered.

Eli grinned. "I know, but we've all been banished. You can see her in a few minutes."

"Fine." Carter leaned back against the couch while Eli chuckled.

"I really never thought I'd see this day, to be honest." Eli angled himself to face Carter more directly, his expression sobering. "I'm just not sure what to think."

Carter nodded. After all, the guys now knew how things had started with Jillian. "I'm not sure what to think, either."

Eli glanced around the room. "We'll have more of a conversation about this later. If you want."

Without a doubt, Carter did want. He needed someone to bounce things off of, even if it meant laying out everything he'd kept to himself for the years he'd been in New Hope Falls.

"I work tomorrow," he said. "But maybe sometime on the weekend?"

"We can work something out," Eli said.

Carter saw Eli's eyes light up and knew without looking over his shoulder that Anna had stepped into the room. Eli got to his feet and walked to his wife.

After a short discussion, he said, "Alright, everyone. Sounds like dinner's ready."

They all got to their feet and followed Eli and Anna into the dining room. The large table was set with lots of autumn style decorations. In front of each plate, there were turkey-shaped place tags with their names written on them in a flowing script. The table was also laden with many bowls and platters of food.

When he found his name, Carter wasn't surprised to see that Jillian's place tag was right next to his. Though he'd begun to wonder if Jillian—by her actions during the times they were apart— wanted distance from him, it apparently wasn't going to happen that day.

Glancing up, he spotted her coming in from the kitchen with a bowl in her hands. Her gaze met his, and when she smiled, it released the tension inside him that he hadn't even realized he'd been carrying.

She came around to where he stood. "Happy Thanksgiving."

Carter wanted to pull her into a hug. To press a kiss to her cheek.

Instead, he settled for responding with a holiday greeting as well. For once, remembering the manners his mother had taught him, Carter pulled out Jillian's chair for her. Once she was seated, he settled onto the chair beside her.

Eli said a prayer for the food, then they all began to load up their plates. As they passed the food, Carter took a look around the table to see who all was there and saw that their guesses of the invitees had been pretty much spot on. Cara and Kieran weren't there, however, so they'd obviously had plans with Kieran's mom. The only people he hadn't expected to see were Pastor Evans and Beau's grandfather, both of whom had already been seated at the table when he'd come into the dining room.

"How was your week at school?" Carter asked Jillian, figuring that might be the better question to ask rather than how she'd been that week.

"It was good." Jillian grinned. "We did a Thanksgiving art project, which was fun. Lots of funky looking turkeys went home yesterday with the students."

"I'm sure the parents were all pleased," Carter said, remembering the fridge in his mom's kitchen that had always been covered with an assortment of art projects he and his siblings had brought home from school.

"I hope so."

They were both drawn into other conversations as the meal progressed. After everyone declared themselves full, Eli got the guys up to help clear the table. Nadine followed them into the kitchen to supervise as they brought in stacks of dishes and the nearly empty food bowls.

Once that was all taken care of, they returned to the table. Carter was sure dessert was still to come, but he was glad it didn't appear that was going to happen right away. He was still way too full from all the delicious food they'd already eaten.

"Before we have some dessert and coffee," Eli began from where he sat at one end of the table with Anna to his left. Nadine sat at the other end, her attention on her son. "I thought maybe we should take some time to share what we're thankful for." He shrugged. "I know it's cliché, but I also think it's appropriate. I'm not going to force anyone to share, but if you'd like to, please feel free. I've asked Pastor Evans to close our sharing time in prayer."

The first to jump in was Beau's grandfather, who shared how thankful he was to have his grandchildren in his life. It was easy to see how much the man loved Beau, Julianna, and Rhett. After he spoke, Beau added his thanks for the older man and for Sarah and the new family and friends he'd found in New Hope. That led to Sarah expressing her gratitude for Beau and her show at the art gallery, as well as her friends and family.

Anna also shared, as did Nadine. Carter wasn't sure if he felt comfortable sharing. This was something he'd done with his family growing up, but over the past decade, he hadn't had the desire or the opportunity to do it.

"This is my first year celebrating Thanksgiving without my grandma," Jillian said after there was a brief pause following Nadine speaking. "I wasn't sure how I would handle it, but I'm so thankful for the love and support I've felt from my friends since coming back to New Hope."

Hearing the emotion in her voice, Carter rested his arm along the back of her chair. For a moment, he thought she might start to cry, but she didn't. And as he thought about what he'd come to know about her and his own experiences with her, Carter realized that even though she'd been through a lot, he had never seen her break down and cry.

She was a lot stronger than she gave herself credit for. No doubt, she looked at her panic attacks and anxiety and saw only weakness and a messed-up life, but in truth, she was stronger than a lot of people—even him.

"I'm especially thankful that Sarah, Carter, Cara, and Anna have been there for me when I've struggled." She glanced over at him. "Carter especially has stepped up in a way he probably never thought he'd have to, so I'm very thankful for him."

At her words, he brushed her shoulder briefly with his fingertips, letting her know through his touch that he was still there for her.

When she was done, Eli spoke briefly, then silence stretched out for a minute or so before Carter finally got up the nerve to speak.

"My parents used to make us do this each Thanksgiving," he began, a smile tugging at his lips at the memory. "But back then, the extent of my thankfulness was usually that I'd had an overnight with my best friend or that Mom had let us have an extra treat." His smile faded away, and his chest tightened. "For a long stretch in my life, I didn't feel like I had much to be thankful for, but God's been working in my life lately. I'm very grateful for Eli and Kieran and the role they've played in helping me refocus my life.

Carter let his fingers lightly touch Jillian's shoulder again, needing even that faint connection with her. "Then, quite unexpectedly, I was introduced to an amazing woman. In her, I saw strength and perseverance. In spite of rough moments, she has continued on. God has used her, as well, to show me how to trust Him more. How to find laughter once again. How to be open to a future that I wasn't sure I'd ever want. So today, I'm very thankful for Jillian, someone who is truly beautiful, inside and out."

"Amen!" Sarah said from across the table. "I'm thankful for her too."

Jillian ducked her head, and Carter was sure she was embarrassed by both his and Sarah's words, but none of them had been a lie, and she needed to know that. He left his fingers resting against her shoulder, waiting to see if she shifted away from his touch. When she didn't, he felt his heart swell with emotion.

After another pause once Carter had finished speaking, Pastor Evans closed their sharing time with a brief prayer. As the other women got up from the table, Jillian joined them. She gave him a quick smile, but there was worry in her eyes, and Carter wished he knew why.

Unfortunately, it wasn't the time or place to ask her about it. That seemed to be the case with so much of their relationship. Always the wrong time and the wrong place for heavy conversations.

Dessert ended up being an assortment of enticing sweets, but Carter didn't even hesitate before choosing a piece of pumpkin pie with whipped cream since that was something his mom had always made for their Thanksgiving dinners. It was as good as he'd remembered his mom's being, but that was no surprise since Nadine and Leah were amazing bakers.

Jillian had a piece of the chocolate cream pie—which would have been his first choice if he hadn't been feeling a bit nostalgic—and a cup of coffee. Despite the weighty moments not that long ago, she seemed relaxed.

He didn't know if it was an act since he was coming to realize that she put on a front a lot of the time. Otherwise, how would she be able to function when she dealt with panic and anxiety on a daily basis?

Midway through her dessert, she turned toward him. "How was your visit?"

"It was good," he said. "Evelyn and Garth were both there since it was a holiday, and they always spend those days with Suzanne."

"Is Suzanne doing alright?"

Carter thought about how she'd looked that morning and shrugged. "She seemed okay. She's not dealing with any infections at the moment, so that's good."

"That's an answer to prayer. I'm sure her parents are relieved."

He still found it a bit weird to talk to anyone but Evelyn, Garth, and his own family about Suzanne. And it should have been weirder that he was speaking to the person he was dating—even if it was *casually*—about her. But Jillian didn't seem to be bothered by it, so he wasn't going to let it bother him either.

"They are very relieved. I mean, they're realistic about her situation, but at the same time, they want every moment with her that they can get, as long as she's not in any pain."

"I think most parents would want that," Jillian said. "Well, any loved one would, most likely. I felt that way with my grandma. I wanted her to stay around forever, and at the end, even though she was in a lot of pain, she hung on. It got to the point where each day, I was telling her it was okay for her to go."

When her gaze dropped, Carter reached out and touched her hand a moment. "I'm sure that was the hardest thing you've ever done."

"It really was, but I know she'd be happy if she could see me now. Her biggest worry was that I'd be alone once she was gone, but like I said earlier, I'm not." She glanced up at him and smiled. "And I'm very thankful for that."

"I know that technically, I'm not alone because I have a large family, but I've kind of forced myself into isolation, you know." She nodded, understanding in her eyes. "So this past year or so has sort of been an awakening of sorts, and I've finally allowed myself not to be alone. Or rather, Evelyn and Garth have been prodding me to not be alone."

"They care about you," Jillian stated.

"Yes. I'm very thankful that in spite of everything, they still love me and want me to live my life."

"They sound like special people."

Carter nodded. "And if you'd ever like to meet them, they'd love that."

She didn't immediately say no. Instead, she turned her attention back to her pie and ate the last bite. After taking a sip of her coffee, she glanced at him again. "Maybe in the new year."

For a moment, he thought that was just her way of putting him off indefinitely, but then it came to him that the new year was only a matter of weeks away. He really hoped that things might be a bit more settled with Jillian by that point.

When Eli got up and began to clear away the dirty dessert dishes, Carter joined him, as did Beau. Though the deal had been for the guys to clean up if the ladies prepared the food, it didn't take long for the women to get up and help as well.

Once the meal was cleaned up, and all the leftovers put away, Beau and his siblings left to take their grandfather back to the personal care home. Pastor Evans also left after thanking the McNamaras for inviting him.

The rest of them settled into seats in the living room while Eli got a fire going in the large stone fireplace. Jillian was seated next to him on the couch with Sarah on her other side.

As Carter watched Anna snuggle into Eli when he joined her on the loveseat, he felt a familiar pang of longing. It was one he'd experienced often over the past year or so as he'd watched his friends find love. The difference this time was that while in the past, he'd felt a longing to share that experience with Suzanne, this time, he could imagine himself sharing a moment like that with Jillian.

He waited for the guilt to come. It had always been the hardest thing to imagine, moving forward while Suzanne was still alive. It helped a bit to know that he was doing so not only with Evelyn and Garth's blessing but with their encouragement. Now he just needed Jillian to consider that life with him was something worth pursuing.

The following Tuesday, Carter yawned as he walked from his bed to the kitchen, stopping on his journey to pick up the remote to turn on the television. After a busy night with several call-outs, he'd had to have a meeting with Stuart about some personnel issues before he could come home and crash. It wasn't often he slept the day away, even after a twenty-four-hour shift, but he had that day.

He hoped it didn't mean he was going to be up all night, but it was a possibility. Hopefully if he skipped coffee, he'd be okay. Skipping coffee was doable, but he was starving, so skipping food wasn't.

His fridge was pitifully empty, so he had to pull a container of chili that he'd made a couple of weeks earlier out of the freezer. He dumped it in a pot and put it on the stove to defrost it and heat it up, half-listening to the news on the television.

"In a shocking turn of events, a judge has granted the appeal of Roger Pearse, better known as the Portland Predator. And in an even more shocking development, he also set bail for Pearse, granting him freedom as he awaits a new trial. One of his two surviving victims released a statement that she was horrified that the judge not only allowed his appeal but also let him out of prison."

Carter turned from the stove, frowning as he watched images of the man flash on the screen as the newscaster continued to talk about the latest developments. As many in the Pacific Northwest had, he'd watched as the events had unfolded a couple of years earlier.

The details that had come out in the trial had been horrible. Eight women dead over the course of four months. Torture. Sexual assault. Murder. All committed by a rich, handsome playboy who'd found his victims through dating apps.

How he'd chosen his victims was a mystery that he'd never revealed. Plenty of stories had come out after his arrest from other women who had been on dates with the man, relieved that they'd survived their close call with death when other women hadn't.

When his phone rang, Carter hit the TV mute button and picked up his phone. Seeing Kieran's name on the screen, he answered it.

"Hey, man," he said, tapping the screen to put it on speakerphone before setting it on the counter so he could stir the chili. "What's up?"

"Hey...uh...Has Jillian told you anything about her past?" Kieran asked.

"What?" Carter stirred the chili then set the wooden spoon aside.

"Her past. Has she talked to you about it?"

"Not in great detail. Just enough for me to know she was attacked and that the guy was in prison. Why?"

"Her attacker's appeal for a new trial was upheld, and he's going to be released on bail."

Carter turned back to face the television, a sick feeling growing in his stomach. *No.* It couldn't be. *No.* Not his Jillian.

"Carter?"

He cleared his throat and swallowed, trying to keep nausea from rising. "She didn't tell me who the attacker was, but I just saw on the news... The Portland Predator?"

Kieran was silent for a moment, then said, "Yes, and I think she needs you."

"I'll be there as soon as I get changed. I just woke up." Carter swung around and turned off the stove.

"Cara and Sarah are on their way to her house too. They'll meet you there."

"Okay." Numb, Carter hung up, then headed to his dresser and pulled out a pair of jeans. Within minutes, he was out the door, his sole goal to get to Jillian as quickly as possible.

CHAPTER THIRTY

The pain in her chest took Jillian's breath away. The frantic thudding of her heart made it feel like it was going to pound right out of her chest. She panted, trying to catch her breath, convinced she was going to die. Hoping she was going to die.

Panic and fear had taken control of her mind. Her thoughts were a wild jumble of messages to hide...to flee...to hide...to flee...to disappear...to just vanish, so she didn't have to face the fear. The overwhelming fear of history repeating itself.

Her body shook. Drawing a breath seemed impossible. Her heart had never pounded so hard in her life. Was she going to die? Continuous tremors battered her, rendering her unable to function. Weak... Vulnerable...

And there was the fear again, making her keep her eyes closed tight.

Would she see darkness or light if she opened them?

She pulled her arms close to her chest, trying to stop the shaking that threatened to break her apart. But nothing worked. Nothing stopped the pain or the fear.

Over the panicked pounding of her pulse in her ears, Jillian heard a loud banging followed by the sound of the doorbell. It was a familiar sound, but all it did was spike her fear.

She tried to breathe the way the therapist had taught her to because if she was going to escape again, she needed to be in control. To be able to think straight.

But it didn't work. All she could do was take panting breaths.

"Jillian!" The man's voice, though muffled by the door, sounded loud to her. "Open the door, sweetheart. It's Carter, and I have Cara and Sarah with me."

Carter. The shaking increased as new emotions were dumped into the mix. She wanted him there with her, but she knew it wasn't right. Wasn't fair to him.

"Jillian! It's Sarah. Can you open the door for us?"

Swallowing hard, she anchored herself to the sound of her friends' voices and slowly opened her eyes. Her living room. She was in her living room with the television playing against the far wall.

She was on the floor, her back pressed to the wall near the short hallway that led to the bedrooms. Looking to her left, she stared at the front door. Solid, but not impenetrable. And so far away.

"Jillian, can you breathe with me?" Carter's voice again. "Deep breath in, two, three, four. Let it out, two, three, four."

Jillian closed her eyes, keeping her arms tightly wrapped around her body, while focusing on Carter's voice. No matter what else might be part of their arrangement, she trusted him.

He continued to count, she continued to breathe. The panic didn't leave. The fear didn't vanish. The world wasn't suddenly right. But the people she trusted were close. She just needed to get to the door to let them in.

"You're strong, Jillian. You can do this."

She realized then that Carter didn't know for sure that she was even hearing him. He was doing this without knowing for certain that she was even in the house.

He started counting again, so she focused on that, keeping her gaze on the door. Carter believed she was strong enough to get there and let them in. She would do this for them because they believed in her.

If they were here with her, maybe he wouldn't come, even though he knew where she was from—she'd *told* him that herself on their date. The date she never should have gone on, but he'd seemed so good. Handsome. Rich. Friendly. Too good to be true.

Resolved to reach the *actual* good people in her life, Jillian began to crawl to the door, unwilling to trust her legs just yet because she was still trembling uncontrollably. She was weak. Carter may have thought she was strong, but she knew better. She'd fallen into a soul-crushing panic attack after getting the phone call from her lawyer, which proved how weak she truly was.

But she wanted to be strong. So she forced herself to cross the short distance to the door. When she got there, she reached up but then hesitated. Was it really Carter?

"Carter?" Her voice was hoarse and sounded barely over a whisper to her ears.

"Jillian? Jillian, I'm here. We're here. Can you open the door for us?"

She trusted Cara. She trusted Sarah. And most of all, she trusted Carter.

Reaching up a trembling hand, she prayed she was doing the right thing and unlocked the deadbolt.

Because she was off to the side of the door, it didn't hit her when it began to slowly open. Carter immediately dropped down in front of her, his eyes full of concern.

"C'mon, sweetheart," he said. "Let's get you to the couch."

Jillian would have almost preferred to crawl, still not trusting that her legs would hold her, but the three of them helped her up, and Carter and Sarah supported her as she shuffled to the couch. She hated that they were seeing her like this, but they had offered their support, and she knew that she needed it.

Once she was seated on the couch, Cara and Sarah settled on either side of her while Carter sat on the coffee table in front of her, his legs on either side of hers. Reaching out, he took her hands in his. He held them lightly, letting her choose the intensity of their connection.

"You're safe," Carter said as she tightened her fingers around his, holding on to the strength he offered. "He can't hurt you."

"He knows where I live," she told him. "I told him. I told him where I lived."

"He knows your address?" Cara asked.

Jillian shook her head. "Not my address, but I told him I'm from here. He could find me."

"We'll make sure that he can't hurt you again." Carter's voice held a surety that Jillian wanted to take into her heart and cling to. "You'll be safe."

"But he might hurt you. All of you," she said, voicing a growing worry. "I don't want that to happen."

"It won't," Cara said, sliding her arm around her. "Kieran will make sure we're all safe. We'll make sure you're safe. You're not alone, Jillian."

Tremors continued to shake her body, like shockwaves, starting at her core and moving out to her fingertips and toes. But the tremors didn't stay gone once they'd reached her fingertips. Another one started, rolling through her in an uncontrollable fashion.

Sarah leaned her cheek against Jillian's shoulder as she too wrapped her arm around her. "We're here for you, sweetie. Always."

"They're right," Carter said. "You aren't alone."

"But you can't always be with me. You have jobs." She swallowed hard. "I have a job."

"Why don't we pray about this," Carter suggested, watching until she nodded.

They gathered closely around her, and Jillian clutched Carter's hands more tightly as she closed her eyes.

"Heavenly Father, we come before You tonight, asking for Your protection and Your peace. We don't understand—we *really* don't understand—the decision by the judge, but You know...You understand...what's happened. Nothing about this has taken You by surprise the way it has us." Carter paused. "I pray especially for Jillian right now. You know the state of her mind and her heart in the midst of this, and I pray that You will give her the peace that passes all understanding. I ask You to calm her heart and mind so that she can have a clear perspective on what's happening and for any decisions she has to make."

Tears pricked at Jillian's eyes as she listened to Carter's words. Some of the panic began to fade away, and the trembling didn't make her feel like she was going to shatter into a million pieces.

Was she at peace? Not entirely, but the absolutely broken feeling she'd had earlier wasn't as overwhelming.

No one moved, even after Carter said *amen*, but then Cara's phone rang. She shifted to look at it. "It's Kieran." She tapped the screen and put the phone to her ear. "Hi, babe."

No one said anything as Cara listened to whatever Kieran was saying. "Okay. See you in a few minutes."

After she ended the call, she said, "Kieran's on his way over."

Now that clarity was starting to return to her mind, Jillian was faced with the realization that Carter knew. He, like everyone else who had watched information from the trial, now knew the horrors she'd endured. At least he'd finally understand why she'd been so onboard with a relationship that would never go beyond casual dating.

"Let me get you something to drink," Sarah said as she stood up.

Cara stood as well. "I'm going to wait for Kieran."

Carter still held her hands even after the two women had left. "What's your anxiety level at?"

She closed her eyes briefly, searching within herself as she took a breath and let it out. When she opened her eyes, she said, "Out of ten, probably a ten. But considering that it was close to fifty earlier, I'd say that's a win."

"It's definitely a win," Carter said with a nod. "You're so strong."

Jillian shook her head. "A phone call sent me into the mother of all panic attacks. That's not strong."

His fingers tightened on hers a bit. "You survived. You picked up the pieces and moved forward with your life."

"Only to fall apart over and over again," Jillian reminded him. He'd been there for several of those moments, after all.

"Don't discount the progress you've made." Carter's voice was firm. "We all have setbacks, but you've recovered from yours. You might still have setbacks in the future, but as long as you pick yourself up, he doesn't win."

She wanted to say that he'd already won. He'd left her with a fear that robbed her of something she'd always hoped to have: a husband and a family.

When Cara and Kieran appeared, Carter let go of her hands and stood to greet Kieran. Sarah came back with a glass of orange juice and pressed it into Jillian's hands as she sat down beside her again.

"How're you doing, sweetie?"

Jillian took a sip of the juice, appreciating the coldness of it as the liquid slid down her throat. "Better than I was an hour ago."

"That's good. As soon as I heard the news, I tried to call, but you didn't answer."

She couldn't remember even hearing her phone ring after that first call from the lawyer. "I'm sorry."

"No. Don't apologize," Sarah said with a shake of her head. "*I* need to apologize because when I couldn't get hold of you, I called Cara and told her what was going on. Then, she told Kieran, who called Carter. We all just felt the need to rally around you. To let you know that you were not alone. But I'm sorry because I'd told you I wouldn't tell anyone."

"It's okay." Jillian squeezed her hand. "You only told people that I would have told eventually anyway."

"I was just so scared when I heard the news and then couldn't get hold of you."

"I'm glad you're here."

"And Carter?" she asked, her voice low. "Is it okay he's here?"

"It's fine," Jillian assured her. "He knows how to deal with my panic attacks, and I think I probably needed him here."

"He's such a sweetheart," Sarah said. "I never realized."

Jillian couldn't argue with her in that regard. He'd only ever been good to her. Good *for* her. But now that he was moving beyond his hang-ups from his past, it was only a matter of time before he would want something more serious in their relationship. Just the fact that he'd been engaged in the past showed that he was the sort of guy who wasn't afraid of marriage.

It seemed that he had finally accepted that he didn't have to let Suzanne go completely, even while he moved forward. The next step would be to find a woman with whom he could move forward.

But that wouldn't be her. Even if she thought she could get to a point where she'd be able to have a healthy physical relationship, it would require him to wait...possibly indefinitely. And after he'd waited so long already, that really wasn't fair to him.

It would be selfish of her to continue to rely on him when she could offer him nothing in return. Pain shot through her heart, robbing her of breath for a moment. She pressed a hand against her chest, feeling panic rising within her again.

No.

She wouldn't allow panic to overtake her yet again, especially over this. She had lived without Carter before, and she could do it again. She might not want to, but she would.

Cara came to sit beside her while Kieran took the spot Carter had been seated in earlier. Carter stayed standing beside him.

"Listen," Kieran said, his gaze serious. "I've been in touch with the Portland police, and they have someone on Pearse, plus he does have an ankle bracelet apparently. I have also asked a couple of my guys who I absolutely trust for confidentiality to alternate watching you. Cara has explained that you didn't want people to know about what had happened to you, which I completely understand. These two guys will not reveal any details of this. We want you to be safe, Jillian."

"Thank you," Jillian said. "I really appreciate that."

"For tonight, however, Cara and Sarah have said they'll stay here with you, as will Carter."

Jillian glanced around at them. "I don't have enough bedrooms."

"I'm sleeping on the couch," Carter said. "Not that I'll sleep much since I just got up an hour or so ago."

"If need be, I could sleep with you, Jillian," Sarah volunteered. "I'm used to sharing a bed with Leah. We're full up with a retreat of some nature at the lodge and cabins, or you could have gone there. You could still come and share my bed."

Jillian shook her head. "I don't want to put any of your guests at risk. I don't want to put *any* of you at risk." She let out a shaky breath. "He's so much worse than Martin. *So* much worse."

"Honestly, I don't think anyone is at risk tonight," Kieran said.

"Unless he's had someone working on the outside to get him information." Jillian recalled all the devious things the man had put into place in order to carry out his diabolical plan over and over again without the police catching up to him.

"But he's under surveillance now." Kieran leaned forward, resting his elbows on his knees. "And you will be too. Don't let him mess with your mind."

"Until he's back behind bars, I won't be able to truly rest. While my name might never have been released, *he* knows who I am. He made sure to find out as many details as he could about me on our dates, and then he used it against me. My grandmother. Even Dolly. He was a sadist on every level."

Carter turned away, running a hand through his hair. Jillian watched him for a moment before looking back at Kieran.

"He's a smart man with a cunning ability to plan and manipulate." Jillian felt a bit of frustration bubble up within her. "The first, and possibly last, mistake someone would make with him would be to underestimate what he's capable of."

Kieran stared at her before nodding. "Then, we'll take whatever steps we need to in order to make sure you're safe."

Jillian wanted to take comfort in his reassurances, but when it came to Roger Pearse, she would never feel safe as long as he was on the loose. If it weren't for her job and her class relying on her, she would have left town and gone into hiding until he was back behind bars.

But what if he was somehow found innocent in another trial? What if they got a jury and another judge who were sympathetic to Roger Pearse? If he walked free, no woman would be safe.

"You guys don't need to stay here," Jillian murmured. "If he's being watched and someone's watching me, everything should be okay."

She didn't feel totally confident about that, but she also felt bad that her friends had to go out of their way to make sure she was okay.

"We're staying," Cara said. "I think Carter would end up camped on your doorstep, regardless, so he might as well be comfortable, and it works out since Sarah and I would also like to stick close to you for the night."

Jillian nodded, dropping her gaze to her clasped hands. She rubbed one thumb against the other, wondering again if it would just be best for everyone if she disappeared until he was back behind bars. Given everything she'd experienced at his hands, she wouldn't put it past him to use those closest to her to cause her more pain.

She hadn't even thought about how having friends could be a vulnerability. But then, she hadn't really thought that he'd get out of prison. That she'd have to worry about being vulnerable to him ever again.

"Jillian?" Carter's voice was gentle, and when she looked up, she found that he had taken Kieran's place in front of her once again. "Where's Dolly?"

"Dolly?" She frowned, blinked, then looked around. Panic started to rise again. What had happened to Dolly?

"What were you doing when your lawyer called?" Kieran asked.

Jillian took a deep breath then blew it out. "I was cleaning. Vacuuming. She said she'd been trying to get hold of me. I hadn't heard her first call because of the vacuum." She paused. "Oh. Dolly hates the vacuum, so I put her in my bedroom."

Sarah stood up. "I'll let her out."

Within minutes, Dolly was in her lap, purring madly. Jillian ran her fingers over her soft fur. The soothing motion tamped down the panic that had started to rise when she'd thought Dolly was missing.

"Hello, Dolly," Carter said, reaching out to scratch behind the cat's ears.

A small smile tugged at Jillian's lips. She watched Carter's hand, remembering the strength of it as he'd held hers, but it was the gentleness of his touch that lingered more in her mind.

"Is the plan okay, sweetie?" Sarah asked.

"It's fine. I just don't want to put anyone out or put you guys in danger." If Roger were to seek her out, it would likely be when she was in her own home, so those there with her would be at risk.

"I wouldn't let Cara stay here if I thought she—or you—were in immediate danger," Kieran said. "We'll take it a day at a time, okay?"

Jillian nodded. "Thank you."

She still wasn't sure about having her friends stay in the house with her, but there was no denying that it gave her comfort and a sense of security.

"Do you need to go back to the lodge to pack up some stuff for the night?" Kieran asked Sarah.

"Maybe I should," she said.

"I'll drive you out there," Carter volunteered. "If you'd like."

"That would be good," Kieran said. "I'll stay here with Jillian and Cara until you two get back."

With that decided, the four of them got to their feet, leaving Jillian on the couch, Dolly in her lap, wondering how she'd ended up living in fear of Roger Pearse again. His multiple life sentences should have meant she never had to fear him again. She was only glad that her grandma wasn't there to have to endure even more worry about her granddaughter.

"Can I get you something to eat or drink?" Cara asked as she sat back down beside Jillian.

She'd planned to heat up some leftover soup from the night before once she'd finished cleaning. However, her appetite had long since fled. Still, she felt like she should offer her friends some food.

"I'm not hungry, but I have soup, if you would like some."

Cara shook her head. "I'm good. I had already eaten when Sarah called me."

"If you want dessert, there's cookies and some banana bread in the kitchen. Or coffee." She glanced at Cara. "Do you want coffee or tea?"

Jillian set Dolly on the floor and stood up. She needed to do something. Though she didn't really want a cup of coffee herself, maybe Carter would like some when he got back.

"I could go for a cup of tea," Cara said. "Kieran, do you want coffee?"

"I wouldn't mind some."

Grateful for something to do, Jillian walked to the kitchen. She pulled out the decorative box that held all her teas. When Cara settled on one of the bar stools at the island, Jillian placed the box in front of her.

"Want to choose something from those?"

"Wow," Cara said as she opened the lid of the box. "I'm always impressed by your selection of teas."

"I'm more into coffee, but my grandma was a tea lover. I've gotten into the habit of keeping a bunch on hand for other tea drinkers."

By the time Sarah and Carter got back, she had a pot of coffee ready and had put out the containers that held the cookies and the banana bread. No one broached the subject of Pearse again, but he wasn't far from Jillian's thoughts as she poured coffee and set out cream and sugar.

CHAPTER THIRTY-ONE

Jillian ended up making a cup of tea for herself, choosing a blend that was supposed to help with sleep. She'd considered drinking several cups of coffee in hopes the caffeine would keep her awake since she was pretty sure the nightmares would be back in full-strength that night.

Though it might have been easier to just not bother with trying to sleep, she wanted to go to work the next day. If for no other reason than to prove to herself that Roger Pearse wasn't going to impact all areas of her life.

Once Kieran and Cara had finished their drinks, they left so Cara could grab some stuff from her apartment. It seemed overkill to have the three of them spending the night with her, but Jillian knew that Carter couldn't stay alone with her in the house.

She should have been strong enough to insist that none of them needed to be there with her. Only they wouldn't believe her because they'd seen the state she'd been in when they first arrived. Nothing she could say would convince them she was stable enough to stay on her own.

"Would you like some soup?" Jillian asked Carter as he sat at the island, sipping at his second cup of coffee. "Although, if you just woke up, maybe you'd rather have eggs or cereal?"

"Soup would be fine. If it's not too much trouble."

"It's no trouble at all." She turned to Sarah, who was drinking some hot chocolate while she texted someone—likely Beau—on her phone. "You want some too, Sarah?"

"No, thank you. I'm interested in more banana bread." She grinned as she pulled the container closer to her and lifted out another slice.

Jillian retrieved the tub of soup from the fridge and ladled some into a large soup bowl before putting it into the microwave to heat it up. Sarah and Carter were discussing something related to Beau's new place, but Jillian only half-listened as she went about getting crackers and some bread out, not sure which Carter would prefer with his soup.

She was just grateful to have something to keep herself busy as the minutes ticked by until bedtime. Once Carter had his food, she turned her attention to Dolly, putting food and fresh water out for her. Then she went to the linen closet and pulled out a couple of blankets and a pillow and put them on the couch for Carter in case he did want to try and sleep.

Though she was sure that Carter and Sarah were worried by her silence, she couldn't find it in herself to talk, just to try to assure them that she was okay. Or maybe they knew she wasn't okay and were doing their best not to focus on her silence, knowing that's what she preferred.

When Cara and Kieran returned, Kieran hung around for a bit, then he said goodnight, promising to be in touch the next day.

Though it wasn't that late, Jillian was exhausted. It was an expected outcome after having a panic attack of the intensity she'd experienced.

"I think I'm going to go to bed." The concern on the faces of her friends was instant. "I'm just really tired, and it's probably going to be a rough night, so I'd rather have a couple of extra hours to try and sleep."

"Do you want me to sleep with you?" Sarah asked. "To keep you company?"

Jillian hesitated then shook her head. "Thank you for wanting to do that, but I think my sleep will be worse if I'm worried about keeping you awake with my tossing and turning and nightmares. No sense in both of us being up all night."

"Oh." Sadness settled on Sarah's features. "I wish I could help you in some way."

"Just you being here is a big help," Jillian said.

"But I want to do more."

"If there was something you could do, I would tell you. Knowing you want to help me means a lot." She gave Sarah a sad smile. "I'm just really messed up."

Carter frowned. "You're not messed up. What you're struggling with is not your fault."

Jillian appreciated his words, but they both knew the truth. They'd even talked about how God used messed up people. So while Carter might want to make her feel better by saying that, he knew the reality, and that was, yes, she was a mess. Rather than argue with him, she just gave him a small smile.

"Anyway, I think I'm going to head to bed, if that's okay. The beds are made up in the other bedrooms, and hopefully, the couch will be comfortable for you, Carter, if you want to sleep."

"I can sleep pretty much anywhere if I'm tired."

"There's a bathroom by the mudroom, plus another by the bedrooms, and feel free to help yourself to anything if you get hungry or thirsty." She paused to look at the three of them seated on the stools watching her. "I'm sorry to leave you—"

Sarah held up her hand. "You need to do what's best for you. We're here to support you, so don't worry about us."

Going around the island, Jillian gave Sarah and Cara hugs, then paused briefly before approaching Carter. She stared at him for a moment, uncertain of what to do, but then he reached out and took her hand.

"I'll be praying you sleep well," he said, giving her hand a light squeeze before letting go. "You know where to find me if you need anything."

She nodded then said goodnight before retreating to her bedroom. Usually, she would have taken Dolly with her, but when the cat didn't follow her, she figured she'd be okay hanging out with Carter.

Once in the sanctuary of her bedroom, Jillian stood for a moment, letting the weight of what had happened press down on her. Then she took a deep breath and let it out before heading for her bathroom.

In an effort to help induce sleep, Jillian filled her tub with her favorite scented bath oil then turned on her worship playlist before climbing into the water. As she sat hunched forward in the water, she wondered what the weeks ahead would hold. Having to go through another trial without her grandma's support would be so hard, and the chances of her identity being revealed would increase.

Her lawyer hadn't given her any idea of what was to come, just said she'd be in touch in the coming days. She was glad she already had an appointment with her therapist for the next evening. It was likely that her need for sessions would increase, just when she'd finally been able to cut down on them following the situation with Martin.

Please, God. Give me the strength to deal with this. Help me, I pray, to trust in You. To not rely on my own strength and wisdom. Please place a hedge of protection around Stef and me, that he won't be able to hurt us again. And protect those who are close to us. Those who are helping us.

And please, please, please, help me to sleep tonight so that I can have a clear mind as I deal with everything. Thank you for bringing me through this the first time, and I ask for You to carry me through it again.

Tears slid down her face, dripping into the water, as pain, fear, and anger swirled through her. She'd lost so many hopes and dreams for her future because of the attack. And now, just when she was starting to realize new hopes and dreams, they were all being threatened again.

Maybe she just needed to accept that this was her life, and to hope for more was a direct path to pain.

~ * ~

Carter dragged a hand down his face, letting out a long sigh. He dropped his head forward, trying to control the anger that coursed through him.

"You okay, Carter?" Sarah asked.

"I'm fine," he said. "Of course, I'm fine. Don't worry about me."

He felt a hand settle on his shoulder and squeeze.

"We do worry about you," Cara said. "Because we know that you care for Jillian."

Care for Jillian? "I love her."

He heard the swift intake of breath, and he didn't know if it was from Sarah or Cara. Jillian should have been the first person to hear that from him, but he wasn't sure when—or if—she would ever be willing to hear those words.

Still, saying them for the first time—even if it wasn't to Jillian—loosened a knot in his chest. He hadn't allowed himself to think too much about how deeply his feelings for her went. Considering how things between them had started, love seemed an unlikely place for him to end up. A place that he now understood even more, Jillian might never reach.

And with that acknowledgment, the knot slowly tightened again.

"We're praying for you guys. You've been good for her."

"She's been good for me, too." Carter knew that people might not see it, but that was only because they didn't know his past. But she did. She knew it all. In some ways, he felt like she'd helped him more than he'd helped her.

"You'll need to be patient with her," Sarah said softly.

"Always." Carter would never force her into something she wasn't ready for. Whether that was a hug or just holding hands. Nothing would happen without her being okay with it.

Right then, he just wished he could take away the pain she was feeling. The anger. The fear. The anxiety. The helplessness. The hopelessness. He'd seen it all on her face, and he wanted to shoulder it all for her.

But he couldn't take any of it away. Though he wanted to assure her that she wouldn't walk the journey alone, Carter knew that the roughest part of the path would be where she had to do the hard work herself. The therapy. The processing of everything that had happened to her.

She'd never be alone, though. Never alone. At least, not if he could help it.

"What did Kieran say about protecting her?" Sarah asked as she got up and walked around to the sink. She turned on the water and rinsed her mug.

"Until we have a better idea of what's going on, he'll have his officers keep an eye on her, just like the Portland police will be keeping track of Pearse. No one can understand how this happened."

"I can't understand how they allowed his appeal," Cara said. "Wasn't there a ton of evidence against him?"

Carter hadn't followed the exact details of the trial, but he'd heard enough to know that evidence or not, the man was dangerous. An absolute menace to women. How a judge couldn't have seen that, he didn't know.

"The worst part is that while the first trial moved fairly quickly, I have a feeling that this next one will drag out a long time." Cara sighed then shook her head. "I just couldn't believe it when Sarah called me with the news. Jillian had told Anna and I that she'd been raped, but not that she'd been one of the Portland Predator's victims."

Sarah turned from the sink to stand on the other side of the island. "She didn't want anyone to know. She didn't want people treating her differently."

Carter understood that—he absolutely did—because now that he knew, it was hard to not want to treat her differently. To try to protect her from everything and everyone who might hurt her. He dropped his gaze again, staring at the remnants of the banana bread on his plate.

"I do think we need to circle the wagons, so to speak," Cara said. "As much as she'll allow us to. She doesn't have her grandma anymore, so we need to step up and be the support for her now."

Carter wanted that too, but he'd seen firsthand that her initial inclination was to try to deal with things on her own. The situation with Martin was proof of that. No one knew she was having problems with him until Carter had witnessed Martin's harassment himself.

"I don't know how receptive she'll be to that," Carter murmured. "She's very independent."

"That she is," Sarah said. "I've really noticed that about her now."

Cara nodded. "All we can do is make sure she knows that we're there for her in any way she needs us."

Silence fell between them. A silence that Carter didn't know how to break. He had so many things he wanted to mull over, and yet there were also things he didn't want to think about.

Soon, Cara and Sarah decided to head to their rooms, or maybe they were going to go talk in one of the rooms away from his morose mood. He didn't blame them one little bit, and honestly, he wouldn't mind being alone with his thoughts.

After they said goodnight, Carter went through the main part of the house, checking windows and doors and turning off lights until the only light left on was the lamp next to the couch. He sat down with his phone and was immediately joined by Dolly.

She settled on his lap and started purring as he ran his hand over her fur. With one hand on the cat, Carter stared at his phone for a moment before bringing up his browser app. He needed to know, but he didn't want Jillian to have to tell him.

The first links that came up had to do with the latest news on Pearse's appeal and release on bail. It became clear pretty quickly that the outrage he and Jillian's friends felt was mirrored by many others. From what he was reading, while some might feel the appeal was warranted, no one thought he should have been granted bail, given the money he had access to.

Carter moved past those articles after reading the first couple. There was a smattering of articles updating the appeal efforts over the past year or so, but it was the slew of articles dated around the time of the trial that he finally zeroed in on.

Taking a deep breath, he tapped on the first headline and promptly fell down a horrifying rabbit hole of things he could never have imagined. That a man could come up with such cruel and humiliating things to inflict pain and suffering on women was beyond Carter's comprehension.

His parents had brought him and his siblings up with a sense of respect for others and for the sanctity of human life. They'd risked punishment if they had intentionally hurt each other—emotionally or physically. He'd chosen the career he had in order to save people from harm.

Carter's stomach threatened to empty itself as he read more about the torture Pearse had inflicted on the women he'd kidnapped and imprisoned. That he'd inflicted on *Jillian*, the woman Carter loved.

He flung his phone onto the couch beside him, startling Dolly, who jumped from his lap. Surging to his feet, Carter shoved his hands into his hair. He didn't know what to do with all the ugly emotions swirling within him, looking for an outlet.

With his emotions swinging widely from anger—violent anger—to sorrow and agony, Carter stalked around the house, making a loop around the open floorplan. Living room...kitchen...dining room. Living room...kitchen...dining room.

Carter didn't know how many laps he made of that route. He only knew he needed to vent his emotions. Had he not been worried about the security of the women in the house, Carter would have gone for a run or lifted weights. Anything to release the maelstrom of emotions.

Instead, he paced the house, his mind supplying detailed images—thanks to the articles—of the torture that Jillian had endured. He understood now with stark clarity why Jillian struggled with anxiety and panic attacks. Pearse had preyed on her mind as much as he had preyed on her body. Scarring her inside and out.

His respect for Jillian had skyrocketed with everything he'd learned. She was stronger than she gave herself credit for, and he would keep telling her that for as long as it took for her to see that for herself.

Still, even with that bright thought, the dark ones continued to swirl around. He could only assume that the judge knew all the details that Carter had found, which only intensified Carter's desire to understand why the man had been willing to release Pearse back into society. If he attacked any other women, it would definitely be on that judge's head.

On one of his laps, Carter paused long enough to pour the remainder of the coffee from the pot into a mug then stick it in the microwave to heat it up. With the mug in hand, he left the kitchen and went into the dining room to look out at the back yard.

He noticed a garden door leading from the dining room out to what he assumed was a deck. But when he peered through the panes of the door, he saw it was another room. He opened the door and discovered that it was a sunroom. After groping around on the wall beside the door, he found a light switch and flipped it on. Soft lights came to life, illuminating the room.

There was an abundance of plants scattered around the space. In one corner, there was a wood-burning stove with a bin filled with wood logs next to it. There was a comfortable-looking loveseat and a matching armchair angled to face each other and also the back yard.

He walked over to the loveseat and sat down on it, letting out a long sigh as he settled back. It was peaceful there. Calming even. Maybe it was because the other part of the house had endured his frenetic pacing, but this place felt a bit like an oasis.

Though he couldn't see the yard since it was swathed in darkness, Carter was sure it was beautiful. Everything about the house showed that Jillian was making a home—a sanctuary—for herself. He could see bits of her in the personal touches within the home.

Dolly wandered in and jumped up on his lap again. A weary smile tugged at his lips as he stroked the cat. The cats that had been around when he was a kid hadn't been nearly as affectionate as Dolly was. Maybe she really was a dog in a cat's body the way Jillian thought.

He continued to stroke Dolly's fur, finding something soothing in the repetitive action. Setting his empty mug on the nearby end table, he leaned his head back on the couch and closed his eyes. In the stillness of the room, he found himself turning to prayer in search of peace and wisdom.

He wanted to beg for God to remove the images that had taken root in his mind, but that was hardly fair when Jillian would likely never be able to forget what had been done to her. So instead, he just pleaded with God to help him help Jillian. That God would use him to support and protect her the best he could.

"I see you found the rain room."

CHAPTER THIRTY-TWO

Carter opened his eyes and straightened up, looking over to see Jillian in the doorway, a thin blanket wrapped around her shoulders. She wore a pair of loose sweatpants, and a T-shirt showed between the edges of the blanket. Her hair was pulled into a messy knot on top of her head. She shuffled into the room and curled up in the armchair.

"The rain room?" he asked. "I thought it was a sunroom."

She smiled faintly. "My grandma called it her rain room since she spent most of her time in here when it rained. It was the only way she could enjoy the outdoors when it was raining."

"I guess this is a good room to have in this part of the country."

Jillian nodded. "We used to spend a lot of time in here. It's the one place I didn't renovate. It was just perfect the way it was. I mean, I had to get a bunch of new plants because the ones Grandma left here died when she came to Portland to stay with me."

They sat in silence for a few moments, Jillian staring at the unlit stove.

"Did you have a nightmare?" he asked gently.

Without looking at him, she nodded. "Not unexpected."

"Do you want to talk about it?"

This time, she shook her head right away, then shifted her gaze to meet his. "You don't want to hear about that."

"If you need to talk about it, then I want to listen."

Her gaze dropped as she twisted the edge of the blanket around her finger. "I hate him. He took so much from me. Every nightmare is a reminder of that."

Carter searched for the right words to say, but he was at a loss. Everything seemed too cliché. Too placating. How could he offer comfort to her?

Please, Father, give me wisdom.

He saw her begin to tap her finger against her leg. "Just breathe. In and out."

When Carter saw her shoulders moving in time with his counting, he continued on. That she trusted him, felt safe with him, was a relief. Knowing what she'd been through, he accepted this as the precious gift that it was.

"You're safe here," he told her after several minutes.

"I don't understand," she murmured after a few moments of silence, her fingers still once again.

He wanted to ask what exactly she didn't understand, but he didn't. Instead, he just said, "I don't understand either."

That was the most truthful thing he could say at that moment. There were so many things he couldn't comprehend.

"I want to understand why God allowed this to happen to me," she whispered, as if afraid to say it any louder. As if she was scared God might strike her dead for even having such a thought.

"It seems there are things that we will never understand while here on earth." Carter thought of his own life and the questioning he'd done over the years. It had taken so long for him to move from questioning to...he didn't want to say acceptance because he wasn't fully there yet. And maybe he never would be, but he understood her desire to understand why.

"My therapist has told me I didn't do anything wrong, but sometimes I wonder."

"You think you did something to deserve what happened to you?" Carter could hardly believe that.

"I wanted a boyfriend...a relationship...so badly that I looked at someone who was too good to be true and went for him anyway because he made me feel like I was special."

Carter wanted to tell her that she *was* special, but he sensed that right then wasn't the time. "Lots of people want that. Lots of people use dating apps to find that special person. Lots of people are good...maybe some even seem too good to be true...and yet they're still good people. You did nothing wrong in wanting what you did and how you went about trying to get it."

She glanced at him before turning her gaze back to her hands. "When I see Sarah with Beau and Cara and Anna with Kieran and Eli, I'm happy for them, but I feel like I made a huge mistake by taking the path I did to try and find a relationship. And now I'm being punished for it."

"Pearse is a horrible man. That is the only reason you ended up suffering. Nothing that you did caused your suffering. Absolutely nothing." He wanted to tell her she could have what Sarah and Beau and the others had, but once again, he knew it wasn't the time. "Lots of people use dating apps to find love and don't encounter someone like Pearse. It wasn't your fault."

"You sound like my therapist," she said. "It's just really hard to accept that I didn't play a role in what happened."

"Do you think the other women he captured played a role in their torture? In their murder? Did they deserve it?"

Jillian looked at him then, her eyes wide. "Of course not."

"But he got them the same way he got you, right?"

Her eyes closed briefly, and when she opened them again, she kept her gaze lowered. "Maybe it's easier to think that it happened because of something I did than to accept that it was truly just an act of senseless violence."

Tears slipped down her cheeks, and she lifted the edge of the blanket to wipe them away. Carter scooted to the end of the loveseat so he could be closer to her. Reaching out, he touched her hand where it was fisted in the blanket.

"This doesn't have to define you," Carter said. "Let the evilness of what happened define *him,* but don't let that define you. You may have been victimized, but you don't have to stay as his victim."

"That's easier said than done," she said, a spark of anger in her voice.

"Yes. I know it is, but don't let him win. *He* wanted you to be his victim. Don't give him that."

She stared at him for a moment, her brows drawing together. His heart thumped against his ribs as he waited for her to respond. He didn't want to upset her, but he needed her to know that he thought she was strong enough to rise above the victimization that Pearse had subjected her to.

In his heart, Carter was sure that she would never be able to move forward, to find freedom and to love, if she wasn't able to see a reason to fight to be more than just Pearse's ninth victim. Her identity might not be public knowledge, but it was enough that she thought of herself that way.

"I know you're right," Jillian said, her gaze lowered again. "But it's so hard. So very hard."

"You are strong, Jillian, and I'll be with you every step of the way."

She took a deep breath and let it out. "I can't ask that of you."

"You're not asking it of me. I'm offering it to you."

"Why?" she asked, her brow furrowed. "This wasn't part of our agreement. I don't expect you to deal with all of this. You need to find someone who you can have a real relationship with, if that's what you want."

Carter hesitated, still convinced that her mind wasn't in the right place to hear how he truly felt about her. "It may have not been part of our agreement, and though I wish you'd never gone through what you did, I'm still going to stick by you unless you tell me you don't want me around anymore. Don't tell me to go for my sake.

Don't do it because you think I'd be better off with someone else. Only do it because you really don't want me in your life anymore."

"Why? I don't understand why you want to have to deal with my panic attacks and all the stuff that comes from me having gone through what I have. You've had so much stress and sadness in your life already with Suzanne. You don't need my complications."

"You've come to mean a lot to me," Carter said hesitantly. "I *want* to be with you through all of this."

Jillian let out a long breath. "If there comes a moment when it's too much, I want you to know that I'd never be mad at you or fault you for walking away."

"That's not going to happen," Carter said with a confidence he felt right down into his soul.

As silence took hold again, Carter noticed there was a bit of a chill in the air. "Do you want me to light a fire?"

She looked at him as she said, "Do you know how?"

"I not only know how to put fires out, I also know how to start them," Carter said with a grin. "So, if you'd like a fire, I can get one going."

"That would be nice."

Carter stood up and approached the box of logs, opening the door of the stove to begin building the fire. Soon, it was crackling to life, and warmth spilled out into the small room.

As he settled back on the couch, Carter noticed that Jillian's gaze was on the fire as it danced behind the glass in the door. Her blinks were slow, and it didn't surprise him when he glanced at her a short time later and saw that her eyes were closed. He stayed quiet, unable to fall asleep himself as his thoughts continued to spin with what he'd learned that day.

He didn't know how the next little while was going to play out. There wasn't any way for him to stay with Jillian each night, as much as he would have liked that. He doubted Sarah and Cara would be able to move in with Jillian indefinitely, which was the only way he could spend nights in her home. Plus, he had shifts at the firehouse that he still needed to cover.

Carter hated the idea of having to trust the Portland PD to keep track of Pearse, but he really had no choice. Unfortunately, his level of trust in the justice system wasn't exactly high at that moment. However, he was pretty sure the cops weren't any happier with the way this situation had played out than he was.

The thing that bothered him the most about it was knowing that Pearse had access to a lot of money. That kind of wealth, in turn, gave him access to people and things that could help him to either track down Jillian and the other woman who'd survived or escape justice altogether by fleeing the country.

Neither of those options would allow Jillian to live in peace.

The sound of increased breathing drew Carter from his thoughts, and he moved closer to Jillian again. He didn't know whether he should wake her up or not, so he settled, at first, for taking her hand in his.

Stroking his thumb across the back of her hand, he softly murmured, "You're safe, sweetheart. No one can hurt you. You're safe."

Her hand clenched his as her movements became more erratic, and she began to whimper softly. "*No. Please. No. I just want to go home.*"

Her words broke Carter's heart. "You *are* home, Jillian. Wake up and see that you're home. Nothing can hurt you here."

Her grip was tight on his hand, but he wouldn't have it any other way. Over the next few minutes, he continued to talk to her as she murmured and whimpered, sweat beading on her forehead. He braced himself for a scream or crying, but she never got louder, which was all the more heartbreaking. It was as if she knew that being loud wouldn't lead to her rescue.

When she finally woke up, it wasn't a gentle waking. Her eyes popped open as she sucked in a huge breath. Her gaze was unfocused, but when Carter spoke to her again, she turned her head to look at him. "Carter?"

"I'm here," he said. "You're safe."

Her eyes fluttered shut as she dragged in several erratic breaths, visibly trembling. He counted with her, sensing a panic attack was lurking. He was grateful to see the counting was working when she loosened her grip on his hand and her expression relaxed a bit.

"Thank you," she said, opening her eyes again after awhile.

"You're welcome." This time he didn't ask her about the nightmare since he was pretty sure he'd get the same response. "Can I get you something?"

"I can get it."

"No. Let me. Just tell me what you need."

"A glass of water." Her gaze dropped. "And a cookie."

"I'll be right back." Carter went to the kitchen and quickly found the glasses and filled one with water. When he opened the cookie container, he ended up taking two—one for her and one for himself.

When he got back to the sunroom, he handed her the glass of water and one of the cookies. "I decided to join you in the midnight snack."

She gave him a small smile. "I usually eat a piece of chocolate or something like that after a nightmare. It helps to ground me. Gives me something good to focus on."

"That makes sense," Carter said as he broke off a part of the cookie then popped it into his mouth.

"I don't know if it's a good thing to do or not, but it seems to help me."

"Then I would say it's a good thing."

She took small bites of her cookie between sips of water until both were gone. Letting out a sigh, she rested her head back, her eyes sliding shut. Carter could see the utter exhaustion on her face, but he doubted that she wanted to fall asleep again.

"Is it better if someone wakes you up from your nightmare?" he asked. "I wasn't sure what to do when I realized you were having one."

"Whatever you did was fine," she said. "It doesn't seem to matter much whether I wake myself up from the nightmare or someone else does. I usually end up having a panic attack afterward, especially during high-stress times like this." She sighed. "When I'm in a more stable place mentally—like I was before the harassment happened with Martin—my nightmares are infrequent and not always followed by a panic attack.

"But all of this, on top of still not feeling completely back to normal...or whatever my normal is now...has really set me back. It's almost like being back to the weeks immediately following my rescue."

"Were you in the hospital long?" Carter asked hesitantly, not sure if she was able to talk about that time or not.

"Two weeks. I was dealing with infection, dehydration, and starvation." She hesitated. "I was up next."

A pit formed in Carter's stomach. "What do you mean?"

Jillian stared vacantly at the stove. "He kept two girls at a time, but we were staggered. The girl who was there when he kidnapped me said that she was going to die next. That was how it worked. When she disappeared, a new girl showed up. That's when I knew my time was coming. He only gave us enough water to keep us from dying right away, but we weren't fed, hardly at all. It meant we were weak. Pliable."

Carter wanted to throw up at the thought that a man could be so twisted.

"The girl who was there with me at first was named Leanne. She made me memorize the names of the other girls who had already died by his hand. *Amy. Jan. Lizzie. Lena. Marianne. Tanya. Yvette.* She shared them with me. I shared them with Stef, the girl who was kidnapped after me. We wanted to make sure that if anyone was ever rescued, they'd know who else he'd killed."

"They were able to find all the bodies, though, right?"

Jillian nodded, still not looking at him. "We didn't know he was...disposing of them in such a way that they would be found. That's the only good thing in all of this. That the families of the other girls were able to have closure. Leanne had a message for me to pass on to her family, just like I gave one to Stef for my grandma."

"Were you able to talk to Leanne's family?"

Her gaze finally met his. "Her father. Her mother had passed away a few years earlier. She was all her father had left."

She didn't have to say how difficult that conversation must have been. He could see it in her eyes. It was just one more horrible thing she'd had to endure.

"I hate him." She looked away again. "I wish he was dead, just like the girls he killed because of his sick, twisted mind."

Carter completely understood why she felt that way. Just knowing how the man had hurt Jillian made Carter want him dead too. He didn't want to think about the damage Pearse could do now that he was out of prison, even if he was wearing an ankle monitor.

"My therapist said my hatred of him will only end up affecting me more than it ever would him. That it will only eat at me." Jillian paused, biting on her lower lip as she once again stared at the fire. "I'm sure she's right, and I know the Bible says we should forgive, but I struggle with that where he is concerned."

"Forgiveness is a tricky thing. Whether it's forgiving someone else or forgiving ourselves, it's hard."

"Have you forgiven yourself?" Jillian asked, looking back at him. "For what happened with Suzanne?"

Carter didn't particularly want to discuss that. But given how forthcoming Jillian had been about her own trauma, it was only fair. "I don't know that I'll ever not feel responsible for what happened.

It was at my insistence that we go to my folks' place that night. It was about an hour away, so Suzanne wanted to go the next morning. I was upset that while I had put off leaving in order for us to attend the dinner put on by the company she worked for, she changed her mind about leaving later that night like we'd agreed.

"She eventually gave in, but she wasn't happy about it. Because of that, it's hard not to feel responsible. If I'd just agreed to leave the next day, we wouldn't have been on the road at the same time as the drunk driver who hit us. Plus, we were arguing as I drove. I was distracted."

"Do you think the guy wouldn't have hit you if you hadn't been distracted?"

Carter let the events of that night play through his mind, something he rarely allowed, then he sighed. "No. He still would have hit us. If I'd been focused on the road, I wouldn't have seen him at all. The only reason I saw him was because I was turned toward Suzanne."

"From what you've said, it doesn't seem like Evelyn and Garth hold you responsible. I would think that if they did, they wouldn't let you near their daughter."

"Yeah. They've never said anything that suggests they feel that it was my fault. The prison I've been in for the past ten years has been one of my own making."

"Maybe you need to go to counseling, too," she said. "I can recommend a therapist."

They shared a smile then. "Maybe I'll take you up on that recommendation."

Jillian fell silent then, and Carter didn't pursue any more conversation. It wasn't long before he glanced over and saw that Jillian had drifted off to sleep again. He was surprised that she was able to fall asleep so quickly. But having seen her exhaustion earlier, it was possible it got to the point where her body won out over her mind. At least for long enough for her to fall asleep.

He prayed that she would rest peacefully. That she would have no more nightmares.

But despite his prayer, about an hour into her sleep, he watched as another nightmare crept up on her. He did the same thing that time around as he had the first, and once she woke up, without her asking, he went to the kitchen to get her another glass of water and a cookie.

After that nightmare, he didn't pursue heavy conversation, hoping she'd fall back to sleep again even though he knew it might bring on another nightmare. Still, she needed the rest, especially if she planned to go to work the next day.

As she sat curled up in the chair, her gaze on the flames that he'd brought back to life, he told her stories of his growing up years in a small town in Florida. Soon, she had drifted off again, and Carter stayed close, keeping watch over her in a way that was similar to how he'd kept watch over Suzanne over the years.

By the time six AM rolled around, Jillian had slept a bit more, but she still looked exhausted when she finally gave up on sleep and went back to her bedroom to get ready for her day. Carter stayed in the sunroom for a few more minutes, thinking back over the night.

When he'd made the decision to stay the night he hadn't expected to watch over Jillian as she slept. But even though it had meant no sleep for him, he'd done it gladly. With that knowledge came the realization that he would always want to stand guard over Jillian, to protect her from whatever might want to hurt her...whether that was nightmares or someone like Martin. He wanted it to be his responsibility to care for her in that way. His heart pretty much demanded it.

Carter was in the kitchen when Cara made an appearance. She looked more rumpled than he'd ever seen her, but she gave him a friendly smile as she approached the coffee pot.

"How was your night?" she asked. "Anything happen?"

"Jillian was up with nightmares."

Cara turned from where she'd been doctoring her coffee with a frown. "I figured that would happen."

"Once she got up, we just sat in the sunroom with the fire on. She dozed off and on, but I don't think she got much good sleep."

Carter took several sips from his mug, feeling the need for an influx of caffeine if he was going to be able to face the day. He was going to need to sleep at some point so that he could be in a fit state to work the following morning.

He was debating what he should do about breakfast when Jillian reappeared, followed shortly by Sarah. The three ladies huddled over mugs of coffee at the island, clearly none of them having had a restful night. Carter stood opposite them, watching how they interacted.

"Are you sure you should go to work today?" Sarah asked.

"I need to. They're counting on me, and I refuse to let that man take this away from me, too."

"I love you." Sarah slipped her arm around Jillian's shoulders and leaned against her. "You're so strong, and I'm glad you're my friend."

"I'm so glad you're my friend too," Jillian responded, resting her head against Sarah's. "Both you and Cara." She looked up at Carter and smiled. "And you too, Carter. I appreciate all you're doing for me."

Carter felt warmth spread through him. He didn't know what lay ahead for them, but in his heart, he knew he was there for the long haul.

CHAPTER THIRTY-THREE

Jillian got through the day, going to school as planned, despite feeling emotionally and physically worn out. Carter drove her to her therapy appointment that night, even though she'd told him she could go on her own. Thankfully, he'd stuck by his guns.

Her session had been exhausting. That wasn't anything new, really, but because of the recent events, it seemed entirely too much. The therapist had strongly suggested that it might be time to go back on some medication, and though Jillian wasn't thrilled at the idea, she had to admit that maybe it she was right.

She was glad that Carter was there to drive her home, and she was very glad that he didn't ask any probing questions. He offered to stop and get her food when he discovered she hadn't had supper. She only thought about it for a moment before taking him up on his offer.

They pulled through a fast-food drive-thru since she preferred not to have to deal with people, then they headed back to New Hope. She munched on fries and nuggets as Carter drove. He'd had something to eat while she'd been in with the therapist, so he hadn't ordered anything for himself.

"I wish I could stay at the house again tonight," he said when he pulled to a stop in her driveway a short time later. "But I have a shift tomorrow, and I need to get some sleep."

"I'll be fine," she assured him. "Sarah said she'd come to stay with me again in case I need someone, plus Kieran said he still has officers outside the house."

"Yeah, he told me that the Portland PD has been keeping in touch with him, and Pearse hasn't left his family's house."

Jillian forced back a shudder at the thought of his family. His rich and powerful family that had shown up in court each day to support their evil, sadistic son. Considering everything he seemed to have going for him, it still surprised her that the prosecution had managed to get a guilty verdict on the first trial. Something told her they might not be as lucky this time around, especially if there were some issues with the evidence.

"You okay?" Carter asked.

Jillian realized she'd just been sitting there staring at her garage door. Normally she would have just brushed aside anyone's concern, but this was Carter. She'd already told him more than anyone else about her ordeal.

"Just wondering what the chances are of getting a second guilty verdict."

"Did your lawyer tell you what the judge's reasons were for granting the appeal?"

"Something about police procedure."

Jillian hadn't wanted to hear too many details, simply because she was already so discouraged and upset about the whole situation. She didn't want to hear that there was no chance of getting a guilty verdict because of something the police might or might not have done. It was bad enough she had those doubts because of the influence of his rich and well-known family.

"Well, we'll just have to pray that God will make sure that doesn't happen."

Jillian had been struggling with God's role in the whole situation. Why had He allowed the judge to grant the appeal? Why had He allowed him to set bail for Pearse? None of it made sense to her.

Pearse was an evil man. There was no way this latest decision was beneficial to anyone. Not her and Stef. Certainly not to any other innocent women who were now at risk because he was free. The only person it benefited even remotely was Pearse.

The thing was, she didn't doubt that God could make all of this turn out in a way that saw Pearse back where he belonged. But she already knew that sometimes God worked in ways no one could understand. So while she didn't doubt that He *could* make sure the next trial saw Pearse back in prison, she wasn't as confident that He *would*.

"Are you sure you're going to be okay tonight?"

Jillian sighed as she realized she'd spaced out yet *again*. She needed to rein her thoughts in long enough to get inside the house. "I'll be alright."

"You can call me if you need to talk," Carter said. "Even tomorrow. As long as I'm not out on a call or in a meeting, I'll answer."

"Thank you," Jillian said, truly appreciating that he made himself available for her in that way.

"Ready to go in?" he asked.

She nodded and reached for her door handle. He met her at the front of the truck and walked with her to the door.

"When is Sarah coming?"

"I told her I'd text her when I was home." She punched in the code to unlock the front door then did the same with the alarm once she stepped inside the house.

Though she didn't feel at all safe with Pearse out of prison, she didn't feel particularly unsafe once she was within the walls of her house, especially after the alarm was reset. This house had always been a place of safety and security for her. The world, however cruel or unkind it had been, had always ceased to exist once she stepped into this house. That had been true for her as a teen, and it was true for her now.

"Do you want me to hang around until she gets here?" Carter asked as he followed her into the house and closed the door.

Jillian thought about it then nodded. "If you don't mind."

When Carter didn't respond right away, she turned to look at him to find him staring at her, his expression serious. "I don't mind. If I offer to do something, you can bet that I don't mind. At all."

"Okay. Then yes. I would appreciate it if you could stay." Jillian pulled her phone out as she headed to the kitchen. "I'll send her a text now, so you don't have to wait long."

Carter slid onto one of the barstools. "Sticking around isn't a hardship."

His words warmed her in a way they shouldn't have. In a way, she shouldn't have let them. But none of that mattered, apparently, because more and more, she was letting him into her life and into her heart. Unfortunately, she was more convinced than ever that going down that road was going to lead to heartache...for both of them.

"Want some coffee?" she offered, feeling the need to do something for him. Something more than breaking his heart.

"I'm going to have to pass on that," he said with a shake of his head. "I need to sleep tonight if I'm going to be able to function at work tomorrow."

"So would a glass of warm milk work better?"

Carter visibly shuddered. "Nope. Let's not go there. That was my mom's go-to when we couldn't sleep. Unless she put hot chocolate mix in it, I could barely gag it down."

"Let me guess," Jillian said as she pulled out her box of teas. "She didn't let you have the hot chocolate."

"No. She did not." Carter sighed. "That was only for special occasions."

"I'd offer that to you, except there's caffeine in chocolate too, so if you need to sleep, that's not going to help either." She set the box of teas in front of him. "But if you'd like a nice tea without caffeine, I have a few options."

He eyed the box like he expected a bunch of snakes to begin crawling out of it. "Uh."

"Not a tea fan?" Their conversation was shallow and a bit light-hearted, but it was what Jillian needed right then. No more talk of Pearse or trials or what she'd endured.

"Not really, no."

"So it's coffee or water?"

"Basically. I also like apple and orange juice."

"I do have orange juice if you'd like some."

"I'm fine."

Jillian turned her kettle on to boil some water for herself. "I don't know if this tea helps me sleep or not, but I drink it anyway. I figure it can't hurt."

"It's probably better for you than coffee regardless."

They passed the time waiting for Sarah to arrive talking about food preferences and other mundane things. Though she could still see a shadow of concern in Carter's eyes, he didn't voice it, and for that, she was very grateful. After her intense session with the therapist, she needed an escape from the past even though she was still mired in it. Those moments of reprieve were like an island oasis in the midst of an ocean of awfulness.

When the doorbell rang, Jillian was a bit disappointed because she knew it meant Carter would be leaving.

"I'll get it," Carter said as he got up from his stool.

Jillian watched him go as she lifted her mug to take a sip. When she heard the murmur of conversation, she could only imagine what was being said. At one time, she might have taken offense or gotten upset that they were talking about her. However, right then, she knew that they were talking out of concern for her, and given what all she'd gone through, she could hardly blame them.

When they appeared a couple of minutes later, Sarah smiled broadly and came to give her a hug. "Ready for another sleepover?"

Jillian returned her hug, then stepped back. "As ready as I'll ever be. I have to say, though, that our sleepovers in high school were a lot more fun."

Sarah sighed as she settled on a stool, bracing her chin on her hand. "True. But I guess it's a bit difficult to stay up all night eating junk food and watching rom-coms when there's work the next day."

"Yeah, I've got to be alert enough to deal with all the little ones. They keep me on my toes, that's for sure."

"Well, since I'm not invited to this slumber party," Carter began as he pushed away from the island where he'd been leaning, "I'd better head out. Morning will come early for me too."

"Being an adult sucks sometimes," Sarah said.

Jillian couldn't help but smile at her friend's expression. "But the good part is that you get to date an amazing man like Beau."

Sarah grinned and nodded. "That is definitely the best part."

"Well, I hope you're both able to sleep well," Carter said. "Have a good night."

Jillian trailed after him as he headed for the front door. "Were you able to sleep today?"

"Yep. I crashed for a few hours this morning, which was enough since I want to be able to sleep tonight."

She watched as he slipped his feet into his shoes and then pulled his jacket back on. "Thank you for chauffeuring me around to-night."

When he met her gaze, his features held an expression she didn't want to name. "Any time. Just give me a call." He opened the door. "I'll talk to you tomorrow."

"Yep. Bye." Jillian stepped into the doorway, leaning against its edge as she watched him walk across the porch and down the steps to the sidewalk that ran around to the driveway where his truck was parked.

She didn't close the door until she saw him back out, and the taillights of his truck disappeared down the road. With a sigh, she stepped back into the house and locked the door before turning to arm the alarm.

When she went back to the kitchen, Sarah was in the process of preparing herself a cup of tea. It made Jillian happy to see her friend making herself at home in her house.

"How was your day?" Sarah asked as she dunked the teabag in her mug. "Did the kids behave?"

Grateful that Sarah was asking about the one part of her day that she was happy to discuss, Jillian launched into a few stories about how the kids had been. "What did you do today?"

"Helped out with meals and just hung around in case people needed something. It's kind of weird when we get a big group like we have right now. They all know each other, so that means they're hanging out everywhere in the lodge. The living room. The dining room. The porch. It's so much crazier than when all we have are small groups of people who don't know each other."

"Hopefully they're nice."

"Yeah. They are. Can't complain about that."

They chatted a bit more before Jillian caught herself yawning. She was tired, but she was also a bit worried about going to bed. The night before, the nightmares had been familiar, but no less terrifying than they usually were. But waking up to find Carter in the chair beside her had made it more tolerable.

"You look like you're ready for bed," Sarah said.

Jillian nodded as she put her mug in the dishwasher. "It's been a long day."

"I'm sure. Is there anything I can do to help you sleep better?"

"I wish there was, but all I can do is just hope for the best. There are things I do to help me relax and focus on positive and uplifting things. But..." Jillian shrugged. "Usually, the nightmares are stronger than anything I do."

Sarah's brow furrowed. "Even prayer?"

"Seems like it," Jillian said with another shrug. How did she explain how she struggled with that? "I pray and recite verses and have worship music playing. Anything that I can think of to try to protect my mind from the nightmares, but nothing works. I don't know about others in situations like mine, but I can't even take sleeping pills because they just make me sleep deeper so that I can't free myself from the nightmares as quickly."

"I'm sorry to hear that." Sarah stared down at her tea. "I wish I could do more than just pray for you, but that's all I've got to offer."

"And that's enough," Jillian assured her. "I understand that you probably feel like you can't do anything to help me, but just being here. Supporting me. Hugging me. Praying for me. It all really does help. Without you guys...well, I'd be all alone now that my grandma's not here."

"Then I'm doubly glad that you're back here where we can care for you."

"I'm glad too. When the doors started opening for me to come back to New Hope, it seemed like this was where God wanted me to be, and now I can see why. He knew what was going to happen and that I'd need the support New Hope had to offer when the tough times came."

Sarah blew out a long breath. "Still. I wish this wasn't happening to you. What went through that judge's mind that he thought the release of Pearse was a good move? I just can't even imagine."

"If something happens to another woman..." Jillian couldn't even allow herself to think about that possibility.

The conversation faded after that. Really, what more could they say? Though she wasn't eager to go to bed, Jillian knew it was time. Sarah said she was going to read for a while, so she picked up her bag while Jillian turned off the lights. She went into the den that looked out on the front street, checking for the presence of the car she knew belonged to the cops before heading into her room.

Even though she knew it probably wouldn't do much to ward of the nightmares, she took a bath then went through the rest of her bedtime routine on the off chance it would work that night. After she crawled into bed, she spent time praying that God would guard her mind as she slept.

By the time Friday afternoon rolled around, Jillian was glad the week was over. As usual, the kids had been full of life, which had made her alternate between being grateful for the distraction and being exhausted from their rambunctiousness. She'd also had another therapist session the night before, so that had added to her feeling of being rundown.

Though she hadn't planned to do anything more than take a hot bath and crawl into bed, Cara and Sarah had insisted that they have their regularly scheduled Fondue Friday. They'd said they'd provide the food, so all she had to do was open the door and let them in.

Jillian had agreed only after they'd promised there would be no discussion of the events of the week. She hadn't seen Anna since hearing the news of Pearse's release, so Jillian had thought maybe she would mention it. However, the only thing Anna did when she arrived was give her an extra tight hug while she whispered that she'd been praying for her.

After that, the evening progressed much the same as their other Friday night fondues had. They'd ended up just ordering pizza, so no one had to cook, which was fine by Jillian since that was one of her favorite foods.

They were partway through their fondue when the doorbell rang. Jillian froze, fear spiking through her. A few seconds later, Cara's phone chirped, and she picked it up to read the screen.

"Kieran says it's him at the door." She got up from where she'd been seated on the floor across the coffee table from Jillian. "I'll go see what he wants."

Jillian dipped the banana she'd taken into the chocolate but then just set it on her plate, listening to the murmurs of conversation from the front door. When Cara returned, she had Kieran with her.

Jillian's heart skipped a beat at the unexpected sight of Carter with the couple. She hadn't seen him since he'd dropped her off after her therapy session on Wednesday night. Glancing between the two men, Jillian saw a curious mix of seriousness and relief on their faces.

"What's going on?" Sarah asked.

"We need to talk to Jillian for a minute," Kieran said.

With fear pooling in the pit of her stomach, Jillian got up from the floor to face him. "What's happened?"

Carter came to stand next to her and took her hand. She gripped it tightly as she waited for Kieran to speak.

"I received a call from the Portland PD a little bit ago, and they told me that Pearse is dead." Kieran paused. "He committed suicide."

Jillian shook her head as she sank down on the couch, still clutching Carter's hand. She stared at the piece of banana sitting in a puddle of chocolate on her plate. "That's not possible."

"Why do you say that?" Kieran asked.

"There's no way he would have committed suicide." Jillian paused, allowing herself to remember things he'd said as he'd tortured her. "That's not the type of man he is. *Was.* That's not the type of man he was. He was a sadistic narcissist. Probably a psychopath as well. He thought far too highly of himself to believe that his own life was expendable."

"So you don't believe he committed suicide?" Kieran asked, settling onto the couch beside her while Carter sat down on her other side.

Jillian shook her head, her thoughts processing what Kieran had told her along with everything else. "I thought that his family must have paid off the judge to not just grant the appeal but to let him out on bail."

"And you don't think that now?"

"Oh, I still believe that, but now, I'm wondering if they did it for another reason."

"Like what?" Kieran prompted.

"What if his family saw this as a way of clearing the family name, so to speak. Him committing suicide conveys that he felt remorse for what he did, though he never—through word or action—showed that previously." She frowned. "What if they paid the judge to let him out so that they could stage a suicide? What if his own family killed him?"

Jillian looked over at Kieran to find him regarding her with a small smile. "Maybe I should hire you as a detective."

"Are others thinking that too?"

"It is by far the most popular opinion held among the Portland PD at the moment," Kieran said.

She stared at him for a moment before asking, "Are they sure he's dead? Like they saw his body and everything? If his family staged his suicide so that he could escape, more women will be at risk."

"The detective I spoke to said that they were taking DNA samples, and his body won't be released until they confirm a match. They did an initial comparison of photos taken of him when he was first arrested to compare tattoos and scars. All of that lined up, but they're covering all their bases. The detective knows what's at risk if they let this man slip through their fingers."

Jillian rubbed her fingers against her lips. Was it possible that he was truly gone? That he would never again be able to threaten her? Even as relief flowed through her body, she knew that it didn't mean everything else would suddenly return to normal. She still had to deal with the lasting effects that his kidnapping and assault had wreaked on her mind and body.

"So, it's really over?" Sarah asked. "No second trial? Nothing like that?"

"As long as they verify the DNA, there should be nothing further."

"Will they try and find out if he was actually murdered?" Jillian asked.

"The detective said that nothing at the scene led them to believe it was anything but suicide. The reason they suspect it is fake is that, like you, they don't believe he was the sort of person to take his own life. However, if his family doesn't press for further investigation, they won't really have any proof that it is anything but a suicide. It will be a closed case."

"I can't believe it's over." Jillian slumped against Carter, feeling all the tension she'd been carrying since Pearse's release drain from her body.

Of course, things weren't completely over. The case with Martin still had to be dealt with, but thankfully, that had become more than just a *he said-she said* sort of case because he'd shot a police officer. He'd been released from the hospital, but he was still in custody. Even though bail had been set for him, he hadn't posted it, and no one had come forward to post it for him. Knowing where he was made her feel more secure.

Though she wasn't looking forward to his trial, she would do what she had to in order to keep him behind bars. She'd testified against Pearse and survived. She could testify against Martin and survive too.

CHAPTER THIRTY-FOUR

The next few weeks passed quickly for Jillian. With Christmas approaching, she'd been involved in several events. The elementary school Christmas program had been followed by Cara's Christmas recital for the students from her dance studio. On top of that, there had been the Christmas Fair.

And through most of it, Carter had been by her side. He hadn't been able to attend the Christmas Fair with her since he was scheduled to work, but he'd attended in an official capacity. So he'd been wandering around the booths, much like Kieran had been.

Jillian had helped the McNamaras with the three booths they had set up, circulating between them as they'd needed help. Sarah and Eli each had one for their art and woodwork. The other booth was for the Christmas baking Leah and Nadine had done. It had been a festive day that she had enjoyed very much.

Interspersed amongst the Christmas events had been lots of therapy appointments. That meant more hard work for her, but she'd pushed through as best she could. The frequency of her nightmares had fluctuated, often depending on how stressed she was by the therapy or by her life in general. Thankfully, the medication she'd finally agreed to take once again had started to help ease the anxiety and panic attacks.

As Christmas drew closer, Jillian struggled with moments of intense grief since it would be her first one without her grandma. But her girlfriends had dropped by to help her decorate, clearly determined to let her know that she wasn't alone.

If someone had told her back in high school that this would be her life, she wouldn't have believed them. She'd operated with a *that will never happen to me* mindset back then. Or maybe she'd just hoped that because she'd already suffered through parental abandonment and the loss of her grandpa that God wouldn't send even more suffering and hardship her way. How wrong she'd been.

But those thoughts were for another time, Jillian reminded herself. She was among friends, celebrating Christmas Eve at the lodge. They'd invited her to be there for all their Christmas celebrations, including spending that night with them. Though she'd accepted the invite for Christmas Eve get-together and Christmas Day dinner, she planned to go back to her own house to sleep.

"Merry Christmas!" Sarah sang out as she looped her arm around Jillian's shoulders.

"You've already said that," Jillian said with a grin. "Several times."

"You really can't say it too much." Sarah dropped her arm. "Are you having a good time?"

"I am," Jillian assured her. "It's been wonderful. Thank you for inviting me."

"You're welcome." Sarah gave her another hug. "I just wish Carter could be here."

"He'll be here tomorrow. Ready to eat lots of yummy food, I would imagine." She knew she would be.

A lot of the same people were there who had been present at the Thanksgiving dinner. People like her who had nowhere else to spend the holiday. Not for the first time, she was thankful for the generosity and kindness of the McNamaras.

"Hey, Carter!" Sarah said, her smile widening.

For a moment, Jillian thought she was joking, but when she turned toward the entrance to the living room, her heart skipped a beat when she spotted him. He headed straight over to where she stood with Sarah.

"Hey!" She smiled up at him. "I thought you were working."

"I am. I just took an hour off to drop by." His expression was soft as he looked at her. "I wanted to see you."

His words made her heart swell with emotion that she didn't want to feel. And yet... "I'm glad you came."

"Me, too."

"Do you want something to eat?" she asked, wanting to make sure he had food in case he was missing dinner at the station.

"I'd be a fool to pass up any food offered in this place," Carter said with a grin and offered her his arm.

"Yes. You would be," Jillian agreed. After a moment's hesitation, she wrapped her fingers around his arm. "Let's go see what we can find for you."

Carter reached over and covered her hand with his, a bit of cold still lingering in his fingers. He led her through the living room, saying hello to people as they passed them.

In the dining room, he seemed reluctant to let go of her hand, but he did. Picking up a plate, he waited for Jillian's comments on what foods she had enjoyed. There was a huge variety of appetizer-style finger foods spread out on the large table. Some of the platters were half empty, but there was still plenty of food left.

When his plate was filled, he took her hand again, and they returned to the living room. They settled on chairs near where Sarah now sat with Beau, Rhett, and Julianna.

"It's so nice you could come by for a bit," Sarah said. "Were they having special food at the station tonight?"

"The guys were cooking a ham and scalloped potatoes, and there are quite a few baked goodies. Some of the guys' wives sent cookies decorated by their kids. They had so many sprinkles on them," Carter said with a laugh and a shake of his head. "*So* many sprinkles."

"I got a few of those cookies on the last day of school," Jillian said with a chuckle.

"We've had lots of baked goods around here." Sarah glanced over to where Leah sat with a couple of their cousins. "Thankfully, they have been basically sprinkle-free."

Jillian couldn't believe how happy she was to have Carter there, even if it was just for an hour. His presence made the evening even more enjoyable for her.

When his time was up, Jillian walked with Carter to the front door. "Thank you so much for coming."

"It was definitely my pleasure. I guess I'll see you tomorrow for dinner." He hesitated for a moment. "I'm going to Seattle in the morning to see Evelyn, Garth, and Suzanne, but I'll be back in time for dinner."

Jillian thought for a moment then said, "Would you like company?"

Carter's brows rose. "You want to go with me to Seattle? You want to meet Evelyn and Garth?"

He seemed so surprised that Jillian wondered if maybe she shouldn't have said anything. "Uh...maybe? If you want?"

"I do," he said quickly, as if sensing that she was close to backing out of her offer. "I would love to have you come with me."

"Are you sure Evelyn and Garth wouldn't mind?"

Carter gave a quick shake of his head. "They wouldn't mind at all. In fact, I know they'd love to meet you."

"What time do you need to leave?"

"Around ten."

"When were you planning to sleep?"

"I was hoping to sleep some tonight, then just run on caffeine and adrenaline for the rest of the day."

"Why don't we take my car?" she suggested. "Then I'll drive so you can sleep?"

He stared at her for a moment before a smile broke across his face. "Sounds like an excellent plan. I'll come to your house a little before ten."

"I look forward to it." Those words were the truth, even if she did have a little flutter of nerves in her stomach at the idea of meeting the people who, had things gone differently, would have been Carter's in-laws.

Carter pulled the door open, and a gust of cold air swept in. "See you tomorrow."

After he'd gotten in his truck, Jillian closed the door but kept her hand on the smooth wood surface. Her feelings were a bit like clothes in a tumble dryer. Excitement. Worry. Hope. Fear. They all tumbled around inside her. Oh yeah...and doubt.

Maybe she shouldn't have offered to go with him. She wasn't any closer to being able to engage in a real relationship than she had been at the beginning of their agreement. But she counted Carter as a friend—a really, really good friend—and she wanted to be a part of his life.

Carter hadn't said anything about changing the terms of their casual dating arrangement, even though he'd truly become more than just a casual person in her life. He knew so much about her life, she'd thought that maybe it was time she knew more about his. Had that been a mistake?

"Everything okay, Jillian?"

Sarah's voice had her turning from the door with a smile that probably looked as fake as it felt.

"Everything's fine." She moved toward where Sarah stood, a mug in her hands. "What have you got there?"

She lifted the mug. "Hot chocolate. Want some?"

"I think I do." Jillian followed Sarah into the kitchen, her thoughts still lingering on Carter and what the next day would hold.

There were others in the kitchen, most of them relatives of Sarah, who made room for them so Sarah could ladle some hot chocolate from a large pot on the stove into a mug. "Marshmallows?"

"Sure," Jillian said. "Why not?"

She still wasn't paying all that much attention to calories, maybe in the new year. Or maybe not.

"Why not, indeed?" Sarah grinned as she handed her a mug with several white lumps floating in the hot chocolate. She picked up her mug and tapped it against Jillian's. "Merry Christmas!"

Jillian laughed, so grateful for the joyful nature of the woman she considered one of her best friends. Over the past few weeks, she'd experienced—yet again—a roller coaster ride of emotions. The hardest part of being on the upswing of the roller coaster was knowing that there would be an inevitable downswing.

Having just gone through a horrible downswing, she'd spent a lot of time wishing she could just get off the ride. It was hard not to want to find a way to maintain a more even keel, so that even though she wouldn't have the highs, she also wouldn't have the horrible lows.

But as she watched Sarah smile and listened to her laughter, Jillian knew that that was never the life she'd wanted for herself. Was she going to let Pearse take away even the possibility of having a life where the highs consisted of smiles and laughter and the happiness of being with friends, just to avoid the lows?

No.

She would just have to embrace the highs, and if she had Sarah, Carter, and their other friends on the ride with her, she thought maybe she'd be able to survive the lows.

The next morning, Jillian was up early to get herself ready to meet the people who were important to Carter. She knew he had a family in Florida, and thought maybe she'd meet them some day—or maybe not. But for the moment, she knew that these people in Seattle were very important to him, so she just hoped that they liked her.

With that in mind, she'd taken forever to decide on what to wear. Her clothing options at her current size weren't anywhere close to the possibilities she'd once had. She'd gotten rid of all those clothes since she'd had no intention of dieting back down to that size. And that decision hadn't changed.

Though her reasons for gaining weight hadn't been based on health, she couldn't deny that not focusing on every single bite she put into her mouth had made her less stressed. And if there was one thing she didn't need more of right then, it was stress. So even if she was going to return to a healthier way of eating, it wouldn't be during the Christmas season and probably not until she was in a more settled mental state.

In the end, she settled for a pair of fitted black pants with just enough stretch that they would still be comfortable after she ate the big meal that was coming later that day. In celebration of the holiday, she chose a long, dark green sweater that ended just past her hips. It had a cowl neck that draped low on her chest. For jewelry, she chose a pair of earrings that had tiny wreaths dangling on silver chains.

By the time Carter arrived, she was battling nerves, but she was ready to go.

"Merry Christmas," he said when she opened the door.

Smiling, she echoed the greeting. After he had greeted Dolly, they walked through the house to the garage, where she turned on the alarm and locked the mudroom door. As the garage door rolled up, she shivered from the chill in the air. She could see a bit of snow scattered on the ground, but it wasn't a white Christmas by any stretch of the imagination.

Once they were in the car, Carter helped her put the address for the care home into the GPS navigator. "If you want me to drive once we get closer, we can switch."

"I think I'll be okay," Jillian said as she backed out of the garage then pressed the button on the remote on her visor to close the door. "I don't imagine there will be too much traffic today."

"That's probably true." Carter moved his seat back a bit.

"Feel free to sleep, if you need to," Jillian told him, hitting a button on her steering wheel to turn on her radio. Christmas music softly drifted from the station she'd had it set on since the beginning of the month.

"I was actually able to get a few hours sleep last night. We only had one call out."

"Hopefully nothing serious." There were times she forgot about the dangers of his job.

"No. An alarm came in from one of the apartment blocks, but when we got there, it was a false alarm. Some kid decided to pull the alarm in the hallway." Carter gave an exasperated chuckle. "Either the kid figured his gift from Santa was already a lost cause, or his parents didn't tell him that he still had to be good after midnight on Christmas Eve."

Jillian grinned at the image of some kid deciding that he didn't care what Santa thought, he was going to pull that fire alarm. "I'm guessing he got a bit of a lecture?"

"Just a bit," Carter said with a laugh. "I left that to one of the guys who actually has kids. I figured he would know better how to get the point across without scaring the kid."

"Did you want to have kids?" Jillian asked, only realizing after she asked the question that maybe it wasn't past tense for him.

"Sure. I'd always hoped to have a couple kids."

She wanted to ask if he still hoped for that, but she kept her mouth shut. She'd also hoped to have kids, but she'd let that dream die, choosing instead to focus on the children in her classroom. Bracing herself for Carter to ask the same question of her, she was a bit surprised when he didn't. Although, as she thought about it, he probably already knew what her answer would be.

"Does your family have a big celebration at Christmas?" she asked, steering the conversation away from a subject she wasn't comfortable pursuing even though she was the one who'd brought it up.

"Yep. Now that some of us are married, Mom has to juggle time with in-laws. That means that if we can't get everyone together on Christmas Eve and Christmas Day, she picks two other days, and they become Christmas Eve and Christmas Day.

"When was the last time you were there?"

"For Christmas, it's been about ten years. I have been back during that time for a couple of family weddings."

"What was your favorite part of Christmas as a kid?" Jillian always found it interesting how others had experienced the holiday as a child. While her grandparents had done their best to make things special, being an only child had meant that Christmas was fairly low-key.

They spent the rest of the trip talking about various Christmas memories. Hers weren't anywhere near as exciting as Carter's. Still, right then, she needed a distraction from what awaited them when they arrived at their destination.

As they neared the care home, Carter directed her to the right parking lot. It was only about half-full, so she had no problem finding a spot close to the entrance.

Her anxiety was rising as she turned off the car, and she was wishing she'd never suggested coming along with Carter. Maybe Christmas Day hadn't been the best day to meet these people who were so important to the man who had become so important to her.

"Hey," Carter said softly as he reached out and took her hand. "I would never take you somewhere that I wasn't one hundred percent certain you'd be okay."

"I'm sorry," she said. And she was... Sorry for not trusting him. Sorry for freaking out *yet again.*

He rubbed his thumb across the back of her hand. "You don't have to apologize. I just wanted to offer you some reassurance. We can sit here as long as you need to. There's no rush to get inside."

She nodded and stared down at their clasped hands. The feel of his hand holding hers was becoming familiar, and she found that it gave her a sense of peace.

As they sat there, Carter spent the time sharing more stories about his family and also slipped in a few about Evelyn and Garth. Her anxiety eventually settled, and she felt like she could handle the meeting with the couple.

"I'm ready," she said, tightening her hold on his hand for a moment.

"Are you sure?"

She nodded, wanting to show Carter that she could do this. That she could stare down something that caused her anxiety—although not without her meds.

"Okay, then." He flashed her a smile before opening his door. "Let's go."

CHAPTER THIRTY-FIVE

Jillian was a little slow to get her door open then she turned to grab her purse from the back seat. By the time she climbed out, Carter was there waiting for her. He offered his hand, and she took it without hesitation, falling into step beside him as they walked toward the entrance.

The three-story building was set on acreage that gave it a park-like setting. Its exterior was a mix of stone and siding in neutral shades, and it had tons of windows. While she knew it was a functional medical facility, it looked like it was a nice place for the residents.

A welcoming warmth greeted them as they stepped into the building. There were a lot of plants scattered around the foyer area as well as a large, brightly lit Christmas tree. Instrumental Christmas music played softly as they made their way across a large open space.

"Merry Christmas, Carter," a middle-aged woman called out with a smile as they neared a reception desk.

"Merry Christmas to you too, Megan."

Jillian braced herself for an introduction, but before it could come, another woman approached Megan and drew her attention from them.

Carter led her to a bank of elevators that took them to the third floor. When the doors slid open, they stepped out into another open area that had a smaller Christmas tree and a nurses' station.

A couple more people greeted Carter, which he acknowledged as they moved toward a wide hallway. The floor to ceiling windows at the end of the hallway allowed in copious amounts of sunlight.

They had almost reached the windows when Carter slowed in front of an open doorway.

Jillian took in a quick breath, realizing that she was about to come face to face with the woman Carter loved. The woman he'd wanted to spend his life with.

"Carter!" A petite woman rushed over to greet them with a beaming smile. Her dark hair was pulled back from a face with delicate features, expertly made up. She gave Carter a quick hug. "Merry Christmas, sweetheart."

A tall man approached them as well, a friendly expression on his face. He also gave Carter a hug. "I'm so glad you could make it."

"And you must be Jillian," Evelyn said, her smile—if possible—growing even larger. "I'm so happy to meet you."

What anxiety had been lingering inside her slipped away at the look of genuine joy on Evelyn's face. "I'm happy to meet you too."

"Come on in and have a seat," Garth said as he held out his hand to Jillian.

Jillian shook his hand then followed Carter to a small loveseat near the window. As she settled down next to him, she allowed her gaze to sweep the room.

With large windows, it was brightly lit, and there was a medium-size tree set up in the corner with lots of lights and color-coordinated red and green decorations. There was a coffee table in front of the loveseat as well as a couple of armchairs. The room was a good size and almost looked like what she envisioned a studio apartment to be.

It was hard to not stare at the bed that jutted out from the corner of the room, facing the windows, but Jillian managed to keep her gaze on Evelyn and Garth.

"I'm so glad that Carter brought you today," Evelyn said as she perched on the armchair closest to Jillian. "We've been so anxious to meet you."

Jillian knew that Carter hadn't told them about how things had started between them, and there was a part of her that understood that them seeing her there would no doubt make them think things were more serious between them than they were. Still, seeing their joy and happiness made her realize that they only wanted good for Carter. She wasn't sure what they'd think of her if they knew everything she struggled with and why.

"How is Suzie doing?" Carter asked, his attention going to the bed.

"She's doing good," Evelyn said. "No further infections or sickness this month, which is great."

"And you're feeling better?"

"I am. Still a bit tired at times, but I'm so much better than I was. I'm just glad Garth and Suzie didn't come down with whatever I had." She turned her attention to Jillian. "I'm sure this is kind of awkward for you, but I think that if you're going to be part of Carter's life, it's important you know about Suzanne."

Jillian nodded because she agreed, even if it was a bit of an odd situation. "I understand that."

"Come meet our girl," Evelyn said, getting to her feet.

Nerves flared to life within her because she wasn't sure what she was going to see, but she stood up as well. Carter got to his feet too, keeping his hand on her back as they approached the bed.

As she got her first glimpse of the woman who held Carter's heart, Jillian wasn't sure what to feel. She forced herself to keep her gaze on Suzanne and not glance at Carter to see what was on his face as he looked at the woman he loved.

Even though her features were slack, Jillian could see the resemblance to Evelyn. There was no doubt that Suzanne was a beautiful woman with dark hair, delicate features, and long lashes that fanned out over her cheeks.

Evelyn rubbed Suzanne's arm as she smiled down at her. "Hey, sweetheart. Carter's here, and he's brought a special friend to visit. Her name is Jillian."

Jillian shifted, a panicked feeling coursing through her. She'd read that people in a coma might be able to hear what people were saying to them. If Suzanne could hear what her mom was saying, was it upsetting her? Suzanne loved Carter. How would she feel hearing that Carter had a *special* friend?

Although what they really were to each other was...unknown.

They were definitely friends, but *special* friends? What exactly did that mean?

Perhaps standing at the bedside of a woman whose life was essentially over, wasn't exactly the best place to be having a relationship crisis. She looked up to see Evelyn watching her with a warm expression. Clearly, she didn't have an issue with imagining something more serious between Jillian and Carter.

Evelyn reached for a tube of lotion on the stand next to Suzanne's bed. She squeezed some out, then began to massage it into her daughter's hand.

"I used to do that for my grandma," Jillian said softly, remembering the times she'd sat at her bedside and done for her what Evelyn was doing for Suzanne.

With a smile, Evelyn held out the tube. After a brief hesitation, Jillian took it and squeezed some lotion into her palm. Lowering her gaze, she looked at Suzanne's hand before reaching out to take it in hers. Her fingers felt frail, and as Jillian began to rub the lotion into her skin, she noticed Suzanne had no ring on her finger.

By no choice of her own, Suzanne no longer wore the engagement ring that Carter had given her. Sadness swept through Jillian as her movements took on a familiar rhythm. She used gentle strokes to work the lotion into Suzanne's fingers, palm, wrist, and forearm.

"Tell me about your grandmother," Evelyn prompted.

Jillian looked up and saw that Evelyn regarded her with compassion. Carter had once again taken his seat near Garth, though when she glanced at him, she discovered that his gaze was still on them.

"My grandma became my mother when her daughter—my birth mom—didn't want the responsibility for my care. When my mom left with her new husband and daughter, she terminated her parental rights. Grandma and Grandpa adopted me and raised me with all the love a child could ever need."

Jillian continued to lightly massage Suzanne's hand and arm. An ache opened in her chest at the memories that came to her then.

"My grandpa passed away when I was younger, so it was just Grandma and me for a lot of years. I moved away to Portland for college." Jillian paused, not sure she wanted to divulge the details of her kidnapping. "A couple of years ago, I was going through a really rough time, so Grandma came to live with me, to help me. A little while after she'd been in Portland, she was diagnosed with advanced cancer. She went quickly."

"I'm so sorry to hear that," Evelyn said, her voice soft. "It sounds like she was a wonderful woman to take you in like that."

"She was. The absolute best. I don't know where I would be without her." Jillian lowered her gaze to Suzanne's face once again. "What was Suzanne like?"

Evelyn reached out to tuck a strand of hair behind Suzanne's ear. "Lively. Energetic. Funny. She could also be stubborn and opinionated, and she had a bit of a temper too. Definitely got the stubbornness from me, but the opinionated stuff? That's all Garth." She laughed softly then sighed. "Since she was our only child, we spoiled her, and sometimes that showed, but she had a good heart."

Jillian kept her touch gentle once the lotion was gone, listening as Evelyn shared more memories of Suzanne. She understood the desire to talk, to share insights about someone who was important to them.

In the background, she could hear the deep rumble of conversation between Carter and Garth. It seemed a bit surreal. Confusing, too, she was willing to admit to herself. She'd thought that maybe Carter viewed her as more than just a friend. Still, Jillian had a hard time believing that someone who had been attracted to a vibrant woman like Evelyn had described Suzanne to be, would be drawn to someone like her.

"Thank you," Evelyn said, her voice low.

Jillian stared down at where she was massaging Suzanne's arm. "You're welcome."

"Not for this," Evelyn said. "Well, yes, for this, too, but mainly, thank you for Carter."

Jillian paused in her motions, holding Suzanne's hand, and looked up Evelyn. "Carter?"

"We've been trying to encourage him to move forward with his life for several years now." She straightened the blanket covering Suzanne. "Only one life truly ended on that tragic night, but Carter has lived the past ten years like it was two. Suzanne would never have wanted that for him. *We* have never wanted that for him."

Jillian admired them for feeling that way, considering there were plenty of people who would have been happy to blame Carter for what had happened. At the same time, having had conversations with Carter about the accident, added to her own experiences, she knew where Carter was coming from.

"It's just been so nice seeing him over these past few weeks. He's smiled more. He's laughed more. He's just been more relaxed and open in a way he hasn't been since the accident."

Jillian wanted to laugh, finding that hard to believe, given what all had transpired since he'd gotten more involved in her life. It seemed unlikely that it had been his involvement with her that had caused those positive changes in his life.

"I just hope things work out for you two." Evelyn leaned over and rested her hand on Jillian's arm. "We're praying for you both."

"Thank you," Jillian replied, not sure what else to say in response.

"And I want you to know how much it means to Garth and me that you came to meet us. All of us."

Jillian still wasn't sure how she felt about seeing Suzanne, but she couldn't deny that meeting Evelyn and Garth had been a lovely experience. They seemed to genuinely love and care for Carter.

"He's a good man. A very good man," Evelyn said. "We thought so when Suzanne first introduced us to him, and we know so even more now."

That was something Jillian could agree with her on, one hundred percent. Carter had proven many times over the past few months that he was, indeed, a very good man.

"We should probably head back to New Hope," Carter said a short time later as he got to his feet.

Garth stood up as well. "We really appreciate the two of you spending part of your Christmas Day with us. It's been wonderful having you both here."

Jillian and Evelyn moved back to where the men stood, the older woman slipping her arm around Garth's waist as he drew her close to his side. "I hope the rest of your day goes well. You have plans for Christmas dinner, right?"

"Yes." Carter reached his hand out to her, and Jillian didn't hesitate to take it. "We are invited to dinner with some of our friends from church."

"That's wonderful." Evelyn smiled broadly. "I'm so glad you have the day off for a change."

"We'll have to have you to our place for dinner in the new year," Garth said.

After agreeing to set up a date once the holidays were over, they said goodbye and left Suzanne's room. They walked in silence down the hallway to the elevator, pausing only long enough to wish a few people Merry Christmas along the way.

"Want me to drive?" Carter offered as they walk out of the building.

"I don't mind driving," Jillian said as she pushed the button on the fob to unlock the doors of her car. Hopefully, driving would give her something to focus on besides her confusing emotions over meeting Suzanne and her parents.

Carter didn't argue as he opened the driver's side door for her. By the time he slid into the passenger seat, Jillian had the car running, and heat was flowing from the vents. They might not be having a white Christmas, but they were certainly having a chilly one.

CHAPTER THIRTY-SIX

Carter took a deep breath and let it out. He hadn't been sure exactly how the visit would go. Not that he'd expected anything but warmth and compassion from Evelyn and Garth. It had been Jillian's reaction that he hadn't been sure about.

He'd appreciated her willingness to meet them and see Suzanne, but he hadn't known how she'd deal with the reality of it. Thankfully, she appeared to have taken it all in stride, interacting with surprising ease—at least outwardly—with not just Evelyn and Garth, but also with Suzanne.

The visit had held a high potential for awkwardness. It was why he had never asked her to go with him to the personal care home. He'd wanted her to meet Evelyn and Garth first. But when she'd asked to come along, knowing he was going to see Suzanne, he hadn't been able to say no.

Their time there that day had just reinforced what he'd come to know about Jillian over the past few months. She was a gentle and caring woman who underestimated her own strength. And all of that deepened the feelings he already had for her. The day, so far, had been as close to perfect as it could possibly be. He only hoped that his gift for Jillian didn't change that.

Remembering the card Garth had handed him before they left, Carter pulled it out of his jacket pocket. They usually gave him a card with a gift of money at Christmas and on his birthday, which he always appreciated even though he told them repeatedly that it wasn't necessary.

Sliding the card out of the envelope, Carter smiled as he took in the festive front with the greeting for a son. Not even "son-in-law." Just *son*.

Opening it, he wasn't surprised to see a folded check inside the card. He read the message which was written in Evelyn's familiar script.

Darling Carter ~ It has been such a joy over the past few months to see the changes in your life, embracing all that God has planned for you. We have always appreciated your love for Suzanne and for us. Your willingness to take responsibility for what happened and to help shoulder the expenses for Suzanne's care speaks to the man you are. Now that you are moving forward in your life, we want to once and for all, end the obligation you feel for helping with Suzanne's expenses. We pray that you'll have a need to financially support a family in the future.

To that end, we are gifting all the money you have given us over the years, back to you. Though we have never needed the money, we accepted it since it seemed that doing so met a need in your life. Now we want you to be able to start this new chapter of your life on sound financial footing.

Frowning at the words, Carter opened the check and gasped at the amount he saw there. He had never kept track of how much money he'd given them over the years, so seeing the full amount stunned him.

"What's wrong?" Jillian asked.

He looked over to see her shooting him worried glances as she drove on the highway. "Nothing's wrong exactly. It's just that I've been giving Evelyn and Garth money each month to help with Suzanne's expenses, and they just gave it all back to me."

"Wow. All of it? They didn't need it?"

"No. I wasn't giving it to them because they needed it. I gave it to them because I felt the need to shoulder some of the responsibility for Suzanne's care. They never asked me for it, and in fact, they tried to get me to not give them anything. But I persisted, so they relented."

Carter stared at the check, then pulled out his phone and called Garth.

"Don't argue with me, son," Garth said by way of greeting. "If you don't cash the check, we'll just find another way to get you the money. We won't give up, so you might as well just accept it."

Carter let out a huff of laughter as he ran a hand through his hair. "Okay. Thank you."

"No. Thank *you*," Garth said. "You've been a blessing to Evelyn and me, and we appreciate your determination to help Suzanne. But, son, it's time for you to move forward. Not that we want you to leave us behind—we still want to be a part of your life—we just want you to forgive yourself and embrace the future God has planned for you."

He sighed. "I appreciate your support. I will always consider you both my second set of parents."

"We love you," Garth said, emotion choking his voice.

"I love you guys too."

After hanging up, Carter closed his eyes and tipped his head back. He was grateful for the softly playing Christmas music so that the silence didn't compel him to try to fill it. With so much emotion threatening to choke him, he wasn't sure he could hold a conversation with Jillian right then.

Her presence didn't make him feel uncomfortable, but he always wanted to be strong for her, and right then, he was feeling a bit weak with emotion. Jillian seemed to sense that he wasn't in the mood to talk because she didn't say anything more.

Soon, his thoughts moved from the shock of the check to the gift he had for Jillian. Carter was sure that she wasn't going to be as excited to receive it as he was to give it, and that was okay. He was prepared for that response. He just wanted her to know where he stood.

They were almost halfway home before Jillian said something. "Did you talk to your family today?"

"Yep. Thankfully, they're three hours ahead of us, so I called right when I got off work. Everyone was with my folks, so I talked with each of them." Carter hesitated. "Several of them asked about you."

"About me?" Jillian shot him a look. "You told them about me?"

"Sort of," Carter said. "Evelyn told Mom, so then Mom called me to ask about you."

"Oh." She stayed focused on the highway, but he could see that her brow was furrowed.

"I sent Mom the picture of us from Eli and Anna's wedding. She said you're beautiful."

Jillian glanced at him again, a flush of pink on her cheeks. "That was nice of her."

"It's true, you know." Carter figured she'd brush aside his comment, and she didn't disappoint him, but that was fine because at least he'd said the words, and they were the truth. Whether she believed him or not.

"Do you wish you were in Florida with your family?" she asked, obviously trying to change the subject.

Carter considered the question for a few moments. For the first time in a long time, there was actually a part of him that wished he could be there with all of them. To hug his parents and hold the newest members of the family.

"I kind of do, but at the same time, I'm happy I'm here. I've enjoyed spending time with you, Evelyn, and Garth, and I'm looking forward to the rest of this day. Maybe next year, I'll go see my family."

"I'm sure your parents would love that," Jillian said.

"You're right about that. My mom expresses her disappointment each year when I say I'm not able to make it home."

Jillian fell quiet, and it dawned on him then that she didn't have any family. Or at least none that were interested in spending time with her. His heart ached for her because of that, and it made him more determined than ever to let her know that she wasn't alone and never would be—if he could help it.

"Did you need to go by your place?" she asked. "Or should we go straight to the lodge?"

"We can go right there. Help out with dinner prep if they need it."

When they arrived a short time later, there were several cars already parked in front of the lodge, and Carter had a feeling that a lot of the same people from the night before would be there. It was great that the McNamaras had opened their home to those who would otherwise be alone for Christmas.

Voices, music, and laughter greeted them as they walked in the door. Carter inhaled deeply, appreciating the scent of burning wood from the fireplace mingling with the tantalizing aroma of food they would be eating soon.

The warmth of the lodge was welcoming, and with Jillian's hand in his, Carter felt like he was where he was meant to be. He'd finally allowed God to truly take hold of his heart, and he'd finally accepted that the future he'd once hoped for was gone, replaced by a new future. A new opportunity for a fulfilling life. He felt a peace and a hope that he hadn't experienced in a very long time.

Sarah greeted them with smiles and hugs, her joy and happiness bubbling over as she spoke with Jillian. Carter was so glad that Jillian had someone like Sarah in her life. He knew that the therapy appointments she was going to left her exhausted and worn out most days, but it seemed that Sarah always managed to cheer her up.

It turned out that there wasn't a need for their help with meal prep, so they spent time visiting with the other dinner guests until Nadine called them to sit up at the table. The large dining room usually held a single long table, but that day, they'd added another table on one end.

Like at Thanksgiving, the table was elaborately decorated, and there were place name cards at each seat. It didn't take long to find his name next to Jillian's, with Michael Reed on his other side.

"How're you doing?" Carter asked Michael as they ate. Jillian was talking with Cara, who was there with Kieran, his mom, Rose, and Mary Albridge, who owned the antique shop in town.

"I'm alright."

"Taylor not here?"

Michael frowned. "She wasn't feeling up to it."

Carter thought about the night after Eli and Anna's wedding when he'd seen the two of them arguing in the parking lot. "I'm sorry to hear that. Is everything okay?"

This time the man sighed. "I'm not sure. She's been dealing with something lately, and it's starting to affect the business. We need to sort it out, but she won't talk to me."

"Do you guys have family around here?"

Michael shook his head. "Thankfully, no."

Carter paused in lifting his fork to his mouth and turned his attention more fully to Michael. "You don't get along with them?"

"Nope. Never have. Never will."

The guy hadn't talked about his family at all in the times they'd been together in the men's Bible study. It made Carter feel bad that Michael didn't get along with his family. While he might not be physically close to his parents and siblings, he loved them, and he knew they loved him. It didn't seem that Michael had that level of family support.

"If there's anything I can do for you, let me know," Carter said. "If you need someone to talk to, I'm here for you."

"Thanks, man," Michael said.

Though he was usually a fairly upbeat guy, Carter could see that Michael was struggling. His shoulders slumped as he pushed around the food on his plate. Carter wanted to ask him more about the situation with Taylor, but perhaps Christmas dinner wasn't the place for that conversation.

With that in mind, he directed the conversation toward other not-so-emotional topics. But through it all, his thoughts lingered on what was to come with Jillian. He had a knot in his stomach—partly from anxiety, partly from excitement—so he found it difficult to focus too much on what was going on around the table.

However, his nerves didn't make him unable to eat more than he should have of all the wonderful food on the table. It was a joyous occasion that he was happy to be part of, and he knew that he owed a lot of his changed outlook to Jillian. She'd deny she had done that for him, but he knew it was true.

She was the person who made him smile the most and laugh more than he had in years. She was also the person who he talked to more than any other. He felt a connection with her that he'd never thought he'd feel with a woman again. Though she hadn't said she felt the same connection, there were times when he was totally convinced she did.

And it was those times that had brought him to the point where he was ready to take a step forward to the future he now wanted. A future with Jillian. However that might unfold. However long it might take. He wanted to do whatever was necessary to be with her. To support her. To love her.

If only she'd let him.

CHAPTER THIRTY-SEVEN

Jillian was happily tired when they finally said goodnight to the people at the lodge. The day had gone so well. Better than she could have ever imagined.

Given that she'd kind of been dreading the day since it was her first Christmas completely alone, her expectations for the day had been rather low. Instead, she'd had a great time with the people who had welcomed her, without reservation, into their lives.

"It was nice of Nadine to send food home with us," Jillian said as Carter drove her car along the winding road back toward New Hope.

"I'm so glad she did because all of it was delicious. Reminded me a lot of Christmas dinners with my family. Such good food and so much of it."

Jillian leaned back in her seat, relishing the heat that flowed out of the vents. "Can you come in for a few minutes? I have a gift for you."

"You do?" Carter asked, sounding surprised. "You didn't have to do that."

"I know, but I wanted to." She hadn't known exactly what to get him at first, but she'd felt like she needed to get him *something*. They were, at the very least, friends. And since she'd gotten something for each of her other friends, she'd decided to get a gift for him too.

"Well, that's good because I have a gift for you too."

Jillian turned her head toward him and frowned. "You didn't need to do that. You've already done so much for me."

"And you've done a lot for me too," Carter said, his tone matter of fact. Like he really believed it.

"I haven't, really," she murmured. That knowledge had weighed on her a lot since the very beginning of their friendship. She felt like all she did was take from him.

Carter didn't respond to her comment. He just kept driving slowly through the streets of the town, humming along with the Christmas carols playing on the radio.

Jillian turned to look out her window, forcing away the thought of how uneven their friendship...relationship...seemed to be. Instead, she tried to focus on the beautiful Christmas bulbs that adorned the houses, and the warm light that spilled from their windows.

When Carter pulled into her garage a short time later, Jillian had a moment of doubt thinking that maybe Carter wouldn't like the gifts she'd gotten for him. It had been hard to know what he might like, but she hoped that she'd nailed it.

After she unlocked the house, Carter followed her into the mudroom. It was just a matter of seconds before Dolly appeared, meowing loudly as she greeted them.

Carter hung his jacket on a hook in the mudroom then took off his boots before bending over to pick Dolly up. Jillian found it amusing how much the two of them seemed to have bonded.

"Do you want something to drink?" she asked as she headed for the kitchen. "Coffee?"

"I think I've had enough coffee for awhile," Carter said, coming into the kitchen with Dolly in his arms. "Much as I love your coffee."

Jillian agreed, so she just filled a couple of glasses with water and carried them into the living room where her tree was set up in the corner. The number of presents under the tree had gotten progressively fewer over the years, and now there were just two.

She set their glasses on the coffee table, then went to the tree to pick up the two gifts she'd placed there the day before. "I didn't really know what to get you, so I kind of erred on the side of practical."

"That's perfectly fine," Carter said as he sat down on the couch, setting Dolly on his lap. "You really didn't have to get me anything."

"I know." Jillian brought the gifts to where he sat and put them on the coffee table in front of him. "But if you don't like them, I still have the receipts."

"I'm sure they'll be fine." The smile he gave her was warm and affectionate. A smile she never saw him give to anyone else.

She felt an all too familiar tug-of-war in her chest. One part of her wanted to fall heart-first into that affection, while the other part wanted her to run in the opposite direction to spare them both the heartache she was sure would come.

Settling on the couch beside him, she motioned to the gifts. "You open yours first."

"Off you go, Dolly-girl," Carter said as he set the cat on the floor. She gave him a disgruntled meow before heading for the kitchen, no doubt in search of food.

Jillian shifted on her seat, anxious about Carter's reaction to what she'd chosen for him. She'd done a lot of online browsing, hoping to get him something that he would use.

"Open this one first," Jillian said as she picked up the larger package and held it out to him.

Carter took it from her and laid it on his lap. With careful movements, he slid a finger under the edge of the wrapping paper and separated the tape from the paper.

When he finally opened it to expose the white box, he glanced at her before opening it. Inside lay a jacket, black in color. Jillian had noticed that the jacket he wore most of the time was faded and had frayed cuffs. It had taken her awhile to decide on a new one, but in the end, she hoped that the all-weather jacket with a removable lining would be something he'd be able to use.

Carter lifted it out, holding it by its shoulders as he looked at it. "This is perfect, Jillian. Thank you."

"I hope it's the right size," she said. "I snuck a peek at your jacket when it was hanging in my closet one day."

Carter unzipped the jacket then stood up to try it on. Jillian smiled when he shrugged it up on his shoulders and zipped it up.

"It fits perfectly."

"I'm glad. It's supposed to be water-resistant, too, so you won't get wet when we have our rainy days."

"It's really nice. Thank you very much." Carter took it off and laid it across the arm of the couch before turning his attention to his other gift. "You really shouldn't have gotten me two gifts. The jacket was more than enough."

Jillian bit her lip, worried that he might think the contents of the next gift was too extravagant. And maybe it was, but she wanted to be able to show him how much she appreciated him and what he'd done for her. Now that she knew how he'd spent much of his money each month, she was doubly glad to have spent the money she had on his gifts.

She could only hope that perhaps he wouldn't be aware of what his gift cost. It was something else she'd spent a lot of time researching before she'd made her final decision. And though she could have gotten a cheaper one, she'd noticed he didn't wear a watch at all, so she'd wanted to get him one that would work for his job.

Her hope that he wouldn't know the value of the watch was dashed when he sat staring at the box for a long moment before he finally said, "Jillian... You shouldn't have."

Jillian squeezed her hands together. "Do you like it? Is it okay? I wasn't sure if it would be okay for you for your work."

Carter reached over and laid his hand over hers as he met her gaze. "It's perfect. Way too much, but perfect."

Her shoulders slumped in relief. "I wasn't sure. I just wanted you to have something useful."

"Both of these things are very useful. Thank you so much."

"You're welcome." Joy filled her that the gifts she'd chosen for him were things he seemed to deeply appreciate and could use.

He returned the box containing his watch to the coffee table then shifted to face her, hooking his leg up onto the cushion between them. With a faint smile, he reached out and took her hands. She unclenched her fingers and let him hold them. His grip was loose as always. It was like he never wanted to hold her too tightly in case she needed to be free of their connection.

"I want to talk for a minute before I give you your gift." Carter's expression was serious, which brought about flutters of anxiety in Jillian's stomach, making her wonder if she should go take a calming pill.

"Okay?"

"I want you to know that I'm not giving you this gift with any sort of expectation. Hope, yes, but I don't want you to freak out."

Carter's words brought forward a new level of nerves, and Jillian fought the urge to jerk her hands away from his.

"Jillian, I know that you've resisted the idea of a more serious relationship, and I completely understand why you feel that way. The thing is, you've made me happier than I've been in a long, long time."

A sick feeling started to grow within her because she had an idea where this was going, and she was going to have to disappoint Carter. She didn't want to, but she wasn't sure what the alternative was.

When Carter let go of her hand and reached into his pocket to pull out a small box, Jillian pressed her fingers to the base of her throat. Her pulse fluttered as her heart pounded.

"Jillian," Carter spoke her name gently as he opened the box and held it out to her.

She stared down at it, observing the ring that was nestled in the velvet insert of the box. It was a narrow gold band with a single dainty red stone set on it.

"I'm not proposing," Carter said softly. "I know that we're not anywhere close to that level in our relationship and that we might never be."

Jillian looked up and met his gaze, uncertain about what he was saying. Her throat was too tight to speak, so she just waited for him to clarify.

"This is a promise ring, not an engagement ring."

"A promise ring?" Jillian had heard of them, but she wasn't sure exactly what they signified.

"Yes. I want to give you this ring as a promise that I will always be by your side." He hesitated then said, "Do I hope that our friendship might turn into something more? I'll be honest, yes, that is my prayer. But that's not what this ring is about."

"But why?" Jillian whispered. "Why would you want that? I can't guarantee I'll ever be ready for something more. Right now, that seems impossible."

"I know it does." Carter's expression softened, and there was that look in his eyes again. The one she'd been trying not to notice. "I felt the same way when we agreed to our casual relationship. It felt impossible to even consider a future with anyone but Suzanne. But God has worked in my heart, freeing me from the guilt and anger that had kept me ensnared to the past. However, regardless of where I am in my own personal journey, I just want to be there for you."

Jillian stared again at the ring and the blood-red stone that she was sure represented her birthstone since it was a ruby. It blurred for a moment, and she blinked away the moisture that had gathered in her eyes.

"You deserve better, Carter." Keeping her gaze averted, she forced the words past the tight muscles in her throat. "So much better."

"Can you look at me, Jillian?" Carter's fingers gently touched her cheek, not forcing her to look up, but encouraging her to meet his gaze. After a deep breath, she looked up at him. "Here's the thing. There's only one person who can determine what I deserve, and that's me. You might feel that I deserve better than you, but I don't feel that way. If we're going to say one of us doesn't deserve the other, it should be me who doesn't deserve you."

Jillian stared at him in shock. "Why on earth would you ever say that?"

"I come with a lot of my own baggage. My past will always be intrinsically mixed in with my present and my future." Carter gave her a weak smile. "So maybe those are things you need to consider as well. Not exactly things that are in my favor."

Jillian wanted to tell him that none of that mattered to her, but she had a feeling that he would just tell her that all of the things she considered as issues about herself didn't matter to him.

"I haven't even stopped to consider whether or not I deserved better than you," Carter said, his expression serious. "Because I know there's no one better than you for me. I understand that you see your panic attacks and anxiety as negatives, but when I look at you, I see a woman of strength. Someone fighting to overcome what's happened to them in order to live the life they want."

She swallowed hard at his words. It wasn't the first time he'd said that about her, but she didn't find it any easier to hear, even when she was having a particularly good day.

"This ring can mean as much or as little as you want it to. But at the very least, let it mean that I'll be there for you. I'll do whatever I can to help you through the ups and downs of life." He hesitated for a moment. "I'm not asking you to wear this on your ring finger like a pseudo engagement ring. You don't have to wear it at all, if doing so makes you uncomfortable. The ring and its meaning will still be there, at least for me."

"So you don't care if I actually wear it or not?"

"My hope is that you will so that you have a visible reminder of the promise I've made to you. But if you choose not to, I'll understand. I'm not going to get mad at you about it. The ring is yours, regardless of whether you wear it or not."

"Really?" She looked down again at the ring. "It's beautiful."

"It's your birthstone," Carter said, confirming what she'd suspected. "And like I said, yours to keep regardless."

Her heart pounded as she shifted her gaze to meet his. "I don't know what to say."

"You don't have to say anything. Not now. Not ever. But if there comes a point where you want to trade this ring in, so to speak, for one that represents a more significant commitment, all you need to do is tell me that you're ready."

Jillian sat there for a long moment, once again staring at the ring as she mulled over his words. Oh, how she wanted to agree to what he was offering, but it just didn't feel fair. What if she never felt ready, and he'd spent all that time waiting for nothing?

She took a deep breath and blew it out. There was only one way she could do this. She had to give herself a deadline, and if, by that point, she still wasn't able to see herself having a physical relationship with him, then she needed to let Carter know that. To set him free to find someone who could give him everything he deserved.

It wasn't that she didn't think he loved her. In fact, she was quite sure he did. The way he looked at her...the way he treated her with such care...the way he was always there when she needed him... All of that spoke of love—a love he probably didn't voice because of how skittish she was. So, while he hadn't actually said the words, she didn't doubt his love.

And though she'd been scared to actually admit how she'd been feeling herself, Jillian knew that she loved Carter too. But the question was...would love be enough to get them through the tough spots that lay ahead?

A year. I'll give myself a year.

Having resolved that, she looked up at him. "If you're sure..."

A smile broke out across his face. "I am *very* sure. Absolutely sure. Never been more sure of anything in my life."

She had to laugh then, the tension of the past few minutes dissipating. "So, I guess you're really, officially my boyfriend now?"

"Yes," Carter said with a decisive nod. "Though, to be honest, I've kind of felt like that for a couple of months already."

She could only hope that he'd still feel that way in a year's time.

CHAPTER THIRTY-EIGHT

July

Carter struggled to push aside the exhaustion that followed the huge spike in adrenalin that came with a serious call-out followed by the physical strain of fighting a big fire. He was just glad that one of the other guys was driving the truck back to the fire station because he wasn't sure he had the energy to do it himself.

They'd been called to an apartment fire in another small town in their district just after coming on shift. The bad thing was that the fire had started in an empty apartment that was being renovated, and the fire detectors hadn't been functional for some reason. As a result, by the time the residents of other apartments were aware of what was going on, the empty apartment was fully engulfed, and the fire was spreading rapidly throughout the rest of the building.

The good thing was that enough people in the building had still been awake to alert others when the fire was discovered. No lives had been lost, but there had been a lot of property damage, which meant many people would need to find new places to live.

"Good work, guys," he called out as they all piled out of the truck once it was back in the station.

Unfortunately, their day wasn't over. It seemed to take forever to get the truck and their equipment back in order, but eventually, that was done. There was food waiting for them since it was already past lunch, and most of the guys headed for the kitchen.

"Hey, Carter," Stuart said as he came out of his office with a container in his hand. "Your lady stopped by while you were out and left this for you."

Hearing that, all the stresses of the morning slipped away, and Carter smiled as he walked over to the man and took the small container from him. They had plans for the following night since it was Jillian's birthday, but now that school was out for the summer, she occasionally stopped by the station for a few minutes on the days he worked.

Sometimes she brought him treats, usually including enough for others at the station too. This container didn't look like it held more than a few of whatever she'd brought him that day, however. There was a card on top of the container with his name written out in her familiar handwriting.

He went over to the table and sat down, eager to see what Jillian had dropped off for him.

"Did she not bring enough for all of us?" one of the other guys at the table asked. He had a plate full of food in front of him, and Carter looked forward to filling one for himself as soon as he saw what Jillian had brought him.

"Not this time, apparently." Carter set the card aside and opened the container. Inside were two cupcakes that looked to be his favorite lemon-raspberry combination, and each one had a chocolate heart on top.

Emotion swelled within him as he took in the hearts. So much had changed in the past six months. From the moment she'd shown up at Cara and Kieran's wedding with the promise ring on her finger, she'd seemed determined to try her best to move forward.

It hadn't always been easy. Having to testify in Martin's trial had brought back bad memories, but she'd pushed through. She seemed well able to judge when she needed additional therapy sessions and adjusted accordingly.

Even though they still hadn't exchanged *I love yous,* it seemed they were each aware of the other's feelings. The fact that she did things like put hearts on the cupcakes she made for him spoke loudly to Carter. And he'd tried to make sure that his actions also showed how he felt for her. But still, there had been no words.

A couple of months ago, however, she'd asked him if he'd be willing to attend some therapy sessions with her. That had been an answer to prayer for him because it showed that she had taken him seriously when he'd said he'd be there for her.

Going to therapy with Jillian had been interesting, and, at times, painful. Surprisingly—or maybe not...—it had led him to meet with the therapist on his own for the issues he still struggled with off and on. All of it had left him feeling confident that they were both in an even better place than he would have imagined they'd be back when he'd given her the promise ring on Christmas Day.

Picking up the envelope, he opened it and slid the card out. His jaw dropped a bit as he stared at the front of it.

To the man I love.

Carter's heart began to pound. It was the first time she'd come right out and said that, and suddenly, a weight he hadn't even realized he'd been carrying lifted from him. Though he'd never allowed himself to dwell on it, there had been a small part of him that worried that Jillian would give up on them, and he wouldn't have a chance to love and care for her the way he longed to.

But now...hope burned brighter than it ever had before that things would work out for them. Maybe that engagement ring that had been sitting in his drawer since the middle of January would see the light of day sooner or later.

Flipping the card open, his heart seemed to stop for a moment before it began to beat at an alarming rate.

I'm ready! 💚

"Hey, Carter? You okay, man?"

He looked up to find all eyes on him. "Uh. Yes. Why?"

The guys exchanged glances before one of them said, "I don't think I've ever seen you smile like that before. Like...ever. Right, guys?"

Carter just shook his head as the other guys voiced their agreement, but he couldn't wipe the smile off his face. "Sometimes, a smile is called for."

Getting to his feet, he snagged the container and card before abandoning the table. Lunch could wait. He had a phone call to make.

He headed out to the small patch of grass at the back of the station where there was a picnic table that they used when the weather permitted. Thankfully, it was currently empty. No doubt because the sky looked like it was going to open up at any moment.

After setting the cupcake container on the picnic table, Carter pulled out his phone then settled onto one of the benches. Without hesitating, he tapped the screen to call Jillian.

"Carter?" she said after the first ring.

"I love you too." The words came out in a rush and probably would have made a teenager proud. The rush of emotion he'd experienced at seeing her words on that card refused to be contained any longer.

Jillian laughed, the sound light and airy. "I love you too."

"I know you do, and but hearing you say it feels amazing." Carter felt like the journey to get to that point had been very difficult—especially for Jillian—so to hear her say those words felt like he'd been gifted something truly incredible. "Thank you."

"What are you thanking me for?" Jillian asked. "If anything, I need to be thanking you."

"I know it would have been easier for you not to have to deal with everything that you've had to in order to consider a life with us together. So thank you for being willing to do the hard work. If I could have done it for you, I would have."

"I couldn't have done it without you," she said softly. "Having you by my side through all of this without pressuring me for anything has made everything so much easier."

When he'd given her the ring, Carter had thought it would be easy to not have much physical contact with Jillian. After all, he'd gone ten years without hugs and kisses from the woman he loved. The problem was that he found that the more his love for Jillian grew, the more he wanted to be close to her.

It wasn't that he wanted to cross any lines. He'd just wanted to be able to hold her close, but that had been something they'd had to work up to because for Jillian, being held felt like being restrained, and that was a definite trigger for her.

Thankfully, they were to the point—with the help of the therapist—where hugs from him that lasted more than a few seconds were tolerable for Jillian. Carter had struggled at times, not truly understanding why his hugs would trigger a flashback. He loved her, after all, and had never done anything to hurt her.

In one of his solo sessions with the therapist, he'd voiced his struggle. Thankfully, the therapist hadn't told him he was wrong for being frustrated with that. Instead, she'd taken the time to explain that a mind exposed to trauma—significant trauma—the way Jillian's had been didn't always respond the way a pre-trauma mind would.

It wasn't about who Carter was or what he had or hadn't done to her. It was about the message Jillian's mind was feeding her, based on the trauma she'd endured.

With a better understanding of what it all meant, Carter had been able to put aside the feelings he'd been having and just focus on doing what made things comfortable for Jillian. And it was paying off for her—which was the most important thing to him—but it was also paying off for them as a couple. Allowing them to have a slowly deepening physical connection.

"I wish I was off," Carter said. "I'd love to see you right now."

Jillian sighed. "I know that it wasn't ideal to share my feelings this way."

"It was perfect, sweetheart. The way we've done things so far in our relationship has been uniquely us. This is no different, and I'm fine with that. More than fine with it." Carter stared up at the sky as a drop of rain hit his hand. He got up from the table, picking up the cupcake container and card once again. "And I'll see you tomorrow for dinner, right?"

"Definitely. The girls still want me to spend the evening with them, but I'm holding strong."

"Good because I have plans." He pulled open the door to the station and stepped inside. "So prepare yourself."

"I'll try."

"I gotta go, sweetheart, but I'll talk to you later." He paused, unable to keep a smile from spreading across his face. "I love you."

"Oh! I love you too."

~ * ~

Jillian stared at herself in the mirror, wanting to look perfect for her evening with Carter. He'd told her they weren't going anywhere fancy and to wear something comfortable. She'd ended up choosing a pair of white capris and a pastel floral blouse with a peplum waist and loose sleeves that ended at her elbows. White strappy sandals and her usual jewelry—including her promise ring—rounded out the look. Hopefully, it would work for wherever they ended up.

Nerves fluttered in her stomach even though she knew she really didn't have anything to be nervous about. Still, seeing Carter for the first time after telling him she loved him was bringing butterflies to life in her stomach.

She turned away from the mirror and left her room with Dolly at her heels. With Carter's arrival imminent, she made sure her purse and phone were by the front door, then went to fill Dolly's food and water dishes.

When the doorbell sounded, Jillian took a quick breath as her pulse kicked up a notch. At least it didn't mean a panic attack was coming. This time around, it was excitement, not anxiety that made her heart pound.

She hurried to open the front door, eager to see Carter. Her excitement over spending time with Carter had grown a little more each day during the past several months. She had reached a point of comfort with him she hadn't thought would ever be possible with any man—a point at which she was ready to consider even more with Carter in the future.

Gripping the doorknob, she jerked the door open, a smile already forming on her lips. Carter stood with a hand braced on the door frame and a grin on his face. He wore a pair of blue jeans and a black T-shirt.

"Hi." She suddenly felt a little shy and unsure of how to act.

Carter didn't seem to feel that way, however, as he reached out and gently cupped her face in his large, strong hands. Leaning forward, he brushed his lips against hers. Kissing was something they'd started just a month ago, and it always caused a rush of butterflies within her.

She hadn't understood, at first, why kissing would be a trigger. But her therapist had helped her come to understand that it wasn't necessary the kiss, but the fear that it wouldn't stop there, and that she wouldn't be able to stop it. Never had she feared for herself with Carter before, but she'd long since accepted that her mind didn't work the way she wanted it to anymore.

She pressed her hands against his, holding them to her cheeks as she gazed up at him. "I love you."

His expression softened at her words, his eyes alive with emotion. He swallowed audibly before he said, "I love you too, sweetheart. So much."

He kissed her again, just light brushes of his lips against hers, and for a moment, it was just the two of them alone in the world.

When he finally stepped back, Jillian let out a contented sigh.

"Oh. By the way," Carter said, his grin returning as he lowered his hands, though he still held onto hers. "Happy birthday."

"Thank you." Already this birthday had far exceeded any of her expectations.

"Are you ready to go?"

She nodded and grabbed her purse and phone before setting the alarm. Holding hands, they made their way to Carter's truck. She'd asked him if he planned to get a new vehicle with the money Garth and Evelyn had returned to him, but he said that what he had worked fine.

He'd also stayed in his studio apartment and didn't appear to have any plans to move. She had to admire his wisdom when it came to finances. She wasn't sure she'd be as wise if she'd been in his position.

"So, where are we going?" she asked after they were in the truck.

"It's a surprise," he said as he held out a sleep mask.

She took it, giving him a curious look. "What's this for?"

"To cover your eyes, so you can't see where we're going."

"Really?"

He nodded. "Really. We're not moving 'til you put it on."

With a sigh, Jillian slipped the mask over her eyes. "Happy now?"

"Yes. You have no idea how happy," he said, and from the sound of his voice, he was being one hundred percent serious.

Jillian was glad that being blindfolded hadn't been part of her kidnapping experience—Pearse had just relied on drugs to knock them out and remove their sight—or she likely would have been fighting a panic attack. And the fact that she was comfortable with being blindfolded and driven to an unknown location was proof of how far she'd come and how deeply she placed her trust in Carter now.

"So, where are we going?" she asked.

Carter chuckled. "Still not telling."

Jillian grinned then said, "How long 'til we get there?"

"Oh, I've heard that one before." He paused. "Come to think of it, I've *said* that one before."

"So, is that your answer?"

"Only one you're getting, sweetheart."

She could hear the laughter in his voice and giggled too. "Okay. I'll stop asking questions, but that just means you have to entertain me."

"Oh boy. Maybe we should go back to questions."

"How about you tell me how your day went?" Jillian suggested.

And so he did. But as he talked about the call they'd gone out on to the burning apartment building, she almost wished he hadn't. It wasn't like she forgot what Carter did, but sometimes she forgot how risky his job could be since most of the calls he went out on didn't seem to be too dangerous.

"Was anyone hurt?"

"No. Everyone got out, and we put the fire out without any injuries."

"I'm so glad to hear that."

She told him a bit about what she'd done that day—cleaning, a bit of gardening, a little shopping—as he continued to drive. She'd barely finished when the truck slowed and made a turn but didn't pick up speed again.

"Are we almost there?" she couldn't help but ask with a grin.

"We are, in fact."

When they came to a stop, Jillian didn't make any move to get out of the truck since she couldn't see. She heard Carter's door open then close. It didn't take long for him to get around to her side.

Once she had her feet on solid ground, she touched the blindfold. "Can I take it off now?"

"Nope." Carter took her hand then wrapped it around his bicep. He moved slowly as they walked along a sidewalk then carefully led her up a short flight of stairs.

She heard a door open, and then they were out of the breezy air and inside whatever building was their destination. Though there was the scent of food in the air, there was a surprising lack of conversation which surprised her since she figured they were in a restaurant.

"You can take it off now," Carter said, squeezing her hand lightly.

Reaching up with her free hand, she hesitated a moment, bracing herself for what she'd see when the blindfold was removed. As she lifted it, two things happened. The familiar living room of Beau's house came into view at the same time as a loud chorus of *Surprise!* rang out.

She pulled the blindfold the rest of the way off as she stared in shock at her friends. The very same friends who had been pestering her to spend the evening with them.

"What's going on?" She glanced over at Carter, who was smiling at her.

"It's your birthday, sweetheart. Who better to spend it with than the people who love you?" His expression turned a bit more serious. "Is that okay?"

"It's perfect." Jillian blinked back tears of happiness.

Carter once again took her face in his hands and gave her a soft kiss. "You're not disappointed that it's not just the two of us?"

"No. Not at all. This is wonderful."

Sarah came over to where they stood and gave Jillian a hug. "Were you surprised?"

"Extremely! You guys did a great job of keeping a secret."

There was much laughter as the evening got underway. The large table had been beautifully decorated. They'd gone all out for the occasion with a catered meal, which was great since none of them had to spend time in the kitchen.

Once the meal was over, they headed out to the backyard, where Beau had installed a large brick fire pit. There were a bunch of chairs around it that they sat on as the sun began to sink, settling twilight over them.

Jillian watched as Carter and Eli worked to get the fire going. It had been a cool day, so the warmth from the flames felt good.

They hadn't been out there long when Sarah appeared with a cake glowing with lit candles. They all sang *Happy Birthday* to Jillian, then waited as she blew out the candles before Sarah took the cake away to cut it.

While they ate the cake, Jillian opened the presents they'd piled in front of her. She hadn't expected any of this and found herself fighting tears yet again.

"You guys have been so generous," she said after opening the last present. "Thank you so very much."

Standing up, she hugged each of the women.

"Jillian?"

Hearing Carter's voice, she turned and froze. There, on the brick surface of Beau's back patio, was the man she loved. Down on one knee with one hand lifted toward her. A ring held between his fingers.

In the flickering light of the flame from the fire, he smiled up at her. "Not sure if you expected this so soon, but sweetheart, I've had this ring since January. Just praying and waiting for the right time."

The tears came again, and this time, Jillian couldn't hold them back.

"I know we got off to a bit of a weird start, but it didn't take me long to see you as someone I couldn't wait to get to know more. And every minute we've spent together since has proven that I was right to want that. You quickly became more important to me than I could ever have imagined, and I'm so thankful that you were willing to give me a chance. To give *us* a chance."

He got to his feet and came closer to her. "I love you, sweetheart, and nothing would make me happier than to spend the rest of my life with you. And just like when I gave you the promise ring, I'm not expecting a wedding to happen right away, but I want you to know how committed I am to you and our future together. Will you marry me?"

Jillian swallowed past the tightness of her throat then tried to brush away the tears from her cheeks. She held out her arms to Carter, and he moved to gather her close, gently wrapping his arms around her. His gentleness was just one of the reasons why it was so easy for her to whisper *yes* in his ear.

"I love you so much, Carter," she said when she finally got her emotions under control. Moving back a bit from his embrace, she looked up at him. "I would love to be your wife."

As their friends whooped and cheered around them, Carter kissed her once again.

They still had work ahead of them, but Jillian was at peace because she knew that Carter understood that and yet was still willing to want a future with her. It was more than she could ever have hoped for, and she was so thankful that God had brought them together and was guiding them along the path He had for them.

She couldn't wait to see where that journey would take them.

EPILOGUE

Carter paced around the small room, stepping over Eli's legs when he came to them. The man was currently relaxing in his chair, arms crossed with a smirk on his face.

"Not sure why you're so nervous, dude," Eli said. "You've been waiting for this day forever."

Eli was right. It felt like ages since the night of Jillian's birthday when she'd agreed to take this step with him. In reality, it had only been nine months. At times, those months had seemed to drag, and Carter had wondered if they'd ever get to this day. But now that they had arrived, he was worried that it was too soon.

Jillian had dictated each moment of the journey. They hadn't set a wedding date until she had reached a point where she could handle what doing so truly meant. As a result, they'd thrown together their wedding in the space of two months. Still, even though Jillian had told him she was ready for this step, even though the therapist had also agreed that the progress Jillian had made was incredible and that she believed she was prepared to move forward, Carter worried.

He wanted this special day—and night—to hold only happy memories for Jillian. Over the past week, he'd found himself constantly praying that God would bless this day and their coming together as a couple.

"You ready, son?" Pastor Evans asked as he walked into the room. "I've been told we have about seven minutes left. Your wife has got this planned down to the minute, Eli."

"She's definitely good at organization," Eli said as he pulled his legs in and got to his feet. "I'm rarely late since she got hold of my life."

Pastor Evans chuckled. "If I recall, you were rarely late even before that."

Eli gave a shrug and a grin. "True."

"How is Jillian?" Carter asked. "Did you see her?"

"I did see her," Pastor Evans said with a nod. "And she's doing just fine. Looks beautiful and happy."

That helped to ease the knot of tension in Carter's gut a bit, but he was still harboring worry that probably wouldn't be completely gone until the next day. He loved Jillian more than he'd ever imagined he could, and the more time they'd spent together—in and out of therapy—the more his love for her had grown.

After all she'd gone through in her life, all he wanted was for her to be happy. And if there was anything he could do to make that happen, he'd do it.

"Why don't we say a word of prayer before we head out?" Pastor Evans suggested.

The three of them huddled together, then the pastor prayed for God's blessing on the ceremony and on Carter and Jillian as they began their lives together. He was aware of Jillian's history and all she'd gone through, so he knew what a big step this was for them.

When he finished praying, he led the two of them out of the room and through the door that led to the front of the sanctuary. Music was playing softly as they walked up the stairs to the platform that held an arch covered in a variety of spring flowers.

Standing with one hand clasping the wrist of the other like Anna had instructed, Carter looked out over the people gathered there. The sanctuary wasn't full by any stretch of the imagination, but that wasn't a surprise since they'd decided to keep their wedding and reception small.

They had also decided to each only have two people stand up with them. He had Eli and Kieran as his groomsmen, and Jillian had Sarah and Cara as her bridesmaids. Beau was an usher, while Anna had organized everything for them.

Carter's own family made up a large part of the wedding guests, and it warmed his heart to look out and see them smiling at him. Though he and Jillian had only made two trips to Florida, one just before school had started and another at Christmas, video chats had allowed his parents—especially his mom—to get to know Jillian better. And they'd voiced how much they loved her and how pleased they were for the two of them.

The sanctuary doors opened, and Carter grinned when he saw his parents standing there. The smiles on their faces were broad as they walked to the front where they'd be sitting, his mom giving him a little wave as they got close.

Next came Kieran and Cara, followed by Sarah. Behind her came two of his brother's children. His niece carefully dropped rose petals while his nephew proudly carried the pillow that contained the rings they would exchange.

When the doors closed again, Carter took a deep breath and slowly exhaled, bracing himself for the rush of emotion that was sure to overtake him at the first glimpse of his bride.

"You ready, bro?" Eli whispered as he jostled his elbow.

"So very ready," Carter said.

The music changed, and *Ode to Joy*, the song they'd chosen for Jillian to walk down the aisle to, began to play. A few long moments later, the doors opened to reveal Jillian standing there with Evelyn on one side and Garth on the other.

Carter swallowed hard and blinked rapidly as he watched her begin to slowly walk toward him. She looked absolutely beautiful in her wedding dress. Her hair hung in loose waves over her shoulders and a light veil started at the crown of her head and lay down her back. The dress flattered her curves, and Carter was glad to see that she hadn't tried to hide what she'd at one time seen as a negative about herself.

The fact of the matter was that Carter loved her curves. It had taken him quite a while after realizing he loved Jillian to acknowledge his physical attraction to her. Given everything that had happened to her, it felt more "right" to focus on the things that had initially drawn him to her—her gentle, strong spirit—than on her physical attributes.

That had changed with an offhand remark she'd made about losing weight, so she would look better. Carter had quickly let her know that while he would support her efforts if she truly wanted to lose weight, he liked her just the way she was. That he loved how she looked.

Her surprise had quickly turned to pleasure as her cheeks had pinked with her blush at his words. It was then that he realized that she needed to know that he found her physically attractive in addition to the other qualities he loved about her. That was no hardship for him, and he made sure that he told her she was beautiful, often.

As she walked toward him, her gaze holding his with that smile that she reserved for only him, she was the most beautiful woman in the world. And soon, she would belong to him just as he'd belong to her.

And as her slow and steady steps brought Jillian closer to him, he found he couldn't wait for what was to come.

~ * ~

When Jillian reached the front of the sanctuary, she turned first to Garth, who gave her a tight hug before kissing her forehead. Emotion clogged her throat as she then turned to Evelyn and welcomed her embrace.

"We are so proud of you," Evelyn whispered. "And we love you as if you were our daughter alongside Suzanne."

Jillian blinked back tears as she shifted so she could see Evelyn's face. "I love you both, too. Thank you for stepping in and filling the void I've had in my life since my grandma died."

"You're welcome." Evelyn smiled through her tears. "And now it's time for you to take this step with Carter. I'm so glad you're both ready and willing to move forward together."

With their blessing, Jillian turned from Evelyn and Garth to see Carter standing just feet away, a look on his face that both calmed and excited her. When he held out his hand, like he had so many times over the past year and a half, she took it without hesitation.

He drew her toward him, and when they stood close with him looking down at her, Carter said, "I love you, and you look absolutely gorgeous."

There were titters of laughter as they stood there for a moment before Pastor Evans cleared his throat. Carter's smile turned into a playful grin as he said, "Let's get this show on the road."

Hand in hand, they climbed the steps to join Pastor Evans and their friends in front of the beautifully decorated arch of flowers.

Jillian wanted to remember every single minute of the ceremony. However, if she couldn't recall everything, there were definitely moments she hoped would remain in her memory forever.

Like when Eli read from I Corinthians 13. So much of that passage on love applied to Carter. *Love is patient. Love is kind. Love always protects. Love always trusts. Love always hopes. Love always perseveres.*

He embodied those words when he cared for her, and that was how she knew, more than anything else, that he truly loved her. She just hoped that he saw her in those verses as well because that was how she always wanted to be with him.

Then came their vows. They'd debated over whether they should just go for traditional vows or try to get through more personal ones without crying. Jillian hadn't thought that Carter would break down, but as she stood facing him and listened as, with tears rolling down his cheeks, he told her how much he loved her and how committed he was to her and their future, she felt tears gather in her eyes before she'd even said a word.

With gentle movements, she used the tissue she'd been clutching in her hand to dry the tears on his cheeks. As he finished his vows, he grasped her wrist before she could lower her hand and pressed a kiss to her palm.

Her tears flowed before she'd even begun to speak, and it had been a struggle to speak the vows she'd written out. The ones that told him how much he meant to her. How she always felt safe with him. And how she appreciated that he was a man of God who encouraged her in her spiritual walk.

What had taken her just a few minutes when she'd practiced at home took much longer as she struggled to get the words out between gulping sobs of emotion. This time, Carter took a handkerchief from his pocket and dabbed at her cheeks and occasionally at his as well, since he was crying again too.

When it was Pastor Evan's time to speak again, he had to clear his throat a couple of times before he could talk. "I'm always moved when I perform weddings, but these two..." He rested one hand on her shoulder and the other on Carter's. "They've shown me that God can shine brightly through even the most difficult circumstances. That even when it seems that the road ahead is impossible to travel, with God's help, anything is possible."

He had them exchange rings, then, as they lit the unity candle, Leah sat at the piano and sang *When I Say I Do* by Matthew West. Tears pricked at Jillian's eyes as Leah's voice brought to life the words of the song she and Carter had chosen.

But soon enough, the emotion gave way to rejoicing. Pastor Evans pronounced them husband and wife, and they shared a kiss to seal their vows in the presence of those who had loved and supported them over the past many months.

As they turned to face their friends and families, Jillian knew that all the pain she had had to endure to get to that moment had absolutely been worth it to finally be able to claim this man as her own.

How she wished that her grandma had been able to be there to see that she had been able to overcome the darkest of days to find joy and light once again. But just as God had guided her and Carter over the past year, He had provided people who loved and supported her in her grandma's absence.

The hours of the day slipped by as they had their pictures taken, then joined their friends and family for the reception in the church hall. Through it all, Jillian was aware of a flutter of nerves slowly gathering in intensity in her stomach. She could barely eat any of the delicious dinner that they'd had catered.

They cut the cake. Tossed the garter and the bouquet. Visited with the people who'd come to share their special day.

Eventually, it was time for them to leave. She fought the urge to insist that they stay and help to clean up, knowing that her friends would see it for what it was: putting off what was to come because of nerves.

When they finally stood on the porch in front of her door—their door—Carter cupped her face in his hands. He bent and brushed a light kiss to her lips. They would be leaving the next day for their honeymoon in a cabin in British Columbia, but they'd decided that the familiarity of her own home and bed might make things more comfortable for Jillian for their first night together.

"Remember, there are no expectations for tonight, sweetheart. Whatever you want. Whatever you're comfortable with. That's all we do."

Jillian leaned into his touch, feeling strength there but also feeling safety and security. "Thank you."

"No thanks are necessary. I love you. Whatever makes you happy makes me happy."

She knew how he felt because she felt the same way, which was why she really wanted that night to go well. They had discussed it at length with the therapist. Jillian wasn't sure about other couples, but their conversations with the therapist about the physical intimacies of a marriage following trauma like Jillian had experienced had been frank and in-depth.

It had been a bit uncomfortable at first, but Carter had never made her feel like he viewed their discussions as anything more than something that would help enhance their marriage someday. He didn't use them as a license to push the physical aspect of their relationship, always respecting the boundaries they'd put in place. Boundaries that she hoped they'd be able to move past that night.

"Are you going to let me carry you over the threshold?" Carter asked, a smile on his face. "And no comments about you weighing too much. If you're up for it, I want to do that for you."

Jillian hesitated for a moment because she really did worry he wouldn't be able to carry her, but she also really wanted this with him. Finally, she nodded and punched in the code to unlock the door, then opened it.

Carter bent down a little. "Wrap your arms around my neck, sweetheart."

She did as he said, feeling one of his arms go around her back, and the other scooped her dress and legs up. Letting out a little squeal, she tightened her hold on him. Carter just grinned and stepped through the door of their home and into the next phase of their life.

Jillian woke with a start the next morning, and it took her a moment to orientate herself. The feel of someone pressed against her back and the weight of an arm across her waist was so foreign, her mind had started to panic, but then other memories had pushed the panic aside, drawing her back to reality.

Moving slowly, she slid out from under Carter's arm. After watching him sleep for a moment, sprawled out in her bed—their bed—she went to the bathroom then pulled on her robe. With silent steps, she left the bedroom and headed for the kitchen to make some coffee.

Dolly immediately greeted her, meowing loudly, clearly put out that she'd been banished from the bedroom the night before. Once she had the coffee going, Jillian scooped the cat up and nuzzled her.

"Sorry, Dolly-girl. But your favorite guy is here, so just you wait. He'll give you lots of love."

After putting some food in Dolly's bowl, Jillian went to stand at the sink, staring out at the back yard. The nerves from the night before had settled, leaving her with only a deep sense of peace.

Had it been the perfect wedding night? Some might say no, but it had exceeded her expectations. When she'd had moments of feeling overwhelmed, and anxiety had started to rise, Carter had soothed her in a way only he could. Over and over, he'd proved how committed he was to her and their relationship...now their marriage.

She felt a light touch across her back before Carter's hand settled on her hip. "You okay?"

She knew that he hadn't wrapped his arms around her from behind because he hadn't wanted her to feel caged in. However, after last night, Jillian knew with one hundred percent certainty that from that moment on, Carter's arms would only ever be a place where she found safety and security.

Turning toward him, she slipped her arms around his waist before lifting her head to kiss him.

"I'm more than okay," she said as she rested her head on his bare chest, loving the feel of his warm skin beneath her cheek, and snuggled close.

He wrapped his arms around her, rubbing her back with his hands as he nuzzled her hair. "So am I."

They stood in silence for a moment before Dolly joined them, meowing loudly as she wove her way around their ankles. Carter didn't step away from her to give Dolly the attention she clearly wanted. Instead, he just said, "You're going to have to wait a few more minutes, Dolly. Gotta cuddle with my number one girl."

Jillian laughed but didn't let go. She cherished the closeness she felt with Carter, something she had been so sure she'd never get to experience. To love Carter and be loved by him in return was the most beautiful thing.

As she stood there wrapped in Carter's arms, Jillian felt a pang of sympathy for Suzanne, knowing that if it hadn't been for the accident, she would have been the one enjoying Carter's embrace. There had been times when she'd been at Suzanne's bedside rubbing cream into her arms, talking to her, that Jillian had felt guilty. Like she had taken something that belonged to Suzanne.

When she hesitantly voiced that to Evelyn, the older woman had assured her that it was what Suzanne would have wanted. In their current circumstances, she would have wanted Carter to live his life. Evelyn had been adamant that Jillian not allow those thoughts to dampen her joy and love for Carter.

Over the past year and a half, God had renewed both her heart and Carter's. They'd both given up hoping that love and a relationship could be part of their future. It was only with God's help that they had been able to find what they had with each other.

Jillian tightened her arms around Carter. "I love you."

"I love you, too, sweetheart," Carter murmured. "I'm so glad that God brought us together. He knew that I needed you in my life."

"And that I needed you."

Carter hummed in response then said, "I can't wait to see what lies ahead for us."

Jillian couldn't either.

They'd already decided that depending on how things went for them, they wanted to try for a baby in the next year or so. Whatever their future held, she knew without a doubt that the work God had begun in her and Carter's lives—together and separately—would continue. Maybe that meant that someday she'd share her story or find a way to minister to others who had experiences similar to hers, she didn't know.

All of it was both scary and exciting, but Jillian knew that with Carter by her side and God directing their path, they'd be able to handle anything that came their way.

ABOUT THE AUTHOR

Kimberly Rae Jordan is a USA Today bestselling author of Christian romances. Many years ago, her love of reading Christian romance morphed into a desire to write stories of love, faith, and family, and thus began a journey that would lead her to places Kimberly never imagined she'd go.

In addition to being a writer, she is also a wife and mother, which means Kimberly spends her days straddling the line between real life in a house on the prairies of Canada and the imaginary world her characters live in. Though caring for her husband and four kids and working on her stories takes up a large portion of her day, Kimberly also enjoys reading and looking at craft ideas that she will likely never attempt to make.

As she continues to pen heartwarming stories of love, faith, and family, Kimberly hopes that readers of all ages will enjoy the journeys her characters take in each book. She has no plan to stop writing the stories God places on her heart and looks forward to where her journey will take her in the years to come.

Printed in Great Britain
by Amazon

38083191R00223